Made in the USA
Middletown, DE
20 April 2018

To the Billionaire Buddha's awakening!

Other Works
by Rivera Sun

Novels, Books & Poetry
The Dandelion Insurrection
The Dandelion Insurrection Study Guide
Steam Drills, Treadmills, and Shooting Stars
Skylandia: Farm Poetry From Maine
Freedom Stories: volume on
The Imagine-a-nation of Lala Child

Theatrical Plays & Presentations
Jimmy/Joan
Stone Soup
The Imagine-a-nation of Lala Child
The Education of Lala Girl
The Emancipation of Lala
The Courage & The Calling
Sweet Angel Fire
Morning Dove

RISING SUN
PRESS WORKS

A Community Published Book
Supported By:

Atlantis Thyme & Art Hinojosa
Annie Kelley
Abbi Samuels
Anne Meador
Ashley Olson & Carol Smith
Dolly and Adam Vogal
Beverly Campbell
Burt Kempner
Bill Moeller
Bob Banner / HopeDance FiLMs
Bob Simonds and Leslie Cottrell Simonds
Carmen Lavertu
Casey Dorman
Clifford and Lesley Scott
Cindy Barnes
Christine Upton
Crystal Marie Ramos Saldana
Carol and Romaldo Ranellone
Czikus Carriere
DeLores Cook
Dianna Lightfeather
Debbie Hibbert
David Haddock
Debra and Lauren Fuller
Dariel Garner
Elizabeth Murray
Grant Baldwin
Genevieve Emerson
Gloria Switzer
Josie Lenwell
Jerry Monroe Maynard
Jim Dreaver
Joshua Pritchett
January Sadler

Jonathan DeJong
Jeanette Colbert
Jazzan Precious
Jack Payden-Travers
Jillian Cornell
Julie and Melissa Quinn-Huffman
and daughters Grace and Madilynn
Jack Tracey and Paula Iverson
Kevin 'StarFire' Spitzer
Leah Cook
Lauren P Vines
Elliott Skinner and Linda Hibbs
Laurel Thomsen
Land Cook
Lynne A. Dews
Taos Sage Waters Massage
Marada Cook
Maja Bengtson
Michelle Dalnoky
Michael Veloff
Martine Zundmanis
Kevin Zeese and Margaret Flowers of PopularResistance.org
Mary Pendergast, RSM Sisters of Mercy Ecology, NE
Community
Marirose NightSong & Daniel Podgurski
Nickie Sekera and Luke Sekera-Flanders
Neshamah Sparks
Nanci Gosling Blackmarr
Philip J. Byler
Rob Garvey
Michaela Carrière
Susan Carroll
Sheila Ramsey
Steven Kenneth Carter
Sharon and David Hoover
Ted Cook

Billionaire Buddha

by
Rivera Sun

CHAPTER ONE

. . . . .

The hills lay golden, ancient in their stillness, cracked with drought. Crisp grass stems stubbed the contoured cheeks of hillsides. Cattle lipped the blades with caution as the sun baked their black hides. Twisted oaks, gray and gasping, withered under the relentless assault of unbroken sky. Tired clusters of leaves dotted the fingertips of their branches, offering one last breath to the earth before they toppled. The crumbled bodies of their brothers lay sprawled across the California foothills.

The dirge of the cicadas sharpened. Tension quivered in the hills. The haze of dust froze. Tears of crusty sap ached from an old tree. A groan wracked its wooden torso. The roots surrendered their tenacious grip on the bone-dry soil. The oak fell in a retort of snapping, brittle limbs. The thunder of its trunk exploded across the hillsides.

"You missed," the man said.

Inches from the crushing weight, he spoke the words simply, without rancor. It had been a valiant act, a desperate sacrifice by the tree.

The man sat down beside the fallen trunk, leaning his back against the armored bark. The fall reverberated in the tree. The man waited. The air stilled. He watched the dust settle back to earth. The trunk trembled. The man placed a hand upon a limb.

This was not the first time a tree had tried to kill him. The man's eyes swung the length of the foothills, falling beyond the oaks and cattle to the seam of a once great river, now dry. The winding curves muttered and glinted, but there was no water there. Instead, a line of cars rushed up the canyon, flashing

1

metallic. The engines mimicked the tumult of the river as they defied gravity to scale the slopes.

The man spoke.

"Look at them," he said. His voice slid out soft and quiet, muffled by the expanse of hills and endless sky. "Rushing, always racing, spending the hourglass of their lives in pursuit of phantoms, sucking the lifeblood of the future to gain speed in the present, climbing highways desperately, trying to get to the top."

A sting of bitterness laced his tongue and he paused to swallow it. He stared at the cleft where the road passed between the slopes and vanished. Beyond the rising foothills lay Gold Mountain.

The man bent and removed his cracked and dust-lined shoe. He peeled off a sweaty sock and poked ruefully at the holes. His second shoe had split; its sole flapped like the tongue of a thirsty dog.

A cow lowed resentfully at him. The man looked up.

"This mess began in haste," he said. "It will not end by rushing."

A branch splintered as if to reply that every day the trees were falling; time was of the essence. The man nodded in agreement, gazing at the glinting thread of cars below.

"The view from the top is not what they think," the man said to trees and cows that had never dreamed of Gold Mountain; never yearned to climb it; never begged, borrowed, lied, or stolen. Yet, the oaks were dying from those that had sought its luxury . . . including him. He had not built the road, but he had sung the praises of Gold Mountain. Yes, he had lured the never-ending stream of pleasure-seekers with his siren's call.

"You were right to try to kill me," he said, patting the

lifeless bark. He pushed himself to standing. His bare toes splayed in the bone-dry dust. His shoes hung from his hand. He bowed his head to the fallen oak. Then he turned and started walking.

CHAPTER TWO

· · · · ·

Seven years ago, the stars sat like diamonds in the crown of the High Sierras. Moonlit snow burned white against the night. A young woman in a black silk dress leaned her bare shoulders over the balcony rail. Her short hemline rose. The conversations faltered. The sounds of the swing band swept out the open doors of the resort. The men cast furtive glances at the length of her pale thighs. The women pinched their lips together and hid their middle-aged glares from their husbands. The girl's companion laid a possessive hand on her waist. A flurry of strained voices leapt falsely into small talk.

The girl sighed at the black and silver majesty of night.

"Come inside," her partner commanded, laying his hand on hers. "I want you to see Gold Mountain."

She resisted. His grip tightened. She looked once more at stars and darkness then yielded, allowing herself to be led into the shine of silver rings and crystal glasses. Her bare back turned on the stars that gleamed like diamonds, but twinkled out of reach; stars that could not be bought or sold; stars that would never touch a human finger; stars that belonged to no one, but blazed equally for all.

Beneath the strum of music, a dragon burned inside Gold Mountain. The beast roiled in haste and fury. It roared of work, work, work! And while it guarded the treasure troves of those above, it terrorized those below. The kitchen raged, aflame with cursing shouts, igniting entrées, foaming tureens, whirling chefs with bloody knives, red-faced managers mopping sweaty brows - and all this was normal, just an ordinary evening in the bowels

5

of Gold Mountain. The well-groomed wait staff ignored the turmoil as they whirred, impassive and obsequious, through their endless rounds like human automatons. Their charming smiles vanished as soon as they turned their backs on the wealthy. Seemingly subdued beneath their black clothes and long white aprons, arrogance brimmed beneath their masks of servility. They treated the kitchen staff with unflinching disdain, and received nothing less than hatred in return.

All this festered beneath the marble floors as polished shoes tapped in time to the manicured swing of the band. Gold-plated platters of hors d'oeuvres glided on white-gloved palms. Wine ran like rivers and champagne bubbled in a constant stream. While the hell realm of the kitchen seethed, the hall gleamed in perfect splendor, a cathedral of the rich, a holy place with a high, arching ceiling that touched the heavens and proudly proclaimed its place among the steep, sweeping peaks of the Sierras.

Behind the mosaic inlaid panels, the master carpenters and masons had signed their work, reverently emulating their forbearers who built the churches of old Europe. These modern masters laid the final veneers into place and vanished, forgotten into history. The wealthy told the legends of the stone, but never the names of the workers who wrested them into place. They praised the woodwork, the famous architect, and the ancient Mayans who first used this wood in temples. The brown, splintered hands that sliced chainsaws into old growth trees remained invisible, irrelevant. The wealthy chanted the ritual recitation of praises honoring the seventy-foot, four-sided fireplace that rose from the center of the room to pierce the vaulted ceiling. They laid perfect manicures on the same stones that had built Aztec pyramids. They toasted the man who built Gold Mountain and owned an entire quarry of the marble that lay beneath their feet.

"Grant Rose Marble, named after Mr. Grant, himself," they whispered to one another. It's impossible to buy, they claimed - but nothing is impossible if you can pay the price.

The girl from the balcony basked in gold-leaf glow. A champagne flush drove the cold clarity of the night from her mind. She turned her star-struck eyes to the profile of her tuxedoed companion and vowed to love him all her life.

"She'll never keep him," a thin, bitter woman murmured into her wine glass. She folded her spindly arms across her artificial bosom and fingered her gold necklace. She and her friend scrutinized the couple across the room, shrewdly unsympathetic. Both wore the pinched and stiff expressions of middle-aged women who have clawed their way up steep barriers and planted themselves firmly in position. They stood elbow to elbow, heads tilted toward each other's ears, wine glasses in hand, bosom friends aligned in the cruel social landscape that ran jagged beneath the polished small talk of the party. Each tight-lipped woman bore her secret scars. They tucked their betrayals, hatreds, and disappointments into hidden places with the skill of plastic surgeons. They analyzed the girl like old battleships, scornful of the newest model in the fleet. Her hull lacked titanium. Her heart was too vulnerable. Her shining youth held a touch too much naivety. She didn't have the grit, the engine, or the drive to hold a man like that.

Yet, neither woman discounted the threat of such a girl. They tracked their wandering, restless husbands from the corners of their periscope eyes. They had built fortunes and empires out of the raw material of a man. The most dangerous moment of their campaign was now at hand. A girl like that glittered young and fresh. She cast the older women in an unflattering light. Their relationships held sharp edges, unpleasant memories, distasteful shows of forcefulness, and the taint of the subtle control the women had exerted all these years. A girl like that could never hold a young man poised to build an empire, but she could grab a man's midlife crisis by the balls. In a fluttering of eyelashes, she could wreck decades of careful manipulations.

The women lifted arched eyebrows at each other. The skinny woman pinched her lips together as her husband boisterously greeted the young couple.

"I say you should divorce him," her friend muttered. "Take half of everything and let him waste it all on some flibberty-git."

The thin woman said nothing. She was calculating risk assessments, mergers, portfolios, and net worth faster than a stockbroker. She compressed her husband into a series of numbers as deftly as he tallied human lives in mortgages and interest rates. Love was an externality that rarely crossed their minds.

"Never mind my husband," the bony woman said dismissively. "What are you going to do about yours?"

Her friend laughed nervously and toyed with her gold wedding ring.

"Oh, him. He won't leave me, not with the money hemorrhaging left and right."

"Business is bad?"

"No, just floundering in delays," she confessed, looking for sympathy. Instead, she found a distracted twitch clicking in her friend's face . . . calculating, always calculating. Her chest constricted, panicking over a friendship that had been secure for thirty years. She turned the conversation back to her friend.

"What you should do," she declared, "is divorce your wet blanket of a husband and marry Dave Grant."

A surprised burst of laughter erupted from them both.

"Not a bad idea," the thin woman said, "except for his wife."

Their eyes flicked across the room. Dave Grant's wife was listening with commendable attentiveness to the usual blustering of the Senator.

"And now they want to see the stars!" the congressman burst out. "Imagine! Suing me for negligence over those smog regulations - they say they have a right to see the stars!" The Senator delivered the words with the perfect touch of patronizing arrogance and indignation. He had rehearsed the line all day, polishing it through repetition. He waited expectantly for the sympathetic burst of laughter at the preposterousness of the situation.

Susan Grant regarded him impassively.

"Well, don't they?" the short, formidable woman asked.

"My house in Los Angeles is just as smoggy as theirs - "

Susan's lips twitched. That might be a good reason to pass smog regulations.

" - but you don't see me whining about the right to see the stars!" the Senator concluded with an aggrieved air.

"The urban poor, Senator, don't have second homes in the High Sierras. Technically, the smog is denying them the right to see the stars."

"They have national and state parks," the Senator replied sternly. "They can visit just like I do. Stars, Mrs. Grant, are not a right. They are a privilege in the modern world, a reward for hard work and diligence."

His eyes darted around the room, beginning to strategize an escape from the awkward conversation. Susan sighed and applied damage control.

"Never mind the lawsuit, Senator. People just like to complain, don't they?"

She smiled, patted his arm, and excused herself before he

could leave her standing alone.

The Senator watched Susan Grant's retreating back, wondering why the woman continued to make him nervous after a decade of acquaintance. She was just too damn smart, he decided. She should have been a doctor or a scientist . . . thank goodness she hadn't gone into politics. She'd be giving him a run for his money instead of financing his next campaign. He'd have to have a chat with Dave Grant, though, see if there was a problem with the smog regulations.

The Senator took a swig of Scotch. Everybody likes to complain, he thought. He snorted as he swallowed the alcohol and eyed the room. The women socialized in designer dresses. The men stood clustered in tuxedos. The band riffed in a clarinet-saxophone duo. Across the hall, his wife peered at a silent auction for some charity or another. He harrumphed. Fundraisers and benefit dinners were just high-class ways of complaining. What was the matter with people? Petitions, protests, phone calls, lobbyists: everybody wanting something! Didn't they have enough already? Take those plaintiffs. It wasn't enough to have low-income housing; now they wanted to see the stars!

The problem, he thought as he swigged another mouthful of Scotch, was that people didn't understand the value of hard work any more. Take any one of those urban poor and put them in his office - hah! They'd be back flipping burgers in a week. The stacks of legislation, bureaucratic reports, endless meetings, flights to Washington, D.C., his accountants, the IRS, campaign financing - it was a headache, the whole damn job! The only benefit was for his business interests . . . and if you didn't have those, there was no point in taking public office. Politicians have a fifteen percent higher likelihood of heart attacks than bus drivers, he grumbled, a hazard of a high-stress profession. The diet wasn't great - too rich, too much oil - he drank too much, didn't get enough time at the gym or the spa. Then there were the assassination attempts! He sighed. The job would be the death of him, one way or another. He downed the rest of his Scotch.

Across the room, Susan Grant was not amused. Her temper crackled like a pitch-pine log thrown on hot coals. Sparks leapt impatiently left and right as she forced her smile into position and gritted her teeth.

Where was he?

The party rose to a frenzied pitch. The wine, the libations, the carefully arranged tempo of the swing band's ever quickening set; the elements of the ritual were peaking. She had one eye on the CEO of a prominent tech firm and the other on the district judge, that obnoxious Senator was getting chummy with her competitor's lobbyist, and where was Grant?

"You are such a lucky woman," an insipid social climber fawned, "to be married to a man like Mr. Grant."

"Indeed," Susan replied tersely. Her list of excuses for his absence had escalated from *he'll be right along* to *he's somewhere around here* and she was about to employ *he's feeling ill* when the woman's eyes darted to the left, the conversations halted, the swing band climaxed . . . and Susan knew without turning that Grant had arrived.

"There he is," she announced.

The room sprang back to life. The whirl of voices and handshakes resumed. Susan pivoted and crossed to her husband's side.

"Where have you been?" she muttered as she accepted his perfunctory peck on the cheek.

He laid a palm on the small of her back. Susan gritted her teeth. Twenty-three years of marriage, forty businesses under their belts, millions - billions! - of dollars flowing through their hands; here they were fabulously wealthy, owners of the most exclusive resort and golf course in the western United States, and look at him!

His tailored suit hid the bulk of his three hundred and sixty-five pounds of flesh, but his corpulence climbed his neck and puffed out his cheeks, narrowed his eyes into little slits, and lined his pudgy hands. His face flushed red. His palms sweated. His sleep apnea forced him to hook up to a machine each night. He took so many pills and supplements it was a wonder they didn't pop out of him like a Pez dispenser. The man was a physical wreck - a walking disaster - a heart attack bomb waiting to explode! Their sex life was nonexistent. He wouldn't exercise. He just kept shoveling food in like -

"I lost track of the time," he said suddenly.

Susan frowned.

"Doing what? The office is closed - "

"Watching the stars."

A blaze of irritation ignited inside her.

"Oh, that's nice," she snapped caustically. "You have three hundred and sixty-four other nights in a year to go star-gazing, Dave. You could have waited - "

"They're different," he muttered. "Each night."

"So be an astronomer when you retire," she said, forcing a sentimental tone into her voice. Heads were starting to turn.

He pinched his lips together. Great, she griped silently, just what I need, a petulant little temper tantrum. He left her side abruptly, moving over to speak with a young man. Susan watched him out of the corner of her eye as he greeted the youth with magnanimity, every inch the booming, laughing, boisterous host, delighted with everyone and everything, pouring the champagne himself, insisting that the star-struck girl taste a strawberry along with the foaming champagne, gesturing to the young man to snag one from the platter and feed it to the girl.

Susan sighed. He could be so wonderful when he tried. All these years together and sometimes Susan looked around a crowded room without seeing a man that was half the equal of Dave Grant. Despite his flaws - the stubbornness, the bullheadedness, his irascibility, his blatant masculine manipulations, his extravagance and wasteful tendencies, his weight - she stopped.

It's a fatal flaw, Dave, she warned him silently. Either you'll lose weight or - she didn't finish the sentence, but the echo crept treacherously around her hidden thoughts . . . or you'll lose me.

"I envy you, Mr. Grant, I really do," his personal physician sighed as he checked his client's pulse.

Dave Grant sat like a stone on the examining table, his eyes squeezed into tiny cracks in his face.

"A beautiful wife, a fortune, a booming empire . . . "

The words entered Grant in a low rumble of meaningless phrases as the physician's monotone washed by in a stream of nothings. The doctor's brow folded downward as he jotted a note on the chart, murmuring incessantly.

"I picture you in ten years, standing on the veranda of your mansion, sipping cocktails in the sunlight, laughing with your wife."

The physician sighed and pulled off his glasses to look Grant in the eye.

"The only problem is that you're not going to be there."

No reaction.

The physician blinked and hastened on.

"Your blood pressure is through the roof, your heart is palpitating, your full body edema is reaching the limits of control, you've got severe sleep apnea, I've got you on every pill I've got, but - "

He broke off, searching for a sign of life in the moribund man.

"If you don't lose weight, you're going to die."

The stony bulk of the man shifted. His eyes flicked to the side, considering this information. The doctor pressed for an advantage.

"If you keep gaining weight, you're not going to be around to enjoy this fortune of yours, your lovely wife, your - "

Sharp blue eyes leapt up in the puffy sockets to pin the doctor. Three hundred and sixty-five pounds of bone, muscle, and fat remained motionless. Only the eyes moved.

Oh, those eyes! The physician suppressed a shudder. He knew eyes, this doctor. He met his patients through the catalogue of glances: cold, worried, tense, scared, sad, haughty, calculating, longing, hopeful, despairing. Grant's eyes unsettled him. Sitting in that torpid body, clenched between the puffy bags and rotund cheeks above the man's double chin, narrowed by the rolls of fat that squeezed his face together, those eyes were alive! The doctor shivered. Those eyes should be bleary with lack of sleep, reflecting the rotting of the inner organs. The light in them should be flickering or fading. Instead, Grant's eyes met the doctor's gaze with unblinking clarity. No pleading, no fear of death, no compromise.

"Grant," the physician begged softly. "Please, you've got to change. Your body is falling apart. You're going to die."

Something hard glinted in those eyes. Realization swept like sunlight through the shadowed countenance of the man. A bite of harsh laughter grunted through his throat.

"Did it ever occur to you, Doctor, that I want to die?"

CHAPTER THREE

· · · · ·

The tempering of time had notched the years in lines across his face. Seven years beyond his early grave, he walked back toward Gold Mountain, resurrected with every breath of life that flooded into his lungs. Every step became a prayer in a long pilgrimage of transformation. The beating sun loosened the incense of the sweating hills. The cicadas chanted. His footsteps unearthed memories that irritated his serenity like grit and thorns inside the shoe. Gravelly images collected from the erosion of his life rubbed him uncomfortably raw. The past is a blister on the mind, he thought. The hills stood mute, but echoed in the silence, *you* are a blister on our sides. A buzzard wheeled in black circles overhead. All things shall pass and so will you. Your memories will vanish with the light in your eyes. Your flesh will erode beneath the buzzard's beak. The hills shall swallow your bones. No blisters, no memories, nothing.

The man shook his head sharply - once, twice - to clear the buzzard's warning. It's not the past that matters, but the present - this breath, this step, this moment. The man stretched his lungs and with the grim determination of a samurai began to hack his memories as they arose.

Gold Mountain.

Slash! Chopped in half by the knife's edge of the mind. Only the sea of hills remained, every yellowed spike of grass sharp with detail. Their subterranean fingers reached skyward, long spindly hands like Susan's -

Slash! With ferocious vehemence he swept her from his mind - too late! A deluge of images assaulted him. Hornets of the past stung him violently. The host of memories swarmed,

17

infuriated at his attempts to annihilate them.

Susan - wife - house - mansion - money - wine - fights - caviar - soirees - resorts - yacht - he never had a yacht! - the red Porsche - spa - golf course - High Sierras - wealth - Gold Mountain - Dave Grant.

His name was Dave Grant. He owned Gold Mountain.

The past arranged its baubles of information like a child's mobile spinning overhead. Dave Grant paused in the dry wash. The crunch of gravel silenced. Phantom music echoed eerily in his ears, along with the clink of crystal glasses and the sound of voices.

Chills ran up his arms.

He was struck by the memory of cold: icy air, sharp nights, hardened diamond stars, and hearts like lumps of coal compressed. He had nearly killed himself because of coldness. The frozen hearts on the high pinnacle of Gold Mountain chilled his soul to within a hairsbreadth of the rigid state of death. He ate to numb the daily assaults. Emotional razor blades sliced his sanity to shreds with the coolly calculated cruelty of that thin-aired world. No warmth, no love, no kindness . . . he had learned harshly, painfully, that he could not live without compassion.

In the dry wash, Dave looked up at an old, twisted oak that clung to the crumbling edge of the riverbed. He eyed it warily. How many times had he brushed up against his own demise? Too many, he shuddered. Death by gluttony, high speed races along cliff side roads, alcohol, misery, starvation, trees that tried to murder him . . . when would he stop hurtling his flesh under Death's scythe?

He continued walking. The sun dropped lower in the sky and flooded gold across the hills. Twilight, the time of nostalgic melancholia, lowered its shroud upon the world. The shadows lengthened in the hills. A sense of impermanence filled the air. Each day, the sun sets out the pageant of our mortal lives, rising fresh and newborn rosy, then blazing at the prime, mellowing with age, and finally submerging into darkness.

Dave squinted to the north. One more hill before sunset?

He shook his head at the bittersweet analogy. Humans always long for one more hill, one more adventure, one more mountain, one more love before the sunset, one more vindication or reconciliation, one more whatever it is we're seeking, one more day, one more breath. Look at this modern-day Odysseus on his long journey back to where he began. The years spread vaster than the seven seas, each one crossed with many storms. He was lashed to the tiller. His compass pointed north. Gold Mountain crested on the horizon . . . but it would not be reached tonight.

No, better to hunker down and sit quietly in the sunset than to go stumbling over cows. The cooling warmth seduced him like a lover's last farewell.

Strange, he thought, that he had come so close to death and still missed the point of life. It took years of near misses and close encounters for him to understand the simple truth . . . life is the point unto itself: to live, to sense, to see the golden slant of light, to watch the dance of lengthening shadows, to hear the solitary lowing cow, to catch a scent of night in your nostrils, to be the conscious eye of the Universe, the mirror of the world.

Oh human, look beyond your limbs. Your body is the looking glass of the One. Self knowing Self, loving what Self sees.

There is more to life than vanity, Dave gently chided the Universe. He climbed the slope and settled down in the brittle grass as shadow conquered light. There is suffering, pain, and ignorance. We're here to ease our agony and end the causes of poverty, sickness, and destruction. We're not just here for navel-gazing narcissism -

Who says? the Universe mocked him.

I do, he replied, and that's good enough for me.

CHAPTER FOUR

. . . . .

"Dave."

Her tone sounded as bland as reconstituted potatoes. Flat starch, no emotion, no cream, no milk, no salt of anger, not even a pinch of pepper. Dave pretended to ignore her as he crammed an oozing sandwich in his mouth. A tomato slipped out one end. Bacon slid out the side. Dave tried to remember the sandwich's official name - the chef called it the Gutbuster. Aha! The Eureka Sandwich - that was the name - the signature lunch special of Gold Mountain's five star restaurant: turkey, roast beef, ham, bacon, mozzarella cheese, cheddar, caramelized onions, sweet coleslaw, and mayonnaise.

"Dave!"

She wanted his attention. He gave it to the assorted fries. Ordinary guests at Gold Mountain - senators, executives, trust funders - could choose between garlic, French, or sweet potato fries. Dave Grant ordered and received all three. He chose a long orange sweet potato fry and held it up to the light, admiring the sheen of grease.

"Dave!!"

He smacked his lips as he crunched down on the fry, studiously ignoring his wife. He licked his fingers. He dabbed his lips with the linen napkin.

"Hmm?" he finally replied.

Their home stretched desolately around them, a wasteland of ivory carpets and statues in recessed alcoves. Through the wide window, he could see the kitchen staff boy zipping back to the resort in a golf cart after delivering their lunch. The hall clock ticked loudly in the vacancy of affection. Grant regarded

21

his wife's stony face.

"I want a divorce."

Nothing moved.

"No," he refused.

She erupted. A volley of resentment cracked around his ears. She flung the shards of their failing marriage at him like an expert knife-thrower drunk on rage.

"I want a divorce," she insisted.

"Over my dead body," he answered, and to prove himself intractable on the subject, he devoured a garlic fry in one gulp. He coughed on the pungent jab. She smirked.

"No need for divorce if you're dead," she pointed out nastily, watching his pudgy fingers cram fries into his sweaty face.

"Exactly," he agreed, swigging a swallow of wine. "Death before dishonor. Marriage is a sacrament, a holy vow until death do us part."

She slid her lunch plate across the mahogany table.

"Eat up, then. You'll be dead of a heart attack in a year."

"Marriage counseling?" he suggested.

She stared at him coldly.

"What do you want, Susan?" he sighed.

"A divorce."

He threw his sandwich down.

"No."

He walked out, pushing over the wooden chair and slamming the side door so hard the framed art beside it crashed to the floor. He strode across the lawn, wheezing as he stalked past the resort. It was not because he was obese, he fumed to himself, she hated him because . . . he paused.

She had loved him, once. She had loved the challenge of Dave Grant, the empire building, the heat of the chase, the ambition, the amassing of the fortune. She loved all that - the risks, the losses, the near disasters, the saving graces, the triumphant climaxes. Grant tried to catch his breath. His chest heaved as he stood under a tree, its pitch pine aroma tangy in his rasping throat. His flesh rode the bellows of his lungs.

She didn't hate him, he thought. She just . . .

Just what?

A golf cart zipped past along the trail. A figure raised a hand. Grant did not respond. He surveyed the expanse of Gold Mountain's luxury. Only a fraction of the extravagance was visible to the eye. Every beam and joint, veneer and finish reeked of custom design. From the golf course to the restaurant to the spa to the high-end subdivision, the development bore the sheen of high-class art. Even the native grasses had been specially sowed into microclimates that blended seamlessly through a series of carefully designed, biomimicry patterns.

Wasn't this enough? This kingdom in the crown of the High Sierras, this jewel of a resort . . . wasn't that enough for her?

No, he decided. Susan's heart had borne the pinpricks of a thousand lances as they climbed the fortresses of wealth. Her heart leaked, riddled with holes that left her feeling hollow despite the constant rush of income. At first, the sharp hunger in her soul made her a perfect partner: energetic, determined, obsessive. She had built their fortune, brick by brick, deal by deal. But that hole inside her . . . nothing filled it, not wealth, not alcohol, not love.

She had consumed him, he cursed. Like a locust, she had gnawed at him and cracked his bones to suck the marrow dry. Now she wanted to be unleashed from his carcass. She thirsted for more fresh blood.

Divorce her, you idiot, he told himself sternly.

But then she'd win, he complained. She'd have his honor, his broken vow. If a man can't stand by his commitments, what good is he?

"Duck!"

He startled. A golf ball whizzed past his head. His fury boiled. That sycophantic, moronic, imbecile! He cursed the golfer and all the others with their weak libidos and repressed existences that drove them onto the fairways to wing metal clubs at white balls, cursing the course for their own stupidity, drinking until they couldn't see straight, let alone knock a ball off a tee or into a hole!

Dave glowered at the retreating polo shirt, then swept his scowl across the golf course that wound serpent-like through the sculpted forest, opening onto stunning views and equally mouth-dropping golf terrain. Grant had designed every inch of the world-class course.

He hated golf.

Even the twenty million dollar tax write-off for the private course failed to amuse him. Gold Mountain had to have a golf course, though. It was the summer sport of the wealthy, when the skiing turned to slush and the yacht lost its seafaring charm. Golf courses brokered deals, cemented alliances, and negotiated contracts.

The course consumed a million gallons of water per day.

While the wild slopes of the mountains were crisped yellow with drought, the golf course pulsated under a lush, green carpet. To the south, the farmers plowed their dried-up orchards under as Texas, Colorado, and Los Angeles threatened water wars, but the playground of the wealthy oozed with all the green that money could buy.

What good is a man if he cannot keep his word? A marriage vow entailed all the sanctity of God and home, love and commitment. He never reneged on business deals; he refused to break his marriage vows. Grant drew a ragged breath on the wealth-encrusted pinnacle of success. Three hundred and sixty-five pounds of flesh, a marble and mahogany resort, enough money to bury himself encased in a solid brick of gold, the whole range of the Sierras under his feet, his artery-hardening, grease-dripping lunch churning in his gut . . . yet here he stood feeling hollow as bird bones.

His marriage had shriveled up like worms after a rain. The relationship had bloated on the money that flowed like water, growing pasty and white. When the storm of ambition plateaued, they were left high and dry, dead on the asphalt of their lives, slowly shriveling into red-faced husks of human beings.

Divorce her, he told himself.

No.

You'd kill yourself first? he scoffed.

Stubborn silence answered.

He turned his hollow gaze to the resort.

I'll think about it after I have a decent meal, he decided. Can't think straight on an empty stomach. He strode across the lawn toward the restaurant, shoving the litany of excuses aside until he could eat himself into oblivion.

CHAPTER FIVE

· · · · ·

Years later, a lean-carved version of Dave Grant lay on his back under the canopy of stars, awakened from the nightmare of his past. Cold sweat shivered his skin. The night stole the beads from his brow. His eyelids rebelled against the weight of sleep. The memory of those three hundred and sixty-five pounds of flesh choked his consciousness. Loathing swamped him along with his recollections of that period of his life: the stubborn, bull-headed choice of death before dishonor; the china plates smashing as she furiously flung them against the wall; the ironic fear that she would pump his body full of bullets before he had a chance to torment her with his slow death by gluttony.

If love is madness, hate is insanity. For months, a silent raging scream rang in his ears. A crazed fog hung over his eyes. His heart pumped a biochemical blend of adrenaline and stubbornness. He wouldn't let her win, not her way. He'd rather die, his way.

On it went, a storm thundering in the silence, through the mundane days of business meetings, charity fundraising events, social functions, and staff meetings. He kept his stomach overloaded to shut down his mind. White noise reverberated in his tense muscles and clogged arteries. And the pills! God, the pills he swallowed without knowing - or caring - what they were! Handfuls in a single gulp, washed down with Bourbon or wine.

It's a miracle he was alive.

His back crinkled against the dry grasses that formed his bed.

"Life is a miracle," he whispered to the night. Every day is a sheer symphony of the miraculous, but we're drowning in so much oblivion that we're deaf and blind to it all.

The urge to weep welled up in his chest. His ribcage ached for the old Dave Grant and for the waste of those years of his life. He would be dead but for that one touch of kindness that finally broke through.

He breathed deeply as the silken caress of wind traced his body, carrying the vast coolness of the sky and the warm heat of the valley. The somber outlines of the hills stretched for miles in all directions, but he was not lonely. Loneliness is being untouchable on the top of the world. Loneliness is lying invisible as you starve on the streets. Humanity was a master chef in the flavors of loneliness. He counted his blessing not to have tasted them all. He had never swallowed the loss of a motherless child, or the ache of an old man by the grave of a fresh-buried wife, or the desperate aloneness of a destitute woman as she submits to the thrusts of a stranger.

He knew only his own nuances of the vast tragedy called loneliness: the isolation of wealth, the subtle space carved around him by power, and the hesitancy of connection under the pressure of prestige. He should have kept a calendar, he realized belatedly, a notched stick of days like a man marooned on an island, one tick for each time the sun set without a single touch from a human. Susan's sharp-edged nails had sliced him once, but for years, the softness of a hand had not touched his body, not from her or his peers, and not from the staff, who revered and feared him.

If not for that new hire hostess from the town, he'd have gone to his grave touched only by EMTs, the coroner, and the mortician. But that woman - all wrong for the high class resort, untrained, flurried, doing her best to impress and falling miserably short - had reached out her hand as she showed him to a table and touched her fingertips onto his back.

Like a plunge in a pond, the touch exploded through his body! He gasped, but no one noticed. Even the hostess walked briskly back to her station, leaving Dave Grant having an attack of the heart. A resurrection of hope detonated in his body. The lightning strike of that touch hit the gong of his soul, and understanding reverberated inside him: *I am human! I am here! I am alive! I can love! I can be loved! I can live!*

His knees melted. He sat. He stared at the white linen, stunned. The waiter stepped lively and solicitously asked what he desired.

"Lemons."

The waiter blinked.

Dave blinked back.

A shocked eternity passed in a half-second.

"Just lemons, sir?"

Dave smiled.

"Yes . . . quartered . . . on a plate."

The waiter inclined in a terse fifteen-degree bow. No questions. Just get it. He knew his training.

In the kitchen, the chef froze over the flaming pan.

"What do you mean, *just lemons?*" the chef demanded.

The waiter shrugged.

The chef's eyes rolled heavenward and then back to earth. He sliced and arranged two lemons, quartered. He added some parsley. The waiter took it back to the table.

"Anything else, sir?"

It was almost a dare.

"Yes," Dave answered. "More lemons."

The waiter's lips twitched. He turned. His eyes flicked back to the table. He saw the inexplicable, indomitable founder of

Gold Mountain lift up a lemon wedge with a jubilant expression and pop the whole quarter into his mouth.

Dave Grant had decided to live.

Flushing, purging, devouring lemons: rumors of his madness raced over the golf course. Resort guests eyed him nervously. The fever of determination reeked off him. He turned pale, blotchy, red as tomatoes, yellowed with the churnings of a liver on overdrive. He drank water like a fish and consumed only lemons. He shed weight by the hour. He ran the kitchen by his nose. Not one morsel they produced entered his stomach.

One afternoon, he took his master chef down to the cold storage room in the basement.

"See that?" he asked the chef, a young whiz with top marks from the most prestigious culinary institute, a kid who rivaled Dave Grant in girth and obesity. "Those are fifty pound cubes of lard, ordered in bulk."

The kid shrugged. The ubiquitous cubes arrived by the pallet. The one in the kitchen would be gone by the evening, simmered in stocks, slathered in pans, whipped into desserts, and dissolved into sauces. The kitchen staff sliced off chunks by the minute.

"Pick it up," Dave urged him.

"Why? There's a cart by the elevator; that thing could throw your back out."

Dave shot the chef an impenetrable glare. Already, the lines of his round cheeks caved and collapsed. The puffy flesh choking his eyes relinquished its squeeze. The startling glint of blue remerged like sky between storm clouds.

"That," Dave said emphatically, pointing at the lard, "is how much fat I've lost already."

The kid whistled appreciatively, shifting his own bulk.

"That," Dave repeated, "is only a third of what I'm still hauling around, every single day."

The master chef threw him an alarmed look. Dave stared at the lard.

"What kind of idiot," Dave grumbled, "gets up in the morning, picks up one hundred and fifty pounds of lard, and carries it around all day long?"

Silence answered the question.

Dave clapped the kid on the back.

"You're not an idiot, and neither am I," he concluded.

They said nothing further. The chef took the elevator. Dave shook his head and started up the stairs. He climbed five steps and wheezed. He took three more steps and gasped. He managed two more then stopped halfway up the flight of stairs. His heart hammered. His ears rang. His breath struggled to reach the full circuit of his limbs. Blackness swarmed. Dave gritted his teeth. He refused to pass out and roll down the steps.

Someday, he vowed, I'll take these stairs three at a time.

He paused twice more on the climb, counting his blessings that the kid had taken the elevator and saved him some pride. When he reached the top, he gave orders to the staff to leave three blocks of lard in a corner of the cold storage room. Every day, he made a pilgrimage into the basement where he sliced off the amount of fat he had lost and heaped the lard onto another pile. Then he wheezed and huffed back up the stairs. The staff shook their heads. The master chef said nothing. He watched Dave grow thinner like a skeptic looking for hope.

Dave ate nothing but lemons for two and a half months. For another six weeks, he consumed only a few hundred calories a day. His doctor kept him on vitamins and electrolytes. The wealthy elite watched him furtively. Susan returned their whispered compliments with a tight-lipped smile. One day, she

31

looked up from her reading in the living room, realization dawning across her expression.

"You're going to lose all that weight and then divorce me," she said.

Dave didn't pause on the treadmill.

"I hadn't thought of it, but that's a good idea."

Astonishment burst through her face. Her jaw dropped. She shut it. Her eyes narrowed. She slammed her book shut and stormed out. Dave quickened his pace. He needed his strength now. In that slip of the tongue, he had made a serious tactical error. He had just declared war with a superpower.

Overnight, the battle erupted. Lawyers, documents, statements, alimony: she attacked fast and furious, determined to get the best of him while he was still in a weakened condition. She remembered the young Grant with his unstoppable will. Quickly, she unleashed the Hounds of War, sent forth the Riders of the Apocalypse, gathered her commanders, and rallied her troops.

Dave watched in horror as she intentionally sabotaged their business projects. He gritted his teeth and attacked back, burning bridges to prevent her from crossing into more wealth. She sank contracts, blew up deals, and cut off his supply trains. Dave considered calling a ceasefire and drafting a reasonable treaty. He discarded the notion. She started this warpath . . . he was determined to come out the victor.

The battles flared into the civilians. She laid off a quarter of the staff. Dave's righteous temper erupted.

"Do not make them suffer!" he roared at her. "This is between us. Don't destroy everything we've built here."

"I'm not," she smirked. "I'm going to run you into bankruptcy, buy Gold Mountain back for a profit, and rebuild it all."

Dave swore. She would do it, he knew. This was war. She'd invade, destroy, and profit from the reconstruction, while the lives of the employees reeled in upheaval. Dave put on the armor of justice. He strode full-force into battle, using righteousness to justify new levels of cruelty. As with all war, it was pointless. The situation was hopeless. The staff fled the disaster. The empire toppled. She gouged him. He burned her. They raked ugly, gaping wounds into one another. They detonated psychological bombs in each other's hearts. They dropped missiles of guilt, laid landmines with words, and hazed each other with the firebombs of anger. They circled in duels. They crushed unfortunate bystanders. They slammed swords. They deflected blows that lodged in their business partners. They parried thrusts that sliced their employees to shreds.

Finally, Dave threw down his sword in disgust. The resort lay in paperwork ruins. The empire verged on utter collapse. Smoke burned out of their investments.

"Take it," he mocked her. "Take it all. Just leave me alone."

Dave fled. He leapt into his red Porsche with a suitcase of clothing and a well-stashed bank account. He sped away from Gold Mountain, refusing to look back.

CHAPTER SIX

. . . . .

Dave woke at dawn. Grass stems pricked his body. He rolled over with the ache of regret that comes from sleeping in a field of memories. Bright sunlight hit his eyes. He winced, hung over from the folly of his past. Silently, he apologized to Susan not only for the cruelties he had inflicted during those years of war, but also for the years he spent reciting the story of Susan the Monster, portraying himself as the champion of the employees, the defender of the realm, the resort, the fortune . . . Christ, he had even claimed to have protected the dog - the dog she loved and kept and cared for after he fled Gold Mountain without a backwards glance. She made good on her promises, bringing everything to the brink of collapse then resurrecting it all while profiting like a victorious warmonger. Even so, she ruled Gold Mountain generously, employing two thirds of the locals and supporting charities while he pissed his millions away, repeating his sob story to anyone who would listen until one day he was forced to confront the truth of all wars: there is no good side, no righteous reason for the violence, no justification for the hurt and damage that war inflicts.

Even his pathetic claim of "death before dishonor" had been empty valor. He had used the phrase to hurt her. He abandoned chivalry the moment they stepped into battle. He had fought dirty, aimed for her eyes, and thrown salt in her wounds. He kicked her when she was down. He spat on her misery. He had even threatened to strangle the dog.

"There is no honor in war," he admitted to the honest light of a new day.

He rose like a veteran, stiff with remorse, unable to find an absolution for his crimes. He stood still as the earth stirred. Flies lifted in crowds, swarmed in the sunlight, and then vanished on the wind.

Life is creation. Life is destruction. Our footsteps annihilate the existence of others. Our actions ripple the web of connection. We cause harm even as we eat to survive. Around and around the cycle goes, but what is needed? What is not? How much destruction must come to pay the cost of our lives? *Do no harm* sounds noble, but *do less harm* is more practical. Our lives are borrowed for a moment - that is all.

"You'll have me one day, worms," Dave promised.

He stretched and stepped forward. The last foothills lay before him. In a few days, he would be climbing Gold Mountain. A swarm of misgivings rose inside him. He sighed. Calculating the cycles of suffering caused by one's actions was a tricky business. After a lifetime as a serial entrepreneur, Dave dreamed in the second language of cost-benefit analysis, but capitalism's clumsy dialect lacked the vocabulary for analyzing the economy of the heart. It had no words for externalities like love and regret.

A poetics was required, Dave thought, a song of the world to describe the causes and conditions of the heart, soul, and emotions. How else can we calculate the risks of one action, the benefits of another, the cascades of reactions, and the ripples of change?

Trust, the wind whispered. *When the fledgling leaps, the wind catches.*

The song of the world is not something to calculate. Economics and science will never speak in this language. The song of the world is not an equation or explanation; it is something you join into and lose yourself in. You leap and it catches. You ride in its current. Right and wrong are but two strands of the stream. Humans were not born to live outside this song, rationally calculating its twists and its turns, trying to fathom economics and budgets.

Give it up! the wind laughed.

Dave smiled in response. Just give it up, he echoed, give up wanting to know all the gears and the cogs, surrender to your place in the whole. He climbed the hills, a small solitary figure outlined against the curve of earth and sky. Seven years of giving it up had emptied his pockets, his bank accounts, and his mind. No baggage, no illusion of safety; just a raw flesh-and-blood figure walking the Earth, empty even of his concepts of that. He had given up fear, desire, anger, hatred, the urge to control, and the longing to know.

How much more must I give up? Dave asked silently. He squinted into the expanse. The weather lines on his face splintered like cracks in dry earth. The blue of the sky met his eyes. The answer returned from the unblinking Universe.

Everything.

CHAPTER SEVEN

· · · · ·

Fleeing the aftermath of the divorce, Dave Grant tore off Gold Mountain like a jailbreak convict headed toward freedom. The local cops blinked as his red Porsche whipped past in a blur. They didn't bother to give chase. Ninety miles an hour in a forty-five zone didn't justify the expense of dealing with Grant's lawyer. The local kids with souped-up junkyard remodels would pay three hundred dollar tickets for their shenanigans. Dave Grant was a card-carrying member of the Friends of Police Officers. He made the annual, tax-deductible donation, had his secretary stick the special decal on his license plate, and was never pulled over by the cops. Only once in a decade had he been stopped for his hundred mile per hour drag races with death - and that poor rookie had been transferred two counties over after bragging about ticketing Dave Grant.

Nothing stopped him but the slow crawl of tourists as he left the clogged arteries of the town. By sunset, he was cruising the winding coastal highways of Big Sur, looking for a hotel or a house. Over dinner, he found both. He slept poorly in a high-class oceanfront resort then met the realtor in the morning to sign the papers on a cliff-top mansion he saw from the road. He threw down his wallet at ten a.m., and settled into the furnished, sprawling house that was perched on a ridge surrounded by nothing but sky. The land fell away in all directions, down into the ravines and redwood forests, tumbling toward the distant, thundering ocean. Dave soaked his battle wounds in the Jacuzzi, determined to heal and enjoy his new lease on life.

It was a shame about losing Gold Mountain, but hell, there

were other mountains to buy, resorts to build. He had erected one empire; he could do it again, faster. His whole life - the whole world - everything stretched out before him!

Dave joined the club of Big Sur playboys, luxuriating in their wealth in the Eden of the elite, picking up young women with jewelry and luxuries, ditching them when they grew too demanding. He poured money into classes at expensive retreats, becoming a semi-permanent fixture improving himself, making up traumas for the catharsis of therapy, rolling in the hot tubs to the throb of didgeridoos, studying massage to meet women. He invested a little, pissed away fountains of money, and invented excuses for his continued inertia.

Years passed senselessly, metered out by splurges and occasional trips to foreign shores, incidental love affairs that never lasted, and the monotony of luxury. A brief and disastrous relationship climaxed dramatically three days before his fiftieth birthday bash. He cancelled the bacchanalian affair as his girlfriend slammed the door and left. He had despised the idea from the start. The party soured their relationship like fine wine spoiling into vinegar. Her sneaky maneuvers to trick him into agreeing to a small gathering (just a couple hundred), and a band (flown up from Los Angeles), and caterers (celebrity chefs), and so on - the manipulations and obnoxious cajoling infuriated him. Seething tensions exploded. She stalked out. He called the event off, shelling out a hundred thousand not just for the band and caterers, but also for the tent company, the photographer, the cake artisan, and the lighting design team.

The evening of his birthday came thick with silence. The plague of loneliness refused to leave his side. The windswept cliffs howled in the night. The raging gusts tossed the ocean up to soak the stars before hurling the waves back down in thunderous booms that shook the foundation of the mansion.

Dave threw his soul into the tempest, pacing the glass deck with a thousand dollar bottle of vintage wine clutched in his fist. He railed against the world that night. The elements lined up to battle his mortal flesh. Wind whipped his hair and slammed into his chest. The air split between the far off threat of rain and the hot breath of the drought-parched mountainsides. The stars glared above, hard and inscrutable, refusing to hint at fate or destinies tonight.

"Cold, unfeeling stars!" he shouted, but the depth of the black sky wrenched his words from his throat and left him mute. He chugged a mouthful of the wine. The burning flush inside his belly reminded him of his flesh and blood, and willful human determination.

"I want love!" he hollered in the lion's roar of men. He stood wide-legged and arched his barrel chest to the heavens.

"Is that too much to ask?" he cried. "You see this body? I am a man. I am alive. I roar with life and yet you send me skim milk substitutes for love! You send me hawk-women whose talons search my wallet! You send me beautiful facades to storefronts that have nothing of substance behind the window dressings."

He howled these accusations to the powers that listened silently in the black heavens. His soul wearied of the courtship dances that led to shallow affairs that dissolved like sea foam on the ocean. He had come from the jaws of death back to the realms of the living. His blood and breath could take no weak substitutions for the nutrient called love. He had to have it!

"I want it!" he roared. "I want the love of legends!"

The furious night wind smacked him for his impertinent demands. He glared and shouted back, undaunted.

"I want real love! I want to meet the one you're hiding!"

The universe stirred uneasily. He chugged the wine for

courage. Out there, in the masses of seven billion human beings, was a woman destined for his soul. He knew it; he had sensed the fates laughing at his confusion as he stumbled through the clutches of other women. He suspected the twisted destinies of stars snatching her from his sight. Even now, as his bold words hung on the thrashing night, he heard the hints of whispers and the tone of consternation lacing through them.

"What must I do?" he asked, nearly wailing. "Travel to foreign countries? Put out want ads? Help me!"

He pleaded with the universe. He offered a guzzle of his rare and vintage wine to the night. The ruby liquid of the drink of the gods tipped over the glass balcony rail and disappeared into the darkness. He could not hear the splatter on the rocks below. The night drank the offering on the wind.

"What must I do?" he asked again.

The night stilled. The wind halted. He hairs stood on end.

Give it up.

He heard a voice so ancient its depth defied the confines of gender and language. The stars shuddered overhead. He knew without a word the sacrifice the voice demanded.

Give up your wealth.

Dave flung back from the railing; back from the night, the wind, the voice, stunned not at the demand, but the immediate retort of agreement that sounded through his synapses. Money bound him in its embraces, defining him from head to toe. Before a stranger saw his face, the subtle mask of money reached out to shake the stranger's hand. Wealth suffocated his humanity and slid adulterously into bed with his lovers.

But now, Fate was robbing him at gunpoint: your money or your love. He could not have both. This woman existed beyond the beaten path of luxury. She hid behind a door his gold-tinged eyes could never see. His money clung to him worse than

his earlier obesity, driving a wedge of gluttony between them.
Drop it. Shed it. Toss it vehemently from your life.

He heard the message loud and clear. Make the sacrifice, he told himself. Money is nothing . . . but love! Love is a treasure worth seeking, a good fortune worthy of great sacrifice.

He swore. He paced. He growled incoherently at the night.

"Fine," he spat out, "I'll do it. I'll give up my money to find love."

Burning with passion, he swigged the last gulps of thousand-dollar wine. He rolled the dregs on his tongue and then threw the bottle into the darkness. He spun around and jabbed an accusatory finger at the Jacuzzi glowing in the night. He warned it silently, *your days are numbered.* The pool bubbled. Steam curled sinuously from the surface. He staggered to the edge and peered over the rim, expecting to see his reflection. A bubble burst. Sharp, hot water slapped him across the eyes. Howling, he smacked the pool. He swung his fist for a second blow, unbalanced his precarious crouch, and toppled in.

Flailing in the churning heat, he floundered to the surface. Gasping, he ripped the clinging silk of his shirt from his chest and threw it onto the deck. He belligerently pulled off the dead weight of his shoes and launched them over the railing. He stripped to nakedness and then leaned his forehead on the cool rim of the hot tub.

It has begun, he thought, sighing into the steam of his unexpected baptism. From the clothes on his back to his last dime and dollar - he would give it away to charity, to start-up businesses, to homeless beggars, to hippie chicks hiking up the coast. He would sell the mansion and move into a small apartment. He would downsize his possessions, wear ordinary clothes, blend into the masses.

He would shed his wealth and dive into humanity,

searching for his love.

CHAPTER EIGHT

. . . . .

The fear of having nothing hurts worse than the reality, Dave reflected as he slipped his ragged shoes back onto his leathered feet and scrambled up an embankment toward a gas station. Broken glass and the treacherous tongues of sardine cans glinted in the noonday light, threatening his soles. Grimy plastic bags waved weakly from their tangled positions in the weeds. Mysteries of human stories lined the slope. Dave paused beside a teddy bear that bore the marks of a child's love along with its weather-matted fur and sun-bleached hairs. He stared at it, humbled by the unknown tragedies that sweep the lives of billions. The bear's leg sank halfway into the dust, paying tribute to the duration of time it had lain forgotten on this slope. The child that once clutched its stubby body might have grown into a teenager now, clutching a cellphone for comfort instead of a bear. That awkward adolescent might be eyeing his parents suspiciously, haunted by murky childhood memories of tears and loss and his parents' refusal to turn the car around, resentful of the inherent injustice that scarred his capacity to trust and love.

Then again, the arc of the Universe is long. Dave crouched down by the bear and pulled it from the dust. He tenderly brushed the lumpy fur. Perhaps this battered bear was a great sacrifice in the Universe's grand design. Perhaps that boy, imprinted early in the aching pain of injustice, did not accept it as humankind's fate. Perhaps that boy, now churning hormonally through his rebellious teenage years, was wearing black and soaking up anarchist philosophy, playing hooky from the tyranny of teachers and public school dictatorships. Perhaps he is, at this very moment, trembling in a fifteen-year-old blend of desire and awe as the radical college girl cries revolution and justice at the local cafe. In his yearning, perhaps he dares to love, dares to believe in what she says, dares to think that tyranny and dominance are not the fate of humankind, dares to imagine that cruelty and violence are not inherent to human nature, but inimical to our souls. That boy - despaired of by his parents - was probably failing in his courses for refusing to memorize the litany of wars that pass for history and demanding to know why they were being taught the supremacy of capitalism when he and his generation would be chained to debt for life.

Somewhere, Dave encouraged the forlorn bear, your boy might be growing into a courageous spark of change.

Dave set the bear upright among the weeds and gathered up the other sacrificial losses that had been tossed out from car windows: a baby's shoe, an illegibly wrinkled notebook, a set of earphones, a lottery ticket stub. He loaded his hands with remnants of broken hopes and dreams abandoned on the littered slope. Each carried the echoes of a thousand stories and too many possibilities to discern. Dave knelt before his roadside shrine and murmured words to all the gods and spirits that might be listening: *May the losses of these people give rise to great awakenings, may we grow stronger despite our suffering, and may our painful moments lay the foundation for courage in our future.*

He sat by the shrine until the sun slid past the zenith and tapped him lightly on his westward cheek. Then he rose and took the last few steps up to the gas station. He threw his legs over the guardrail and stepped onto the asphalt of the parking lot. Suffering lives in gas stations, Dave decided as he glanced around. It takes up residence in overweight diabetics struggling to rise from beat-up cars; in bleary-eyed truckers buying half-gallon sodas; in squabbling children and exasperated mothers; in pained-looking men filling up sports cars, anxious to speed away from the masses and forget the uncomfortable faces of poverty.

Dave crossed over to the station and swung open the glass door. He courteously held it for the line of people waiting to come out: a big bellied man who barreled through without a glance; a mother hauling two kids, a bag of chips, her purse, and a newspaper who muttered a sound of thanks through the car keys clenched in her teeth; and a shuffling old woman. He waited patiently for the old woman while two more travelers shouldered in through the door, ducking between old age and celebrity magazines in a rush to the free coffee.

She paused on the threshold, head bent down, looking at the metal strip on the floor as if it were the Great Wall of China. She swayed and her gnarled claw snatched at the door jam. She sighed. One foot lifted a quarter inch and slid over the metal. Dave offered his hand. She looked up owlishly, her eyes magnified by the thickness of her glasses. She took his hand. Her left foot made the crossing. She stared wearily across the wilderness of the gas station.

"Where's your car?" Dave asked quietly.

She pointed her nose toward the air pressure station. An idling delivery truck blocked the handicapped parking. The driver dipped the handcart and rolled boxes of sodas toward them. Dave held the door with his foot and helped the old lady shuffle out of the way. With a thrust and a grunt, the deliveryman passed into the store.

"Maybe we could borrow his handcart to roll you over to your car," Dave chuckled.

The old woman wheezed with laughter.

"You get to be so old that traveling to the bathroom is like climbing the Himalayas," she rasped out. Her smile crinkled her face into hundreds of wrinkles.

"Come on," Dave offered, "I'll walk you to your car."

"Oh no," she protested, "that could take all day. You've got places to go."

"No," he answered with a shrug. "Not really. I'm not in a rush."

"Well, that makes you, me, and the dead," she snorted, "because the living are all trying to get nowhere, fast."

He walked her to her cantankerous-looking station wagon and practically lifted her into the driver's seat. He paused; he had serious misgivings about her ability to make it down the road.

"Are you going to be alright?" he asked anxiously.

She waved her hand at him as she dug in her purse.

"It's my balance, is all. Can't stay upright, but get me behind the wheel," she boasted, patting the steering wheel, "and you'd be amazed at how fossil fuels can power an old dinosaur like me."

She pulled out a twenty from her wallet.

"Here."

"Oh no," he began.

"I insist."

"I don't - "

"Don't tell me you don't need it. Your shoes look like you walked up this mountain."

"I did," Dave answered.

She blinked.

"Whatever for?" she snorted.

"Long story," he replied with a sigh.

She shook the twenty at him. He took it. They exchanged the routine thank you's and goodbyes. Dave walked back to the station and gave her a wave from the door. She hadn't even started the car. He shook his head and entered the station.

"Where's the rest - "

"They're for customers only," the cashier snapped at him, cutting off his question.

Dave looked around. Sodas, candy, a poisonous-looking apple that could have been straight out of Snow White: there was nothing to eat in the whole place. He bought a newspaper. He tucked it under his arm and held out his hand for the men's room key.

"Gas customers only," she qualified.

"I don't have a car," he told her.

"Then I don't have a restroom."

"You're joking," he exclaimed.

She pointed to a sign in the window: *Hitchhiking is strictly prohibited on this highway.*

"I'm not hitchhiking. I'm walking," he explained.

She raised her penciled eyebrows in her puffy face.

"We don't serve vagrants," she informed him.

"I'm not a vagrant," he answered.

"You look like it," she retorted.

"Look," he sighed, "water and bathrooms are human rights."

"Go talk with the United Nations," she snapped back unsympathetically.

"Couldn't you just - "

"No."

"Ma'am, I'm not going to graffiti the walls, shit on the floor, shoot up heroin, plug up the toilet, leave the water running, or spend all day in your restroom - "

She craned her neck and looked past him.

"Can I help the next person in line?"

Dave pivoted. Four people glanced away in an mixture of embarrassment, pity, and irritation. He stepped back from the counter.

"The dignity of all human beings," he began softly, "resides in our kindness to one another. The refusal of common decency does not lower my dignity; it lowers yours."

"Next!" the cashier barked, blushing red.

"The same is true for all who witness cruelty and stay silent. Your honor falters when you remain neutral toward unnecessary suffering. It would be easier for me to leave, shame-faced, and go defecate in the bushes than to cause a stir in our well-ordered world. But who will speak up for the next person in line? If I don't say something, how long will culturally-approved cruelty continue to mire this gas station in shame - "

"I'll call the police," the cashier threatened, tired of his sermonizing.

"You would use law enforcement officers to deny my basic human rights?" he questioned.

"Go shit in the bushes," she snarled back.

The line of customers stirred uncomfortably. Dave looked sadly at the cashier. She glared angrily back at him. Beneath her scowl, he could see the flush of embarrassment intermingling with her irritation, and also worry. Her eyes glanced at the security camera, wondering what her boss would think. She scowled at him, just wanting him gone.

A thick hand fell on the counter.

"Give me the key to the john," a trucker muttered.

The cashier hesitated.

"I ain't got time for this crap," the man growled. "I gotta take a piss and get back on the road."

She handed him the key. He gave it to Dave.

"Get in there and be quick," the trucker warned.

The cashier started to object.

"Shut up," the trucker snapped. "You'd probably make Jesus go shit in the bushes."

He stalked toward the restroom, jerking his head at Dave to follow.

Dave pissed, shit, washed and dried his hands in record time and handed the key to the trucker with a sigh of thanks.

"Don't mention it," the guy said as he shut the restroom door.

Dave slid out the glass door without looking at the cashier. He paused. The old lady's station wagon was still parked by the air pump. He walked over.

She had dozed off.

Dave hesitated. He shuffled. Finally, he sat on the concrete curb to wait. In twenty minutes, the old woman's eyes fluttered open. She blinked in astonishment, peered around, and scowled at the gas station. She saw Dave sitting on the curb, pursed her lips, and rolled down the car window.

"What are you still doing here?" she demanded.

"I was going to ask you the same question," he replied.

A grin of wrinkles contorted her face.

"You want a ride someplace?" she offered.

"Not with you," he answered.

"Afraid I'll keel over going sixty on the freeway?" she demanded.

"Something like that."

"You offering to drive?" she asked, squinting suspiciously at him.

"I would never presume," he replied. "You'd probably think I was a serial killer."

"Posh!" she exclaimed. "I know you're not."

He looked at her curiously.

"How?"

"You're Dave Grant."

He startled. His heart struck the gong of adrenaline and reverberated furiously.

"Yep," she continued, "took me this long to place your face, but now I'd know you a mile away. I'm Edna Lawrence."

"Oh lord," he sighed.

He had never met the shrew who had lambasted the owner of Gold Mountain in the local paper's weekly letters to the editor. They had not crossed paths at the contentious town planning meetings about the resort. He'd received handfuls of missives from her, decrying his capitalist invasion of the mountain town. She'd organized the local efforts to drive out the development . . . and lost.

They stared at each other over the halfway rolled down car window until she finally spoke.

"Why don't you get in and I'll give you a ride up to Gold Mountain. That's where you're headed, isn't it?"

"You'd probably drive off the road just to see us both in the grave," he complained.

She cackled.

"Hadn't thought of it. Good idea, though. I'd love to watch the Devil rake your soul over the coals."

"Careful," he warned. "We'll be neighbors in Hell."

"I'm a Buddhist," she sniffed. "I don't believe in that nonsense."

"Me too," he replied.

She sat back in her seat and regarded him with a curious expression.

"You're a Buddhist?" she asked.

He nodded.

"Well, I'll be darned."

She stared at him a moment longer then popped the door open with her gnarled hand.

"Alright then, you drive. You do me any harm and karma'll hurt you worse than the Devil. Truth be told," she said as she laboriously got out of the car, "I'm blind as a bat soon as the sun gets halfway to dark."

"Are you sure?" he asked as she made her way around the tailgate.

"'Course I am. I want to hear all the trouble you've been up to. We've got eighty miles and seven years of gossip ahead of us. Get in."

He complied with her imperious command. She settled into the passenger seat with a flurry of sighs and groans, taking her time as she clawed the seatbelt into position. He turned the ignition. The engine coughed and sputtered awake.

"Be a gentleman," she warned. "This wagon's nearly as old as I am. No fast stops or taking the turns too sharp. Her undercarriage is liable to snap like old lady bones."

The station wagon creaked and rattled up the winding highway. Edna kept her eye on his driving until, satisfied, she folded her hands in her lap.

"So . . . how'd the billionaire end up a bum?" she asked.

"Am I a bum?" he replied quietly. "I never begged or asked for anything."

"No, true enough," she conceded, "but you look like you've been dragged through the gutter."

"That might be true," he agreed with a short laugh.

"So . . . ?" she pressed.

He sighed.

"The gutter isn't what people think."

"So tell me what it is," she urged him.

And the gutter years flooded back into the present.

CHAPTER NINE

· · · · ·

Rain. He stood like the sandstone monoliths that dotted the central California coast, eroding under the pounding demands of poverty. Two years had slipped through his fingers since he began to give up his wealth. Now he stood in the downpour and shivered. Rain spat in his face and he no longer bothered to wipe away the insult. Shame stuck to him tighter than his wet clothes, but numbness rendered him oblivious. Cold has its blessings.

He squinted up through the scanty shelter of the tree's leaves. Smack! A fat drop waterboarded him between the eyes. He dropped his head and swore. The downtown was a deserted stretch of gray, flooded concrete. The storefronts valiantly attempted to fend off the winter gloom. The gutters ran with water. Dave leaned against the aching cold of the tree trunk. A shiver whipped through him. He contemplated ducking into the grocery store and taking a garbage bag from the bottom of the can where the cleaning lady kept her fresh supply.

He decided to wait. The store was slow; someone would notice him. Better to try in half an hour when the downtown shop clerks dashed in to grab deli sandwiches on their dinner breaks. Dave knew the tides of the street: the early morning trickle of workers, banging garbage trucks, clerks rolling up metal storefront gates, the scratching brushes of brooms sweeping up the trash and flicking cigarette butts into the gutter; the slow mid-morning ebb of people; the noon tide peak; the slight ebb in the afternoon; and the resurging tide of evening that led to the darker currents late at night.

Back when he had money and nice shirts, he would stroll

the avenue for hours just watching people, sitting quietly, and thinking. The hospitality guides knew him by sight; they assumed he owned commercial real estate or one of the businesses downtown. He watched them nudge the sleeping bundles of the homeless, telling them to move on. He saw them blow their whistles at skateboarding teenagers and issue tickets to the dreadlocked hippies who dared to coast their bicycles down the sidewalk.

He sat unquestioned and non-harassed for hours on the main street of town. The roll of cash in his gold money clip earned him this privilege even when he didn't spend a dime in the downtown shops. His fresh shave and tailored clothes allowed him to sit in the outdoor seating areas.

The politicians rotated. New policies crept into the downtown. He watched the city maintenance guys remove the benches up and down the avenue.

"Why are you taking out the benches?" he asked them.

"Beats me," they answered with a shrug. "It's like the big wigs don't want people sitting around any more."

Next, they ripped out the short rails that protected the raised gardens while allowing people to perch on the concrete garden walls. The rails were reattached in the middle of the narrow retaining walls, effectively blocking off the seating areas.

"No more sitting on the garden walls," the maintenance man grumbled, even though they were designed as benches, even though the blueprints specifically stated that the walls were meant to foster community and conversation, even though the architect had won a prize for the design. "City council thinks it encourages unseemly elements to hangout downtown."

"Who? The locals?" Dave asked with a short laugh.

The maintenance man shrugged with a commiserate grin.

"Yeah. Apparently the ridiculously high rents aren't enough

to drive out the punks, hippies, Rastafarians, anarchists, surfers, and artsy types. Got to make downtown downright unwelcoming so this place seems normal."

"You mean, like a sterile shopping district for the wealthy?" Dave asked. He had taken girlfriends shopping in dozens of those expensive streets - hell, he'd owned one, once. They were all the same: pristine little playgrounds, modern day promenades where the rich could see and be seen, obscene prices for boutique clothing, outdoor cafe seating at expensive dining restaurants. He rolled his eyes.

"This isn't exactly Beverly Hills," he pointed out.

"Not yet," the maintenance man agreed, "but they're working on it, just wait and see."

"I doubt the locals are just going to vanish without a fight," Dave commented.

"Oh, but they will," the guy countered, wrenching down a bolt. "They're working six jobs just trying to make the rent."

An attitude of detached curiosity swept him up. Dave observed both the changes in the town and in his own life like a coolly scientific anthropologist. He even started taking notes: *bank account dwindling, probably should start a new business; that new city statute requires permits for street performing, busking, or sidewalk vending - guess I won't learn to play the violin, haha; really should find work; new city plan says no music within ten feet of storefronts, garbage cans, or parking meters . . . what does that leave? - There's a new sign up about recent ordinances. Seems like the locals are thinning out, nothing to do downtown but shop, no music, no places to sit and talk. Only people left are bums and tourists. Better make some money soon, maybe sell those paintings and Asian art pieces, not sure where the rent is coming from this month. That's it; they've really done it now. Homeless meters? Are these people insane? Put a quarter in the red meter, folks, feed the homeless, keep them off the streets, put a quarter in – Jesus! The funds won't go to drunkards or druggies, it says. Huh, I bet the funds go to some nonprofit director's salary to be spent on wine and anti-depressants. – Look at that! Can't help but smile. Somebody ripped out those f-ing meters. Good. – Found a little teahouse to hang out at – wonderful place! – and the woman . . .*

Dave truncated the memory and scowled into the rain. He spat his bitterness onto the sidewalk. Raindrops pummeled his saliva into oblivion in the blink of an eye. His little notebook had cut off abruptly, but his downward slide had continued, inexorable. Winter came, along with rain and misery. The TV news station at the bus terminal blared out that the Supreme Court had ruled that waterboarding wasn't torture. Dave, the bums, and the Guantanamo prisoners all lifted bleary eyes and dared the judges to try it out for themselves. The prisoners went on hunger strike; the bums just went hungry. The torture didn't stop for either group. Cold laced his marrow until he stopped bothering to shiver. He could chatter his teeth into pulverized bits before he warmed up in this downpour. Cheap alcohol worked, but even that ran out.

He stood in the gloom of the rain under a tree downtown, cursing Gautama Buddha for his bourgeois privilege of living in tropical India. The Buddha didn't awaken in the monsoon season, Dave thought belligerently. No one gets enlightened in the rain . . . they just get wet.

A couple of Hare Krishna devotees dashed up the street, the hems of their orange robes soaked from the flooded gutters. Their funny, half-shaved heads remained dry under a solid umbrella. Dave cursed them, too. Then he changed his mind. Why condemn everyone just because misery loves company?

His eyes wept rain as he scanned the storefronts trying not to envy the mannequins poised inside the windows or the yapping shop-dog that lived inside the boutique across the street, growing fat on treats from wealthy women who made him dance and beg. The little bastard had bitten Dave once. It ran out and snapped off a chunk of his leg as he admired the window display. He kicked the vicious beast and the shopkeeper screamed bloody murder as if he were the menace to society! The monster had drawn blood! It could have rabies! The cop who came running shoved him down the street and told him to get lost.

Dave flipped the middle finger across the street to where the red-eyed little devil was curled up in a dog bed in the windowsill. He couldn't read it through the rain, but he knew there was a greeting card taped to the window with a Gandhi quote in gold embossed typeface.

"The greatness of a nation can be judged by the way its animals are treated."

The boutique sold those cards at twelve dollars a pop to women who carried Chihuahuas in their designer handbags and walked stiffly past the panhandlers on the street. Dave had heard one woman mutter something about lazy bums who wouldn't work - to which her companion had shrilly laughed.

"But darling," she exclaimed, "you've never worked a day in your life, either!"

"True," the first woman replied, "but I'm rich."

As if that explained everything. Laziness is a sin of the poor. The wealthy call it leisure.

Dave's thoughts turned black. The evening gloom sank deeper into muffled grays. Midnight blue shadows pooled outside the soggy orange streetlights. He needed a drink. He needed food. He needed to get out of the rain for fifteen minutes. The coffee shop down the block would let him stay one hour per cup of coffee. It wasn't whiskey, but it was something. He saw a huddled figure walking up the sidewalk with a long overcoat pulled tight around a set of narrow shoulders. Dave set his jaw and swallowed his pride.

"Hey, could you spare - "

"Dave?"

Shit . . .

Joan.

CHAPTER TEN

. . . . .

The old woman's ears pricked up. She pivoted in the passenger seat. The worn out springs moaned in protest.

"Joan?" Edna repeated, blinking through her thick glasses. "Who's Joan?"

"A friend," he answered.

"Your girlfriend," she said decisively.

"Not - "

"Your lover."

"Uh - "

"Your soul mate."

"Look Edna, I didn't say - "

"I can hear it - everything - in the way you said her name. Joan."

"You're making assumptions - "

"They're right, aren't they?"

He rolled his eyes at the old bat. She cackled and rubbed her hands together.

"Tell me about this soul mate of yours."

"She's not my soul mate," he grumbled.

"Of course not," Edna snorted. "You're a Buddhist. No life, no being, no self, no soul, no mate for the soul that is not a soul."

"Oh stop."

"Well, you're leaving out parts of your story," she protested.

"You asked about the gutter, not Joan. Seven years of gossip won't unravel in one thread."

"You met her as a bum?" Edna guessed.

"No, before that," he clarified.

"When you were still rich?"

"Somewhat." He paused to think. "Did you ever watch a leaf falling? Remember how it plunges down then swoops up as the flat side catches the air? That was me. I met Joan during a brief upswing."

"But then you fell? Did you lose her?"

"For a while," he concurred. "Then I found her. Then I lost her again." He broke off. "It's a long story."

"I've got time," Edna promised and then suggested with vindictive enthusiasm, "Sounds like Joan is all your bad karma come around to whack you upside the head!"

He rolled his eyes.

"No, she's my good karma come around to whack me upside the head."

"Ah," Edna sighed knowingly. She folded her hands in her lap and waited. A man can't help but want to rattle on about the woman he loves, even if she's whipping his sorry rump into shape. 'Course, Edna amended her thoughts as she snuck a glance at Dave Grant, she would bet her winning bingo ticket that those two were like blacksmiths at the forge: anvil, fire, steel, hammer, smith, and smithy all at once.

"So, who is she?" Edna asked.

"Joan's like drowning in the well of truth."

"She'll kill you if you don't learn to swim?" Edna chuckled with familiarity.

"Oh, so you know," Dave replied.

"Oh yes, I know," Edna said, pursing her papery lips together.

They drove quietly for a moment as the sun touched down on the peaks of the hills, spilled its golden farewell, then ducked out of sight, leaving them in shadows. Dave flicked on the headlights. When Edna spoke, her voice was thick with the past and her eyes saw memories invisible to Dave.

"You're just sitting there talking," she murmured, "when the eye of the Universe opens and sees itself looking back."

He nodded. Swallowed. Nodded again.

"Yes," he agreed.

"And you're not sure whether to be terrified," she said, "or fall desperately, madly in love with yourself in ways Echo and Narcissus could never even imagine."

"Yes," he whispered.

"Rumi and Shams, words of the beloved, Ram and Sita: it all makes sudden sense, but you can't find the words to explain it."

"Yes," he agreed.

"You want to shout your discovery from the rooftops, shake people in the street, and say *hello! Hello, my beloved self, hello!*"

"No," he shook his head. "That part comes later. At the moment your eyes meet, you can't bear to look away. You fall into the grace of seeing through her body, through yours, as if eyes and flesh were but ungainly telescopes and you are seeing the face of God mirroring your own because she is the mirror, polished, empty, quietly serving to reflect the truth - and in her eyes, you see - "

" - that you are the mirror, too," Edna finished. "God seeing God, seeing God seeing God."

"But there is nothing there - not you, not her, not God as something other than that reflection of what is."

"The paradox that annihilates us all," Edna whispered.

"And then you fuck," Dave concluded.

Shocked laughter shot out of Edna.

Dave grinned.

"What else is there to do," he said, "except reignite the cosmic spark of creation that turns this whole Universe around?"

Edna wheezed with laughter. Tears trembled in the gutters of her wrinkles.

"What else is there to do?" Dave repeated. "Wash the dishes? Take out the garbage? Get into petty arguments with your neighbors? Come on," he rolled his eyes. "The Universe just said hello . . . the only logical response is to give her a tremendous welcome!"

Edna howled until laughter shook the rattling car. Her gnarled hand patted his arm over and over. Her other hand curled its pale fist to her mouth trying to hold the laughter in, but every time she looked at Dave it exploded from the narrow birdcage of her chest.

"You'd better stop," he chuckled. "You'll have a heart attack."

She cackled harder.

"What a way to go!" she gasped. "I always told this world, sex or laughter, that's how I want to die, but at my age . . . " she trailed off.

His grin crinkled up the corners of his eyes.

"It would be a great inconvenience to me if you kicked the bucket at the moment," he mentioned.

"Me too," she wheezed. "The story just got interesting. Too bad you didn't meet this Joan back in your Gold Mountain days. I like her already."

"If I had known Joan back then, I would never have built that resort," Dave declared.

"Well, sometimes we've got to make a lot of blunders before the eye of the Universe opens," she said. "I know I sure did."

"Who was it for you?" he asked.

"A stranger in a cafe."

He blinked.

"Mmm-hmm," she murmured, "imagine that! Never saw him again, but spent my whole life wondering if I'd look up while I was in the bank or at the grocery store or when the Jehovah's Witnesses knocked on the door, and see the Universe looking back."

"Did it happen?" he asked.

"A few times," she recollected. "We're all the eye of the Universe - just some of us have our eyelids squeezed shut. The trees never blink, you know, nor the stars, or the rivers. Seems like humans are the only ones telling lies to mask the plain and simple truth. I used to go around with my eyes wide open like a submarine periscope, a spy of the divine, undercover in ordinary life."

"But you don't any more?" he questioned.

"Nope," she said shortly. "I got tired of it. It's been mighty sad and lonely saying hello and getting no answer back, only blank stares and scowls." She smiled sadly. "Never got the chance to welcome the Universe as thoroughly as you," she chuckled. She reached out her thin arms with their hanging bags of skin and in the yearning on her old face, Dave could see the woman, voluptuous once, rounded curves, plump breasts, who longed to embrace the divine in human form.

"My husband was an atheist," she said, dropping her arms and becoming a lonely old woman once again. "And that's the worst kind of blindness. He went through life with his eyes shut tight and there wasn't anything I could do to coax them open. You spoke of drowning in the well of truth? Well, he was that kid who scrunched his face up in a pucker when he went underwater. Meanwhile, I was diving in, eyes open in wonder, swimming in the beauty of it all."

"How'd that work out?" Dave asked.

"About as well as you'd expect. He kept yelling at me to

come up for air and sending in lifeguards to pull me out and finally I was ready to leave him when he up-and-had a coronary. Rest his soul."

"I'm sorry," Dave said quietly.

"I'm not," Edna replied. "He may have found answers to his skepticism by now."

They rode in silence for a moment, each lost in thought. Then Edna sighed and shook off the fog of memory.

"So, tell me about your Joan. Where did you meet? Was it love at first sight?"

"Something like that," Dave answered with a wry smile.

"She didn't fall for you right off?" Edna guessed.

"Not exactly," he grimaced. "You have to understand, I wasn't a terribly nice person back then."

She snorted.

"I remember," she said caustically.

"No, no," he protested. "I wasn't the heartless businessman that you knew, but I was only halfway from Gold Mountain to the gutter - and a long way from blossoming like a lotus in the muck. I was reading like a fiend, studying not just politics and economics, but also meditation, heart chakras, natural healing, things like that."

"Ah," Edna chortled, knowingly, "you were a disgusting blend of caterpillar goo stuck halfway in the middle of metamorphosis."

"Minus the chrysalis, which might have spared me the embarrassment of being a walking hypocrisy," he agreed, chuckling at the awkward reality of change. "I meant well," he said in defense of his sincerity, "but that semi-wealthy playboy spouting half-formed spiritual notions certainly was not a match for Joan."

He laughed.

"Of course, fools rush in where wise men fear to tread . . . and if I'd encountered her without that exact cocktail of arrogance and sincerity, I might have turned tail and run the moment I saw her in the teahouse."

"Teahouse?" Edna asked curiously.

Dave smiled. The teahouse marked the turning of a chapter in his life - the moment where the extraordinary took on new proportions and defied the imagination of everyday society.

"Yes, a teahouse," he told Edna. "Or rather, a hidden tea speak-easy off the radar of permits and signs, tucked into an alley behind a thrift shop, marked only by a red door with a small note that read 'Pull' and so I did."

CHAPTER ELEVEN

. . . . .

A slant of light had tugged his eye toward the long branches of an enormous weeping willow hanging over the end of the narrow alleyway. The roots split the sidewalk. The trunk shoved the building to the side. The tree defied a dozen city ordinances as it stood guard over the row of shops. He turned down the alley and strolled the sidewalk booths, curious. He nodded to the shopkeepers perched on front stoops. He pretended to admire trinkets while inwardly marveling at the existence of such an old-fashioned alley in the modern world. The last building sat crammed against the drab beige concrete wall of a thrift store, overgrown with a rambling jasmine vine that ached with longing. Dave eyed it cautiously. Cupid with his arrows could not intoxicate men's hearts more potently than those blushing star-white flowers. This vine twisted human emotions as tightly as it clung to the bricks and beams.

The red door caught his interest. He obeyed the invitation of the small, handwritten sign that told him to pull the door. The springs creaked as it opened. He looked left and right. No one on the alley looked his way. He entered. Indonesian statues stood shoulder-to-shoulder with rolled-up Persian carpets. He squeezed down the narrow aisle toward a hanging curtain, placed his eye against a slit in the fabric and saw -

No one.

He pushed the Japanese curtain aside, squinting as his eyes adjusted to the dimmer light. He blinked slowly, taking in Chinese clay teapots lined up neatly on shelves, Turkish rugs across the floor, rattan stools arranged in clusters around low tables, redwood pillars holding up the roof, and carved doors leaning against deep maroon walls. A record spun silently on an old turnstile. An electric tureen of boiling water hissed on the counter. An open skylight allowed a tumble of jasmine to hang down into the room. The backdoor opened onto a tiny stone courtyard. An errant breeze spun the paper lantern overhead. Behind a counter, a woman crouched under the sink, a wrench in her hand, adjusting the plumbing. A long black braid hung down her white blouse. It captured his gaze for a brief moment before she sensed his presence and whirled.

The arrow of her eyes shot him through the heart.

It's her, he thought.

"We're not open yet," she snapped, crackling with the fire of irritation.

"Oh, sorry. I just wandered in," he stammered.

She stared at him for a moment then pointed to a table with the wrench.

"Sit down. I'll be right with you," she commanded.

He sat, too surprised to do anything else.

She ducked back under the sink. Her arm muscles flexed. He stared at her compact back and thin ankles. She flinched and cursed the pipes. She twisted the wrench then leaned back on her heels. He hastily looked away as she reemerged with a satisfied expression. She washed her hands and glanced at Dave.

"You've got that *Through the Looking Glass* expression. You must be new."

He nodded.

"I'll make you a cup of tea," she decided.

He nodded again.

"That's what we do here," she informed him.

"You make tea?" he repeated dumbly.

"Drink tea, talk philosophy, and greet world-weary travelers rolling in from the road," she said, gathering a pot and cups as she explained. "It's a teahouse."

He shivered. His hair stood on end. His senses went on high alert.

A teahouse.

Up in the mountains, thirty miles east of town, he lived in a tiny Japanese teahouse complete with tatami mats. He had rented it on a whim, intending to live in the main house on the property, but he had rolled a futon out one day to take a nap and that moment of quiet ease became an obsession. Tucked under the towering redwood trees, surrounded by a giant bamboo grove, the Japanese teahouse was a gem hidden from the world. The owner let him rent it for a living space, along with the nearby wooden deck with an outdoor bathtub and a little toolshed converted into a kitchen. He cooked on a hot plate, showered under the stars, ate at the wooden picnic table when the weather turned warm, and shivered under three down comforters when the winter rains came.

It was as if he had never lived before. Years of luxury had dulled his senses, but the cold nip of winter rains and the hot breath of summer awakened his sensuality. The crack of a twig underfoot, the crunch of pebbles, the scrape of dry, papery leaves, the silent settling of the dust - these revived him. He crackled with aliveness. He breathed in the sharp cleansing tang of the redwoods. He watched the ripple of daylight shift through the bamboo grove. He listened to the evening lullabies of blue jays roosting and the soft hush of leaves scraping stone.

Then there were the buddhas.

Thirty carved stone statues stood silently throughout the property, some standing, some reclining, one kneeling; all life-size, six foot tall, imposing figures that watched him mutely, hands raised in mudras, palms outstretched, one up, one down, the old chant on their immobile lips: *Fear not, I shall not*

71

transition without you.

He moved quietly under their unyielding gazes, subdued from extravagance, challenged toward reflection. Dave wondered at them. Their presence pulsed, animate. He bought copies of sutras at old bookstores and read voraciously.

Until his encounter this afternoon, he gave no thought to the significance of the teahouse. It was simply shelter, a novel and unusual retreat. But now, here was another teahouse. He gazed around the room unsettled by coincidence. A teahouse to live in. A teahouse in town. Each one as rare as a river pearl.

He shivered. He forced his gaze around the room, noting the low tables arranged in clusters, waiting for people to occupy them with philosophic musings. A dark bookshelf held stacks of aged volumes. He squinted at the spines of sutras, Taoist texts, Rumi, Indris Shah, poetry, haikus, and Sufi tales. His treacherous eyes darted back to the woman.

She's too old to be the one, he thought. I prefer younger women.

This is different, his conscience warned. This woman is going to rake your soul over the coals and forge you into hardened steel.

I'll skip the coals, thanks, he retorted. She's over forty - see those wrinkles?

Thin tendrils sprouted in the corners of her eyes. Her hair was dark, nearly black. She wore no jewelry. Her skin bore no makeup. The slant of her cheekbones was real, not a trick of powdered blush or cosmetic surgery. Her plain clothes - the white blouse and simpler, loose-fitting cotton pants - rode her limbs and torso. She moved with unerring grace, but with a certain muscular firmness to the motions.

Dave looked away.

"So, what is this place?" he asked to break the silence in the room.

"I told you, it's a teahouse," she responded impatiently.

She carried a small tray over from the counter and set out the most intriguing collection of items Dave had ever seen: a tiny pot, no bigger than a bird's nest, a stack of cups the size of cracked-open eggs, a glass pitcher to match the pot, a strainer made of a small, sawn-open gourd, and a bamboo tray with slats across the top.

"I've died and gone to fairyland," he joked, lifting a little cup. "People drink tea from these?"

"This is gong-fu cha," she told him. "The Chinese tea ceremony."

He pulled the teasing smile off his face and sat up straighter.

"I'll behave myself," he promised.

She smiled in amusement.

"It's more relaxed than the Japanese form . . . I've heard the Chinese smoke cigarettes and crack peanut shells one-handed as they drink tea."

She sat opposite him and warmed the small electric kettle on the low table. When it reached a rolling boil, she began to pour. Dave watched in fascination as the stream of water touched the rim of the clay pot, circling it.

"Warming the pot," she told him.

She moved the thin strand of steaming water into the pot. The aroma of the tealeaves rode the clouds of steam. She poured the dark amber liquid into the glass pitcher, then into the two small cups. He reached. She held up her hand.

"That was just the rinse," she explained. "It opens the leaves. Here, smell."

She offered the clay pot on a small cloth. He cupped it in his hands, feeling the warmth enter his palms. He inhaled the scents of old wood and dried Turkish apricots, along with a touch of peat moss. He raised his eyebrows and glanced up. Her dark eyes regarded him steadily. The corner of her mouth twisted up. Her eyebrows drew together in a puzzled frown as if trying to place his face. He held her gaze a moment, wondering the same thing.

"Have we met?" he asked, though he knew they hadn't.

She shook her head and reached to take the teapot from him. When he released the pot into her hands, his fingertips caught the underside of her knuckles. A tingle ran up his arms. She froze, sensing the same.

"Do you have a name?" Dave asked her.

"Joan," she answered, startled. "Joan Hathaway."

She pulled away and placed the teapot back on the bamboo tray.

"Dave Grant," he offered.

She picked up a pair of bamboo tongs and tipped the tea from the cups into the slatted tray.

"Where did the water go?" he exclaimed.

Joan's laughter drew up the wrinkles in the corners of her eyes. His heart lurched. *Stop that*, his mind chided.

"Everyone asks that," she replied, pointing out a catch basin that slid under the tray. "The tea water is good for the plants."

"Ah," he replied, but could say nothing more as the tea and steam and hot water swirled in a flurry of motions he could not follow. Joan's body flowed with the lifting of the kettle and danced with the pouring of water.

"The Chinese gong-fu tea ceremony," she spoke as she placed the cups on the tray, "evokes the embracing of the Tao, the watercourse way. It flows, splashes, and breathes with the occasion and the ever-changing nature of reality. It asks us to be present, natural, and to simply enjoy the tea."

She placed a brimming cup before him. Dave's eyes leapt from the white porcelain circle to Joan, convinced that the shape of her face framed by the black line of her braided hair would forever be linked to this tiny cup and his first taste of tea.

"What does it mean, gong-fu cha?" he asked, lifting the bird's egg cup with the tips of his fingers and wincing at the heat.

"Drink your tea," she replied.

"That's what it means?"

She shook her head, eyes dancing in humor. She sipped and he copied the motion. His eyes widened at the rumble of taste, deep as velvet, with a dried fruit undertone and an edge of bitter chocolate.

"Now that," he declared, "is tea!"

Every anemic, tea-bagged, sugary, milk-weakened mug of nothingness he had ever grudgingly swallowed in his life was knocked off the pedestal of tea. Even coffee swayed slightly from its unconquerable position in his heart.

"Gong-fu cha," Joan said, replying to his earlier question as if only after tasting the tea could he understand the answer, "means perfection through practice."

"And perfect it is," he declared, lifting the cup appreciatively.

Joan smiled slightly. Her strong arms folded across her chest, puckering the white blouse. She lifted her chin.

"It is not the tea that needs perfecting, but one's self," she pointed out. "Gong-fu, also known to Western ears as kung-fu, literally translates to *skill through work*. Paired with *cha* - the Chinese word for tea - it means *making tea through effort* or, as I mentioned, *perfection through practice*. The tea ceremony, like the kung-fu martial arts, is meant to be a vessel for inner cultivation."

75

Dave swallowed as she glared at him sternly.

"Don't tell me," he said hastily, "that you're also a karate master?"

"Hah!" her laugh leapt out. "No. Tea is the only martial art I practice."

"Thank god," he sighed. "Your tea packs a strong drop-kick. I'd hate to run into it in a dark alley at night."

"It doesn't tolerate much nonsense," Joan concurred.

Was that a warning? Dave wondered. He doubted this compact, serious forty-year old woman took any nonsense in her own life, either.

Joan refilled his cup and looked searchingly at him.

"What do you do with yourself when you're not wandering into hidden teahouses?"

"As little as possible," he replied truthfully.

Her mouth twitched in a quick frown, as if she'd heard that answer before, masking unpleasant occupations. Dave groaned. She thinks I'm a narcotics dealer, he thought.

"I run a small business," he said, which was almost true. He had invested in a small business that was currently roiling in bankruptcy.

She nodded, satisfied.

"And you?" he challenged. "Do you just emanate along with the teahouse?"

"That is a very tantalizing notion," she sighed, "but no, I live and work in the ordinary, modern world most of the time. I pour tea three days a week - "

"Don't tell me any more," Dave joked, covering his ears. "I'd like to continue imagining you're a genie in a bottle."

Her smile curled in amusement. Dave's chest ached as his treacherous thoughts whispered that he could spend a lifetime teasing that hidden curl of a smile out from under the facade of

Joan's severity.

"Perfection through practice," he murmured, remembering her earlier phrase. "Why does that sound familiar?"

"Perfection of Wisdom," Joan answered instantly. "You're thinking of the Buddhist sutras."

She tilted back on her stool and stretched her arm to the bookcase behind her in a yawn of leonine grace. Dave's eyes traced the curve of her body from hipbone to splayed ribs to the small, shapely breast –

"Ah, what?" he stammered, looking away as she swiveled back to the tea table with a book in her hand.

"The Mahayana Buddhist texts are called the Perfection of Wisdom," Joan informed him, sliding the volume across the table.

The Diamond Sutra.

For the second time in an afternoon, every hair on his body stood on end.

"I was just reading this," he murmured, lifting the sutra.

"Really?" Joan asked sharply, her curiosity crackling to attention.

"Yes," he answered absently. "This morning, before dawn."

In the blackness of four o'clock in the morning, he had woken in the Japanese Teahouse, instantly and fully awake. Nocturnal animals rustled through the dry leaves just beyond the plaster walls, creeping to the koi pond for a drink. The blue jays roosting in the giant bamboo nested silently. The blackness cloaked the world, absolute. Dave's eyes blinked, sightless. He rolled over on the futon and snapped the small floor lamp on.

The Japanese Teahouse lit up in the darkness, glowing like a paper lantern before dawn. Inside, Dave listened, uncertain of what had roused him. Then, as if drawn by unseen forces, his hand moved to the stack of sutras piled on the tatami mat next to the futon.

The stone buddhas watched him from the woods. The carved, serene faces of those closest glowed with the soft light of the teahouse. Further in the darkness the statues merged into the silence. All around, they ringed the tiny dwelling, watching . . . waiting.

Dave slid the sutra across the sheets of his bed. He leaned on one elbow as he read the cover.

The Diamond Sutra.

His fingers opened the volume. The pages crackled.

Thus I have heard, the text began, *once, the Bhagavan was dwelling near Shravasti in Anathapindada Garden in Jeta Forest.*

As he had so often done before, Dave flipped to the commentary, leaving one fingertip placed on the printed letters of the translation, licking the forefinger of his other hand to search the pages for explanations. Ah, he thought, scanning the translator's notes, the Buddha was hanging out in a park with his buddies. He ate breakfast, and then they all sat down to talk shop about enlightenment.

The Buddha's disciples were on a crash-course to become spiritual superheroes - bodhisattvas; literally translated, *spiritual warriors* - and they asked the Buddha how they ought to behave.

What you should do, the Buddha suggested, is liberate all beings from suffering and delusion by thinking this thought:

However many beings exist . . . in the realm of complete awakening I shall liberate them all. And though I liberate countless beings, not a single being is liberated.

Huh? Dave frowned and blinked. He scanned the page to see if the rest of the text was as inscrutable as this line. Ah, apparently, he wasn't the only one with a befuddled expression because the Buddha went on to explain:

And why not? No one can be called a bodhisattva who creates the perception of a self, a being, a life, or a soul.

And why not? Dave asked, but the Buddha didn't answer that question; this was advanced curriculum. He was wildly out of his depth. Dave turned to the commentary like a floundering undergrad turns to Cliff Notes. The commentator wrote with a hefty dose of humor:

"Let's start at the basics. The only constant is change. The rocks change, the mountains change, the universe changes; you change. Nothing stays the same. So what are we calling a self? An ever-changing stream of thoughts, blood cells, muscles, bones, etc. Got that? Now, think of this: this stream of a self has inputs and outputs - food comes in, waste goes out; oxygen comes in, carbon dioxide goes out. Check it out. The tree breathes in your CO_2; you breathe in the tree's oxygen. From one end to the other, you are connected to the whole world. So, why limit your self? Where do you stop and where does the air begin? If you're a part of everything else, can you truly call your self this solitary sack of skin and bones? Rather arbitrary, don't you think?

"The bodhisattva lets go of delusions such as a permanent, unchanging, isolated self. Instead, he or she dives headlong into a reality beyond borders, division, or knowing. Here, there is no self, no individual beings, no such thing as a life to these nonexistent beings, and no soul that isn't also changing and connected to this wild transforming nature of reality.

"So, when the bodhisattva enters the realm of complete understanding, he or she lets go of you and me. Fixed and permanent gives way to changing and connected. The perception of many separated beings gives way to one inter-connected being, and . . . voila! There are no beings to liberate from the delusion of separate, fixed, or permanent existence."

It's a joke, Dave realized with an exuberant leap of the heart. You can't liberate a being that doesn't exist! And what's real is already liberated! He laughed so hard the blue jays burst out of the bamboo grove chattering in annoyance.

"What a hoot!" he hollered.

We just forgot the truth. We have no self to suffer, no lives to lose, no beings to enlighten, no souls to save. Self, being, life, soul are all illusions - arbitrary concepts in a teeming, interconnected soup of reality!

He jumped up from the futon and shimmied across the tatami mats in a sideways, shuffling dance.

"Hot diggity!" he shouted. "Let's just enjoy these no selves, then!"

In the dawn grayness, the buddha statues' eyes curled up at the corners. Stone mouths twitched. Dave missed the flick of carved glances and the patient bemusement of the buddhas who watched him as he dressed and showered and took off down the mountain to celebrate the good news of the bodhisattvas. Their buddha breaths rustled through the bamboo and flipped the pages of the sutra lying forgotten on the tatami mat.

Oh, awakening one, they whispered, *this is just the beginning.*

"So," Joan said, returning him to the present, "you read Buddhist sutras?"

Her casual tone was laced with intense curiosity. He glanced up and caught the dark stare of her eyes searching his face. A frown furrowed her eyebrows as if this information had caused her to suddenly reconsider every aspect of the man who had appeared in the teahouse this afternoon.

"I read them every night," Dave joked to break the tension. "They put me right to sleep."

Joan rolled her eyes and released a short laugh of exasperation.

"I'm just kidding," he amended hastily and honestly.

Her eyes kept him pinned.

He paused, soberly returning the gaze.

"This may sound strange," he warned.

She shook her head.

"For the past few weeks," Dave told her, "I've been waking up at four in the morning and reading the sutras - Hui Neng, Vimalakirti, Heart Sutra. This morning, it was the Diamond Sutra."

"All Mahayana texts," Joan pointed out, leaning her elbows on her knees, eyes bright with interest. "And four a.m. is a traditional time for monks to rise and meditate." She bit back a smile. "You're even wearing burgundy and saffron."

Dave startled, glancing down at himself. Sure enough, his buttoned-up shirt was deep maroon, and the scarf he had thrown over it was as gold as Tibetan monks' robes.

"Sounds to me," Joan commented as she sipped her tea, a mischievous grin spreading above the rim of the teacup, "that you're being called onto the bodhisattva path."

"Oh no," Dave objected with certainty. "They've got the wrong guy for that."

He laughed uneasily. Her words had struck a chord of possibility and the resonance unsettled him.

"I'm no spiritual warrior, let me tell you!" he exclaimed, shaking his head emphatically. "I'm lazy, self-indulgent, driven to the sense-pleasures of luxuries, food, drink, sex, music, dancing - "

He broke off. Joan's eyes watered from the effort to hold her laughter in.

"What?" he asked.

"I knew it," she chuckled. "The moment you walked in the door, I knew there was something about you. Your karma's got you enrolled in bodhisattva boot camp. Watch out, Dave Grant, we'll be crossing paths at the Buddhist temple before the year is out!"

"Wait! What?" he stammered.

"The Buddhist temple," she answered. "I'm joining. And I'll bet that - "

"You're joining a monastery? As a nun?" he gasped, horrified. "You can't do that!"

She frowned at him.

"Why not?" she asked.

Because I'm falling in love with you, he answered silently, because the Universe conspired to bring us together, because I feel like I've known you for a thousand lifetimes and you can't possibly be serious about joining a monastery!

"Are you going to take a vow of celibacy?" he asked as his reality ground to a shocking halt.

"That is generally required," Joan pointed out. She narrowed her eyes. "Not that it's any concern of yours."

Dave glared at the Universe. This isn't funny, he warned the laughing fates. He heard them howling with humor, theatergoers enjoying the drama of his life, thrilled with the convolutions of plot, eagerly anticipating his lifetime of longing for the woman he could never have.

That's what you think! he shot back at them.

"Joan," he said calmly, "you do know why all the bodhisattvas come back from the edge of enlightenment, don't you?"

82

"To liberate all beings and end suffering," she replied confidently.

"No," he made a face. "That's just propaganda for the Buddhist temples."

She blinked. He drank his tea and smacked his lips as he waited for her to ask . . .

"So, why do they come back?" she challenged him.

He smirked.

"Sex and chocolate."

She rolled her eyes at him.

"It's true," he insisted.

"That's ridiculous," she retorted.

"Think about it," he urged. "Why else would they come back?"

"To end suffering," Joan answered indignantly.

"Exactly. Sex and chocolate equals no suffering."

"No," she argued, "no suffering equals no suffering."

"Are you saying sex is suffering?" he teased. "Sounds awfully Roman Catholic to me. Have you ever had an orgasm?"

"That is none of your business!" she burst out, shocked.

Not yet, anyway, he amended silently. He drank his tea nonchalantly and put his cup out for more.

"Maybe," he drawled slowly, teasing her with his eyes, "I was meant to come here today and save you from the cloister."

She raised one skeptical eyebrow.

He stretched his hands behind his head and smiled winningly.

"Tell me, Joan, if all beings are liberated already, what good does it do to lock yourself up in the temple?"

"Where do you get this notion of self that's locked up?" she shot back.

"I don't," he laughed. "My notion of Joan doesn't involve

cloisters and locks."

"Your notion of Joan is an illusion."

"Ah, but so is yours," he countered.

Her eyes pinned him sharply.

"Who are you?" she asked him with an intense frown.

He froze. The look in her eyes broke the confines of time and space. Lifetimes unraveled threads of connections. He had known her before - once, twice, a thousand times over. Their fates had spiraled through the centuries. Who was he? Woken before dawn to read the perfection of wisdom, drawn to a red door that said pull, brought to this teahouse to meet her at this moment . . .

"Perhaps," he said softly, "you should think about that before joining a monastery."

Her eyes widened, but the door jingled and new teahouse guests strolled in through the curtain. He drank his tea silently, following her with his eyes. When their glances crossed, sparks flew. An inexplicable fury boiled in her. Unspoken outrage brimmed beneath the surface of her tranquil demeanor. Dave chuckled to himself. A spark of troublemaking ignited gleefully in his chest. The disgruntled fates frowned at him for his intervention. He smiled back at the unseen, invisible realms. Dave Grant had built empires and fortunes; he had challenged the gods, destiny, and the divine. Oh ho! he declared to the smug certainty of karma and Fate, so you think she'll go to the cloister? Not if I can help it - not this time around. He smiled arrogantly at the Universe's annoyance.

But beyond his perception, the Fates maneuvered and laid traps. If Dave had caught a glimpse of their plans, he would have run for cover at once, but instead, he boastfully mocked and challenged their notions of destiny. He flirted with Joan as she studiously ignored him. Joan flicked her dark eyes at him once and pointedly reached to clear his tea tray. He grasped her arm.

"I think," he said as she glared at him, "you're going into the cloister - "

" - monastery -"

" - whatever," he replied. "You're going in because you're afraid."

"Of what?" she demanded indignantly.

"Sex and chocolate."

She glared at him. He spread his hands wide open, innocently.

"How could you live without love?" he challenged her.

"Enlightenment is a kind of love you can't even imagine," she retorted.

"Ah," he shot back, "maybe love is a kind of enlightenment *you* can't even imagine!"

Her mouth fell open. He grinned triumphantly. She glared back and would not speak to him for the rest of the afternoon. Joan leapt to serve the other teahouse guests, carrying water and tea ware back and forth around the room, avoiding Dave except to curtly and perfunctorily refill his electric kettle with fresh water. He caught her eye once and winked. Her arm muscles twitched. Dave ducked, but the jug of water she carried didn't fly across the room in his direction. He lifted a cup of tea in a toast. She ignored him. He had never had so much fun in his life. He stayed until closing time. She pointed to the clock.

"Do you want help closing up?" he offered.

"Not from you," she snapped back.

"Must have hit a vein," he teased.

"The door is that way."

"I'm an expert in sex and chocolate," he mentioned.

"Not interested," she retorted.

"I wasn't offering," he commented smugly.

She glanced sharply at him, hands on her hips, toe tapping in irritation.

Joan, he decided, was far superior to any of the young blondes he had dated. At forty, she had nuances and confidence, self-respect and -

"Don't make me throw you out," she warned, cutting off his train of thought.

He picked up his coat and tossed it over his shoulder. She followed him out with the keys in her hand, ready to lock the door behind him. He turned back to her with a wicked grin, anticipating her reaction to the parting shot he had spent all evening preparing.

"By the way," he mentioned casually, "did you know that I live in an authentic Japanese Teahouse?"

He closed the red door on her startled expression.

CHAPTER TWELVE

. . . . .

Perfection through practice.

Joan's words echoed through Dave as he rose the next morning just before dawn. The eyes of the stone buddhas followed him as he walked the winding path from the Japanese Teahouse to the kitchen shed in the semi-dark, carrying the *Diamond Sutra* in one hand. The redwood mammoths stood still and silent overhead.

His sandals hit the smooth planks of the deck. With a triumphant grin, he clapped one stone buddha on the back and slapped a high-five on the upraised hand of another. He pivoted in front of the outdoor sink that drained into the bamboo grove and picked up the shard of mirror he used to shave. Narrow and small, it barely caught glimpses of his chin. He slowly turned it, assessing the morning and his reflection. His arm hairs stood as alert as sentries. Thin threads of adrenaline crept through his blood. Daybreak hung with a hush on the forest. He could almost hear the invisible world whispering.

He held the shard of mirror up to his face. A stone buddha rose in reflection. He whirled.

There was nothing there.

The bamboo and redwoods turned pale hues in the dawn.

He looked again. A band of sunrise bathed his face in gold. There he was, neither old nor young, neither handsome nor hideous, just a man who wore his life in his lines. He was still overweight - just twenty pounds or so - enough to puff out his cheeks, put bags under his eyes, and to give him a paunch to flop over his belt. He sighed. He'd have to lose that. He'd been meaning too, but there was always another pastry shop or a new

Chinese restaurant to try out. But, Joan's eyes had curtly raked up and down him yesterday. He had felt her unspoken scorn as she swept her black eyes over him cursorily.

He decided to fast. He would let the pounds slide off his body like uncomfortable reminders of the past. He didn't care about the weight, he told himself. It's not vanity; it's . . . he paused, glancing guiltily at the stone buddhas.

It was a spiritual thing.

The wind stirred in the bamboo, demanding honesty.

He wanted Joan to want him.

The redwoods swayed their trunks overhead.

He wanted to tease her, scorn her, and make her hop on coals exactly as she made him.

The buddhas rolled their eyes in exasperation, as if they had seen these two through countless lifetimes of this nonsense. Dave glowered back through the shadows.

"What?" he had the temerity to object. "She started it."

Dave paced back to the teahouse and threw himself on the futon, remembering his intention to give up all his money in pursuit of real love. He groaned. Not Joan! Not sharp-eyed Joan with that smile twisting up her lips as if she'd heard the cosmic joke a thousand times! She was too serious, too severe, too old. Her opinions scorched with fire, her tongue kept him dodging its cutting edge . . . and this was the treatment he got when she hardly knew him!

Or did she?

Dave grew still. He felt the heave of past lives, the eerie déjà vu that defied body and birthplace. He had encountered Joan-before-Joan; before black hair and dark eyes; before teahouses and sharp tempers. Their story had entwined throughout centuries. He shuddered, wondering what he had done to annoy her in the last go-round that had left her in such a pissy mood.

He groaned, remembering how her eyes narrowed like truth-pulled bowstrings before the launch of her quick retorts.

Touché, my love, he conceded, you're more than a match for me. He considered surrendering now, waving the white flag of truce and swearing undying devotion.

No. He rolled over onto his back and laced his fingers behind his head as he rejected the idea. He felt a roar in his guts and corresponding stir in his loins. She didn't come back with fighting spirit just for his surrender. He mused long into the morning, his smile growing wider and more mischievous as the hours passed.

Unseen in the woods, the buddhas sighed. The wind hid their exasperation, but Dave felt the hint of their message brush his mind.

Would it be so hard just to love her?

His mystic understandings dissolved like soggy cereal the moment he turned the corner into the alley. His carefully constructed strategies fled his mind like farm-boy foot soldiers. He barked at them to hold their ground. They vanished. He stood in front of the red door, abandoned by last night's confidence. He considered retreating. He shifted, ready to bolt-

The door flew open, a swing of water swooshed out, and Joan soaked him with a tray of cold tea!

He gasped.

Her mouth flew open in astonishment.

He dropped his head down, looking at his sodden shirt in disbelief.

She stammered out an apology.

"The drain is blocked again - I didn't think - I should have looked - I'm so sorry."

Dave burst out laughing.

"Admit it," he said. "You wanted to throw a kettle of water at me right from the start."

"I did not!" she protested. "The thought never occurred to me . . . though if it had," her mouth twitched as she trailed off.

Joan gestured for him to follow her inside. She grabbed a dry towel from behind the counter and patted his soaked shirt. Her hand lingered on his hair as she tousled the water from it, then darted away. She handed him the towel and spun, but not before he saw the blush on her cheeks.

Oh ho! he thought.

She offered to buy him a shirt at the thrift store next door, but he refused.

"This is proof of my baptism by tea," he joked, pulling the damp shirt away from his chest and fanning it. "I've been anointed by the teahouse goddess, herself."

Joan's grin curved across the sculpture of her cheeks. The lines in her eyes curtsied. Dave's heart flopped over in his chest, forcing him to admit that it was not the shock of cold water that left him breathless and turned his knees weak.

"Bring me the finest tea in the house," he declared. "We'll drink to the occasion."

He leaned his elbows on the counter and pulled out a packet from the collection of fine teas available to purchase.

"Oh, that's terribly expensive," Joan warned him. "You shouldn't - "

"I'll take it. Let's pour for everyone who comes in," Dave suggested magnanimously.

She regarded him with solemn curiosity for a moment then shrugged and prepared the hundred-dollar pot of tea. Dave refrained from telling Joan that the shirt she had just ruined cost twice as much, and that he had uncorked bottles of wine worth ten times the price. Her offer of a thrift shop replacement for his shirt amused him. He had never stepped foot inside a secondhand store. He frowned, realizing the discrete iconic label on the breast pocket of the exclusive designer shirt meant nothing to Joan, nor did the subtlety of the high-quality cloth.

A layer of the teahouse's novelty to him lay in its rejection of the classic elements of luxury that adorned the leisure halls of the wealthy. The tables and stools were egalitarian in their arrangement. There were no sections that could be bought for higher prices or screened off for private parties. In fact, the only extra perks available for purchase in this establishment were the rare teas in the small basket on the counter. Everyone who walked in the door paid the same price for teapots, cups, hot water, loose leaf teas, the old fashioned record player that spun world music albums, the solitude of a solo table or the company of the teahouse guests, and of course, the hospitality of Joan.

"Is it always quiet in here?" he asked, thinking of yesterday's slowness as he glanced around the empty room.

"Oh no," Joan assured him. "Friday through Sunday, the irregulars roll in and stay until closing."

"The irregulars?" he asked.

She smiled, thinking of the odd assortment of human eccentrics who congregated at the teahouse.

"You'll see."

Just as she spoke, a trio of youth burst through the hanging curtain, greeting Joan with familiarity. A dour-looking man crept in before the young students had finished their greetings. Joan invited them to join Dave's table, and quickly laid out cups for them all. Dave watched silently, observing a world so different from his own. The hidden teahouse attracted an odd collection of souls. A school bus driver and a dreadlocked dancer pulled up stools next to each other. A bohemian college

91

student tumbled in from the woods, carrying a wooden flute instead of textbooks and a handmade leather pouch instead of a cellphone. A modern-day nomadic biochemist stopped in for a cup of tea. From the exclamations of the irregulars, Dave gathered that she swung in for tea each time she passed through town on her circuit between laboratories. A farmer arrived, lean as a beanpole and as solemn as the melancholy fogs that blanketed the coastal strawberry fields he tended. A pair of lesbian moms handed Joan a bag of herbs from their garden and updates on their mischievous sons.

Dave listened to stories from the daily lives of people from all walks of life, startled by the honest camaraderie that emerged around the tea ceremony. Joan kept her eye on him, he noticed. Subtly, he tracked her moves, noting when her fingertips touched his shoulder and when her grin turned in his direction. As the table filled with company, their stools scooted closer and closer until he could feel the flushing heat of her thigh and the electric shock of their bodies brushing together. Once, when Joan rose to fetch more water, she steadied her balance on his shoulder and her palm drew across his scapula, leaving a trail of tingles as she passed.

He watched her. Some women would play the role of the hostess with a heavy dose of syrupy mothering, but Joan fulfilled her role like a determined bird kicking the chicks out of the nest just for the joy of seeing them fly. She teased the teahouse irregulars, snapped back retorts to their philosophic challenges, shot out piercing questions, and tore apart assumptions like a defender of the realm of truth. All the while, Joan's hands danced, pouring hot water and laying out fresh cups as more irregulars arrived.

"What are you all doing?" Dave asked, noticing a tapping gesture the irregulars kept using.

"Oh that," Joan laughed. "It's a way of saying thanks for the tea. It's a reference to an old Chinese story."

She tapped her pointer and middle fingers together on the edge of the tea tray then curled them under and gently rapped her knuckles.

"The Emperor wanted to hear what his people thought of him," she explained, "so he disguised himself as a servant and made his manservant dress up as the emperor. This way, he could hear all sorts of gossip - and honest opinions - about his edicts and policies. All went well until it was time for tea. The Emperor-disguised-as-a-servant kowtowed to the nervous manservant and offered the manservant tea. The poor servant panicked! After all, this was the Emperor - a god born as a man - ruler of all of China, offering tea to a lowly servant. The manservant could not even bow or say thank you! Emperors never pay any attention to servants, after all. If he so much as looked at the Emperor-disguised-as-a-servant, he might blow the whole ruse!"

Joan's eyes danced in her face, animated by the story.

"So, the manservant discretely put his fingers together in the shape of a little man," she continued, placing the tips of her fingers together like two legs and standing them on the edge of the tea tray. "And then he folded them onto the knuckles like a man bowing on his knees. In this way, the manservant thanked the Emperor for the unimaginable honor of being served tea from the hands of a god."

Dave smiled at the tale and the use of the gesture.

"So," Joan finished, "when we use it to honor the tea pourer, it is a way of honoring the god-in-disguise in each of us."

"Or the goddess," Dave sighed. Their eyes met for a long moment. He drew a deep draught from the mysterious depths of her gaze. She glanced away.

93

Dave looked around at the miracle of the assembly of gods, drinking tea together in a hidden teahouse tucked in an alleyway of a touristy seaside town. Across from him sat an older man with a long beard and watery blue eyes. To the old man's left, a middle-eastern acupuncturist studied his tea as if searching for the meaning of life. Dave sat among them, a former billionaire in a damp shirt.

"Hey, Joan," one of the students called out, "did you catch the news about the protests?"

"No, nothing today. I've been here," Joan replied, pouring another round of tea.

"What protests?" the bus driver asked.

"Against the rich," the student answered.

Dave froze. He had heard about the demonstrations. He had been tracking the populace's growing resentment of the wealthy ever since he made his first fortune. He sat very still, listening like an emperor-in-disguise.

"There are massive demonstrations happening on the East Coast," the student explained. "The police tear-gassed the crowds yesterday, but I heard they came back even stronger today."

"There's nothing on the evening news," another man harrumphed.

"Of course not," the student scoffed. "The mass media isn't covering it. They never do." Irritation flushed the student's face.

"What are they demanding?" Dave asked.

"Change," Joan answered with a wry grin. "An end to extreme income inequality, unemployment, poverty, the market manipulations of the rich, bank bailouts, and tax cuts for the wealthy."

"Phht," the man snorted. "I've seen the online footage. It's just a bunch of pissed-off college students who don't want to work their way out of debt. They should just get a job."

The student spun in his seat, gaping at the older man.

"You're, like, joking . . . right?" he asked, stunned.

The man folded his arms across his chest.

"No," the man said, shaking his head. "These kids don't understand. They have no respect or appreciation for the fact that the wealthy are the job creators. They build businesses, hire people, create opportunities. They pay the bulk of the taxes - "

"Only because they have the bulk of the nation's wealth," Joan interjected, frowning.

"Billions," the man argued. "They pay billions in taxes. I bet you don't even pay taxes, do you?"

Joan scowled.

"I do," the bus driver said quietly.

"We do," added the lesbian moms.

"Me, too," said the farmer.

Dave burst out laughing.

"The wealthy don't pay taxes," he informed them, speaking from experience, "unless they have a lousy tax accountant. The rich hire lawyers and experts. If that doesn't cover it, they buy a change in the tax code."

He drank his tea and ignored the strange looks his confident statement elicited. The other man resumed his arguments, ignoring Dave's points completely.

"There have always been rich people and poor people. It's the way the world works - "

"That is patently untrue," Joan retorted, her eyes flashing. "The monkeys aren't wandering around rich or poor. At some point, the human species invented money, wealth and property . . . and with those came poverty, the notion of scarcity, and the condition of hunger for some and abundance for others. It was a shell game that paid off well for the elite, so they perpetuated it.

But," she fumed, "what came into existence can fade from existence. Humanity could drop the shell game if it wanted to," she spat out in disgust, "but everyone keeps thinking they're going to win it. Everyone keeps gambling, hoping to get the winning lottery ticket."

Joan threw her leftover tea onto the tray, furious.

"Do you know how the lottery works?" she asked. "Most people lose a little, one person makes a little, and the lottery owner makes a lot. It's rigged. The whole game is rigged . . . same with money, wealth, and poverty. We can't win by perpetuating it. We have to stop hoping to be the lucky winner and recognize that the whole game is corrupt."

Dave regarded Joan with renewed admiration. It had taken him a long time to work that out. When he was rich, the banks called him up practically begging him to borrow money from them. He had a saying; *the first million is the hardest.* Once he had capital, he could invest, start businesses, and then put those businesses up as collateral for more capital. But as he grew poorer, doors shut, opportunities vanished, and the banks wouldn't even set up a meeting. Dave wondered how Joan knew all this. He snuck a glance at her, but her attention was fixed on the other man.

"If it's a lottery, what does that make you, Joan?" the man snidely shot back. "A sore loser?"

Dave bristled at the attack on Joan, but she snapped into fighting position. The sharp edge of her tongue unsheathed as she leapt into battle.

"Hah! It makes me the only fool in the room smart enough not to lay down a dollar for a lottery ticket. No, I don't pay taxes. I don't make enough income. And if I did, I'd refuse to give half of it to a war machine that blows up innocent people in foreign countries so that wealthy weapons manufacturers can detonate their inventory as if war were just a clearance sale making room for new merchandise."

Joan's temper erupted when provoked. Dave watched the other man try to parry her points, but he quickly realized that Joan had been holding back, allowing others to score a few points here and there like an indulgent warrior sparring with village boys.

Watch out, he warned the man silently. Joan's expression indicated that she intended to cut pride and delusion into shreds.

"The rich are only viewed as job creators because they hold all the capital," she pointed out. "If their massive fortunes were dispersed among the people, every Tom, Dick, and Harry would be popping out small businesses, jobs, and stimulus to the economy. The wealthy and their mega-corporations are not - and never have been - job creators. They tend to be poverty-inducing, minimum wage-producing, part-time job-inflicting, union-busting, healthcare-eroding, worker rights-violating, democracy-destroying monsters."

She heaved for breath and the man stole an advantage.

"Well, without those jobs no one would have any work."

"Are you insane?" Joan shot back. "The wealthy elite are sucking up money like water and the whole nation is cracking with drought. The dam of their fortunes is amassing into a huge reservoir that no one has access to, except for the rich. Break the dam, I say! Turn the water into the desert and you'll be amazed at the vibrant economies that will grow."

"You're hardly an economist -"

"No, I'm a Buddhist," Joan retorted. "Which simply means that I observe things as they are."

"I think you're overestimating the size of the dam," the man argued.

"Actually," Dave interjected, "she's underestimating it."

She raised an eyebrow at him, picked up the neglected tea pitcher, and refilled all the cups as he spoke.

"The richest handful of individuals in this country owns more than the poorest forty percent of the populace. How much do you make a year?" he asked the youth sitting next to the college student who had started the conversation.

"On a good year?" the young man pondered, thinking about his three, post-college, part-time jobs. "I'd say about thirty thousand dollars - but only if I get a sweet summer gig with good tips."

Dave calculated rapidly.

"The wealthy make that much in an hour and fifteen minutes," he pointed out.

"You're making that up," the man objected.

Dave smiled grimly.

"No, I can assure you, I'm not."

The number was based on his Gold Mountain income, not including investments or interest from his offshore account.

"You're just parroting the protestors," the man grumbled.

Dave folded his arms across his chest and stared steadily back.

"I have been a serial entrepreneur for over three decades," he stated. "I know more about business and economics than this entire room put together. I have been a multi-millionaire since the age of thirty and I built the most exclusive resort in the western United States. If you knew what I know about the wealthy, you wouldn't be arguing about those protestors . . . you'd be joining them in the streets."

A stunned silence hung on the room. The egalitarian camaraderie vanished. Dave winced. The student's eyes narrowed suspiciously. The other youth's round-as-saucers eyes gazed at him above the dropped oval of his mouth. The white elephant of class and money stood awkwardly in the room. He was rich; they were poor. The emperor had been discovered.

The argumentative man fumed and glowered across the table until a triumphant gleam touched his expression.

"If that's true," he accused Dave, "then why don't you go join the protests?"

Dave stared back steadily.

"That," he replied slowly, "is a very good question."

The evening ground on awkwardly as the irregulars avoided the earlier subjects. One by one, they petered out, making their excuses and saying goodbyes until only Joan and Dave were left. His tea sat cold and forgotten as his mind reeled with thought. Words churned inside him, reflections on the illusion of wealth and money. He folded his hands in a steeple against his lips, staring up at the ceiling. Wealth in this country was inseparable from capitalism. Fortunes grew from the brutal history of stolen capital, first the land of the continent, then the resources, the labor of the enslaved and immigrants, and most recently, the robbery of their potential bound up in loans and crushing debts.

Dave's expression fell into deep shadows as he grappled with the parasitical nature of capitalism. The spine-shuddering vision of a massive beast haunted his thought; he watched capitalism sink its talons into living creatures and suck their blood and sinew until the emptied sack of bones and skin collapsed. In the New World, capitalism had unleashed its seething violence to massacre a continent of civilizations that objected to its parasitic invasion. The coasts of the east, the farmlands, the Appalachia's fell to the all-devourer. No more! the natives cried, but the Spanish conquered Mexico at sword point and sucked up the California coast. The French trappers wormed into the tall forests. The English, the Irish, the German, the Dutch: the hordes continued to advance as greedy European elites consumed wealth, food, equality, and justice, thrusting thousands more into desperation, and ultimately, onto the ships departing for the Americas. Manifest Destiny delivered divine rule to white-skinned masses; opposition was plowed under, along with the arrowheads and blood of massacres and battles. Darwin broke onto the scene and out of a hundred pages of cooperation, collaboration, and compassion, the marketing racket caught the line "survival of the fittest" and trumpeted it from the rooftops of the burgeoning city skyscrapers. Adam Smith's invisible hand met a similar fate as the Wall Street robber barons reached eagerly to strike a deal with a hand that was mentioned only once in the economic treatise. John Locke's theory of the right to private property was truncated at the clause " . . . so long as the well being and good of the commoners is assured." A heartless novelist capitalized on the ill-founded myths and a well-funded foundation ensured her books were read. A thousand false premises paraded around in the psyche of a nation without a single courageous child to cry out, "Look Mommy, the Empire has no clothes!"

It had no clothes, no heart, no decency, no shame, no foundation in truth, no reality. Capitalism was Greed unleashed like Satan's right hand man, justified by convenient misinterpretations of the Bible, and rationalized by sciences that failed to account for the reality of the world. Capitalism had the gall to proclaim its superiority to all other economic systems when Europe lay in crumbled ruins and bombed-out cities after two world wars had tromped across its back. Capitalism dared to vilify its main competition in a twist of bitter irony - the system that lauds competition as its main insignia would not duel fairly with communism or socialism, but instead fought dirty and aimed low. Never has a day risen or set upon an equal opportunity capitalist economy. Never has competition proved survival of the fittest. Instead, the lowest, vilest, meanest, cruelest, most heartless villains who hold nothing sacred and will stoop to anything for a profit have risen and risen and risen.

Including him.

Dave Grant bore no illusions about his former life. From personal experience, he knew capitalism in practice was a vampire wearing the historic cape of colonization and imperialism. Its success was built on others' ruin. Predatory, voracious, insatiable, it devours lives as resources and then moves on to greener pastures, leaving the emaciated in its wake along with toxic wastes, birth defects, poverty, and devastated landscapes. It crunches down the rocks and licks the minerals. It drinks the water. It sucks the air. Then it collapses and finally lies forgotten in the dust of human extinction on a barren, empty planet spinning through the lonely void of space.

All this and more pounded through Dave as his temples throbbed with thought. Capitalism ends in collapse, lives in a state of collapse, and preys on collapse. It is the accountant for the Four Horsemen of the Apocalypse. It is the all-devourer of the ancient spiritual prophecies. Capitalism builds up value, then destroys it, buys it up cheap, resells it for a profit, and builds something new. But in this tidy equation lie billions of lives thrown into ruin. Disaster, debt, imprisonment, and despair: it's all just par for the course on capitalism's green.

As for socialism, communism, he could not say. He could only speak for a system he knew with great intimacy, one he had excelled at, witnessed first hand, manipulated, perverted, dominated, succumbed to, escaped from and been chained to again. He could only speak for himself and perhaps for the creatures without voices, those who were resources or externalities to capitalism's eyes.

"Capitalism will destroy us unless we destroy capitalism," he said, half in a trance.

"What?"

He jolted. Joan slid into the seat across from him. He flushed, disgusted with his thoughts, his past, his own complicity in wealth and vicious cycles. They sat in silence for a moment as Joan heated the electric kettle. It hissed and steamed. She lifted it and poured a pot of tea. The last sweet steeps of the leaves made a light gold liquid. She held it up and admired the color in the light.

"So," she asked softly, "was it true what you said earlier?"

"Yes," Dave confirmed, avoiding her eyes. "I was quite wealthy, once."

"Once?" she probed. "Not any more?"

"Not at the moment," he answered.

"How wealthy were you?" she asked him. "A billionaire?"

"I was only a multi-millionaire." Dave paused, looking up to the ceiling as he calculated. "Actually, I may have been a billionaire at one point."

"You don't know?"

"When you're that wealthy, you don't really know how much you have. A lot of it is moving wealth or assets that rise and fall in value or investments in the stock market. My financial manager had a closer count. I didn't really care."

She regarded him solemnly.

"I'm not rich anymore," he told her. "I lost it all in the divorce with my ex-wife."

He forced himself to be honest.

"No, the truth is that I wasted most of it and haven't made it back. I haven't really tried," he quickly added. "I've always hit bottom before the rebound, then it comes back bigger than ever."

"You've lost fortunes before?"

"Several times."

"Oh," she said in a small voice.

"You can run a computer search on Dave Grant and find out all about it," he informed her. "I've made front page news for decades. Notoriety is the cheapest form of advertisement. I even paid to run a scandal story about myself once," he reflected.

She looked horrified.

"Business was slow," he protested.

She poured the tea and gestured for him to drink it.

"Alright," he said, changing the subject away from him. "Tell me something about Joan . . . apparently, you don't just emanate along with the hidden teahouse. Where'd you grow up?"

"Boston area."

"Ah, East Coast girl, I should have guessed," he said teasingly.

"How?" she challenged him.

"You're smart. I bet you went to an Ivy League school."

"Huh," she snorted, "my family could never have afforded that."

"So, you grew up poor. Did you ever steal things to survive?"

"Dave!" she protested.

"What?" he shrugged. "The wealthy steal billions just to get richer."

"I stole some candy once," she confessed. She squirmed, a forty-year old woman remembering awkward childhood memories. "Not just once, several times. My parents were beans and rice believers. They never bought the trendy cereals or snacks. Mom told us it cost too much and rotted our teeth and she didn't have money for insurance or dentists so tough luck."

"Did you ever go hungry?" he asked, fascinated.

"Sometimes around rent day," Joan answered, the lines in her face deepening with the shadows of memory. "More often, my parents would lie and say they'd just eaten on the way home from work so that my brother and I would have a full dinner." Joan's lips turned thin and bloodless. "My mother cleaned daycare centers. My father did whatever was available. They both had college degrees, but the country didn't have any jobs."

"That was the jobs drought caused by trickle-down economics," he pointed out.

Her eyes flashed angrily.

"Yes, and while I went to bed hungry and missed out on my overworked, underpaid parents, the rich kids rode their yachts around exclusive reservoir lakes. You probably built one," she accused him.

"Metaphorically, yes," he agreed, not bothering to deny the truth.

"Didn't you know what you were doing?" Joan demanded. "Didn't you know that somewhere, children were suffering while you built a playground for the wealthy?"

He shifted uncomfortably.

"The vistas of the rich are designed to mask those realities," he explained slowly. "They hire a legion of staff to maintain the complete facade of their splendor. Sure, some read the statistics and the economic reports, but that's just numbers on a page."

"I was a number," Joan said quietly.

"Yes," he answered, almost harshly, "and so were your parents, your playmates and everyone else you knew."

"And numbers don't suffer," she murmured.

"No," he agreed. "Numbers don't cry at night."

"The people behind those statistics do," Joan told him.

"Did you?" he asked.

"Of course."

Dave sighed.

"I suppose," he mused, "even Cinderella and Prince Charming had class and wealth discussions."

"No," Joan retorted, pursing her lips in irritation. "Cinderella was a disgraced noblewoman clawing her way back up into comfort. She bought the whole wealth concept hook, line, and sinker. Fairytales are almost always a sickening propaganda campaign for the upper class."

"Have you ever been to Disney World?" Dave asked curiously.

"No, we could never afford it."

"I spent a couple of weeks there after the divorce," Dave reflected.

"What'd you do?" Joan snorted. "Ride the rollercoaster for therapy?"

"No, I watched people buying into the illusion that happiness and wealth go hand-and-hand." His tone turned bitter. "You see, I had the real life Disney World - castles, magic, money, princesses, the whole nine yards, but money doesn't bring happiness."

"Then why didn't you stop stealing it from people who didn't want to buy happiness, they just wanted survival," she cried. "Bread, rice, a roof over their heads!"

"Because I lived in a Disney World where poverty doesn't exist."

She frowned at him.

"Did you know," he asked her, "that they repaint the railings at Disney World every night to make sure the illusion of perfection is absolute? Like Siddhartha Buddha before he left the palace of a prince, the rich are sheltered from the sight of poverty by the fortresses of wealth and class. We just don't see it."

"So who has more opportunity to awaken?" Joan asked. "The prince in the palace who never sees suffering? Or the pauper who drowns in the river of life?"

"Neither - both - everyone has a chance," Dave suggested.

"The Buddha was a prince," Joan pointed out.

"But he had only a robe and much knowledge of hunger by the time he awakened," Dave commented.

"Hui-neng, the Sixth Patriarch of the Zen School was poor and illiterate," Joan told him. "His father was a banished bureaucrat, and after he died, Hui-neng had to gather firewood to sell in the market to support his mother."

"Vimalakirti was a wealthy businessman," Dave said. "I always liked him."

Joan raised an eyebrow.

"Trying to have your wealth and get enlightened, too?"

"Some people say the wealthy have more opportunity to reach enlightenment," he said slowly. "But I disagree. They can buy gurus, but most of the spiritual teachers they meet are charlatans who are just after their money. These fakes tell the rich some version of manifest destiny or God's chosen rulers or good karma and fortunate rebirths and that enlightenment can be gained by supporting a temple, but even Jesus said it's easier for a rich man to pass through the eye of a camel than enter the Kingdom of God."

"Needle," Joan corrected. "Camel is a mistranslation."

"Regardless, the wealthy have too much baggage."

"Why don't they put it down?" Joan sighed.

"Some would rather be fat and wealthy here on earth than

go through life thin and poor to get into heaven," Dave tried to explain.

Joan put her head in her hands.

"It's all such idiocy," she groaned. "Religion, eyes of needles, kingdoms of God, heaven. Look," she argued, lifting her head and pounding her fist into her hand. "Jesus taught that the Kingdom of God is within. It's not a place in the sky. It's a living awareness. The reason it's so hard for rich people to enter is because their minds are caught up in a fabricated reality that has nothing to do with God, or enlightenment, or any sort of spiritual understanding. You've got to drop all the nonsense of riches, status, prestige, indulgence, being better than anyone else, and holding onto wealth. In the Kingdom of God, there are no rich and no poor."

"As they say, you can't take it with you," Dave chimed in.

"Exactly!" she cried. "But that's not just about death . . . it's about life. You don't need the Porsche, the pool, the mansion - "

"Nor a beat-up Volvo, a cold shower, or a rundown apartment, either," he countered.

"Yes!" her eyes shone with excitement. "The phrase, *you can't take it with you*, is a reminder to let go of the nonsense of stuff - no matter if you're rich or poor."

She looked at him, hawk-eyed.

"That includes bank accounts," she pointed out.

"It includes collections of rare teas," he shot back, pointing at the teapot.

"It includes living in a replica Japanese teahouse," she argued.

"It includes your self-righteous notion that a rundown apartment is more spiritual than my Japanese teahouse," he retorted.

"It includes your compulsion to 'make it all back'," she claimed.

His finger leapt up to point at her.

"It includes your judgment about my former wealth."

Her mouth dropped open. She shut it. Her eyes narrowed.

"It includes your masculine superiority complex that always has to have the last word."

He burst out laughing.

"Truce?" he offered with an apologetic smile.

"Truce," she agreed.

Her eyes glinted with another thought. Her lips twitched up. She glanced at Dave and he caught the hint of a challenge. Joan rose to flip the record. It was closing time, but she made no move to throw him out.

"So, do you think," she asked him as she examined the black disc in her hands, "that the changes in our lives are inscribed in fate like grooves in a record?"

"No," he answered. "Somebody makes the record, the music, the record player."

"And who is that somebody?"

"Me, of course," he replied. "Why let someone else botch up my life?"

"So, you're responsible for the mess you've made of it," she pointed out.

"Mess?" he protested, indignantly. "I'm not a mess. I consider myself a work of art, a masterpiece, a great epic equal to the Ramayana or the Iliad, thank you very much!"

She rolled her eyes and swept into her seat with a graceful movement.

"Maybe wealth was a rut you needed to jump out of," Joan suggested.

"I wouldn't mind taking another spin on that record," he

joked.

She gave him a fierce look.

"Well, so long as the source of the wealth isn't causing suffering," he amended.

"Wealth is a form of suffering," Joan commented with a small frown.

His breath exhaled in a whoosh.

"It is," he agreed, startled by her remark. "Accumulating wealth is a sickness - or maybe a symptom of a deeper illness, a deficiency of the heart and soul. I was half-dead when I was extremely wealthy, physically and emotionally dead."

He said nothing further. His throat closed tightly over decades of memories. Wealth, like food, had been an addiction with which he drowned out the wailing of his heart. Long before his failing marriage, even before he built his first fortune, his starving heart had found gratuitous satisfaction in his businesses. He celebrated profits instead of birthdays, acquisitions instead of anniversaries. Extreme wealth was an extreme sickness . . . a form of suffering that inflicted endless suffering on others.

"Wealth," he said simply to Joan, "is one of the saddest, most miserable things you can imagine - despite all the glossy advertisements to the contrary."

Joan nodded slowly.

"In Buddhism, there is a parable that says Hell is a sumptuous banquet at which everyone has spoons that are so long they cannot put the food in their mouths. Heaven is when everyone finally learns to feed each other."

Tears brimmed against the floodgates of his eyes. He bit his lip and swallowed hard.

"Yes," he whispered. "Yes."

Joan gave him a moment to recover. She contemplated the

steam evaporating from the sides of the clay pot. He drank his tea, placed the cup on the tray, and lifted his gaze to hers.

"So," he challenged, "if wealth is my rut, what is yours?"

"How about we just drink tea?" she suggested, avoiding the question.

He pointed to the glistening stream of tea.

"What if that's a rut and you need to jump track?"

She raised her eyebrows.

"It's a groove," she countered. "I like it."

"What if you're meant to jump out of it?"

Joan thoughtfully considered the idea.

"I'd have a sign."

"What if you're looking right at it?" he demanded.

"You're not my sign," she huffed, spurning the notion.

"I didn't mean me - "

Joan's dark eyebrows furrowed. She rose swiftly and swept the kettle off the table, turning to refill it with fresh water. Dave observed her smooth motions as she spun from tea table to counter and back again following a path she travelled dozens of times each day.

When the groove works, it sings, Dave reflected. You can go on playing the same beautiful song through your whole life, occasionally flipping the record for variation, or resetting the needle to the beginning.

Then again, sometimes the groove wears out from overuse. It grows scratchy, warped and distorted; the song doesn't sound as beautiful. He watched Joan circumambulate the room in a tiny migratory route. The orbit of her life swung in a comfortable circle. Was she content? She seemed it, he conceded, watching her smile gently as she refilled the electric kettle. Her braid hung over her shoulder, reminding Dave of an ancient statue. Then she glanced up and he dismissed any notion of contentment. A fire burned in her, a fierceness that belied the welcoming image of the teahouse hostess. She snapped her limbs around with a certain impatience. Her eyes scoured for answers. That was not contentment, Dave decided. She quested for knowledge ferociously and argued like a philosophic swordsman.

"Assuming that my life is in a rut is the height of patriarchy," she declared as she returned to the seat across from Dave, pouring out his cold, forgotten cup of tea, and steeping a fresh batch.

"I didn't - "

"You did."

He glanced around, looking for backup or distractions. Nothing.

"It was a philosophical point," he claimed.

"I know. This is, too."

She filled his cup with steaming tea.

"It's hot," she warned. "Don't burn your tongue - "

He drank it and scorched his mouth.

She rolled her eyes.

"There's no such thing as a rut that heads nowhere," she declared, crossing her arms and giving him a hawk-eyed glare. "Ancient cultures rooted in the feminine understand that, in an impermanent world, the new horizon is the same one we look at every day. The world is, in fact, recreating itself anew, right before our eyes. We cannot step in the same river twice, and a groove changes with each revolution."

"Do you realize that there is a whole generation that won't understand that metaphor at all?" he interjected.

"Don't distract me with the subject of obsolete technology," she warned him.

Yikes, he was in for a penny, in for a pound - another

archaic phrase for the average American who would miss the English currency reference.

"Are you listening to me?" she asked.

Oh god, he just committed the seventh deadly sin of men.

"Of course," he answered quickly. To prove his attentiveness, he reached for the teapot to serve her.

"It's not ready yet, I just filled it."

This was not going well. He glanced up, expecting to be met with a tough-eyed scowl, but no, she was laughing.

"So, what do you think? Is the fundamental notion of expansion and growth inherently destructive?"

"Uh . . . " he stammered. Had he missed something significant?

"And is the feminine - the yin - any less destructive? Everyone thinks of nurturing mothers and Kwan Yins, but water is the most corrosive force on earth. Rot, decay, darkness, death, autumn, winter, these are all yin elements."

"I think they're both destructive in the excess," Dave replied carefully.

"Yes," she agreed before emphasizing her point again, "but is it right to think our lives are about growth? Or is that just a left-over concept from the patriarchal invade and conquer mentality: clear the forest, kill the natives, set up the homestead, build a town, develop a city, raise the skyscrapers, consume the world's resources . . . "

"That's just one model of growth," he replied, latching onto the firmer footing of economic models and development plans. "And, if you oppose the global industrial growth society, you ought to stop drinking tea shipped from China."

"I know, it's a moral conundrum, isn't it?" she replied seriously. "Everyone has their indulgences. I wash my plastic bags and reuse them, bucket the gray water into the garden;

support local, organic agriculture; I became a vegetarian because of climate change; I don't drink alcohol because the grain should be used to end world hunger first; I bike around town and never travel on airplanes . . . but I drink tea from China." She frowned. "I suppose shipping tea to the United States is more fuel efficient than flying there to drink it."

Dave groaned.

"There's a lot you don't know about me, Dave Grant," she warned him.

And even more you don't know about me, he countered silently, thinking of champagne Jacuzzi baths, daily massages, and truffles flown in overnight from France. He considered telling her, but quickly decided she would shun him for being the epitome of the self-absorbed, greedy billionaire who had left his wife for a young blonde and drove a red sports car at reckless speeds through school zones. He pictured her bailing out her bathtub and lugging a five-gallon bucket to water the plants, doing her small part to help the ecology in the drought-prone central California coast.

His golf course had guzzled a million gallons of water a day.

From the perspective of his former business and political associates, her lifestyle activism was not only pointless; it was downright pathetic. With a flick of a wrist, legislators could subsidize renewable energy, end fossil fuel use, and free up the billions of gallons of water consumed by coal plants. Wealthy billionaires could write a check to put solar panels on every home and business in the nation, thereby ending the cause of the climate crisis. And here was Joan, bucketing her gray water.

That's how the system works, though, he thought. The powerful do nothing; the powerless labor and sweat and beg and plead for change; using every bit of time, energy, resources, and skills they possess; exhausting all possibilities while the powerful rake in millions of dollars on systems of destruction, sitting in their chaise lounges, sipping bourbon by the pool, criticizing the lazy, drunk, good-for-nothing poor.

"We live in an imperfect world," Joan stated, startling him from his thoughts," a world built on thousands of years of violent domination and exploitation. Our current civilization is laced with the poison of countless rounds of suffering."

"I agree," he interjected.

"You do?" she replied in surprise.

He nodded.

"I'm giving up my wealth," he told her. "I've been working on it for a while now."

Joan's mouth dropped into a round oval of astonishment.

"That's incredible," she exclaimed. She leaned back on her stool and regarded him with fresh curiosity. Dave caught a hint of admiration in her eyes and basked in the rare light of her approval.

"I've never met anyone that understood that wealth is only accumulated through causing suffering," Joan declared.

"Oh, that's not why I'm giving it up," Dave blurted out. He cursed his own honesty as her eyes narrowed. He stammered to explain, "I mean, yes, you're completely right, and I absolutely agree with you, but I had other, perhaps less altruistic - though equally noble - reasons for my decision."

"What were they?" she demanded to know.

He balked. His heart quaked at the thought of revealing the truth of his bargain with the Universe. He shied at confessing to Joan that he had auctioned off his wealth to find not just love, but her. The utter certainty shivered in his marrow, but his tongue refused to spit out the truth. Excuses stumbled through his mind: the hour was late, the heat of the day's conversations still burned, the moment was all wrong for confession -

"What are you doing tomorrow, Joan?" he asked abruptly.

"Nothing. Why?" she asked suspiciously.

"I'll answer your question if you come see my teahouse," he offered, though he meant: I'll answer your question if you come hear my story; come listen to the truth about my wealth; come see me for a human being, not a former billionaire; come give me a chance to be worthy in your eyes.

"I don't have a car," she replied.

"I'll come pick you up."

"You'd drive thirty miles into town, drive back up to the woods, and then repeat such a wasteful trip all over again?" she exclaimed in disapproval.

"Joan," he sighed.

"Dave," she retorted.

"Come on," he pleaded, "the planet will forgive you one luxury car trip to see an authentic Japanese teahouse - a veritable temple of tea - and thirty, life-size stone buddha statues."

"Thirty?" she gasped. Her dark eyebrows leapt to her hairline. "You live in this place?"

"In the teahouse itself," he confirmed. "It's a holy spot, I swear. Come on a pilgrimage and be glad you don't have to fly to Nepal to see Buddha's birthplace."

"India," she corrected.

"Whatever," he shrugged. "Buddhas aren't born, anyway."

She shot him a sharp look, surprised by the level of perception his comment revealed.

"Come on, come visit the place."

"I'm not interested in statues," she replied, dismissing the notion with a wave of her hand. "The buddha is a shit-stick, remember?"

"Okay, fine, no attachment to appearances, the buddha is everywhere. Why don't you come preach the Dharma for my unenlightened sake?"

Joan put her hands on her hips and regarded him seriously. Dave held his hands together like a poor, spiritual seeker who desperately needed the compassionate wisdom of a teacher.

"I think it's closing time," she said without answering his question.

"Ten more minutes?" he tried.

"Goodnight, Dave."

She stood up and walked him to the front door.

"Call me if you change your mind," he urged.

She locked the red door without a word.

CHAPTER THIRTEEN

· · · · ·

She didn't call. She just showed up. Dave heard the soft
scratch of footsteps on the gravel driveway, peeked over the
garden wall, and scrambled to throw the teahouse into order.
He shoved the dirty laundry under the futon cover and piled the
stack of sutras in a prominent location. He peered out the open
doors of the teahouse as she slowly paused on the stepping
stones that led up through the bamboo grove. Her eyes widened
as she gazed up at the long, blue stalks and fluttering leaves.
Dave sighed at the rapture in her face. Her long braid stretched
almost to her knees as her head tilted back in wonder. Dave
quietly spun away and sat cross-legged on the tatami mat,
waiting for her to enter into the pebbled courtyard. He pulled a
sutra into his hands, sneaking glances out the open doors. Joan
walked up to a stone buddha statue and placed her hand
reverently against the cool, carved upraised palm of the buddha.
Her lips murmured a prayer or mantra - he could not tell which.
She bowed her head and retreated back, slowly pivoting on her
heels.

"You came," Dave spoke gently, so not to startle her.

Her braid whipped around as she spun at the sound of his
voice. A smile unfurled in her eyes.

"Yes. A friend was driving up this way. I caught a ride."

"Come in," he invited.

She slipped her sandals off, leaving them on the wide stone
outside the sliding doors. Her eyes swept the tiny structure,
noting the hand-hewn wooden beams, cream plaster walls, the
traditional side door to crawl through, his stack of books, the
carved black lacquered trunk that held his clothes.

117

"It's for real," she breathed in awe.

"Bona fide," he assured her.

Her eyes fell on him then, tracing his cross-legged posture, the upturned tilt of his head as he looked up at her, and falling to the sutra he held in his hands.

"Which one are you reading?" she asked.

"*Heart Sutra*," he replied, holding up the cover. "I thought it would be about love."

"In some ways, it is," Joan mused. A curl of a smile teased her lips.

"In most ways, it's not," he sighed.

A breath of laughter stirred in her chest.

"Please," he invited, "sit down."

She nodded and folded her legs neatly under her as she lowered to the tatami mat next to him. Gracefully, she pulled one foot onto her thigh in a half-lotus position.

"*The Heart Sutra* is my favorite," Joan remarked.

"Why?" he asked.

"The mantra," Joan answered, quoting it. "*Gate, gate, paragate, parasangate. Bodhi svaha!* In English . . . go, go, go beyond, go totally beyond the beyond, all together, go! Whoopee!"

She laughed.

"*Go beyond* has been the anthem of my lifetime long before I ever read it in the *Heart Sutra*. Even as a child, I could feel the rhythm of the mantra pulsing in my blood: *Gate, gate, paragate, parasangate. Bodhi svaha!*"

"Ah," Dave sighed. "Then you're just the person to ask . . . explain this emptiness thing to me. What is that all about?"

Joan looked bemused. Around them, the afternoon lulled and the stone buddhas eavesdropped through the teahouse's paper screens and plaster walls.

"*Form is emptiness; emptiness is form,*" Joan quoted from the *Heart Sutra*. "Everything we perceive - including our perception - has no fixed, permanent, or separate existence. Thus it is said that form is empty. The same is true for sight, sound, taste, touch, scent, thought, memories, concepts, and even the Buddhist teachings of liberation, paths, and enlightenment. If it changes; if it can be perceived differently from viewer-to-viewer; if it relies on air, light, eyes, or anything else for its existence . . . then that object or being is said to be empty of any intrinsic nature of its own. But," she warned, "this does not mean non-existence! Emptiness describes the phenomenon underlying the ever-changing, interconnected somethingness of reality."

"Ah," Dave said, scratching his head. "I'll have to think about that for a while."

Joan grinned.

"Most people do."

"Not you?" he asked.

Joan grew solemn.

"The first time I read the sutra," she told him, touching the cover of the book, "it was as if I had heard the words a thousand times. The meaning unfolded like a lotus, my notions of reality lurched abruptly, and nothing has ever been the same since."

"Is that why you want to join the temple?" Dave dared to ask.

She nodded.

"What I experienced was a lightning flash of understanding in the dark storm of human delusion," Joan explained. "Imagine what the sunrise would be like."

"Probably not much different than this," Dave shrugged.

Joan frowned at him. He gestured to the bamboo swaying over the courtyard and explained his meaning.

"A beautiful afternoon, pleasant company, no suffering, just being. If I was the Buddha, that's how I'd go through this world."

"But," Joan countered, "if you were the Buddha, you would be excruciatingly aware of the vast suffering of your interconnected self!"

"If I were the Buddha," Dave argued back, "I wouldn't suffer the suffering. You've got to stop the suffering in your self, right?"

She nodded.

"So, wouldn't a fully enlightened being view even the hell realms as cheerfully as a sunny afternoon?"

Joan regarded him steadily.

"Someday," she sighed, "you'll have to tell me how a former billionaire comes to such conclusions."

Dave burst out laughing.

"Trial and error and sheer stupidity," he confessed. "I've made more mistakes in this one lifetime than most people make in ten."

Joan smiled.

"I can believe it," she chuckled. She bit back a small smile and asked, "So, why are you giving up your wealth? You promised to tell me if I made the pilgrimage to your teahouse."

Dave drew a breath and looked away from her. His limbs shook slightly. The confessions of his heart trembled in his chest and when he looked back at Joan, her serious, intense beauty robbed him of words.

"Love," he answered, finally. He rubbed his sweaty palms on his thighs and swallowed his nervousness. "I gave it up for love."

Her eyes darted away and she bit her lower lip. A sudden hint of hurt crossed her expression and Dave saw quick thoughts and hidden secrets flash past in a rapid succession that left him wide-eyed.

"Wait," he said quickly, "let me explain. I'm giving up wealth in search of love."

A sharp, curious look crossed across her face.

"On a stormy, windswept night on top of a cliff overlooking the ocean," he began, laughing to himself at the memory, "I realized my life was a disaster. So, I struck a bargain with Fate. I promised to give up all my money if the Universe would show me to the doorstep of true love."

He glanced at her expectantly, but she sat still as a statue. Her eyes locked gazes with his and the world around them slowed as he spoke.

"So, I gave it up - most of it, anyway - and I was guided to a red door that said pull, so I did, and inside . . . was you."

If our lives were fairytales, she would have gasped in delight, leaned in for the kiss, and they would have lived happily ever after.

Instead, Joan frowned.

"That's ridiculous," she retorted.

"Why?" he protested. "It's all true! Didn't you feel it, the first moment that our eyes met?!"

Her mouth dropped open in an oval.

"You - ah - I - " she stuttered. "Dave!"

"Joan?" he taunted back. "Admit it, didn't you know from the start that something truly special was going on?"

"Dave Grant!" she exploded. "I am not the booby prize for your great sacrifice of wealth! You don't know the first thing about me! I'm not your soul mate. I'm joining the Buddhist temple. I've been studying sutras for years - "

"Yes, but then I walked in the door - "

"When you walked in the door," Joan shot back, "I thought,

aha! Here is a fellow wandering sangha member who is looking for connection to the Dharma."

"I was looking for connection, alright!" Dave teased. "Just not to mildewed, old sutras - "

"You shouldn't mock - "

"Oh, don't be such a spiritual prude."

They froze. In their voices, they heard the echoes of a hundred lives, each one chasing the other in and out of marriages and monastic vows, laymen's follies and spiritual austerities. Each had jumped into monastic life; each had begged the other not to go. Once, they lived a lifetime of excruciating closeness, separated by vows of celibacy; once they had raised seven children together, bickering constantly through the years. They had worn a thousand faces. Today, they stared at each other in this lifetime, stunned to see past lives etched in each other's expressions.

"Perhaps," Dave suggested shakily, "we should just sit quietly for a moment."

"Uh huh," Joan agreed.

They said nothing as their hearts pounded and their minds reeled. Joan's fingers curled and uncurled in her lap. Dave drummed his knees. They snuck startled looks at each other. Joan closed her eyes and breathed. Dave sighed. He moved to speak.

"Don't," Joan warned him.

He closed his mouth and let the afternoon settle the raging emotions inside him. In the quiet, the world hovered in anticipation. The stone buddhas leaned in, listening. Joan's eyes fluttered open. She took a breath to say something. He shook his head.

"Shhh," he hushed. "Let's . . . let's just sit here . . . like this."

He could not form the words to explain the aching

tenderness he felt for the woman he had spent so many lifetimes circling, forgetting, finding again, losing. In that sudden flash of insight, he had seen a hundred betrayals, broken promises, and failures in the midst of passionate embraces, clandestine love affairs, vows of honor, tremendous lovers' sacrifices. They sat in silence, not just Dave and Joan, but a husband and wife, lover and beloved, friend and companion who had called each other by countless names through endless rounds of incarnation.

In the quiet, everything settled like the low dip of the sun. Gold slid through the husky blue-green leaves of the rustling bamboo. The blue jays chattered warnings of the lengthening afternoon. The air stilled to a timeless calm. Joan and Dave hung suspended in an eternity, staring at each other as time slowly poured like honey off the spoon of the afternoon. The wind spied on them and whispered gossip to the high branches of the giant redwoods. The bamboo leaves murmured secrets to each other.

A twig cracked.

The murmuring whispers paused.

Inside the thin plaster walls, Dave's fingers reached to touch the end of Joan's braid. He brushed it across the tatami mat like a paintbrush, stroking invisible calligraphy on the floor. She watched him from the corner of her dark eyes. He tickled his palm, then her knee. A bemused curl slid across her lips as if she had seen this maneuver a thousand times.

He slipped the elastic tie off the tail of her braid.

She stiffened.

He glanced up.

Their eyes locked.

Without releasing her gaze, his fingers threaded through the strands of her hair. He splayed his fingers apart. Black silk spilled into his palm. She said nothing. Her eyes darted toward the door and fixed steadily on the sunlight flickering through the maple leaves. Her breath lifted her bosom. Dave stared at her profile then slid his gaze down to the unwinding strands of her braid.

Deliberately, he loosened another twine of her hair. She swallowed. He rolled over onto his side, propping his cheekbone in his palm, his eyelashes cast downward as he slipped the strands loose like buttons on a blouse, slowly, sensuously. She licked her lips.

His fingers paused.

"Dave," she murmured.

"Hmm?" he replied, lifting his gaze.

"Nothing," she finished, shaking her head.

Another set of crisscrossing strands tumbled loose.

Her eyes leapt to the unraveling. With a flash of irritation and grace, her arms curled down, swept the length of her hair over her shoulder, met his eyes, and pulled out the tresses of the braid.

He watched mesmerized.

Pale fingers dove into black coils, resurfacing like skinny-dipping women, working the strands loose until she shook out thick lengths of hair that sighed in release.

His hand touched the satin of her hair.

She stilled.

He slid his fingers along the tendons of her arm, into the warm cascade at the nape of her neck. He rose; she leaned. They met. Their lips touched in a pose that would make sculptors roil in envy - the arch of her bent neck, the yearning of his rising chest, the delicate lift of her hand mid-air - all hung poised, resisting the tumbling surrender to gravity.

An eternity passed in a heartbeat. Their lips separated. Joan sat up. Her hair crackled soft and sinuous around her somber face, eyes luminescent in the dark wreath of her unbound hair.

"Joan," he said, but stopped, for all the intimate secrets men love about women tangled on the tip of his tongue. Gone was the sharp-eyed tea pourer. Before him sat a woman, her femininity breathing in her slightly parted lips, flushing in her cheeks as her hand curled and uncurled in the pulse of her desire and alarm.

The startling blue of his eyes pinned the dark secrets of her own.

"Tell me," he pleaded, "why are you going to the monastery?"

"Why do we persist in doing this?" she asked him in reply. "Why do we continue these countless rounds of lives, loving and losing?"

"How could you tire of it?" he exclaimed, thinking of passionate embraces and heart-shuddering discoveries and love-struck moments.

"It is the heartache that I'm weary of, Dave."

"So, go beyond it," he suggested. "Remember the *Heart Sutra*? *Gate, gate, paragate, parasangate, bodhi svaha! Go, go, go beyond, go totally beyond* – beyond all limitations of what you think this existence is all about!"

The afternoon held its breath. The air suspended in the trees. The birds froze, waiting for her response. She sat on the tatami mat with her black hair unbound, looking into his blue gaze with the dark intensity of her own. He shivered.

Her head tilted slightly as if listening. Joan shifted her eyes to the bamboo outside the door, but she seemed to be seeing beyond the shadows and light into the realms of the unknown. A smile twitched over her lips. His blood throbbed with unexpected nervousness. She nodded as if receiving instructions. He swallowed. She almost laughed and his heart froze. Her eyes refocused and she shook her cascade of hair and blinked as if returning from a deep sleep.

"I'm going to the temple," Joan told him decisively, "for one year."

"What?!" he objected. "How can you?"

"One year," she insisted, holding up her forefinger, "because you aren't done with your promise."

"My what?" Dave questioned with a scowl.

"You promised that you would give up all your money," Joan reminded him. "You're not done yet."

"Oh, come on," he scoffed. "I don't need to be a homeless beggar - "

"Maybe you do," she said thoughtfully. Her grin curled wickedly. She rose to standing. Dave scrambled to his feet as she stepped toward the door.

"Wait! Joan, where are you going?"

"Goodbye, Dave."

He lunged and caught her wrist as she slipped on her sandals.

"You're going?" he croaked out.

"Yes."

He could see her utter determination.

"Don't - "

She slid her fingers behind his bent head, pulling him to her lips.

"I've decided," she murmured. She kissed him, twisted free of his hand, and flew across the stepping-stones toward the bamboo grove as Dave blinked in disbelief.

"You're going to get to the monastery and realize you can't live without me!" he shouted after her retreating back.

Her laughter mocked him as she called back.

"You," she yelled, "are going to get down to nothing but the clothes on your back and wish you had joined me in the temple!"

In the woods, the stone buddhas exchanged glances. With one hand raised, and the other lowered, they silently echoed the couple's words, infusing them with prophecy.

CHAPTER FOURTEEN

. . . . .

"That's it?" Edna cried when he fell silent.

"Oh no," Dave assured the old woman, blinking at the fog of memories. "There's more, but I need directions to your house."

The lights of the mountain town shone in the deepening darkness.

"Right on Rocky Bend Drive," she instructed, "all the way to the end, last house before the mountain turns into a steep wall."

"You were practically my neighbor," he commented as he pulled through the first intersection on the outskirts of town. Gold Mountain resort and development lay right over the shorter crest of the slope that backed up to Edna's house.

"I know," she snorted. "Why do you think I fought the development all those years?"

"Resistance to change," Dave answered.

"Huh," Edna grunted. "Resistance to your pig-headed notion of progress is more like it. I love change; sunsets and the rise of the Milky Way, spring snowmelts and the height of summer dryness. I haven't got any problems with things changing, young man. It was the bulldozing of those trees that ticked me off."

Dave sighed.

"I am sorry about the trees," he murmured.

"You ought to be," Edna sniffed. "Larry's been doing penance all these years for plowing up those trees."

"Larry?" Dave exclaimed. "Is that gosh-darned catskinner still around?"

129

Larry Boggs, the local backhoe and bulldozer operator, had reached the status of living legend by the age of twenty. Give him a backhoe wide enough, it was said, and he could level the Sierras flat enough to build an ice skating rink. He could skin the grass sod off an alpine meadow so carefully that the bumblebees wouldn't even look up from nuzzling the wildflower pollen. Rumor had it that, at nineteen, he stripped the rebellious preacher's daughter with a backhoe, getting her down to bra and underpants before the whole pack of teenage boys was busted up by his loud-mouthed little sister's tattling.

By the time Dave Grant moved to town, Larry Boggs charged a hundred bucks an hour for local businesses and two hundred to environmentally-minded developers who cared about leaving the spotted salamander habitats in pristine condition. He tucked his flannel shirt into his Levis and held them up with an alligator skin belt that he had won off a bet with a Texas oil tycoon after making a bulldozer do a triple pirouette on Main Street. At thirty-two years old, Larry Boggs had matured into the type of young man a newcomer never wants to meet outside a bar late at night. Dave Grant decided to hire Larry at double his normal rate and keep the guy busy to the point of exhaustion - an endeavor greatly aided by the birth of Larry's second son, a feisty fellow prone to howling until two in the morning. Larry took to bolting a car seat on the back of the bulldozer.

"Like father, like son," he grinned to Dave one afternoon as the infant contentedly rode along with the rumbling machine.

Years later, Dave learned that Larry's outrageous rates supported not just his family, but his ailing parents, his younger sister who was raising up her kids as a single mom, and provided scholarships for the local high school students to go to college. Unlike most of Dave's Gold Mountain contractors,

Larry continued living in his small house on Second Street. He drove a truck so beat-up that it often left parts lying on the main road up to Gold Mountain. After the resort and golf course were completed, Larry became the only Gold Mountain employee to buck the dress code with impunity, refusing to don the company jersey and khakis. Daughters of billionaires chased his blue-jeaned ass around the resort, but Larry would have nothing to do with them.

"They just want a piece of something money can't buy," he complained to Dave. "So I tell 'em nice as possible, that Larry Boggs ain't for sale - I gave ex-clu-sive rights to my wife years ago."

Underneath that rough-and-tumble demeanor, Dave Grant saw a living master riding atop a bulldozer. The young man approached his worksite like an artist's canvas. He studied the contours of the land, noted trees and boulders, and scrutinized the blueprints before he fired up his equipment. He'd argue Dave down on points of architectural alignment and once told off the exclusive design firm for having their heads so far up their urban asses that they couldn't see the idiocy of a design that obtusely missed the best view in northern California.

"Two feet," he begged Dave. "Get them to move the resort up two feet higher on the ridge. I promise the balcony view from the main hall will drop jaws."

When Dave frowned, Larry had hauled him up onto the backhoe roof as it sat parked on the side of the slope.

"See?" Larry demanded.

And Dave's jaw dropped.

He'd never regretted a day spent with Larry Boggs, not from the first afternoon they had plowed down the trees.

Long before they had broken ground, when Gold Mountain was nothing more than a blueprint moving through the interminable rounds of public hearings and permit processes, Dave hired Larry Boggs to bulldoze the pine saplings and scrub brush off the proposed area of the golf course.

"This town needs a sign that Gold Mountain is coming whether they like it or not," Dave had growled. "Clear the trees."

Larry set to work. Dave watched as the metal blades ripped into the mountain hillside and pushed the brush over. Grassy clearings rolled up like carpets, exposing the under-soil of the mountain. About half a mile into the project, at the foot of a towering matriarch of a tree, Larry paused. The machine idled while the young catskinnner leaned his forearms on the wheel and scrubbed his face. Dave frowned from his vantage point, but before he could stride across the slope, Larry fired up the machine again. The two hundred year old tree fell with a monstrous groan of ripping roots and snapping boughs. The trunk smashed through the forest, shattering smaller pines and shoving several more trees over as it toppled. The twisted root mass howled in the sunlight. Larry grimly turned the bulldozer toward the next section.

Years later, after they had cleared miles of forests for roads, driveways, houses, pipes, and outbuildings, Larry paused next to Dave after a long day of work.

"Do you ever wonder if we oughtn'a plowed up those first trees?"

Dave had startled at the question. His marriage was collapsing; the empire teetered, unstable. The resort was operating at a sizable deficit. Larry's comment eerily echoed the unexpressed sentiment seething in his own thoughts.

"I almost didn't do it, you know," Larry muttered, swiping off his sweaty baseball cap. "That first afternoon I worked for you, I stopped out there." He pointed to the spot where he had paused. The flag on the seventh tee of the golf course now stood where the giant matriarch once towered. He swallowed hard, but said nothing about the two hundred year old tree. Instead, he gestured to where the saplings had once clustered. "It seemed so unfair, cutting down those thin, little trees. Felt like I was bulldozing the high school graduating class, all those young saplings with nothing but promise ahead of them. And for what? A golf course?"

Larry glanced at Dave.

"No offense, Mr. Grant," he added.

"None taken," the billionaire replied.

Larry Boggs changed after that conversation. Though he continued working for Grant Construction, he bent his skills to new heights of artistry. Not one blade of grass more than necessary was shifted by the bucket of his backhoe. He maneuvered construction sites around boulders and old growth trees. He set up protective fencing so tight to the work zone that the construction workers complained.

"Pretend you're in a historic district," Larry told them unsympathetically. "You don't get much elbow room when you're squeezed between buildings that predate your grandfather. These trees are older than those buildings - and even if grass grows back, why should we crush it if we don't have to?"

Dave had watched him carefully . . . Larry Boggs sobered as he aged. His sons evoked a reverence in him for the sanctity of life. His youthful arrogance matured into the qualities of mastery. Respect infused his actions. His unexpected talent as a teenager evolved into art as he learned to work his craft with humility.

Dave paused at a red light, shaking his head at the memories.

"What's Larry up to now?" he asked Edna.

"Still grounds keeping at Gold Mountain," she replied.

"Really?" Dave murmured.

Edna nodded.

"He's keeping an eye on the trees. Hasn't let the management cut down a single tree for years."

"Good for him," Dave said approvingly. He swung a left through the main street of town, noting the new pizza joint, the closed storefronts, the old Chinese restaurant that had been in town longer than anyone could remember.

Edna pointed to it.

"Pull in there and we'll pick up my special. You'll be staying for dinner," she decided.

"Oh no, it's not necess - "

"Yes, it is," Edna argued back. "I owe you for the drive."

"I got a ride, too."

"I need to hear the rest of the story," she insisted.

"That could take all night," he warned.

"I've got all night," Edna answered with a chuckle. "Some old ladies conk out at sundown, but I always was a night owl. I like the quiet when everybody else stops chattering."

Dave pulled over by Ling's Palace. Edna rummaged in her purse.

"Tell 'em, the Lawrence Special - it's vegetarian, no eggs - but make it double. I've got it all worked out over the years."

She held out a couple of twenties.

"And pay down the five dollars on my tab, too."

"You have a tab at the Chinese restaurant?" he asked in surprise.

"The Lings and the Lawrences have had a tab since 1850, when we founded this town looking for gold."

Dave opened his mouth in astonishment, but Edna waved

off his questions.

"Later, later, we've got all night. Go get some dinner. No chopsticks, I've got plenty!"

He shook his head at the histories he never knew. He placed the order and the young woman asked politely after Edna. Dave assured her that the old lady was fine, just waiting out in the car. The woman expedited the order with familiarity and walked Dave to the door to wave to Edna.

"My great-grandfather hired their great-grandfather and a whole passel more of 'em straight off the boat from China," Edna explained as he climbed into the station wagon. "He needed labor on the claim, but there's no gold here, so he went belly-up on that deal. Most of the Chinese moved on to the railroad work, but the original Ling owed the original Lawrence a personal debt for bringing over his wife. So he and Mrs. Ling stuck around turning the claim into a homestead. They cleared up what they owed just in time for the Lawrence place to burn to the ground. The Lings fed the Lawrences for the winter and it's been back and forth like that for a hundred and fifty years. I'm the last Lawrence, though. The Lings all think I'm a great barren tragedy as if they never heard of women's liberation or birth control!"

Edna shook her head.

"Never had children 'cause I just plain didn't want 'em. Let the Lings inherit the earth, I say. What difference does it make?"

Dave drove quietly up Rocky Bend Drive as Edna continued.

"All that Gold Mountain land used to be Lawrence Ranch, you know."

"I didn't," he said.

"Mmm-hmm," she murmured, "and a right mess we made

of it, too. Hundred and twenty years ago, we clear-cut the place. Hardly a tree to be seen for miles around. Then came the sheep - locusts on the hills - and then came the landslides until the scrub brush hunkered down and held onto the slopes so the trees could get a toehold on nothing. We sold most of it off in the Depression. Trees were too small to lumber and the sheep market had been flooded down to worse than worthless. We were flat broke, same as everybody else."

Edna looked out into the blackness.

"You came along, Dave Grant, and I set out to stop history from repeating. Gold Mountain, indeed! There's never been any gold here. Just lies and fantasies. Gold started a long series of tragedies interrupted by small acts of kindnesses and the miracle of a few babies that grew to adulthood."

She nodded to the porch light up the road.

"There's the house."

It sat low and stoic beneath the dark, looming shape of the mountain.

"There's beams up in the attic that have the original Ling's characters carved next to an X for Lawrence Jr. - he never did learn how to read, though his boys all did. Their names are up there, too. I carved my own in, the first girl to have the gumption to demand her place in the lineage."

Dave parked the station wagon. Edna took an eternity to climb the three steps of the porch. Glaciers melted as she set down her purse. Continental plates inched closer together as she fumbled for the light switches and moved down to the washroom.

"There's plates above the toaster, and chopsticks in the drawer to the right of the sink," she called out to Dave. "Set out that food and turn on the coffeemaker. I'm famished for supper and the rest of that story."

Dave smiled and obeyed. Inside the ubiquitous red and white cardboard boxes, Dave discovered an assortment of vegetables he had never seen outside of China. Edna smiled proudly at his surprised expression.

"Grace Ling grows long beans and Chinese greens for the family to eat. The Lawrence Special is a scoop of whatever the Lings are having, minus the meat dish and plus a fortune cookie. It's one of the perks of cultivating a hundred-and-fifty year old family friendship and being the last in line to reap the benefits. Here, put a little offering out to the kitchen buddha."

She pointed to the round-bellied carving of Ho-tai with his cheery smile and arms hoisting a rice bowl aloft. She insisted on a moment of silent prayer over the food, then filled a heaping plate for Dave and a smaller serving for herself. She let him eat two mouthfuls before hunkering down to business.

"So . . . she rejected you," Edna reminded him.

"Yes," he conceded, "and I didn't take it well. I crashed, utterly and absolutely."

CHAPTER FIFTEEN

. . . . .

Autumn grew sharp and bitter. He spiraled down like a tumbling leaf tossed carelessly into the gutter. Dave fumed and paced and grew morose. Joan didn't return his phone calls. His world unraveled faster than an old sweater caught on a hook. He avoided the teahouse. He started drinking heavily, arguing drunkenly with the disapproving stares of the stone buddhas. He gorged on cheap Chinese food and pastries. He reeled through life, furious and half-conscious. His credit cards dried up. His bank accounts dwindled. He watched it with distaste. He fell from grace. He floundered. He hit bottom and wallowed in the muck of self-pity. He sank into alcohol and poverty, hating his own histrionics. Pull yourself together, he snarled at himself. Yet, the poles that lifted up his life collapsed one by one and he was plagued by a sense that he could do nothing. Forces beyond his control were snapping the pillars of his world like matchsticks. Unseen presences raged, full of fury at transgressions Dave could not fathom.

The owner of the Japanese teahouse did not renew his lease; the property was put up for sale. On the day Dave moved out, an auction company arrived to cart off the buddha statues. With a pit in his stomach, he watched the laborers tip the stone carvings onto handcarts, strap them down, and roll them away. The redwoods thrashed dangerously overhead as he packed up his belongings and tossed them into his car without care. A jade carving cracked in the maelstrom. He flung it into the bamboo grove. He heard a snap above him and leapt to the side. A redwood branch missed him by a few inches.

He bolted, feeling cursed. He sped away from the furious

sound of doors slamming shut and opportunities being lost. Bad luck plagued him. His belongings burned in an unseasonal forest fire that swept the coast. He couldn't find a job. In despair, he drank. Inebriated, he sank.

He crash-landed in the reality of poverty, spinning his mind over and over, wondering how he had tumbled down so low. He ate Thanksgiving Dinner at the homeless shelter. He poked his instant mashed potatoes with the white plastic fork, wincing at the screech of Styrofoam plates.

"You eating that?" asked the thin, shaking guy next to him, pointing to his jellied cranberry sauce.

Dave shook his head. The guy reached a tattooed, filthy arm over and speared the cranberry sauce off Dave's plate straight into his mouth of rotting teeth. Dave leaned back, shocked.

He camped in his car until it was repossessed, then in the woods with a pathetic thrift store tent with a broken pole. One night, the cops raided and threw his gear in the garbage. Dave curled up on cardboard and got drunk with the other bums. He slurred to them that this wasn't possible, he was a billionaire, he was Dave Grant, his luck was all going to change soon, this was some cosmic joke - hah hah hic!

Poverty is a grind, a sinkhole that traps entire families for generations, but at times, Dave could not shake the sense that his poverty was the most self-indulgent act he'd ever committed. It was right up there with commissioning a fourteen-foot tall portrait of himself to hang in the wing of the modern art museum that bore his name. Or the time he tried to persuade the state legislators to create a black hole in the county ordinances so he could fly private jets in and out of the resort while still receiving a tax break for building a "municipal airport" that only the wealthy could use.

His slide onto the street brought him to a new height of egotistic self-centeredness. He wasn't trying to lift himself out of poverty. He believed it was fate and told the homeless shelter's social worker as much. He had condemned himself to pennilessness by making bargains on that wind-swept night on the glass balcony of the cliff-top mansion. His money or his love, the contract stated. He found his love, but he could not keep her until he had rid himself of every penny.

The social worker told him that was nonsense. She berated him for his dramatics. She said he made a mockery of the people scrambling to get out of adverse situations: the mentally ill, the single moms, the struggling addicts, the people on parole caught in the endless cycles of conviction, unemployment, crimes to survive, and more convictions. He was living proof of the conservative nightmare that government welfare turned able-bodied men into ticks on the backs of hard-working citizens.

Dave laughed until he cried and then he wept in disgust. A bed at the homeless shelter, food stamps, panhandling - even added altogether, it didn't break even with a single year's subsidy of rich people's oil, gas, corn, or sugar industries. All the poor people combined couldn't consume more of the taxpayers' money than the military contractors. The conservatives screamed about welfare until they were red in the face as they swilled vintage wines and dined on fine aged beef. Every dollar they earned came from the sweat of the people, from corners cut and healthcare benefits shortchanged. Their profit margins were collected by dumping costs on the public - pollution, health care, research, education, wars to secure economic dominance of the global market - and privatizing the profits.

Dave's body started to shake. He sat down on the curb of the main street of town, even though the city ordinances made it illegal for the poor to stand on the corner, sit on the sidewalk, lie in the bushes, carry a blanket, wash in public, or piss in the back lots. Yet, the public restrooms were closed, the shelters were full or shut down, and the benches had been removed. Tourists and shoppers sat in cafes, never dreaming that they had to pay for the right to sit down. They sipped café lattes while the poor who could not afford coffee or tacos were swept out of sight from a city that denied them their right to exist.

Dave broke the law when he fell to his haunches. He'd broken so many laws in his life: tax codes, zoning ordinances, monopoly and antitrust laws, speed limits, investments in stocks. The wealthy break laws because the laws don't apply to them. The poor break the law because their survival has been outlawed. Dave added loitering to his litany of crimes when he crumbled to the curb, shocked by a memory that symbolized the height of his conceit.

The day had unfolded like any other on Gold Mountain. An armored limousine pulled up. Two men stepped out nonchalantly. The hostess seated them for lunch in the restaurant. Then she scurried to Mr. Grant's office to inform him that the Vice-President of the United States and the owner of the top weapons manufacturing firm would like to play golf after lunch.

He looked up from his desk with a frown.

"Why are you even asking? The guest cards are in the front desk."

"I thought you'd like to know they were here, sir," she stammered.

He waved her out and went on with his day.

Five hundred thousand children were in the process of starving to death. A city would be in rubble the next day. Appalled ministers were practically begging, "there are no weapons of mass destruction here, please!" The two men playing golf raked in millions of profit with each swing. Soldiers' bodies exploded in the desert far away.

The height of conceit is business as usual and the blank eyes that gloss over when war criminals walk in the door. He had the right to refuse service, but he didn't. He had the ability to discuss the war with them and appeal to their consciences in a manner that the hundreds of thousands of citizens marching in protests nationwide never could. But while thousands held candlelight vigils for peace and millions frantically called their senators and representatives, Dave Grant went on with his day as if a war for profit were nothing more significant than the olive in his martini.

His sin of self-involvement shrank next to those two men, yet it loomed large in the list of his life choices.

War is the greatest horror that exists, and one's silence on the subject is the second. For the profits of the wealthy, millions of bodies fall into graves. White phosphorus and depleted uranium disfigure civilians. Women are raped by soldiers from both sides. Young men's minds are destroyed by the brutal acts they commit and witness. Whole populaces are crippled inside and out, the shell-shocked survivors left living, but dead. Hollow expressions haunt their eyes. The people are fed lies to fill their blood with hatred and fear. And for what?

For the sake of men's profits, that's what.

Dave choked on the truth as he sat on the curb. The only ideology great enough to launch wars is that of profit and wealth. Religion and politics are nothing but smokescreens. The chains of the dogs of war aren't released unless personal gain for the owners lies in sight. Offense and defense can be summarized thus: can the rich get richer by invading? Do they have fortunes to protect from attack?

Dave put his head in his hands. A downtown hospitality guide - doublespeak for privatized police - nudged him with the tip of her shoe.

"You can't sit on the curb. Get moving."

He looked blearily up at her.

"You're drunk," she said in disgust.

He pointed to the people stumbling out of the bar across the street.

"So are they," he replied. "Everybody's drunk - on war, money, blood, alcohol. We're all drunkards, louts, winos, beasts, vampires, suckers, ticks - "

"Get out of here," she ordered.

"Where do you want me to go?" he cried.

"I don't care as long as I don't see you."

He rose and gave her a mocking bow.

"Invisibility is not one of my magic tricks."

He walked away before she called the police. Dave was sick of her, sick of them, sick of society, sick of drinking, sick of life, sick of death, sick of dying, sick of hating, sick of loving, sick of caring: sick.

He drifted. He begged for a buck. He took the bus up the coast. He hung out on the sandstone bluffs where the whales spouted in the deep ocean channel that brushed the shore as it skirted the broad bay. He rolled up under a cypress and slept. He mocked Kerouac as he hitched rides to nowhere. He got chased out of state parks by peach-fuzz rangers who couldn't be convinced that public lands belonged to the people - not to the cash-wielding tourists or starched-shirted administrators or salivating, lease-hungry oil, gas, and timber companies. Public lands were held in trust for the lost and as a place for the destitute to rest their feet, he argued. On a continent carved up into private postage stamps, a poor man deserves to take a break on the back of his own country.

"Tell that to the governor," one ranger snarled. "He's going to sell this park off to pay for the roads in the more popular parks."

Dave opened his mouth to disillusion the kid about politics and money - the governor probably had a buddy in real estate who would make a fortune on this ocean-side property - but the kid clenched his fist and told Dave to get moving or he would forcibly evict him from the park.

Dave left. He stumbled through the bushes, haunted by a millennium of conquest and colonization. The belligerent eyes of the strong, pale-faced youth unnerved him. There stood the shadow of Columbus and Coronado, conquistadors, colonists, and countless waves of invaders and immigrants propelled by greed and cycles of injustice. In this new millennium, the genetic and cultural descendants of conquest were using instant communication to repeat the same old story of 'you cannot stand here, you cannot use this land, it does not belong to the common people, it is not yours, it is mine, now get lost!'

Way back in human history, who threw the first stone of property and control? What prophet could predict the enduring ripples of the unknown human who first claimed land, people, and power over both? Beyond the Bible or the Upanishads, further back into the unwritten songs of oral histories, a seed of domination had been planted. From the murky depths of history to Viking ships crashing on Briton's shore, to the arrival of William the Conqueror, to the growth of the British crown, to the rise and fall of an empire, to the eruption of American colonies into independent states, to the evolution of conquest into capitalism . . . the invasive weed grew and grew until it threatened total annihilation of the earth.

The hungry ghost of conquest, forefather to the lusty greed of capitalism, leapt the ocean to North America, unleashing genocide and land theft, privatizing a world that was not owned, but inhabited by the native peoples. And behind the textbook history of the rise of a nation of immigrants lies the less-told story of tyranny that evicted millions from their homelands. We are told of the huddled masses yearning to be free. We are told of the massacres of natives perpetrated by newcomers looking for a bit of land. Yet, who speaks of the robbers of Europe? Who mentions those greedy souls who held the purse strings tight and forced peasants off their land, enclosed the commons, outlawed vagrancy, and loaded the greed-created homeless onto ships to be dumped on America's shores? Hundreds of years of history, dozens of countries, many languages and peoples are swept into this lineage; they all share a tyrant class, one that continues to this day.

"Around and around the old story goes, encircling the globe until civilization implodes!" Dave cackled madly at the rhyme.

He walked out of the public lands and squatted on the vast acreage of an absentee landowner who would never find him sleeping under the branches of a massive oak. Private jets hummed faintly far overhead, traversing from Los Angeles to the High Sierras.

Heave ho! Onward! Dave rose in the morning and set sail for unfamiliar territory, feeling indentured to the hunger that propelled him to hitchhike northward seeking alms. He labored for the wealthy alongside brown-skinned men who lined up outside the hardware store, carrying the heavy loads for lily-white ladies and hopping in the flatbeds of landscapers' trucks.

For six hours of labor, Dave was promised forty bucks. He received twenty and no ride back into town. He walked from the gated community along the highway, speaking Spanish with his fellow migrants, getting drunk on swigs of cheap tequila.

What else can a man do with the tragedy of this world? The land of plenty starves the people so the wealthy can enjoy pristine vistas from their second homes.

"Pristine, my asshole," muttered one of Dave's companions. "Their mansion overlooks a mass grave of the indigenous and the submerged ruins of Spanish missions and the long-crumbled beams of whorehouses."

"Pristine, my ass," Dave agreed, pointing to the towering eucalyptus trees. "Those invaders from Australia are devouring the coast. Where are the indigenous and the redwoods? Gone, rotted into buried bones and roots of three hundred foot giants."

His words slurred with weariness and inebriation. Later, he sat behind a natural food store and watched the lights of SUVs jump as they applied their four-wheel drives to speed bumps. He felt like a stock actor in Shakespeare's Globe Theatre, playing all the roles in the world: men, women, rich, poor, servants, nobles, fools, sages, dogs, witches, villains, and star-crossed lovers - Joan. She flashed like lightning through his mind, electric, then gone - bitter enemies, demons, and demigods. He had played all the characters in the canon of the world. He was weary of strutting and fretting across the stage in the endless repetitions of humanity's folly.

"Stop," he muttered to the incessant traffic. "Just stop." He rose unsteadily. "Just stop! Stop!" he shouted. "Stop!" He waved his arms, caught in a delusion of sorcery, chanting as if he held the power to halt the madness of the world, "Stop! Stop! Stop!"

The motor of the world continued grinding. A few eyes turned, then glanced quickly away from the dirty homeless man on the hill behind the store.

The police came to pay a visit. They rode up in their cruiser, knights of the modern times, as chivalrous as the mead-drunk, bosom grabbing, louse-ridden swine of medieval ages, wrapped in myths and uniforms.

"Be gone," he commanded them.

They ignored him, discussing his fate.

"The jail is full," one commented.

"Just take him out of town and dump him on the side of the road where he can't bother anyone," the second cop suggested.

Dave was unceremoniously evicted from a town of tourists getting sloshed in local bars. He didn't have the qualifications to stay in town - no home, no clean clothes, no money in his pocket.

The officers drove south and dumped him out. He wandered into the forest, stumbling over roots until, exhausted, he leaned his head against an oak - the property of god-knows-who - and wept into the Spanish moss that climbed its bark.

"You," he informed the tree, "are a slave."

He pushed away from the trunk and pointed his finger at the other silent, gnarled trees.

"You . . . and you . . . and all of you are slaves. The earth - the soil - that your roots curl into is a slave. The water that runs in creeks is enslaved. All of earth is enslaved to humans!"

He climbed onto the toppled body of a fallen oak, carved by chainsaws into sections and limbs and then forgotten by the loggers. The dampness of the coast enveloped them. A dreary bank of rain clouds made the branches shiver and the moss droop forlornly like rags across the thin arms of the trees. Dave tripped drunkenly on his tongue as he addressed the silent oaks.

"Property - hic! - property," he paused, shaking his head. "You live out your days, thinking you are free. Then, one day, you discover you are not. The whole lot of you belong to your owner."

He waited for their gasp of horror, but the oaks stood stoically, barely rustling their tiny leaves. He was, after all, a mere human, drunk on the madness of his species. But, Dave warned them silently, he was a human who had made his first fortune butchering their brothers to the north.

"Ah," he continued, eyeing them shrewdly. "Property is all delusion, you say, but whose? Humanity writes its claim to you on the backs of your parents who were toppled and pulverized into paper."

Again, no answer. Perhaps a sigh of wind slipped through the hanging moss. Dave scratched his head. He examined the grime of his scalp that clung beneath his fingernails. He tottered on the fallen log, grabbing a twisted limb for balance.

"Isn't it wrong," he cried, "to be enslaved to anyone?"

The hubris and debate over slavery merely exempted humans from the definition of property . . . what a failure of vision to have stopped our logical examination. An African should not be enslaved because an African is not an animal, but should an animal be enslaved? Captured, domesticated, kept as house servants or locked in pens, bred not by natural attraction but by the genetic selection of human owners, sent to slaughter by decree of the master: all these are objectionable when applied to fellow human beings, but are they any less objectionable when applied to other species? It defies logic.

Dave's audience stood silent, weighing his words or ignoring his ranting. He could not tell. He did not care. Thoughts burned like fire in his chest and rose in flaming outbursts. Words have made humans more ferocious than dragons - those mythic beasts could only scorch and burn, but with words, humanity has touched the moon and scraped the sky with towers and spanned the ocean with wires and sent satellites into space where once only gods and angels dared to fly.

With words, humanity raises up a single man to rule all others. With words, the ruler kills entire populaces. With a word, the bombs begin to fall. With a word, the nuclear warheads could annihilate the world. They say dark mages are only legend, yet the spells of words still bind us all. Orders, commands, legal words on paper . . .

"And you," Dave said to the oaks, "are caught by words - paper words backed by chainsaws, protected by guns of state, bought by paper money and electronic transfers. You are slaves! The mighty oak has masters! Your worth is calculated by weight and length. You have no value as a living creature. Only your death will turn a profit for your owner, so you live on borrowed time, thinking you are free. You are like cows in a vast range that never see the fence. Or like humans in the modern world who never wonder about these things!"

He wept. The rain drizzled and choked his words. The corpse of the oak grew slick. He slipped, falling painfully on the hard wood, banging his ribs and collapsing in the loam, muddy and moaning, shivering against the decaying bark.

You are not free until all are free. Equality is not a half measure. While the animals cower in the feedlots, and the dogs yap behind the fences, and the trees, rocks, rivers, and valleys are owned by human beings, our species is no better than the plantation slave owner loftily claiming that without him, his negroes would degenerate into wild beasts.

Dave groaned on the ground. The wilds - that which we called the wilds - was nothing more than a perfectly content ecosystem going about its business until our fear came along and choked on it. The wilds once humbled humanity, keeping our species into the natural system of checks and balances. They cast the arrogance of human beings into the democracy of the species, the round table in which elephants and ants are all created equal. And for this reason, humanity holds nature's egalitarianism with deep disdain and lauds the hierarchies of man. But as the slow quest for equality between the human races, genders, and classes begins to bear fruit; humans are also starting to wonder . . . what is humanity doing on a pedestal of our own construction?

The meadowlark, the sequoia, the humpback whale . . . how can humankind maintain its arrogant delusion of superiority when confronted with the truth of every species' beauty? Our scientists prove the language of the birds, the intelligence of the dolphins, the social structures of the bees, the use of tools by primates, the emotions of the elephants, the alteration of environment by beavers. Nothing sets humans apart from the rest of the animal kingdom - except our penchant for folly. At that, our species exceeds all others.

No, we can claim no superiority to other species. Our desire to tame the wilds is nothing but the lust for domination, an attempt to escape the inherent equality of Earth.

Dave laid his head against the damp bark of the fallen tree. The scent of loam swelled up from the disturbed earth. In the aroma of wood, rot, and soil lay the scent of Joan - dark, inscrutable, and woman. In the woman lies the wilds - not the lofty peaks or rocky, windswept summits, but the hollow places twisted with bracken, damp with hidden streams and fertile with life.

The western man sets out to conquer that, to clear the nonsense, establish order, raze the bushes, plow rows, plant fields, and sit on his porch, the master of it all.

And yet, she seethes. Beneath the surface, the woman pulses with resentment, strapped into corsets that bind her as tightly as the property lines that encircle the Earth, ordered to obey her master-husband's beck and call. The woman erodes him, rots him, pulls him back from lofty quests, clings and burrows into him. The man thrusts out, raises structures, towns, and cities. She holds him back, pulls him down and in, wraps him between her legs, and never lets him go.

Go where, my love? the woman asks. Where are you going without me? The barren moon? The flaming sun? The mountain peaks that hold no seeds of life?

Progress! He shouts. *Onward!*

Onward where? She taunts him. *There is only one place that you and I are headed.*

He sees in her the beginning, the end, the womb, the grave, the endless cycles, the net, the trap - and he struggles to break free. He seeks to fly, to excel, to shine, to live forever, to be omnipotent like the gods. She folds her arms across her breasts and closes her legs to him. He has missed the point completely.

I'm here, she whispers. Immortality, resurrection, birth beyond death, the emptiness that births your form, embraces your form, gives meaning to your exclamation point of existence.

And still, the man rages. He shaves the forests as severely as his culture insists that women shave their legs, armpits, pubis. He blows up mountains in brutal rapes for coal. He pisses his sewage into oceans as if defecating on his lover. He cruelly exhales toxic smoke into her face. He sprays her with disfiguring, cancerous substances. Then he kicks her in disgust, saying she is old, worn out, useless, ugly; her vagina stretches wider than a whore's; her breasts hang like an old sow's.

In her brokenness, she mocks him. Missing a tooth, she sneers at him. *Go find yourself a virgin, fool!* She is the wilds, the woods; the Earth. She says to humankind: in this entire

Universe, I dare you to find another planet as hospitable as I. She stands on rickety knees, naked and hideous. She waggles her flabby hips.

I was beautiful, once, she reminds man. He groans, remembering. She was beautiful once, beyond belief, beyond compare. The very memory of Earth stirs his loins and quickens his pulse.

Dave wept into the forest floor. His mouth grew chalky on the crunch of loam. The musk filled his nostrils. She is there; the maiden, mother, crone; every woman he's ever known, the friends, adversaries, ex-wife, fantasies, lovers . . . and Joan.

Joan with her half smile at the old cosmic joke and with eyes that had seen life and death a thousand times. Joan who hid her softness behind gates of fire. Joan who floundered in the modern world, trying to make sense of womanhood in a landscape built by men. Who was Joan with her hair undone, with the sisterhood of the wilds around her?

He rolled over on his back, staring at the dark swallow of the storm. Suddenly, he stilled. His eyes swept the sodden clouds. His ears tensed. His skin crawled with the sense that something moved through the dark, leaving no footsteps. The mists whispered and swayed in curtains. Pinprick droplets landed on his skin.

"Who's there?" he asked bluntly.

The night stilled.

Dave froze.

Something was out there. If it had been nothing, the mists would have kept moving, brushing, hissing and sliding onward, inland. Yet, at the sound of his voice, the mists hung, static.

Dave clamped down on a shiver. He felt the presence of the unseen growing thicker around him. The sense of invisible forces was not completely unfamiliar. He had felt them during the construction of Gold Mountain, swirling around synchronicities and unusual events. But these were potent, strong, and present. He could feel them rustling out of sight. Beyond the stillness, he sensed the great bank of storm clouds swirling. Images of migrations ghosted in his mind: peoples on the move, armies, peasants, ranchers herding cattle, protesters marching with streaming banners.

Dave breathed in a thread, barely moving. There are layers to life that we cannot see, masked by our focus on reality. The madman's consciousness grows blurred and he stumbles into streams of ghosts, demons, invisible adversaries, seraphim, and angels. Western man tried to conquer the sages, druids, shamans, ghost walkers, spirit intermediaries with the singular dogma of Christianity, but they still lurk beyond our sight, hidden.

It's all true, Dave thought. His eyes darted to the unseen that hung in the night. Every story of ghosts and spirits is all out there in some layer of the Universe, like waves of infrared or sound outside our normal range of sensing.

I'm going mad, he thought. His chest constricted in a fit of panic. I'm unhinging from reality, he worried. He lurched, lunged, and smacked his head against the tree trunk.

"Ooh," he moaned, clapping his hand to the spot and leaning back against the solidness of the trunk to stop the spinning sensation. He squinted into the rain, but he saw nothing otherworldly - only the bulky shapes of oaks.

He sat for hours, listening, but nothing extraordinary occurred, just the sigh of wind through oak leaves and the tap of rain. An occasional animal rustled through the forest. The tang of the sea rode the storm. Salt hid in the low clouds.

Yet, he could not shake the sense of movements, as if out of mortal sight the angels marched and the spirits embarked on great migrations. He listened, wakeful, until he sensed that he sat at an invisible crossroads, leaning against the great oak as if it were a signpost. His arrival here was no mistake, Dave realized with a chill. He had stood at the crossroads of the realms and delivered a speech. He scrambled to remember his drunken rant. His thoughts skittered and dodged beyond his grasp, disappearing into the mists and the night, taking on a life of their own. He remembered only vague concepts of oaks, trees, slaves, property, and the ultimate emancipation of them all.

He woke late, head throbbing, the ocean pulling back the storm clouds along with the tide. He was hungry, hung over, and filthy. Dave staggered to his feet. The oak trees and the tangles of brush seemed demure in the morning light, subdued amidst the ordinary qualities of day.

"Remember," he warned them. "Remember all my words. The days will pass and the loggers will return. Then you will know you are not free."

They stirred uneasily as if wondering what to do. Dave squirmed uncomfortably; he had taken away their illusion of freedom, yet he held no hope of emancipation.

A trickle of blood ran down his cheek. He gingerly touched his head. His fall last night had broken skin and raised a bruise. He scooped the blood onto his finger and stared at the bright scarlet potency. Quickly, before the blood dried, he pivoted and pressed his blood into the soil.

"I will do what I can," he promised, gazing up at the trees.

He rose with the uneasy feeling that the oaks had shouted, *heard and witnessed!* at the crossroads of the realms. Daylight crowned the treetops. Dave looked down at his body.

"I'm disgusting," he said.

Not one leaf on one twig on one branch of the forest disagreed. He thought about the ocean down the cliffs and winced at the remembrance of the itch of salt. He walked deeper into the bracken and brambles until he found a stream. He dammed up the trickle and stripped.

Sitting naked in the shallow rough-hewn bath, he scoured himself with sand and water, running his fingers through the tangled ends of his shaggy hair, wishing for a razor to remove the stubble on his chin. He examined his recent history of bruises and scrapes. Scars of filth marked his skin. He rubbed his flesh raw and shining, then sat in a patch of sunlight, reluctant to climb back into the weary grime of his clothing. Hunger knotted his guts, but he let it gnaw on the bacteria that proliferated in his innards. A solid cleansing inside and out was exactly what he needed.

"Inside and out," he repeated and nodded decisively.

He eyed his grimy clothes distastefully. Impulsively, he threw them in the pool, plunging them in and out as the water turned black and brown. He scrubbed the fabric against a rock, wrung them, slapped them in the pool until he was sweating with exertion. He twisted the water out of his shirt and jeans, broke the dam and let his grime sweep downstream where the clinging moss and rotting leaves along the streambed would decompose the traces of his self-abuse, turning grime into soil, and soil into green curls of ferns. Fresh life emerges from the rotting of the old. Dave's eyes traced the stream down the embankment as he sat on his haunches, panting.

He stood. The sinews in his legs protested. He carried his damp clothes to a sunny patch and laid them out to dry. Glancing left and right in case of wayward hikers, he returned to the grove of oaks, hesitated, then spoke.

"Naked as the day I was born," he told the trees. "Naked as you stand right now."

The oaks said nothing, but seemed to watch him curiously as he scrambled up the side of the fallen oak and sat cross legged on its back. He pivoted to look around at the ring of trees.

"I wish to tell you a story," Dave began uncertainly. "A true story, and an uncomfortable one . . . a tale that has no easy answers, and may be long in telling, but our fates are twined together as deeply as the air we breathe. My exhale is the inhale of your lungs . . . and without your breath, my species will crumble into dust."

Dave trembled at the madness of addressing trees! Now, when he was no longer drunk, but stark and serious, not in the depth of night, but in the morning's clarity and light! He took a breath and plunged deeper into insanity.

"And I will say this at the crossroads," he declared, "inviting all the realms to listen."

The forest halted. The buzzing insects stilled. The wind hung in place. Not a single leaf rustled. A shiver ran down Dave's spine, for this was real; he was not imagining the reaction of the woods. Sunlight touched his back with its warm encouragement to continue. He swallowed, a pale, naked human being, hairless and defenseless, without fire, knife, or clan to back him up.

"If I tell this story right," he murmured, "perhaps it will help you understand."

And perhaps, it would help them all - oaks, humans, animals, and Dave - find the freedom that they sought.

"My first memory of a tree is a whipping stick smacking across my back."

He must have seen a tree before then, but the red welts of abuse drove all other memories from his mind. He remembered crying - and being whipped again for the cry-baby tears. He remembered hating the willow from which his father cut the switch.

"My second memory of a tree," he confessed to the silent grove of oaks, "was hiding in the branches as my older brother lobbed rocks at me."

He swallowed. The memories ached raw and red, swollen with bruises and unspoken words of childhood anger. He had known the taste of hatred long before the taste of love. Even now, the flavor returned to sting his mouth. He winced and continued.

"My third memory of a tree," he told the forest, "is the shaved and sawn up body of a hardwood board of lumber. My father sent me to pick a whipping switch. Fat or thin, stinging or smacking, I was to choose the method of my punishment."

Instead, he had hauled a two-by-four board into the kitchen. Barely six years old, he had struggled with the awkward length, throwing it at his father's feet.

"Why don't you use this, Dad?" he spat out angrily.

His father's face crumpled in dismay.

"My father never beat me after that," Dave said, "so my mother took on the task."

He closed his eyes to the gentle sunlight. His lips tensed and trembled. Mothers are meant to be nurturing, comforting; his screamed with fury, hustled her wayward sons into line, set her mouth in a line thinner than a switch and attempted to beat the impudence out of her younger child.

"I hated her," he whispered.

He hated them all: mother, father, brother, their house with the white picket fence, the dog he was allergic to - that dog received more gentle pats, treats, and cooing words than he did.

"I studied forestry in college," he told the trees. "I applied early, and at the age of sixteen, I was reading instruction manuals on how to murder forests. I read profit spreadsheets printed on the backs of your brothers. At the age of twenty, I wrote my thesis on your mother's skin. The study covered how to take the sapling youths and scrub brushes, grind them into chips, and make a fortune off the paperboard. By the next year, I was verging on making my first million off of flaying trees alive. At twenty-one, I could legally drown the last scraps of my conscience in alcohol."

He could not count the acres he had razed.

"I remember the first time I cut a chainsaw into a redwood trunk," he told the oaks. A primal rage had pulsed in his veins; a sense of power and victory crashed through him as the giant trunk thunderously toppled. "I felt no remorse. No guilt. No twinge of sorrow that I had ended eight hundred years of life." Dave forced himself to be honest with the oaks. The wind shifted uneasily, almost angrily. His naked flesh rose in goose bumps. He held up his hands.

"Hear me out!" he cried. "If my story ended there, I would not be here today."

He had been raised with hatred, whipped and weaned with violence. His mother's accusatory eyes cursed the weakness of his father for refusing to whip their son. He learned at his mother's hand that real men were expected to beat this world. Strength lay in conquering. Little boys must mow the lawn and beat the bushes back from the edge of the house and lift the heavy loads. Men must work and earn good wages, providing amply for the family. No standing in solidarity with those striking for better wages could supersede the importance of a roof over her family's head. No moral quandary must threaten the bread upon their table. Principles were a luxury of the successful or the foolish. His mother was neither. His father worked for the oil company until they fired him six months before he could retire with a pension.

"Pay attention!" she barked at her youngest son. "This world is survival of the fittest. It's dog-eat-dog out there. Work hard, but act smart. A man's got to be on his toes to get ahead."

She laughed when his older brother tortured him, telling Dave to buck up and be a man. She snapped at him to stop being a crybaby when his brother's taunt cut him to his heart. He grew iron armor around his soul. He learned to fight and win.

"You were always an odd child," his mother had murmured as she lay dying. Her eyes had searched his face, hazy with pain medications for the cancer, seeing double visions of the child-son and the man-Dave.

"You were a stoic, remember?" she said.

He had slept on the floor and trained as a warrior, lifting weights and doing pushups, taking vows of silence, jumping in ice cold showers.

I was a child in a warzone, Dave realized all these years later. Given the circumstances, there was nothing odd about imitating Spartans in a suburban San Francisco house.

"Will you be alright after I'm gone?" she asked him anxiously.

"Ma," he said hesitatingly. Perhaps she didn't know . . . "I'm a millionaire."

"Are you?" she murmured, biting her lips in pain.

He nodded.

She closed her eyes for a moment.

"That wasn't what I meant," she whispered.

"There is a point to all of this," Dave reassured the listening forest. "When my mother asked if I would be alright, she echoed the concern of a million mothers in this country. In her eyes welled the sorrow of generations of broken women who came to this continent hoping for a better world, but found hardships and misery stretched from coast to coast. In her heart burned the remorse of all women who learn cruelty to survive. Her determination to succeed came at the price of her compassion. We are the children of these women, all of us in America."

His mother came from the lineage of the New World, a saga of greed and lust, murder, backstabbing lies and avarice, broken hopes and shattered dreams, and worst of all the myth of survival of the fittest in which failure is the fault of personal shortcomings, not the result of systemic oppression. If you fail, his mother told him in a thousand silent ways, good riddance. May your faulty genes rot in the grave, and may only the best perpetuate the species.

So Dave had plundered, robbed, and cheated his way to the top. Forests built his first fortune; computers supplied the second. From there money begat more money. The resort was simply the icing on top of the cake. He strove to prove himself a survivor, to escape beatings and his mother's scorn. He built fortunes to buy access to the golden club of the survivors, the champions of domination.

Then one day, he looked around. On top of the world, part of the elite, he had won - he had surpassed most men of fortune, he owned hundreds of millions to their mere millions.

"Ten thousand years of human evolution," Dave told the trees, "has given rise to this: the socially successful are a set of psychopaths. The richest victors - with few exceptions - are broken human beings. Not one of us had happy families; not one of us understands how to love. We were barbarians on top of the world, cruel and avaricious. Our human hearts had been encased in lead. Our minds were poisoned by profits. Yet, the whole world strives to emulate us. Everyone wants access to the elite. But we are not human beings - we are rotten husks without any hearts. We drown our emotions in alcohol. We numb sympathy and close our hearts to stay at the top. It is insanity! Yet, humanity persists in holding such sickened individuals aloft."

Dave shuddered on the fallen oak. The consequences of this cultural insanity were dire. As long as humanity believed in the colonizing lie that survival came by destroying others, nothing on this planet would survive. The forests would be clear cut, the indigenous mowed down in genocide and wars, the earth torn open in search of minerals, the oil burned into the skies, the people devoured by a machine of greed that knows no bounds or limitations.

"Somehow," he told the oaks, "we must stop the madness of these beliefs."

He fell silent then, for he did not know how to end the delusions of his species. The oaks sat with him, pondering the situation. The morning stretched into the afternoon; the evening rolled toward night. Dave sat like Siddhartha Buddha, naked to the world. His body chilled. His limbs began to shiver. He rose, redressed, and returned, gathering up dry branches. He built a small fire awkwardly, fumbling with half-forgotten methods he had learned in boyhood, cursing his own incompetence until a tendril of smoke finally sparked to flames.

"Do you mind?" he asked the oaks, listening carefully for their reply.

Do you mind, the forest whispered, *if the birds build their nests from the hair that falls from your head?*

"No," he answered, "only if they pluck it from my scalp."

And so it is, the oaks replied, *thus it is so for us.*

Dave crouched by the small fire, slowly feeding it branches and twigs. How does humanity change? he wondered, glancing up at the night. His irises adjusted to the darkness and a single oak loomed, illuminated by the brightness of the flames.

Do not ask how an entire forest grows, the tree suggested, *ask how a single oak emerges from an acorn. You changed . . . how?*

Dave shifted uneasily. His fall from fortune had been propelled by fate and by forces beyond his control.

"I could be up there at the top," he sighed, "except for love. I wanted love, not hard-hearted cruelty and control."

Like a sapling reaching for sunlight, he had begun searching for love, stretching toward the light, strengthening his heart. He had faltered so many times, lost his courage in the thickness of the shadows, but here he was, still reaching.

"I met Joan," he said softly, "and truly understood that there was something I wanted more than money."

He squinted at the flames. A furrow creased between his eyebrows. For a moment . . . he swore he had . . . no, there! Dave dragged his palm across his eyes. When he looked back in the fire, the images remained: a dark haired woman, a twisted hedge of briars, and behind the brambles, him. Dave held his breath as the hairs on the back of his neck raised. The dark haired woman - Joan - pivoted and spun, seeking passage through the bracken, calling out to him in words that made no sound. In the flames, his figure wandered aimlessly - as if sleepwalking - and did not appear to hear Joan's cries. At every twist, the briars scratched her and raked their spines through her clothes. She frowned and her soundless voice repeated the same phrase over and over. Dave leaned toward the fire, desperate to read the words on her lips.

Wake up!

The fire crackled. Sparks shot off like fireworks. He flinched. The flames curled into thick vines; each bramble held dark images inside it. Dave's eyes watered and ached as he tried to make out the forms. The images in the fire reflected on the burning blue of his eyes.

He gasped.

His life twisted in those thorny brambles, every story, memory, assumption, myth, fact, thought, belief, or idea he'd ever conceived. The briars sprouted in his footsteps as he sleepwalked through his days. In the fire, his figure's breath hissed spells of words that clung to the dark vines. Joan struggled to break through, but he spun his stories faster than she could move.

Wake up! her soundless lips cried. *Wake up!*

And still he continued muttering the stories of his past, throwing them up like stinging barriers between them.

The coals of the fire suddenly collapsed. The flames lurched. The images vanished. Dave furiously rubbed his eyes and glanced around at the darkness. He shivered.

"So, my stories are getting in our way," he murmured, thinking of Joan and the twisted brambles keeping them apart. In his hands, he gripped a thin stick - a perfect switch, he thought. The kind of switch his mother preferred for beatings. His knuckles clenched white around it.

Laughter rang like bells through the dark outlines of the oak grove. He spun. Nothing. He recognized that laugh - Joan's laugh.

You're the one holding onto the stories.

"Who spoke?" he demanded.

The trees refused to answer. The night hid itself in silence. He looked down at the switch in his clenched hands.

What would it be like to put the stories down . . . and never pick them up again?

The voice whispering in his mind sounded like his own. He pondered this, staring at the stick, seeing in it all the beatings he had received, his mother's scorn, his brother's abuses, his father's silence.

Why not let it go? he thought.

He threw the stick into the fire. It smoked, fizzled, curled and ignited into flames. He watched it burn and saw his memories char and vanish into ashes.

He sat back.

Why not let everything go?

He reached for another stick, a knobby branch with a whorl that sneered like his brother's face. He dredged up memories - fire ants dumped in his bed, the time he had unzipped his fly and pissed on his brother in retaliation, the day his brother locked him in the closet and told his parents Dave had run away. He let the painful memories roll out and lodge inside the stick. Then he chucked it in the fire, watching the whorl's expression scream and collapse into coals.

He threw his father in the fire, his former girlfriends, and treacherous business partners; all that was a part of his past, every gesture, every thought, every twitch of expression, every sentiment and cliché statement, every slogan, tagline, business motto; every memory of his actions, every motivation, every rationalization for his behaviors both good and bad. Into the flames he tossed the drunkard on the street. The playboy writhed in hot coals. A smoldering fat branch burned up the weight of his former obesity. He threw it all in the fire. Twigs, branches, sticks: a small blaze mounted. He thought of Indian cremations, pyres of logs burning bodies into ashes by the river. In utter clarity, he knew what he had embarked upon: he was incinerating his self, conducting a cremation in reverse. His body remained seated by the fire while flames consumed his inner world.

Time stretched in ancient patience. Those who gathered at the crossroads stood witness. His actions echoed rituals and rites of passage. He evoked older times and civilizations now crumbled into dust. He sat on the ground and stared at the fire like countless generations of human beings who had walked this earth before him.

The flames twisted into shapes and figures. His memories danced for brief moments before vanishing. Long forgotten times and places emerged in the twisting curls of the fire. He saw battles and ceremonies, lovers and bitter enemies. Ten thousand years of human history swirled in the flames, only to fall as still and silent as his own meager past.

Lightness filled his being. A sense of vastness stretched in the silence between his ears. His mind expanded like the night, empty as space with stars of thought scattered across his awareness. One by one, he plucked them from the sky of his mind, turning them like diamonds in his fingers before tossing them into the fire.

Long bouts began to pass between his feeding of the fire. He sat quietly, watching the coals settle in the white ashes. The stillness grew profound. The coals burned down into nothing until only one ember remained, a tiny spark in a vast pool of night, no bigger to his eyes than the stars overhead.

What happens when we let it all go?

The thought streaked across the vastness of his mind like a shooting star. On its heels, the Universe replied.

Everything. Something. Nothing.

The ember flickered. Dave waited. It sputtered. He fixed his eyes on the last spark of existence. The night crept closer. Darkness stretched its fingertips toward the void. The coal blinked. Dave froze.

It died and his self extinguished with the light.

CHAPTER SIXTEEN

· · · · ·

Darkness loses meaning in the total absence of light. Nothing becomes something when that is all that seems to exist. This place would terrify the mind, except there is no mind to experience terror. There is no one to sense the vast eternal stillness. There is nothing to worry, rejoice, or think.

Here, eternity is presence; the present is eternal. Time ticks out the meter of human memory and cognition. When the grip of the mind releases, time dissolves into sheer illusion.

How long did Dave hang suspended in that place? There is no answer, for there was no Dave, no thought of time, no measure, no human self to think of such a concept. But when he woke to breath and body with a diver's gasp, resurfacing, the sun burst over the rim of dawn, and his eyes flooded with golden light. The black and green-gray silhouettes of trees emerged upon his retinas. His sense of self lagged behind. He breathed the crisp air of morning. His chest expanded. He glanced down at the rise of his ribs.

I am here, he thought.

But who is here? What survived this baptism by fire? What resurrected after the extinguishing of his self? His eyes stirred cautiously in their sockets, newborn in this dawning day. He saw the ragged cloth of a shirt, the worn knees of jeans, crossed legs and a bare, leathered foot folded up on one thigh. In front of him, a black ring of charred ground held the remnants of a fire. With a hand he did not recognize, he touched the cold, brittle coals and white flakes of ash. With one finger, he stirred the remains of his own cremation. Like a stranger at a funeral, he searched for hints of this unknown person, clues to this

169

extinguished life. The ash clung to his fingertips. A slight breeze flung the lightest bits into the air.

Once, he thought, *I was a man named Dave Grant.*

But all that was gone on the ashes of yesterday. The past had been buried in the grave. Memories lay dull and lifeless on the furthest peripheries of consciousness.

Who am I without all that? he wondered.

He rose without an answer.

I am here.

He frowned. Who is this I?

Everything. Something. Nothing.

All possibilities rolled into one. He was the breath of air, the inhalation of the trees, the exhalation of humanity. He was the sunlight tapping on one cheek and the cool shadows on the other. He was the sound of the blue jay in an ear, the curve of cartilage and bone, the beat, the throat, the sound, the silence.

But he was not so for long.

The Earth turned and he transformed. One cheek grew hot; he ducked into the shade. He was the echo of the shadows. He was warmth against solid tree trunks. He was the hush of rustling leaves. The settling and the breeze's ruffling return.

I am change, he thought. *I am the river of the world.*

The waters of existence flowed through him, churning his human banks. He was change pouring through change, inseparable from the watershed of life. The tiniest drops on mountaintops rippled changes in his being.

I am awake, he thought - as if Awake was an entity as tangible as a human being. He could not claim to be only a human - not by the limited definitions of that species. Humans box themselves inside their skin and define their parameters by their bodies. He could no longer perceive the great divide where his being stopped and the rest of the world began.

I don't exist! he thought paradoxically.

The small being called Dave Grant had vanished, replaced by a being-ness beyond all limits. Yet, even that conception would not stand still long enough to be named. It brightened, grew, hung poised for a breath of a moment, then dimmed, decayed, stilled, and silenced only to stir again.

I cannot say that I am something, he thought, *but neither am I nothing.*

He was something, everything, nothing all rolled into one. His mind ran clearer than a mountain stream. The past had settled. The future had not been stirred up. A great calm suffused him in the present. The morning sun curved its arc across the sky as that one calm moment stretched into the day.

How long will this spell continue? Dave wondered. As soon as he asked, he knew.

Forever.

Unless he disrupted it, the clarity of presence would simply continue. Suspended from the concept of time, having jettisoned his memories, desires, and fear in the great meditational purge, he would simply exist in the present moment without the burden of a past, without concern for the future. Alive!

Color poured through his retinas. He sniffed the faint whiffs of sunlight heating up redwood sap. He heard the footsteps of deer crossing the meadows. He bent and plucked a wild strawberry from the grasses, felt the stinging burst of sweetness explode across a world. He rolled the seeds across the continent of his tongue.

This, he thought, *is Life.*

To humans, the rest of the animal kingdom is comprised of lesser beasts that lack Homo sapiens' cognitive abilities. Yet, humans are the only animals wandering through life so lost in nightmares of memory and fantasies of thought that they can never truly taste a wild strawberry. They rush past the field, missing the little red berry no bigger than a fingernail. Half-dead to the present, they crave a larger burst of sweetness to compensate for their inattention.

Dave crouched in the grasses among the oaks, rolling the seeds of the tiny wild strawberry in his mouth, following the faintest traces of sour and sweet as they lingered on his tongue. He ate five strawberries as the sun lowered toward the ocean.

This is Life, he thought.

Not 'the life'. Not the glossy advertisement, the pre-packaged fantasy sold to delusion humanity. This was Life! This true aliveness in absolute presence that turned every inch of the globe into the paradise of Eden in which Adam walked with Eve.

He tipped his head back and swallowed sunlight through his skin. He drank the aroma of the grasses. He savored the sounds of birds and the crackles of small animals rustling through the underbrush.

And then, abruptly, he wanted Joan.

His human body roared into focus. His marrow ached to savor a woman with all the luxurious indulgence of a wild strawberry. Not just any woman: Joan with her dark flashing eyes and the faint perfume of meditation incense and the crooked smile on her lips.

The flood banks of presence collapsed and the past came crashing into his mind. Joan in the teahouse, Dave drunk on love, days in the streets, rain freezing his bones, luxury on silk sheets, obesity and hate, accumulating pain and fortune -

"Enough!" he roared.

Memory vanished.

He sat in the meadow, chest heaving. Sweat trickled down

his back. His heart punched the cage of his ribs. His limbs shook with the sudden shock of how quickly one thought triggered the avalanche of memories. A moth fluttered past his gaze. Dust settled on the sunlight. He shifted, frowning. He carefully nudged his mind, trying to pick up one thought without exploding the cascade of all the others.

He sensed the versions of himself hovering on the edges of perception. He could pick up any of them: the businessman, the tea drinker, the drunkard. He refused every one of them. He steeled his mind with the discipline of a warrior, picking up thoughts, examining them, and ultimately putting them aside. All afternoon, he worked his mind with determination, persevering through the ache of ill-used muscles, strengthening his capacity. The sun submerged in the silver ocean and threw its rays up into the clouds like the raised arms of a rejoicer. The world settled into slumber. Ghosts of his past crowded up around him, pushing with unseen hands that passed through air. He faced them, staring at the invisible. He uttered one word.

"Go."

They vanished.

He lay back in the grass and exhaled in a whoosh. The night swallowed the sound and spat out silence. His chest rose and fell. His gaze peered into the deep void between the stars. Something moved at the edge of his eyes.

"Come," he ordered.

Memory slid out of the darkness: Joan.

She stood solitary, strong, unattached to other memories, surrounded by the vast space of possibility. He considered her carefully, examining the string of desire that tied his mind to humanity's delusion of self and other. He shook his head.

"You are an illusion. A story like all the others," he told her.

"Go."

She stood her ground.

"Not tonight," he said. "Memory can eat up one's life, devour the present, make one live like an addict hooked on his dreams."

She smiled.

"You, " he said, pointing his finger, "are not the real Joan. No more than - "

No sooner had he uttered the words than the floodgate of images broke open. Thousands of Joans poured through his mind in a deluge of memory, fantasy, images, sounds, words she had spoken, laughter he had dreamed, twists of humor on her lips, stinging looks from her eyes.

"Enough!" he roared.

The hills shook. The stars trembled. The crickets silenced. His chest heaved.

Just one memory? her voice enticed.

"One drink topples the drunkard," he retorted.

Love is not an addiction, the vision argued.

"Oh no?" he countered. "We drink of each other and grow drunk on the notion of self, spinning the cycle of suffering."

Remember? she teased in the tones of the devil's advocate. Her voice tempted him with hints of her beauty and his desire.

What is life without memories? she challenged him.

"This!" he exploded and the stars blazed, the grass trumpeted, the ink of night spilled across his vision.

"Go," he told her.

Go, go, go beyond, she chanted the great mantra of the *Heart Sutra* at him. *Go totally beyond the beyond –*

"Go," he told her.

She vanished.

His chest ached with an unexpected hollowness. For a wild

moment, he fell in the lurch of a missing step, feeling that something that should be there, wasn't. Then the crickets struck up their symphony and the wind hummed across the redwood branches on the hills. The minutes ticked by, then the hours. The constellations in the sky shifted positions. His eyes felt no need to close. Sharp, awake, he lay with the night and time lost its human meanings.

Enlightenment is a kind of love you can't even imagine, she had told him once.

Maybe love, he had countered, is a kind of enlightenment.

Somewhere in the long stretch between midnight and dawn, when the blackness seems interminable, he stirred. He sat up and ran his hands through his hair. His heartbeat raged in his chest. His body pulsed with sinew and marrow, breath and life. His cells yearned. His blood cried out in the night. His body let loose the howl of human existence.

"Go beyond the beyond," he murmured. "Buddha, human, empty, full, all together, go!"

He loved her.

Enlightenment could go to hell.

CHAPTER SEVENTEEN

· · · · ·

"I knew it," Edna declared, smacking the table with her palm and leaning back in her chair. "I knew you'd go back to her."

Dave startled. Lost in the recounting of his story, he had forgotten the presence of the old woman. He blinked at her satisfied grin, wondering how much he had said out loud, and how much had simply throbbed inside his recollection.

"Did she take you back?" Edna asked. She waved her hand. "No, no don't tell me. Pour me some coffee and get on with the story."

Dave rose to wash the chopsticks and dishes as he stalled for time. He carefully ran the sponge around the rims of the plates. There were layers to this story, stages of awakening and forgetting. He put the leftovers in the fridge and poured a cup of thick coffee for Edna as he decided what to tell her. The old woman's eyes followed him closely, watching the way he turned off the water between rinsing the plates and then carefully emptied the sink strainer into the small compost bin on the counter.

"You have changed, Dave Grant," she conceded. "For the better."

"Thank you," he replied, setting down her coffee cup and searching her wrinkled face. "Are you sure you aren't tired?"

"Look at me, Grant!" Edna exclaimed. "I'm on the edge of my seat. I haven't enjoyed a love story this much since Bogie and Hepburn grew as old as I feel."

He chuckled. Her eyes shone bright and she sat in her chair like she could truly last until dawn.

"Alright then," he agreed, pouring a cup of coffee and inhaling it appreciatively. He hadn't drunk coffee in a long time. He sat down at the kitchen table, brushing aside sleepiness, determined to repay all the decades of headache he had caused this woman with the kindness of a story.

"Eventually, I headed south," he began, "toward the hidden teahouse - "

"Eventually?" Edna interrupted with a snort of disbelief. "Eventually? What were you waiting for?"

"The monastery, remember?" Dave sighed. "She had gone to the monastery for a year."

"Bah," Edna scoffed. "I bet she didn't stay."

A wry twist of a smile twitched in his mouth.

"She didn't," he answered. "But I didn't know that then."

Edna shook her head at the folly. Dave stared at the dark windows of the house, remembering.

"She saw me on the street, that day in the rain. I was drunk - or bitterly sober, I don't remember which - she said my name. I pretended not to know her. I turned away and slunk into the darkness. Later, I learned that she had left the temple and returned to the hidden teahouse."

He paused. In the rain, he had not turned back when she called his name again. He had ducked out of sight, shivering under an overhang for a moment. Then he remembered running - stumbling - tripping on curbs and smashing into flooded gutters. A car skidded to a halt on the slick streets when he lurched off the sidewalk. He crashed into an old man outside the liquor store, begged a fiver off the next guy who pulled up, slapped it down for cheap whiskey, and drowned out the encounter in the misery of the railroad tracks behind the store. A weeping cluster of eucalyptus trees swayed in the gusts of wind. Peeling bark slapped against the trunks and broke off in long strips that whacked him on top the head. The nostril-piercing pungency of the sopping eucalyptus mingled with the harsh whiskey. For months, the smells locked together in his memories, making him queasy at even the sight of those striped trees.

"I was a fool," he told Edna, disgusted at his former self. "That moment in the rain might have prevented months of misery. She reached out and I rejected the outstretched hand of fate."

"Actually," Edna retorted, "it's even worse."

He blinked at her.

"You reached out your hand for help, begging for change. The Universe sent you Joan and you turned away. You're an idiot."

Dave nodded with a sigh. He completely agreed.

"Fortunately," Edna continued cheerfully, "you got a second chance."

"Yes," Dave agreed. "Though it was more like the millionth chance. I stayed up in the woods for months, waiting."

He paused.

"No," he amended. "I wasn't waiting. I was preparing."

He was preparing to meet Joan again. In the end, he didn't wait. Months before the year concluded, he left the oak grove and headed south toward the teahouse. In the back of his mind, perhaps he thought that he would find work and settle into the town. In reality, he had no plans. He left the woods because the moment to leave arrived. Unsure of anything, he walked southward down the coastal highway, determined to find Joan again.

CHAPTER EIGHTEEN

· · · · ·

He entered the town unnoticed, stepping under the threshold of the streetlights. He was lean and browned from the sun, scoured from cold mountain streams and long days of absolute presence. He had stood at the feet of the giant redwoods as the crickets whined long into the night and the spray of stars turned slowly across the sky. He had sat by the roar of the ocean as it pounded the sandstone cliffs. He let his assumptions and thoughts erode until truth swept over him like a tide. He followed a tendril of possibility toward an unknown hope, trekking down the coastal highway to the ragged outskirts of the town. He was taut from simple living, nourished by basic food, thin and muscled from hiking the rolling hills.

The commercial strip ignored him as he strode past. His eyes quietly regarded the folly of concrete and tar and cars and strip malls and gas station convenience stores, wondering why humanity put up with such an assault to their living sensibilities.

He walked without stopping past the last place he had seen Joan. The winter's pouring rain had washed away the shame he had felt on that day. He went directly to the alleyway, past the shopkeepers eating lunches on the stoops, to the little red door.

It was locked.

He sat down to wait. Someone in the teahouse would know where to find Joan.

"It'll be a few hours," one of the shopkeepers called out helpfully. "They're opening late today."

"That's alright," he replied. "It's a fine day for waiting."

It was. The blue sky pulsed with fresh energy. The breeze wafted gently through the alley. The scarves hanging on display at the shop next door stirred in the sunlight and shadows.

Dave sat quietly and watched the world live. When his back grew sore from leaning against the door, he crossed his legs and calmly carried on.

"You look like one of those stone buddha statues," the shopkeeper cackled. Then she frowned in the sunlight and squinted at him. "You seem familiar. Didn't you use to come around regular?"

"It was a while back," he answered.

The shopkeeper nodded and returned to her lunch. The afternoon breathed. A couple of college students wandered up the alley. Friends of the shopkeepers stopped to visit.

How odd, Dave mused, that we can put a man on the moon, but we can't make this calmness a mainstay of modern life.

The afternoon sun slid from east to west as he quietly waited. His mind rested in disciplined stillness. Now and then, the past threatened to swell up like a tidal wave and crash onto him in waves of anxiety or doubt. He firmly refused to let the memories break into the present. He breathed with the breeze and watched the ebbs and flows of the alleyway. He nodded to passersby and smiled at the curious glances of the shopkeepers. His shadow stretched long as he waited. When it reached the sidewalk display of the shop next door, he wondered how long it would take to extend all the way to the willow tree at the far end of the alleyway.

On the heels of that thought, he squinted to the east . . . just in time to see Joan turn the corner. His heart leapt into a chokehold on his throat as a sudden rush of emotion overwhelmed him. Dave leaned his head against the red door. Tears pushed his eyes. He considered scrambling to his feet, but his limbs refused to cooperate. Relief swept over him.

Somewhere deep inside, he had worried that he'd blown his chance; that she'd moved on, or died, or remained in the monastery. Yet, there she was, dressed in somber tones, her coal black hair pulled back in a long braid.

"There's someone waiting," he heard the furthest shopkeeper inform her.

Joan shaded her eyes and glanced down the alley, but couldn't see the features of his face.

"Whoever it is can wait a few more moments," she replied.

Dave would wait an eternity, if that were what it took. Joan exchanged pleasantries with the shopkeeper and then continued toward the teahouse. She called out a greeting to the next woman sitting on the front stoop of her store, turning to laugh over her shoulder at something the shopkeeper said. Dave's breath caught in his chest as the curve of her neck shifted, her profile swung toward him, her eyes narrowed to focus on him -

"Dave."

"Hello," he answered almost bashfully, looking up at her with his knees pulled to his chin and his arms hung over them. Her eyes took stock of him, running the length of muscles he'd never had before, and sweeping along the angles of his cheekbones. Behind the black depths of her gaze, he sensed her calculating the significance of those changes. He leaned his head back against the door and dropped all his thoughts except for a tendril of hope. He let that curl green and vulnerable like a seedling cracking through the soil.

Her eyes widened as she saw the quiet shifting of stories and the dropping of expectations. Here was a Dave she'd never seen, but had been waiting for - no, searching furiously for - through all his nonsense since the very first day they had met. *There you are!* her eyes exclaimed. Beside them, Joan's thin wrinkles curved in the arc of a smile. Her lips twisted. She glanced again at the muscles in his arms. He sternly suppressed his schoolboy urge to flex them. They were too old for that silliness - she, breaking forty, with crows feet dancing in the lines by her eyes; he, nearly a decade older, gray running through his hair - but alive, my god! Alive beyond measure, crackling in this moment with an intensity that twenty-year-old zombies glued to cellphones could not conceive. Alive in ways that Hollywood could never capture, not with a thousand flashing images of sky diving, trick biking, extreme sport footage intercut with bronzed, waxed models licking their tongues over gelatin-injected lips, and underscored with thudding beats designed to artificially increase the heart rates of youths that had forgotten what it meant to be alive!

Alive! In the uncertainty of the next word that trembled in them both. Alive! In the indescribable flood of sensation that evicted blood and replaced it with inconceivable wordless pulsing. Alive! In the excruciating slowness of a moment that hung like thick honey off the spoon of now.

The world is dead until it learns to love. In that moment, two people who had breathed a collective sum of ninety circles around the sun suddenly learned to live.

"Well," Joan said shakily. "You'd better come in."

She dropped her hand down to him - he wanted to kiss it - but at the last moment she rolled her palm over into the extended hand of equals and dared him to take it.

He smiled. He took it.

She pulled him to his feet.

He kept her hand in his and curled it against his chest. Her head tilted up to catch his eyes.

"Joan, I - " he began.

"I know," she replied. His heart had been an open book since the first day at the teahouse. He had only glimpsed the cover of hers and never seen a single word, let alone read between the lines of the book of Joan.

"And?" he asked, breathlessly. His whole life depended on her answer.

"You'd better come in," she repeated with a smile, moving past him and reaching for the keys with her free hand. He held her back.

"If I come in . . . "

"I know," she assured him.

"No half-measures," he warned.

"No," she agreed.

"I don't want to just be friends," he blurted truthfully.

"Neither do I."

In broad daylight, under the narrowed squints of gossipy shopkeepers, against the little red door that framed the blackness of her hair in a hood of scarlet, he kissed her. Their lips met with a passion that put the youth-obsessed world to shame. They kissed with an honesty that burned the retinas of voyeuristic eyes. There is a truth to this kind of love that cannot be watched. Its intensity makes the observer uncomfortable, self-reflective, suddenly aware that they are dead to the world without that passion igniting in their own hearts. No amount of salivating over movie starlets can replace the aching honesty of human love - the inexplicable passion for the rounded curves of an older woman, or the humble sincerity of a man's paunch, or the texture of real life etching its dirt into the skin of your beloved, or the dust of time that peppers the body with seasoning, leaving the taste of aliveness tingling on the tongue and lips.

Joan in her twenties did not have half the beauty of Joan in her forties. There is an aching gorgeousness in the confidence of a woman who dares to press her hips into a man's loins as they embrace in a side alley of a touristy seaside town. There is a glory to her shameless gasp for air and the gleam in her eye that dares him to steal her breath again. There is a solemn truth to the lines in her face that warns the spying eyes of shopkeepers not to waste a moment more! Do not watch us, her older, lower breasts cry out. Go find your love! Time is the essence of love. Each moment stretches into an eternity and yet love is greedy for just one second more.

Go find your love, her body tells the world. We are nothing. We can tell you nothing that will help you in that excruciating moment when you encounter love. For we are each unique, irreproducible, exquisitely perfect snowflakes in the storm of humanity's existence.

"Let's go," Joan said, her voice cracking with longing.

"Where?" he answered.

"Anywhere. Let's walk. We'll go to the ocean," she gasped, flinging out suggestions. She could not - would not - sit quietly in the teahouse pouring tea for the irregulars, biting her tongue on the ten thousand words that pounded in her chest, burning with desire yet bound by the proprieties of time and place, aching for him - and him alone - under the hawk-eyed scrutiny of teahouse guests who would rip apart the sanctity of this encounter with obnoxious questions and prying inquiries as they built up a stockpile of gossip to chew like tobacco and stale gum as soon as her back was turned - no! She would not drag him through the hell of polite conversation - not now, not at this moment when so much raged between them unsaid and yearned to tumble out of their wildly beating hearts!

Joan's eyebrows furrowed as she dug in her bag for paper and pen. She scrawled a note and stuck it in the frame of the door.

Closed due to the inevitable.

"We can wait," he mentioned.

"No," she retorted. "We can't."

The moment was now; the time to leap had come. Joan felt the churning of the crossroads, and intersections of great change approaching. The wind pulled tendrils of her hair loose from her braid as she swiveled in the alleyway.

"Come," she commanded, striding up the street in a furious pace.

He jogged to catch her hand. She pulled away.

"Where have you been?" she demanded, for now she was angry - she had gone to the monastery with her serenity shattered; weeks of silence and sitting did nothing to quiet the tempest raging inside her. Longing ran up and down her skin like ants, and though she knew her task was to endure the sensations, truncate the simmering thoughts that boiled her blood, and restore the equanimity of mind . . . she couldn't. The half-veiled eyes of the Buddha mocked her. The temple bells drove her mad. After each session, she burst out of the temple, catapulting her legs into running. Three times a day, she sprinted up the road and down the trails through the woods, hurtling her body to the brink of a ravine, screeching to a halt as small pebbles scattered over the edge. One afternoon, she churned toward the blue of the sky and knew with stark clarity she would throw herself off. She stopped in one stride. Her blood pounded, *go, go, go beyond*. Heat pulsed in her eyes. Her chest heaved. Shock coursed through her limbs. She left the temple that day. Life is too precious to risk. She cast aside her stubborn commitment to the year in the monastery, laid down her pride, confessed to the head nun that she could not walk this path, and returned to the teahouse to find Dave. The head nun watched her departure with knowing eyes. Below the half-lidded gaze of the Buddha, a slight smile curled imperceptibly.

"Where have you been?" Joan asked him. "I came back to find you, and you had already left."

Again, Dave struggled for words.

"I hadn't left," he began.

"That *was* you!" she gasped, whirling to pin him with accusatory eyes. "That day in the rain -"

"Joan, I - " he floundered.

"You pretended that you didn't know me!" Joan exclaimed. "And then you disappeared. Where have you been?"

In her tone of voice he heard the dangerous riptides of the past threatening to drown the waters of the present.

"Quiet," Dave answered as if quiet was a place. Then, with a sigh, he slowed his pace.

"Lost," he replied truthfully. "I have been lost."

For fifty years, he had wandered through life, sleeping on silks and lying in gutters, absolutely confused about where he was and why. He had built houses without finding a home and traveled the world without knowing where he started. He had bumbled around inside his skin and flesh and bone container all his life, utterly and totally lost.

"Joan," he tried to explain, "the real question is not *where* have I been, but *why* have I been?"

Joan smiled the smile of Gandhi's wife, one of great patience and respect crowned with a determined pragmatism, crested with a humble acknowledgement that yes, Mahatma, that is an excellent philosophical question, but what would you like for dinner tonight?

"Where have you been, Dave?" she asked.

"I have been dropping the juggling balls of my life," he said, "one by one, to see if I survive."

Joan's eyebrow arched, as she looked him up and down.

"Clearly, you survived."

He shook his head, ruefully.

"I'm not sure I did. What's left of me? A sack of sinew and bone, inhabited by someone other than who I once was." He smiled ruefully down at his body. "These arms, legs, and chest are but a costume. You know, a lot of people go through life pretending they are the same stock actor performing the same role, year after year. They tie a thread of memory between each show and call that thread their self."

He paused.

"But what happens when you cut the thread?"

Joan looked sharply at him.

"The fabric of reality unravels," she replied cautiously, for they were trespassing on the territory of the saints and sages, geniuses, madmen, and giants of philosophy.

For weeks, Dave had sat in the woods and audaciously pulled the woven thread of his mind. There were times when he panicked and rapidly rewove the warp and weft of himself. Yet, the sheer skill of his weaving emboldened him. All of his life, with natural dexterity, he had woven the cloth of himself out of notions and memories. Who is Dave Grant? Where is he going? What is he doing? Opinions, ideas, information, knowledge - he wrapped himself in a shroud of his own construction, woven so tightly it would clothe him all the way to the grave.

Yet, under the swaying of giant trees in the gentle spring heat, he had let his fingers fall idle from the constant weaving of his thoughts. In the stillness, he turned to examine the fabric, and, curious about a loose thread, he pulled it.

Oh human! Curiosity is a gift to all creatures, yet you have excelled in its art. To the moon, to deep ocean trenches, to the core of the Earth, to the center of atoms: how far must you go before satisfying your curiosity? Must you explode your whole world before you can enjoy a campfire? Could not a small flame satisfy your wonder? Must you truly unravel the fabric of reality before loving your human existence?

Man, you have always been the incorrigible flirt, a provocative rapscallion! How you love the cliff's edge of danger! You dance on the pinnacles and lean over the abyss. When you succeed, the gods cheer your bravery; your fellow humans emulate your endeavors. When you fail, we mourn your demise; yet look up expectantly for the next daredevil.

But in the crowd, unobserved, is the other hero of humanity: the woman. With children clinging to her skirts, she draws her mouth into a thin line at all of your stunts. One hand on the head of your child; the other placed on her hip, her eyes never leave your teetering body as it runs along the edge of disaster.

Is it not enough? she demands. Your children, home, me, your love? Is the beauty of existence so lacking that you will risk annihilation to catch a glimpse of some other horizon?

No, he replies. It is not enough. The same drive that thrusts him into her arms propels him away once again.

And the physical body of gender and sex is no barrier; there are men who love homes, children, and contentment. There are women who must hurtle the abyss. This is the breath of the Universe: the exhale to go further, the inhale to pull back.

Here they stood, Dave and Joan, her breath catching at the thought of his antics.

"You did what?" she exclaimed.

"I unraveled reality. I took off the shroud, got rid of the warp, cast off the weft. You don't need it. It's nonsense."

Her heart thudded. She touched him to guarantee his solidity. She moved her hand to his.

"You need an anchor to keep your thread of reality tied to

the rest," she warned.

"Why not cast off?" he invited. "The water is warm; the ocean is wide. Unravel your self. Who would you be without Joan?"

"I like being Joan," she said, turning and pacing slowly down the street.

"I like her, too," he confessed, catching up and touching her shoulder softly. "She's a nice story, beautiful, one of the best."

"She goes well with Dave - " Joan began with a wry smile.

"No," he disagreed, shaking his head. "Dave was a disaster, a real problem for Joan, a square peg to the circle she made. A businessman, a rich man, a self-centered lout; I had to get rid of him to get within ten feet of you."

"So, who are you?" she asked, swiveling to gaze at his face.

He laughed.

"I don't know," he answered honestly. "I am. I'm here. Here's good."

"Why are you here?"

Ah, the old showstopper, why?

"I came back to love you," he said simply. He had come back to existence with one purpose: to love. To love the woods, his breath, the crackling intensity of life in human form . . . and to love her.

"I had this crazy idea," he mentioned, tracing the soft hairs on her forearm, "that if I dropped all my stories, and you dropped yours, we would love like no others in the history of the Universe."

He glanced up through his eyelashes, almost daring her to accept.

"Just what," Joan drawled, "do you think will happen if we did?"

"I don't know," he chuckled, "but I think the last time such lovers collided was back at the Big Bang."

She laughed and glanced up at the brilliant blue of the sky. The roar of the ocean touched their ears as they strolled down the sidewalk.

"You think we'll spawn a new Universe?" she teased.

"Something like that," he said with a shrug. "Want to try?"

She thought about it.

"What I would like first," she said slowly and seductively, "is one day just as we are now. Tomorrow, we can consider boldly going . . . "

" . . . beyond the beyond," he finished.

Their teasing dropped into the pool of sincerity and dissolved. She studied the carve of his cheeks, his jawline, the hollows of his collarbone.

"When I saw you sitting by the door," she began.

"Yes?"

She paused, leaning into him, thinking. Dave was in no rush to speed up her thoughts.

"It was as if I had finally found you after all this time. There was a sense of recognition, as if someone I knew had been hidden under layers of disguises in your body and you took them all off."

"Surprise?" he teased.

She shook her head.

"No surprise - that was the surprising part."

"I dropped a lot of layers," he admitted.

"I can see that," she agreed.

"I had built up a lot of nonsense."

"Yes."

"We didn't part on good terms," he reminded her tentatively.

"No," she acknowledged.

"Truce?" he asked.

"Truce."

Missed connections and ruined opportunities came full circle to forgiveness. The gods smiled. The fates aligned. The terrible banishment of the year ended abruptly. She slid her arm around the crook of his elbow. The ocean came into view. The sun tipped low and threw gold along the white foamy lips of the surf. Joan closed her eyes for a moment, remembering.

"I prayed for you, Dave Grant," she sighed. "I actually prayed for you. After the day I thought I saw you in the rain, I felt like it was my fault for cursing you."

"It was," he laughed.

She glared at him.

He reached to curl his fingers through hers.

"But I didn't handle it very well," he admitted, "and that was no one's fault but my own."

He narrowed his eyes, curious.

"What else did you do besides pray for my mortal soul?" he asked, wondering what bargains she might have struck with the Universe.

"Oh," she stammered, turning red. "I made all sorts of promises if only you'd be kept safe."

"I hope you didn't promise your firstborn child," he teased, "because I'm back."

Joan poked his chest at the sight of his arrogant smile.

"You just ought to be glad I have a good spiritual credit rating," she warned him.

"I hope I didn't bankrupt your account," he laughed.

"Close enough," she retorted, "so don't pull any stunts before I can say my Buddhist Hail Mary's and feed the hungry a few times, hmm?"

He clasped her pointed finger in his hand.

"I won't, Joan," he promised. "And thank you."

She reached her free arm around his shoulder and cupped the base of his skull, tilting his head to meet her lips. He felt the tremble of relief that shivered through her and made a note to find out exactly what spiritual bargains she had made to guarantee his safe return from the oblivion of alcohol and despair. He held in his arms a woman he barely fathomed, one who could argue metaphysical philosophy with the Buddha himself, who lived and breathed her practice and who desperately wanted him, Dave Grant, back in her life.

No, he amended, she wanted the man who stepped in the door of the teahouse and met her eyes. Dave Grant was baggage picked up on the traveler she knew from other lifetimes. Put down your suitcases, she had told him, welcome home.

I'm here, he cried silently. The journey had been long and heart-breaking, but he had finally arrived. And the welcome, indeed, was sweeter than he had imagined. Her body surrendered, sinking into his, arms reaching around him, squeezing him tightly. His hand cupped her ribs, slid to her lower back, and touched her braid.

His fingers pulled the tassel of her braid, removing the tie, letting the locks release each other. Slowly, he loosened the plaited strands and ran his fingers through the black hair that sprung to life. Her lips left his and pulled back a few inches. He cupped her face in his hands, marveling at the cascade of hair, the softness to her eyes, the heave of her breasts underneath her blouse, the scent of Joan's meditation incense that clung to her.

"I love you," he confessed.

Her lips twitched in a smile.

"Who is the I that loves the You?" she asked back.

He shivered at the strength of the koan she posited; they could spend their whole lives answering that!

They walked, spiraling like butterflies intoxicated with each other, circling and pausing for kisses on the sidewalk. They strolled along the tiny front yard gardens, peeking in lit windows to see couples watching television from separated armchairs. They leaned against the fences as the ocean pounded the cliffs, locked in long impassioned embraces. Then they would break apart gasping and chase each other down the bike path like a pair of college students drunk on the cheap wine of love. They waved innocently at the cop car that crawled past them, looking for prostitutes and drug deals, finding only a pair of middle-aged lovers.

They grew quiet as the sun plunged into the black ocean. The waves roared loud in the seamless night. The suck and draw of the tide quickened their desire. Their footsteps slowed and their caresses lingered like sea foam trailing over sand. They walked along the cliffs that wound up the coast until they came to a spot Dave knew well.

"Stay here," he whispered.

He hopped the wooden fence, following the footpath down to the rocks below. The tide had retreated and wouldn't return until dawn. Dave scouted for bums, meth addicts, or rowdy college students, but found no one. He clambered back up the slope through the ice plants.

"Come," he invited, offering a hand as she climbed over the fence.

It was there, on the smooth coolness of the tide-swept sandstone rocks, to the ebb and pull of the ocean, the gasp and roars and moans of the waves, that they made love. There, with bodies naked and tender between the solidity of earth and the ever-changing rush of sea. There, with the glare of orange streetlights blocked by the shoulders of the cliffs. There, with the blanket of the dark night shielding them from prying eyes.

195

Bits of sand and seaweed clung to them. The salt of the ocean mingled with his sweat, her tears, semen and dampness. And as they lay shuddering, bodies hot against the coolness of night, Joan looked at the envelope of darkness above, below, and to all sides, and felt safe in night's embrace. Dave listened to the sweep of ceaseless waves, felt the reverberations of their thrusts through the rocks, through his skin, through his own body. And they wondered why humanity had need for anything more than a quiet place to love one another in peace.

The chatter of early morning joggers along the bike path made Joan stir. She rolled over quickly, reaching for her clothes. She pulled her blouse over her dark nipples and stuffed her bra into the pocket of her pants as she closed the buttons.

"Get dressed," she said to Dave, who lay naked in the sunlight.

A garbage truck screeched and banged on the final legs of its daily rounds, taking the scenic route to the dump as a reward for working before dawn. It clattered around the curving ocean road, annoying the rich mansion owners as they vacationed in their second homes on the cliffs.

Dave groaned and reached for his blue jeans. He pulled his shirt over his head. The ocean tide licked the rocks not twenty feet away, sending cascades of saltwater glistening into the air. He grabbed Joan's waist and spoke over the roar of the surf.

"Look!" he pointed to the balcony of the mansion above them, where a man and woman in white bathrobes spoke unintelligibly to one another.

"All the money in the world can't buy the night we just had!" he declared as a crash of seawater leapt up to catch the dawn.

She smiled and turned her head so that her lips brushed the sculpture of his cheekbone.

"No," she agreed. "No one can sell it to them."

"More than that," he answered. "They won't lie in the grit of the sand and endure the smell of seaweed."

"They would send in security to sweep the area," she guessed, "and have their secretaries check the tide, and arrange for their yacht to pick them up for breakfast."

"They'd go get a hotel," he added. "An expensive one."

She grinned and pulled a strand of seaweed out of her hair. They scrambled back up the cliff, startling a pair of moms with toddlers strapped in strollers.

"Where to, love?" Dave asked.

Joan paused on the sidewalk. A girl on a pink cruiser swerved around her. Dave reached out and tugged Joan to the side before the bicyclist could slam into her.

"Where are you going?" she asked him.

"With you," he answered simply.

She grinned.

"That was my answer."

They laughed like a couple of love-struck school kids bent on playing hooky from life as usual.

"Come with me," he invited. "Let's go places where the cops don't run the lovers out of town. Let's go beyond the snobbery of humanity and the prying eyes of prudery. Walk with me into the hills and we'll visit the quiet mountain streams and swaying trees together."

He watched anxiously for her reply.

"I suppose," Joan said thoughtfully, "that it would be a little idealistic to just start walking out of town with you this morning."

He blinked.

"You sound serious," he said.

"I am," Joan answered with a determined look. "I am."

CHAPTER NINETEEN

. . . . .

Pulling Joan out from the web of society took time. The dust of daily life mounted into piles of appointments to cancel, jobs to quit, rental contracts to settle, belongings to give away, social obligations to fulfill, utility bills to pay. Friends demanded explanations and argued against her decision.

"What can I tell them?" she asked Dave later. "They don't like the idea that I've just decided to quit society and walk off into the woods with a madman."

"You're only young once?" Dave offered.

She smiled ruefully.

"We're not that young," she pointed out.

"Tell them it's a mid-life crisis," he recommended.

In the end, she told them nothing. The modern world may scream for rational explanations, but there are forces beyond the mechanistic model of the Universe. Science knows only the limits of its answers; infinity is vast and fecund with the unknown. Joan dropped the constraints of society and stepped into the lineage of wandering saints and mountain sages, ecstatic nuns alive in God, and singing women who walk naked through the streets, clothed only in wisdom and compassion. Throughout all time, they have leapt for love and reached for knowledge of the divine. Societies have mocked and scorned them, bound these women to husbands, children, chains of propriety and property. But when enlightenment comes knocking, how could they refuse to answer the door? When the divine says, leave this life and leap into the unknown, would you protest that the laundry wasn't done? Joan closed up her house, gave away her sparse belongings, quit her jobs, and left.

"It's odd," she murmured as they began to walk out of town.

"What is?" he asked.

"I think I knew," Joan answered. "For months I've sensed that change was coming."

"I was," he laughed.

They carried packs, but their steps felt light. At the last set of streetlights on the northwest edge of town, Joan paused and looked back.

"Goodbye to all that," she said quietly to the traffic, stores, stoplights, throngs of people, congestion, exhaust; goodbye to routines and three-year plans, to expectations of normal life; goodbye to the mantra of the culture: live, work, consume, die.

She turned and greeted the opening of the unknown. The highway carved through fields and forests. The ocean stretched vast to the west. The sun blazed proudly in the blue quilt of the sky.

"Let's go," she said.

The full glory of a California summer spread out in front of them. They walked side-by-side on the generous shoulders of the road, breathless with adventure and wild-eyed from the sudden spontaneity of this unfolding.

"Here, " Dave said, pointing off the road.

It was not his mountain stream, but a cleft between the swelling breasts of hills, ignored by the tourists and surf-seekers whose eyes veered to the westward ocean across the road.

Here, the redwoods hung back, high up in the hills. In a low dip between the rises stood a cluster of oaks and a hidden spring that barely trickled in the height of summer. They scaled the steep side of one hill and tumbled down the next.

"Do you know where you're going?" she asked Dave.

He whirled and held a finger to his lips.

"Yes," he whispered and he turned to greet the tree.

She was ancient, teetering with crooked limbs. Her branches lay across the ground for several feet before lifting their fingertips toward the sun. Dave placed his pack on the ground and walked to the trunk. He laid his hand upon the surprising smoothness of the bark. He waited. Joan waited. The hills leaned in closer, listening.

"We'll stay," Dave finally said.

Joan blinked.

"Did Dave Grant just ask a tree's permission to sleep under it?"

He retraced his steps to her, a smile creasing up the corners of his eyes.

"Not exactly. Dave Grant would never speak with a tree. But, I am not who I once was." He had dropped all stories about his past. Anything was possible. He took her hand and brought her to sit on the sparse grasses under the shaded boughs of the oak. He knelt beside her in the dry, silky dust.

"This is our first day of just being."

He untied the laces of her hiking boots and lifted her feet out. He pulled off her socks and laid her soles in the cool silt of the fine soil. Then he bent to yank apart the gnarled laces of his beat-up sneakers.

"We should have gotten you a new pair," Joan mentioned.

Dave looked up in surprise.

"Oh, these'll last a long time if I don't walk in them."

He swept his hand to the hills.

"It's only the highway that requires rubber soles. The rest of the world is kinder to a slightly calloused foot."

"I'd like to see your feet take on the rocky deserts with cacti and scorpions," Joan countered.

"We are not in the desert," Dave argued.

"Cross that bridge when you come to it?" she asked, raising

an eyebrow.

"It's just a story to us," he commented, "and stories won't hurt my feet."

"We shall see by the end of the summer," she scoffed.

"I have no intention of hiking the entire coast," he laughed. "People are always going, seeing, doing, traveling. I'm just interested in being."

"Like right now?"

"Yes."

They could spend a minute, or a month, or even a whole lifetime under this tree, listening to the whir of cicadas and the wind rustling the grasses on the hills. Dave leaned on his elbow, stretching the length of his ribs into the comfort of the earth. The dust coated his clothes; he did not seem to care.

Joan envied his ease. His comfort with the earth attracted her. It seemed to say, the Earth is my family, my home, my comrade, my village, my body. Dave's eyes moved lazily around the grove. Every now and then, he smiled at something Joan could not see. He nodded once with an upward flick of his head as if greeting someone with familiarity. She craned her neck to look.

"An old friend?" she asked, and a strange sorrow filled her. All at once, she felt the echoes of a long theme in the human story. She was the new bride brought to the man's world, alone, having left her community behind. He rejoiced at his certain welcome; she followed with trepidation and the ache of gain and loss, together.

Perhaps he sensed a hint of her uncertainty for he sat up and pulled her to lean against him as he spoke softly over her shoulder.

"The sun touched the grasses, just so," he answered, "like it has done for millenniums, yet differently each time."

He spoke to her gently, compassionately, in the tones of a tender bridegroom who dearly wishes his beloved to come to love her new home. *Look*, says the husband, see how the old men gather in the evening? That one is my uncle; that one is my grandfather; and that is my brother's father-in-law.

"The beauty of this place is that it is so dry on every hill," he said, pointing to the rising mounds above them, "yet here there is a trickle that makes a green thread between the hills."

He absently drew his hand between her breasts, along her sternum, down toward the thread of her valley in an unconscious gesture, a cartographer tracing a line of a map while following the contours of the horizon with his eyes.

Joan closed her eyes, aflame.

"We humans," he murmured, "are always rushing. We treat our bodies like bulky luggage that must be dragged along as we race toward tomorrow's destination." Dave leaned the flat of his chin on the bone of her shoulder, pressing his head gently against her cheek. She curled her hand behind her to stroke his hair. Dave's arm wrapped around her torso and teased the sensual stretch of her ribs with his fingertips.

"How can we ever learn to love - or live - if our minds are always light-years in front of the rest of us?" he questioned.

"Until recently," she replied, "I'm not sure I've ever been alive . . . not in the sense you mean. I've always had an alarm clock ticking away the end of relaxation and a to-do list being ignored."

Joan followed the journey of a seed puff floating sideways on the wind.

"I've never done this," she said. "I've never walked away from time and schedules, rent, work, expectations and appointments, without a plan or a destination."

"I have a plan," Dave chuckled.

"Oh?"

"To just be."

She pressed down the rebellion of a smile.

"That's hardly a plan," she teased.

"It could take me all afternoon," he protested.

"Or a whole lifetime," she said.

"I'd better get started right away," he replied without making a move.

"You're running late already," she laughed at him.

"Shhh," he hushed, "let's just be."

So they were. With the tree that slowly churned water through her wooden capillaries and pulled sunlight into dark green leaves; with the lone scout of an ant who ran up Joan's leg and down Dave's shoulder; with the shifting slants of sunlight; they were. Dave thought if this didn't last his lifetime, he would treasure this day all his years Perfect presence and contentment are rare in the experiences of humankind.

For days, they spoke only a little. Words were spells that conjured up other places, times, people, ideas, and thoughts. They had no use for those old stories. The simple act of being here and now was unraveling everything they'd ever known in all their decades on this planet. Joan had once excelled at verbal swordplay; now she wondered why she had ever bothered to speak at all. Even their minds ceased chattering in English. The array of images and sounds that incessantly whirl through waking thoughts slowly settled.

They walked deeper into the woods. Oaks and madrones gave way to redwoods as they followed the hidden watercourses winding through the forest. Joan filtered the water, regretting that humanity had turned the streams dangerous all around the globe.

One afternoon, Dave stopped beside a stream.

"Take off your clothes," he offered. "I'll wash them."

"You'll wash them?" Joan repeated back, amused.

"On one condition," he added.

"What?"

He grinned mischievously.

"That you won't put on any others until these are dry."

"Dave!" she exclaimed, looking around as if expecting hikers to stumble out of nowhere. He pulled his shirt over his head and tossed it beside the stream.

"Come on, come on," he urged, holding out his hand for her clothes.

She hesitated.

"Have you ever spent an afternoon naked?" he asked.

She shook her head - of course not. Since toddling out of infancy, hardly any human had let the sunlight touch their hidden parts for fear of other human eyes.

"It's just you, me, and the trees, Joan," he told her.

She shyly slipped out of her clothes and sat on a rock, drawing her knees protectively up to her breasts. Dave wondered at the contradictions of this woman. Joan could seduce him with a yawn and make love like the ocean caresses the shore, yet, here in broad daylight, she blushed and maneuvered her body away from his gaze.

"I'm not twenty," she finally snapped.

"I know," he answered in delight.

"I just mean," she stammered, "that I don't look - "

"- like a twenty year old," he finished. He plunged the clothes into the stream for another rinse. "I suppose you won't believe me," he murmured, thinking of wild strawberries compared to cardboard-tasting, toxic, pinkish strawberries the size of plums in plastic containers in the middle of the winter.

"Believe you about what?" she asked.

"That this," he replied, rising and reaching to touch the lines that gathered in the corners of her eyes. "And this," he touched the extra puckers around her dark nipples. "And this, " he cupped her hip in his hand and ran his thumb down the crest of her pelvic bone, "are all beautiful to me."

He drew his fingers across the curve of her no-longer flat belly, light as feathers.

"This," he said softly, "says that you are a woman, not an anorexic fashion model starved into the shape of a pre-pubescent boy. Believe me when I say that billboards are too flat, and I prefer every line and curve of you, my love."

Dave turned back to the stream and crouched beside it, masking his anger in his studious scrubbing of the clothes. What kind of a world robs women of their confidence in their beauty? And not just any woman, but Joan, who stood so certain in her views and was so assured about her intelligence. If Joan had a line he didn't adore, he hadn't found it yet. He shifted at the stream, no longer scrubbing his blue jeans with indignation at the world, but sneaking glances at her like a schoolboy. He remembered thinking once that she was too old, and the recollection shamed him. Who was that fool who had once thought such a pathetic notion? He scoffed at his nonsense.

Joan's breasts were small, prone to shrinking as she aged. He adored them. They had never swelled with milk, never been pulled or twisted by a child's suckling, never been implanted with silicon to assure artificial youthfulness. They were, like Joan, utterly unique. Comparisons were not even worth remembering. His eyes crinkled, watching her intense focus on the dust motes and the trees. He followed the curve of her breast against her knees, the taut, sculptured muscles of her arms, the violin bow of her collarbones, and the dry wrinkles that gathered between her breasts and fanned out and upward. How could that not be beautiful?

She glanced up. His heart stopped.

"Sometimes," she said, rising in one smooth motion that his eyes followed in fascination, "the stories we tell ourselves get in our way."

"Most of the time," he commented, enjoying the full stretch of her body.

"Who are we without our stories?" she asked.

"Something, everything, nothing," he answered without hesitation. "Just love enjoying itself."

"Love is just another story," she pointed out. "If we dropped all the stories, would there still be love?"

"Why not?" he shrugged. "Or why drop it? If a story is useful, we could keep it around. When it becomes dead weight, chuck it."

"The dharma is like a raft," Joan quoted, "once the river is crossed, it should be discarded."

He nodded.

"Dharma just means thought," he pointed out.

"Or teaching," she amended. "Either way, don't carry it around once you've reached the other shore. Just drop what we don't need and keep what serves."

"I suppose," he drawled, rising with the heap of damp clothes, "that the enlightened masters would say to drop all of it."

He tipped his head toward the meadow, indicating that they should spread the clothes out to dry.

"Wait, you should wring them out," she said, reaching for the bundle.

He swept it high above his head.

"What? And rush the drying process? Never!"

"You just want to walk around naked all day," she accused.

"Wrong," he replied. "I want to walk around like this all summer."

She rolled her eyes at him.

"Come," he invited, "I bet you've never walked as humans were intended through a majestic redwood forest at the height of a California summer."

There they were, Adam and Eve in the twenty-first century, modern echoes of thousands of years of human evolution.

"How can we ever go back?" Joan wondered as twilight shifted places with the afternoon. Her skin tingled with the continuous caress of shade and sunlight, dust and bits of grass seeds. The world of clothes and cars, houses, cellphones and appointments seemed an eternity away and twice as far from being rational. It was all so much nonsense from the vantage point of a naked afternoon.

Dave rumbled his agreement. He lay on his back looking at the blue sky.

"We'll go back, Joan," he murmured, "but not the same as we left."

Suddenly, the evening chilled just enough to raise the hairs up on her skin and remind her that winter follows summer and even the rains of coastal California are cold enough to make warm-blooded humans long for shelter, clothes, and warmth. Though summer hung at the zenith and August seemed beyond the imagination, Joan suddenly knew that it was not. Change was always turning as the earth curved around the sun.

"Now, Dave," she urged. Life is fleeting; time is short.

He tilted his chin down to look at her and then rose up on one elbow. She slid onto her hand, leaning across his legs, hair falling over her back.

"Now what?" he asked.

"Answer my koan."

Who is the I that loves the You?

"Everything. Something. Nothing," he answered.

Joan stared at him with her bottomless dark eyes and shook her head.

"Go beyond that."

Without moving, without speaking, she cracked reality in pieces. She dropped all concepts of Joan and Dave and left them nameless, orphaned, and resplendent: two human bodies in a field of grass.

He shook his head.

"Go beyond," he murmured, and he tied the truth of breath to their bodies, their lungs to the air, the oxygen to the trees, the roots to the earth, the planet to the void of space, and on and on, until they were the entire web of creation hung in the infinite moment of now.

"Go beyond," the One urged.

And the web embraced the emptiness that gave rise to it, held it, birthed it, and took it back without a trace in the eons-long seduction of something and nothing that has continued without ceasing beyond the illusion of time.

The human being who sees this is rare. The being who lives this is rarer still. The couple that loves with this knowledge of reality cannot be measured at all. They cannot be called rare, nor can they be called common, for they have been ever-present in the rise of creation. They do not come; do not go. They encompass all things. They do not appear, nor do they vanish, nor walk this earth, nor cease to walk among us. Nor can they be called people, for they are one and the myriad, the ten thousand things all at once.

And if you taste the sting of a paradox in these words: savor it. For truth is a paradox that explodes the mind's logic, yet by the grace of this truth, we can know it.

CHAPTER TWENTY

· · · · ·

The kitchen hung in the suspension of the witching hour. The hands of the old fashioned clock reached for the sky and tilted ever so slightly toward morning. The old woman sat very still, hands folded over each other, eyes fixed unblinking on the thin-carved man in her kitchen.

"You're not Dave Grant," she said in a voice cracked with age and held together by the glue of realization.

"Aside from the convenience of a name and a driver's license, no. I am not Dave Grant," he admitted. "That continuum of ego ended that night with Joan. The story that was Dave Grant is finished."

"And you are?" the old woman challenged.

"Everything. Something. Nothing," he chanted, "all rolled into One."

She closed her eyes in a long, shaky shuttering of wrinkled eyelids. Her head inclined slightly in the bow of a puppet whose joints have stiffened with age. When the crinoline curtains of her eyelids fluttered open, she pulled her reveal.

Everything, Something, Nothing looked back at itself.

"What are you doing on Gold Mountain?" the Universe asked itself in a thousand tones of curiosity, irritation, and wonder, pondering the motivations of the tiniest speck of dust on the tiniest grain of sand in the tiniest forgotten corner of infinity.

"I vowed to liberate all beings from the causes of suffering," he-that-was-not-he replied.

"We vowed to bring all beings to complete enlightenment," she-who-was-not-she corrected. "And, as it says in the

Diamond Sutra, in the realm of complete awareness, there is not one being to be liberated."

"Doesn't cut it," he shot back. "Wherever there is someone who is suffering, deluded, or unaware, we must go and share the truth. We must remind them who they are."

They circled like eagles around the wheel of understanding, retracing the contemplations of the Buddha, searching for something permanent to lay a finger on, but finding nothing that did not change. They looked for existence and found nonexistence entwined within it. They looked for individuals and discovered an interconnected web.

"Why are you at Gold Mountain?" the old woman asked again.

"Gold Mountain is the seed of a lesson waiting to unfold," he replied.

"You're here to teach the Dharma on Gold Mountain?" she gasped. Then she burst out cackling as if the cosmic joke was on them all - every Tom, Dick, and Harry, every Susan and Joan and Edna, and every Dave Grant who would awaken.

"Not exactly," he chuckled, though his expression grew solemn. "I'm here to end the wheel of suffering that spins the illusion of Gold Mountain."

"Money?" she choked.

He shook his head.

"Wealth," she amended.

He shook his head again.

"Capitalism?"

His eyes turned into half-melons in amusement as she struggled to guess the obvious.

"I came," he said softly, "to end the delusions of separation and permanence that cause people to long for money, wealth, and property; the delusions that cause them to amass fortunes in defense of change; the delusions that allow them to pretend that the suffering of others is not hurting them, as well. I came to teach my wealthy colleagues to unclench the fists of grasping, to release the grip that harms so many, and to trust the nature of reality. To let go and be embraced; to release and find companionship; to rest in the ever-changing, interconnected web that is us all."

The old woman bowed again in a slow blink of eyes, and when she raised her wrinkled lids, Edna Lawrence's gaze crinkled in wry amusement.

"Well," she drawled in her creaky voice, "good luck."

They burst out laughing in a shock of sound that reverberated around the kitchen. It is ludicrous - outrageous - to teach such truths, to intend to say such things to the madness of humanity's delusions. It is audacious to think awakening is possible for the world's wealthiest elite . . . and yet, the Buddha smiles slightly. Because all things are always possible and the audacity of the awakened ones truly knows no bounds.

"So, what," Edna inquired as she gasped for breath, "do you intend to do? Sit in full lotus on the golf course and gather them for a Dharma talk?"

Dave shook his head in merriment.

"I haven't the foggiest idea. I thought I'd walk up tomorrow and let things take their course."

"Hoo-hoo," she wheezed, "you're like a bowling ball of dharma on a crash course with the kingpins of society!"

"That," he said seriously, "is exactly what I am."

"Alright then," she promised, "I'll help."

"You will?" he asked, surprised.

"You'll need a place to sleep, won't you?" she offered.

"No, no, it's warm and the stars are beautiful."

"Nonsense," she waved her hand. "You'll stay in my spare

bedroom. Besides, the night is still younger than me."

She held out her cup for more coffee.

"Tell me what happened next."

CHAPTER TWENTY-ONE

· · · · ·

They stepped down from the golden shoulders of the hills onto the highway, an ordinary man and woman with an extraordinary understanding. They did what all others who have glimpsed the true nature of reality have done: they tried to live this knowledge, tried to inhabit these human bodies, and tried to share a bit of what they'd learned.

The sea of humanity attempted to drown them. On good days, they parted the foolishness of the world like Moses parting the waters. Other times, an overwhelming riptide swept them up. They submerged for a while and then resurfaced with a gasp.

"We're not particularly good at this, are we?" Dave said ruefully to Joan.

"We're better than we were," she admitted, "but there's a long haul ahead of us yet."

They traveled the coast like a pair of mystics on the frontier of a spiritual wasteland. SUVs hurtled past them. The occupants averted their eyes from what they could only see as a couple of dirty hippies begging on the side of the road, suckers on hardworking people.

"Get a job!" students hollered out the windows of cars their parents had bought them as they headed to college dormitories paid for by their grandparents.

Joan and Dave had a job.

"We exist to elicit compassion," Joan said as she thanked a woman who rolled down her window to hand Joan a dollar and change.

"Good luck with that," the woman snorted cynically. The

light turned green and she drove on.

"The opportunity to offer small kindnesses brings great rewards," Dave mentioned to a man who couldn't hear him over the blaring music pounding out lyrics that made Joan blanch.

"It's exhausting," she admitted later, "maintaining a sense of compassion at the filthy intersection of greed and oblivion."

They begged like Buddha, not for their hunger, but to offer their fellow beings an opportunity to be generous, kind, and compassionate.

"Is it kinder," Dave wondered aloud, "to wear ragged old clothes and challenge people to look past appearances . . . or to dress nicely so they offer generosity more often?"

They would circle these themes like koans as they hiked into towns. After a day on the corner, they would split their earnings with other homeless people standing around town holding cardboard signs in grimy hands. Now that they had embarked on the path of the Buddha, holding out the begging bowl in modern America, they could never be certain that winos were just drunkards - a bodhisattva might hide in that body. The jittering meth addict and the tired old veteran could be emanations of the Buddha sent forth to test their compassion and wisdom.

"In truth," Joan mused thoughtfully as they watched a toothless, shuffling woman walk away with a handful of dollar bills, "if the Buddha is the awakened understanding of our interconnected reality, then everything is the Buddha, and we are all bodhisattvas in disguise."

On lean days, they meditated on the practice of non-attachment. On generous days, they passed out handfuls of crumpled bills without a thought of a self, or of a being named Joan separate from the homeless mother who accepted the donation. Dave deepened his understanding of the emptiness of all things as he gave all their earnings to a pair of teenage runaways trying to get home. Sometimes, confusion crossed the weatherworn faces. Occasionally, suspicion flickered in eyes as Joan offered the same money they had just seen her beg. Dave could not catalogue all the different reactions: the rejection of kindness, sudden snatchings and retreats, tears springing into eyes. Once, when they were mugged and shaken down by a brute, Dave gave him every penny they had simply to spare the man the bad karma of robbery and theft.

"No, no, it's a gift, really," Dave insisted to the utterly confused man. "Please, take it all."

Later, they pondered the depth of their practice as they sat on the side of the road.

"Why join a monastery when you can live your enlightenment on the street?" Dave asked.

"Preparation," Joan replied, thinking of her attempt to join a Buddhist temple. Their path was more challenging than Joan had ever imagined. It was one thing to chant *no self, no being, no life, and no soul,* as one struggled to sit upright among wooden beams polished with age and mindfully swept floors. It was another thing to drill one's mind on that concept while burning with poison oak rashes after tripping into the vines. The story of the Buddha's enlightened perspective on the lifetime when an enraged king had cut off his nose, ears, and limbs was all fine and dandy until a crazed meth addict came after them one night and they discovered certain limits to their non-attachment to their forms.

The practice of forbearance plagued Joan as she corralled her quick temper.

"Patience, forgiveness, refraining from judgment," she chanted to herself when a driver spat in her face, when the coffee shop refused to let her sit down, when a cop smacked her ass to tell her to get moving.

Anger at injustice whipped her.

"Dave," she argued one night as they hiked up the highway into the woods, "don't you think that there's a place for righteous outrage when you see suffering?"

Earlier that afternoon, the cops had been hassling a Hispanic woman and her children, asking them for identification. Joan had intervened, telling the police that this woman had rights, it was illegal for the cops to demand identification from someone just walking down the street, and their claims of probable cause wouldn't hold up in court as anything but racial profiling. Joan had snapped so indignantly and articulately that the police had moved on, but Dave later criticized her fury.

"Why not just stop the suffering," he suggested, "and drop the anger part?"

"Because it's fuel for action," Joan countered.

"It's fossil fuel, then, like dinosaurs. It's obsolete. It combusts and puts out dirty emissions that cause their own forms of suffering," Dave commented. He glanced up at the night sky. "Why not simply act from compassion?"

"But what if it isn't enough?" Joan asked.

"Love more," he said with a shrug. "It's like solar panels in Seattle. The answer to the problem of low solar gain is not to rely on coal plants . . . the solution is to put up twice as many solar panels!"

"I shall have to contemplate this," Joan snapped testily, lengthening her stride to stalk ahead of his smug analogies.

He grimaced apologetically, but she couldn't see his expression in the dark. They walked in silence for almost a mile before she dropped back and looked at him thoughtfully.

"I'll give your theory a trial run," she conceded.

"What have you got to lose?"

"Just anger," she sighed, "the bee clenched in my hand, stinging me."

Dave laughed softly in the darkness.

"If I have a bee in my hand, what's in my eye?" he asked her.

"Huh?" she frowned.

He stopped on the side of the road and posed the riddle again.

"If I have a bee in my hand, what's in my eye?"

He could just make out her confused expression in all the lines and shadows drawn by the night. They were headed to a quiet stretch of woods about a mile further up the road. The hour was late, but they were in no hurry.

"Beauty," he told her, tracing the back of his hand down her cheek. "Beauty is in the eye of the beeholder."

She groaned and laughed and grabbed him. They continued up the road, legs swinging in stride, his arm wrapped warmly over her shoulders.

Odd experiences and unusual adventures broke the daily rituals of begging, meditating, living, and being. Whole volumes could be written about those short months of summer when awakening comes more naturally than breathing and the fog of their lives cleared at noon without fail. They never asked how long this existence would continue. They never wondered what would come next or what they would do when winter arrived. Hunger came and went, along with blisters, sunburn, poison oak, grumpiness, bursts of enlightened moments, passion, and love. Everything rose like the dawn and subsided like sunset.

Then, like an earthquake, it ended.

CHAPTER TWENTY-TWO

· · · · ·

They crossed the town line into new territory. The coastal community sat further north than they had ever traveled. With a few bills in their pockets, they headed toward the natural food store for trail mix, a loaf of bread, and hot soup from the deli. Leisurely, they strolled along the sidewalks, stopping to examine the storefronts and front yards of downtown houses. Dave stopped to adjust the strap of his ragged backpack. Joan fanned her sunburned face with her grimy hat, frowning slightly and thinking she needed to give it a good washing. Dave shouldered his pack again, nodded to Joan, and they continued down the sidewalk.

A cop car crawled up beside them. The uniformed man squinted suspiciously at them through the window. Joan waved and kept walking. Through a bullhorn mounted on top the vehicle, the cop ordered them to stop. They halted and waited for him to approach.

"We don't have vagrants here," the cop announced.

"Ah," Dave chuckled wryly, "then we can't possibly be vagrants, can we?"

"You look like a vagrant, smell like a vagrant, and walk like a vagrant," the cop growled. "I'm going to arrest you for vagrancy."

Joan blinked. Dave laughed and held out his wrists as a joke.

"Good way to solve the problem," he chuckled. "The Jail Hotel must be packed with former vagrants."

The officer threw the handcuffs on Dave quicker than Joan could open her mouth to protest. Dave blinked slowly as the cold steel closed on his wrists.

"You got an address?" the officer growled at Joan.

She said nothing.

"Then get a hotel or you'll spend the night in the women's section," the cop warned.

"You're really arresting me?" Dave asked, almost amused.

"I'll go with you," Joan began.

The cop shot her a sharp look.

"It's a five hundred dollar fine," he warned without sympathy. "The hotel is cheaper."

"Five hundred?!" Joan exclaimed. "You can't be serious!"

Dave frowned at the officer.

"How can homeless people afford to pay the fine?"

"They work it off in jail," the cop informed them.

"You're joking," Joan gasped. "It must be costing the taxpayers thousands of dollars to keep people imprisoned while they pay back their fine!"

The cop frowned at her.

"It doesn't cost the taxpayers much extra. We charge the prisoners for the expenses."

"You what?!" she choked. "This is outrageous! I could see this kind of insanity going on in some places, but not here - "

"Lady, I recommend you get a room and find five hundred bucks to get your pal out or he's going to be in there a long time."

"But this is unbelievable! This is criminal. You don't have any proof that he's even a vagrant."

"Get a lawyer and argue it in court," the cop shrugged. "I'm just enforcing the law."

Dave turned to Joan.

"Go get a hotel room. I'll be out in the morning."

The cop pulled Dave into the car. Flashes of the slave trade shot through Joan, images of free African-Americans caught by bounty hunters in the north and shipped south, leaving wives, children, and shops behind. She shuddered as the door clicked shut with Dave in the backseat.

This can't be real, she thought, panicking. She sank to the concrete sidewalk as the cop car rolled away. Dave swiveled in the backseat to watch her through the window.

"Don't worry," he mouthed.

But how could she not?

Dave waited in the main holding cell of the local jail. Weary figures occupied the few concrete slabs that served as benches. Dave squatted against the cool, concrete wall, and watched the parade of people roll through: domestic abuse calls, drunkards, belligerent drivers pulled over for speeding tickets. The cops were tough in this county, everyone moaned.

Dave said nothing. Either the cops were clinical sociopaths or they were all on the take from the lawyers, judges, and private prison system. The SWAT team raid victims started coming in around midnight, protesting that the cops had planted the drugs.

"I want to call a lawyer," Dave told the jail supervisor.

"You and the rest of the world," the supervisor retorted.

Dave kept up his mantra until the supervisor snapped at him.

"You're not getting a lawyer, so shut up."

At six a.m., the jail supervisor informed Dave that he was guilty of vagrancy and would be transferred to the prison. Dave's jaw dropped. He asked about lawyers, trials, judges and juries. The supervisor and the guards gave him an exasperated look. Dave argued that being a vagrant wasn't a crime - the whole town was a vagrant traversing the solar system on the back of the Earth.

"He's crazy," one guard muttered to the other.

"Absolute lunatic," the second agreed.

The entire human species is insane, Dave realized as he overheard them.

Half lost in thought, he hardly noticed that the officers were shoving him through the protocol of booking him. He turned obediently to the barked commands, nodded at appropriate intervals, and only when they shaved his head did he realize he had just been incarcerated without judge, jury, or trial.

"Wait, there's been a mistake," he tried to inform them.

"Don't listen to him," one guard told the next. "He's completely crazy."

His clothes were taken into custody. A drab gray jumpsuit was handed over to him. He slid the thin cotton over his limbs. He was taken into the main section of the jail, scalp tingling, and assigned a bunk in a gymnasium-sized room filled with triple decker bunk beds, each occupied by a man who sat or lay in various states of muscular or scrawny. Eyes rolled toward him in weary curiosity.

"This can't be legal," he choked out.

The guard shoved him toward his bunk.

"Take it up with a lawyer," the guard barked as he left.

The man on the bunk directly to Dave's left rolled onto his elbow.

"Take it up with the lawyer you can't call, that is," he muttered.

"You can't call a lawyer?" Dave repeated. "That's unconstitutional."

"Take it up with your lawyer," the man countered. "They come around once a year, like Christmas."

Dave frowned at the angular man. The fellow was thin as a

rail. His elbows and knees jutted sharply through the cheap fabric of his gray jumpsuit. His cheeks collapsed into caverns beneath the bones of his skull. The man's humorless smile stretched hollowly across his teeth. His tongue licked his bloodless lips. He sat up, and his long, puppet-like limbs slowly folded under his curved torso. The man's fingers hung from his hand like twigs on the end of tree branches. He pointed to Dave's bunk.

"That three-by-seven bunk may be your new home for the rest of your life. Stare up the ass of the man above you. Endure the wanking off of the guy below you. Get up for meal times, work times, and an hour in the yard, once a week."

Dave stared at the thin mattress steadily.

"It's not even tall enough to sit up on," he commented.

"Nope, and your feet won't reach the floor without stepping on the guy below you - for which he'll hate you and take advantage of every opportunity to beat you senseless and use the bottom of your mattress for a punching bag at 2:00 a.m."

"Do you have a name?" Dave asked.

"P240010."

"That's not a name; it's a number."

"That's all we got here. We are numbers - numbers of beds, numbers of man hours, numbers of profits and expenses."

"So, even on the smallest score of a name, you'll let them win?" Dave sighed.

"Game's over," the man muttered. "They already won."

Dave squatted down on his haunches and looked at the hard, concrete floor for a moment.

"Tell me something," he asked the man. "If it's game over, why are you still alive?"

"Haven't figured out how to die of despair," the man replied.

"Stop eating," Dave suggested.

"Tried it. They used the old Gitmo on me."

"Torture?"

"Force-feeding tube, a double torture robbing you of the chance to die with the searing pain of injecting food through your nose and throat."

Dave pondered this.

"It hardly seems worth the expense," he reflected, thinking of the jail's profit margins.

The man snorted.

"I earn the prison company a hundred grand a year just laying here wasting my life away. If I sit my ass on a work bench ten hours a day, I make even more for the prison industry's supply company."

"That would be good money for a free man," Dave pointed out.

"Sure would, but instead, it all goes to the Man."

Dave flinched at the twisted, bitter expression on the other fellow's face. The Man had a name and a face; Dave had met a few in his Gold Mountain days. He had considered them small fry in the ranks of the wealthy. He calculated the Man's possible net worth and scorned him as nothing more than a two-bit thug in the relative scheme of fortunes.

"So, what should I call you?" Dave asked. "I can't just call you a number."

"Call me the Number then, 'cause that's what I am."

Dave sighed.

"I'm Dave," he told the other fellow.

"No, you're P108514," the Number replied, pointing the number on Dave's prison uniform.

"I'm Dave Grant," he insisted.

"Oh, like the billionaire?" the Number joked.

Dave froze.

"You ever heard about him?" the Number asked, clearly rejecting the shared name as anything but coincidence.

"Sounds familiar," Dave replied carefully. "I might have heard of him before."

"He lives up on Gold Mountain, one of the richest guys in California."

"Heard anything about him lately?" Dave asked cautiously.

"Nah, I've been in jail for ten years."

"That's a long time to be nothing but a number," Dave said, turning the conversation away from billionaires.

"It's long enough to forget you ever had a name," the Number retorted. "And what's to remember about that name? Nothing but misery and failure."

The Number's eyes stared bleakly back at the past.

"What about a new name?" Dave suggested.

"Who would use it?" the Number shot back. His angular arms swept a gesture to the row of bunk beds and concrete walls.

"I would," Dave promised.

"Fine. You can call me whatever you want. Everyone else does."

"I'll have to think about it," Dave replied.

"You do that P108 - "

"Don't call me that," Dave implored.

The Number laughed harshly.

"I'll call you whatever I want . . . everyone else does."

"Look," Dave sighed, "I'm not your enemy."

"I know," the Number replied.

"So, stop fighting me," Dave urged him.

"It makes you stronger," the Number insisted.

Dave shook his head, disagreeing.

227

"Less than half as strong as you'd be if we worked together," he pointed out.

The evening whistle blew. Dave climbed up onto his bunk, leaving the Number calculating the logic of cooperation.

Long into the night, the rumble of breaths kept him awake. He stared at the mattress above him, listening to the unconscious voices of three hundred men stacked like sardines in the tin can of the jail. Snores reverberated the bunk frames in long rhythmic pulls of breath that sawed impossibly at concrete and iron bars. Muffled snorts, gasps, and moans fell out of men's mouths. Restless insomniacs tossed on creaking mattresses, rolling one way and then another, searching for the comfort of oblivion.

Dave lay sleepless on the sagging foam pad. He steeled his mind against running endless circuit races around the pointless tracks of what ifs? He firmly truncated his yearning for Joan. He banished thoughts of the past and locked his mind on the here-and-now with iron resolve. Sanity lay in maintaining discipline of the mind, ceasing all desires for what was not and eliminating the fear of what could be.

He was not the only man who lay awake that night.

In the gloom, he could feel the heat of bodies, the smells of human beings confined in a room, the scent of men dehumanized, frustrated, trapped like animals, slumbering like oxen uneasy in the stall. Some fell dead into weary sleep; others shifted restlessly in their bunks. He heard the low moans and sighs of injustice that sat clamped behind bitter expressions during the day.

Dave took a deep breath.

Injustices festered in the prison like pustules on the skin of society. Every man locked up had a story; every story contained a million shards of injustice.

"Like grains of sand along the Ganges," Dave murmured. The phrase from the old sutra refrained its poetic calculations through his mind. If one took all the grains of sand in the Ganges and filled as many Universes full of sand as there are grains of sand in the Ganges . . . such are the heaps of injustices in a world of seven billion people, each perpetrating tiny acts of unfairness until injustice lines the banks of the River of Life, impossible to count.

Dave was five hundred dollars in debt for walking down a street like a tourist in the wrong clothes. He could not call a lawyer. Every day sunk him deeper into trouble. Just nights ago, he was a free man, owning little, owing nothing, traveling as he pleased, sleeping when he was tired. Now he was locked in jail, doomed to work every day of his life, accumulating nothing but more debt.

What good could a lawyer do, anyway? he sighed silently. He was a vagrant, and escaping the fate of his fellow vagrants did nothing for their plight - though joining them in a lifetime of debt slavery and imprisonment didn't resolve anything but a guilty conscience, either. There were little things that a lawyer could argue in court - that the cop had no proof of vagrancy, that the cop had not read him his rights, that the law had been selectively enforced - but these were just oozing scabs on a body of rotting flesh. Picking at them would not heal the problem; it would only make the blood of injustice run fresh down the festering systemic crisis.

At the root lay an ancient unfairness that had embedded itself in the psyche of generations, passed from father to son like blonde hair and blue eyes. For millenniums, humankind had believed that one man could rule another, own another, or set himself above another. According to the rule of law, a cop could snatch a man off the sidewalk and press him into servitude.

Dave saw his freedom gone forever, stolen by the iron weight of convictions. The cop had stolen his ability to live as he pleased and forced him to bend his labor to the will of society. He had stepped into a cycle as old as Viking ships and galley slaves chained to oars to provide manpower for the captain's voyages. It was as old as conquerors and kings; as old as the abolishing of the Commons. It was as old as the Great Enclosure that kicked the people off the land. It was as old as Columbus claiming the New World for the Old. It was as old as the genocides of native tribes. It was as old as the conscripted labor that built the Great Wall of China. It was as old as slavery on the Nile, Russian gulags, plantations in the South, and the warring tribes of Africa.

Dave traced the threads of imprisonment and enslavement back through history, pondering each era like a bead on a meditation mala. He saw bodies stretched in bunks, in rows, shoulder-to-shoulder tight, three layers high in chains, the dead rotting above the dying, the living sickened and terrified. He saw bodies thrown in graves, lining the ditches of every war. He saw pale bodies emaciated into bones, the white snow of the German winter tight around them, the smoke of incinerators black and churning. He saw mounds of Jewish hair, heaped like bodies in the ditches, stacked like bison skulls, piled up in mountains. He saw the heaps of bison bodies, dead across the plains; the bodies of the people who held them sacred, dead across the continent. He saw the herding of human beings in long lines, on the Trail of Tears, into ghettos, into camps, into gulags; train loads to Siberia, busloads across America.

He saw rare emancipations sparking moments of freedom in this world: Moses raining down God's plagues, parting waters, leading Jews from slavery; Frederick Douglass revolting from chains and death; Sojourner Truth and Harriet Tubman racing through the darkened woods; indigenous uprisings, the Levelers and the Diggers, the workers' movements for cooperatives, the cry to occupy for equality in wealth. On and on, the recitation went, one prayer bead recollection at a time. The mala stretched longer than the night without scratching more than just the surface of the truth.

There were the women standing throughout history, thin-lipped, frowning, subjugated to the men, imprisoned in obedience.

There were the slave-wage workers chained to a paycheck, selling their labor to the owners, their sovereignty and dignity eroded by the economic grind of titans who forced generations into poverty.

There were the masses of animal species, locked into pens and pastures, driven off cliffs, chained to plows to labor for human beings, caught in nets to be devoured.

There were invisible ropes of property lines, binding up the planet, this great round orb of Earth which existed long before humanity walked the surface, which will exist long after the last human falls extinct, upon which the mightiest man of wealth and power is but a flea in the circus of humanity . . . a flea devouring the globe's skin, sucking the blood, leaving poison, itching this great mother to no end.

And there was himself, imprisoned for existing in a society gone insane, locked up to labor for a lifetime because he would not own another being. He had been locked up for refusing to own property, a home, or rent one from a richer man. He walked the Earth and slept in forests, performed small tasks to buy some bread. But freedom is an illusion in a world bound up in chains. The flea upon the slave's back becomes the property of the master, as does the child in the slave's womb, the knowledge in the slave's head, the songs in the slave's mouth.

The worker is a slave to the business owner; the prisoner is a slave to the jail.

"We are not free until all are free," Dave murmured, thinking of animals, land, forests, fields, women, children, and planets.

A set of eyes flew open in the bunk nearby. The breath of a man without a name paused. His muscles tingled. His eyes rolled to the side, wondering. The silence stretched long as he waited for the next word to be spoken.

But Dave lay quiet, his mind spiraling through the ages, watching empires rise and fall. Over and over, the old cycle of enslavement continues, taking freedom from the people and forcing their muscles to labor for the profit of another. With wealth, humans buy power; with power comes authority; with authority comes law; with law comes control; with control comes more profit, more power, more authority, more law, more control, more profit.

So rise the kings, the tyrants, the presidents, the Pope, the tycoon, the billionaire, the chief, the Queen, the Empress, the noble, the nouveau riche . . . they are lifted on the backs of the masses. Both willingly and through coercion, populaces raise one man above another and surrender themselves to be ruled. Some people fawn like lapdogs, groveling, and unashamed. Others conduct themselves like dignified hounds and offer unquestioning loyalty to authority. But a third set are wolves, imprisoned and starved, viewed as dangerous because they yearn for freedom.

Freedom is ferocious, wild and uncivilized. It will never be part of respectable society. Freedom cannot be controlled or forced to build fortunes for others. Freedom will not die for another man's profit. Freedom will not starve children to put feasts on the tables of the wealthy. Freedom will not tolerate classism, racism, sexism, or discrimination of any kind. It will ever advance the concept of radical equality, for one who is free cannot condemn others to slavery - to chattel, debt, work, marriage, or prison - no form of enslavement is tolerable to the free.

Freedom is not a concept that swears allegiance to any flag! It defies nationalism! Patriotism! Boundaries and borders! The wild birds are free! The wild fish are free! But the wild human? Such creatures have gone extinct. Out of seven billion humans, not one knows the meaning of freedom. Humankind enslaves their species by culture, society, history, and law. In blind ignorance, they utter the word, *freedom,* to launch wars, spend money, make laws, and imprison others. Freedom is not free, their bumper stickers read . . . but such a twisted convolution of logic baffles the brightest thinkers.

Freedom is free, you fools! It is war that is costly, that takes your sons' lives. It is protecting the empires of the rich that is expensive to the people. It is the fortunes of the few that enslave the lives of the many. It is the imprisonment of your mind that bankrupts your freedom.

As such thoughts rolled through Dave, a sense of ancient injustice opened its maw and swallowed him whole. He sat in the cold prison while he fell into the hell of human history that stretched back through thousands of cultures. What was the point of hiring a lawyer to argue a mere technicality of an unjust law when the entire system of law, order, nations, and ownership of other humans, animals, plants, land, or the planet was fundamentally unjust. The notion of property was nothing more than a euphemism for ownership and enslavement.

Dave began to laugh in silent consternation as the construct of his society collapsed like an imploding building. His eyes darted around the jail as if the solidity of concrete might dissolve along with his delusions. The concept of a jail to imprison wandering human beings lost its moral authority. The system of government that imprisoned a man who had caused no harm to others fractured its legitimacy. The society that blindly obeyed and upheld the laws of such a government toppled from the grace of his respect.

The people of the nation fell from his esteem. One by one, they would have to redeem themselves in his eyes. One by one, they would need to decry the injustice of their society. One by one, they would have to take action to undo it. Only then would his respect for his nation return. The fire of conviction stirred in his guts. He slapped the mattress with the flat of his palm and heard a few bodies shift in the semi-darkness. He glanced around. A pair of eyes stared blearily at him, lost in the hell realms of delusion and injustice, so deeply entangled that Dave nearly lost the courage to attempt to speak truth.

What did Moses say to the Jews who argued that they would never be free of the Pharaoh? What did the African mothers whisper to their sons and daughters who had been born into slavery? How did they convince their children that they were not property even though the slash of the whip, the gunshots of the masters, the fearful obedience of even their own mothers told the children they were slaves? What did Mother Jones say to the laborers who deserved more than misery in the workplace? What did Gandhi say to the naysayers who believed the British would rule India forever?

Dave sighed. It is one thing to realize truth . . . it is another to help others awaken.

"We are not free until all are free," he repeated in the barest whisper of breath.

The ears in the next bunk caught the sigh of the words. The Number's eyes leapt in Dave's direction.

Ah, the thin man thought, he's here.

The Number's heart grew tight inside his chest, bound by hope and fear, sadness, prophecy, and loss. The churning wheel of causes rolled the world forward through the night; old debts unpaid for actions taken lifetimes ago came closer to collection. Long into the night, the Number lay awake. As the breaths of imprisoned men dropped into the slow rhythm of slumber, the two men lay silent, listening.

CHAPTER TWENTY-THREE

· · · · ·

Before the sun broke free of the horizon, the prisoners were ordered out of bed.

"In the winter," the Number remarked as he and Dave dressed in thin, gray cotton pants and shirts, "you rise in the darkness, dress in the darkness, eat in the darkness, go to work in the darkness, and hope that the sun catches up with you before lunch."

The Number stuck close to his side, explaining the protocol of the jail.

"Don't speak to the guards unless spoken to. Don't argue. Don't complain. Oh, and don't eat too much at any meal," the Number whispered as they stood in line for lumps of oatmeal. "The food is drugged to keep the men complacent."

The Number's eyes switched across the rows of men.

"It's the lean ones like me the guards keep an eye on. The heavy-set guys can't think straight enough to raise a fist, let alone plan a prison riot."

"Did you know," Dave murmured as they sat down, "that monks eat lightly because overeating dulls the mind? Extreme hunger does the same."

"That's why the Middle Path," the Number remarked.

Dave looked up sharply. A crooked smile hung from the corner of the other man's mouth.

"There was a Buddhist fellow who used to teach meditation," the Number explained. "That was back when the jail was halfway normal - by which I mean, absolutely corrupt, but only in the usual ways of all prisons."

Dave put his spoon down in the gray lumps of oatmeal.

"What are you here for?" he asked the Number.

"Murder. I killed a man. And you?"

"Walking down a street," Dave replied.

"Ah," the Number sighed, "there's been crime wave of pedestrians lately. Happens every time the bosses have a big work contract lining up."

The Number watched Dave's reaction with a bemused look. The florescent lights chiseled shadows under the man's eyebrows, chin, and nose. His cheekbones and forehead glared white. Stubble and skin pores, nostril hairs and moles stood out in sharp, relentless detail. The Number dropped his eyes and poked disinterestedly at his breakfast.

"I was locked in solitary, once," the Number remarked in a reflective tone. "While I was in there, it occurred to me that monks and prisoners are both kept in cells."

He pointed his spoon at Dave.

"Did you ever think about that? Cells are compartments, separations. Now, take the biological cells of plants and human beings. They're just tiny compartments, but out of them comes consciousness: minds, thoughts, memories . . . or so we think."

The Number leaned his elbows on the table, eyes dark as black diamonds set in the carved hollows of his skull.

"That Buddhist teacher," the Number said urgently, "he claimed that it was all delusion, that there is no self, no consciousness, no mind . . . "

"Nothing fixed, permanent, or separate" Dave clarified.

"Ah, see," the Number sighed in relief, "I had a feeling you were the guy to ask."

He's up to something, Dave thought, frowning. The scrappy man was dodging around words, maneuvering the conversation in an indiscernible direction like a night ferryman poling through dark fog. Dave narrowed his eyes.

"But I can't figure it out," the Number complained, shaking his head ruefully. The craggy man held up one long, bony finger and turned it from side to side.

"What is the delusion?" he asked. "The cell in my finger? Or the body to which it belongs?"

I'm being tested, Dave realized with a start. Here in the concrete cafeteria, under the harsh glare of fluorescent lights, surrounded by smudged, whitewashed walls, over a bowl of drug-laden, lumpy oatmeal, a man without a name was testing his Buddhist wisdom.

"What do you think, Dave?" the Number questioned with a wry smile. "Is the cell the delusion? The monastery? Or the prison?"

Dave saw the thoughts teeming behind the Number's eyes like schools of fish beneath the surface of a pond: cells and monasteries, suburban houses, cars, offices; little cells inside a pulsing body of civilization; cells unaware of any identity beyond the scope of walls and membranes; cells inextricably linked to the lifeblood of every other cell throughout the massive body of reality that broke through every barrier of conception; cells, tissues, organs, bodies, humans, home, neighborhood, city, country, continent, planet, solar system, galaxy, universe. Even the infinite, endless Universe became a cell of the unknown.

"The self that has the thought of cell and whole is the delusion," he answered.

The Number's thin lips dropped apart. A flash of perception shot through the black caverns of his eyes. He rubbed his bony fingers across the black stubble of his cheeks. His head bowed. His gaze rose to beseech Dave.

"Really?"

Dave nodded.

"If you have no self, you have no delusion," he added.

The Number's eyes closed. His mouth twitched. Emotion trembled across his expression. Dave's chest ached inexplicably. He wasn't just being tested, he realized. The Number had posed a question at the limits of his awareness, hoping to escape the chain link confines of his mind.

"It all makes sense now . . . it all makes sense," the Number whispered. A review of memories paraded through his thoughts: his rough childhood, the murder of the man, his long imprisonment, his encounters with the Buddhist meditation teacher, his sojourn in solitary confinement, the long nights spent pondering the teachings . . . every event and action had been calculated, poised to bring him to this moment. Everything was preparation for this encounter.

The Number opened his eyes and looked at the man sitting across from him. The fathomless gaze of this hollow-cheeked prisoner traced the newcomer's freshly shorn head, dropped to his folded hands on the table, and finally met the steady gaze of Dave Grant.

"Picture a large wall," the Number urged him. "A wall so high, you can't see over it, and so wide, you can't get around it. You wonder what's behind the wall. If there's a corner that bends away, you assume there's something inside the wall. If the corner folds toward you, you assume that you are contained within it, while the rest of the world is on the other side."

Dave nodded.

"The thing about walls," the Number went on with a voice that cracked with anguish, "is that they confine people on both sides. Inside or out, it makes no difference. As soon as you build a wall, both sides are trapped. Some walls you want to escape; others you want to get into. Freedom and imprisonment swap sides in a flicker of the mind."

The Number heaved a deep breath. Dave waited, listening. The Number leaned the knobs of his elbows on the hard, white table, and jutted his shoulders forward as he spoke.

"I spent six weeks on water rations in a concrete cell without contact with any human being," he said.

"What for?" Dave asked.

"Organizing a work strike," the Number replied. He ran a hand wearily across his eyes. "I organized a work strike because the whole world is a prison and I didn't believe in breaking my back to continue its delusion."

The prisoners sitting next to them on the long bench shifted down a few places. Uneasy glances leapt between them. Burly prison guards in khaki uniforms prowled the cafeteria.

"Perhaps, we should stick to philosophy," Dave suggested carefully.

The Number nodded in agreement.

"Did you know," Dave remarked slowly, "that in the Old West, no one fenced the cattle in? If you wanted a garden, you had to put up a fence to keep the cattle out. You penned up your vegetables and your petunias against the wilds and the open range. Just imagine - the vast prairie stretched out hundreds of miles in all directions, teeming with bison and badgers, hawks and antelope, and the settlers lived in tiny patches, enclosing their sod houses behind fences and walls."

He paused for a moment to see if the Number understood. The other man watched him solemnly, saying nothing.

"But nowadays," Dave continued, "the whole country is crisscrossed with fences - wooden ones, barbed wire, visible and invisible - and it is the wild spaces that are hemmed into little postage stamps not much bigger than the homesteads that the settlers fenced off. And freedom? Where does freedom stand? Show me a place where a free man can exist! You can't! He is always trespassing on someone's property. There's no place on Earth that's not fenced in by humanity. You can't go north. You can't go south. You can't go east or west. The only place you might find freedom is within."

The Number's eyes lit up.

"Yes!" he cried. "In solitary, I sat locked up behind countless sets of locks, no more or less free than we are right at this moment."

"Or before," Dave pointed out, referring to the world outside of the prison. "Our world is a thousand sets of walls and fences, little boxes, jails, and prisons. We've snatched up land and forced others off. We've fenced in our minds with a million barbed-wire thoughts, starting with concepts of me and you, then going right on up to mine, yours, theirs; money, wealth, profit, prisons, work camps."

"There were times," the Number said, "when I sat in the darkness in solitary, not knowing if it was night or day, and just cried with pity for all of the imprisoned souls outside of my cell; the guards, the inmates, the warden, the judge, the lawyers, the cops, the legislators."

His voice choked on a nameless emotion, a deep primordial regret for the endless destruction wrought by human folly.

"We're all so locked up in our delusions," the Number cried, "that we can't think straight. So it makes sense to people that we've got poverty and crime, justice systems and criminals."

"The crime," Dave shot back, "is that the real criminals - the wealthy elites throughout history - have not only gone unprosecuted for creating poverty, homelessness, and starvation; they have been lauded by society for the riches they stole by pushing people off the land and claiming it as their own."

Dave plunged his plastic spoon into the cold oatmeal in disgust.

"People will hear about this prison," he said, knowing that one day the horrific injustice of the jail would be exposed, "and they will be outraged, thinking that this one jail is a unique example of corruption. They'll call for tighter regulations and reforms. They'll petition and protest until they get this place fixed. They'll donate to nonprofits who work for prison reforms, call their senators, email the Department of Justice, fast in solidarity, picket outside the capitol building, lock down to the chain link fence outside the prison." Dave turned his gaze to the stark walls and the heavy metal doors. "But this one jail is not the problem. The problem is the imprisonment of humanity. Those people outside the jail are just as much prisoners as the men and women behind bars. The only difference is that we know it . . . and they don't."

Dave rubbed his hands across his face.

"In prison," he said, "the obedient are rewarded and the disobedient are punished. How is that any different than the rest of society? There are many walls in a prison and just as many illusions of freedom. To the man in solitary confinement, a row of bunks three high seems like freedom; to the man on the middle bunk, the top bunk is freedom. To the man at work, quitting time is freedom. To those stuck inside the house, the yard is freedom."

His metaphors reached beyond jails to touch the ordinary lives of people world over.

"There will always be jails and corruption as long as the minds of people are bound," he said. "Solitary confinement exists because we lock ourselves up. We imprison our yards with fences, then our neighbor's, and the next neighbor's down the street. The money is locked up by the wealthy, poverty chains the masses, crime becomes the only option for survival, prisons make profit for the wealthy, and our entire economic system turns into a racket where humans equal numbers, bodies equal profit, one man's labor becomes another man's wealth; and eventually the comfortable existence of a powerful class relies on the misery of imprisoning not just the poor, not just whole cultures, but the land, the animals, the trees, the air, the water, the mountains, and the minds of every sentient being in existence."

He trembled with the words. His fist curled and clenched on the table.

"So, sure, tell people to call the senators, the Supreme Court, the Department of Justice, the President. People should call and tell them it's a waste of our tax dollars to lock people up behind bars when the real prison surrounds our whole world."

The Number stared at Dave, realization illuminating his expression.

"You're not in here because you were a vagrant," the Number murmured. "You're here because your very existence threatens every wall, cell, and barrier that exists."

"Well, yes," Dave agreed softly. "That's what all awakened beings must do."

CHAPTER TWENTY-FOUR

· · · · ·

The work whistle blew. The prisoners stirred from their seats in a flurry of noise. Dave and the Number sat staring at each other. Dave's mouth curled into a small smile and his eyes crinkled as if to say, *surprise!* He reached out a hand. The Number shook it. Laughter rumbled in the cage of his ribs. He opened his lips to speak -

Two burly hands clamped down on Dave's shoulders and hauled him forcibly out of his seat by the fabric of his cotton shirt.

"P108514," the guard barked. "Up to the Warden's office."

"Why?" Dave asked.

"If I wanted questions, I would have ordered you to ask them. Get moving," the guard commanded.

Dave was marched to the Warden's office, handcuffed to a metal chair that was bolted to the floor, and forced to wait for an hour before the Warden arrived. Dave heard the man coming down the hall, preceded by a sharp retort of snapping commands. The door to the office flung open behind him and crashed shut with a bang that rattled the old prison photos hanging on the office walls. The Warden was a narrow man, tight as a wire. He ran the prison brutally, tolerating no infractions against his strict rules, punishing unflinchingly, turning a blind eye to the violent abuses of the guards. He moved with the precision of military officers. His eyes could turn a man to stone, but he possessed a knack for appearing mild-mannered at dinner parties with politicians and prison corporation directors. The Warden brushed past Dave without a glance, smacking a stack of files on the desk before snapping up the metal blinds on the window. A stab of sunlight forced Dave to squint.

"Ah, sir," Dave said as the Warden settled into the chair behind his desk. "I'm glad we have a chance to speak - "

"Be quiet."

"But, there's been a mistake, sir," Dave pointed out. "I've had no trial or conviction."

"There's no mistake," the Warden replied without glancing up from his papers.

"I haven't been allowed to speak with a lawyer - " Dave added.

"I said, there's been no mistake," the Warden's voice was soft and chilling. He picked up a file from his desk and glanced at it.

"You were charged and found guilty of vagrancy," he commented, reading the notes.

"That's impossible," Dave argued.

The Warden glared at him. Dave's stomach sank. He realized with a shudder that not only were convictions without trials possible, they might be routine in this system.

"P108514," the Warden remarked warningly as he examined Dave's file, "you haven't been in long, and I'm already hearing rumors about you." The Warden looked up from the papers on his desk, catching Dave's eyes. "Are they true?"

"What are the rumors?" Dave asked.

"Oh, we don't need to go into details," the Warden said, waving his hand dismissively.

"Truth is finicky," Dave replied. "It's best to know the particulars before verifying what's true or not."

The Warden picked up a sheet of hand scrawled notes.

"At 9:20 p.m.," he read, "Prisoner P108514 said, 'we are not free until all are free'."

"It's a philosophical statement," Dave objected. "Every great thinker from Socrates to Siddhartha Buddha said something to that effect."

"Sounds like code for jailbreak and prison riots to me," the Warden growled.

Dave sighed. One man hears philosophy; another interprets schemes.

"Are you planning a jailbreak?" the Warden asked bluntly.

"Not at the moment," he answered.

"But for some other moment?" the Warden grilled him.

"The phrase references Buddhist philosophy," Dave attempted to explain. "In it, words such as freedom and liberation are directed at the delusional thinking that plagues human beings."

"Are you thinking that you could plot a jailbreak and get away with it?" the Warden questioned sharply.

"That could be considered delusional from many angles," Dave replied carefully.

"Indeed," the Warden agreed, pinning him with a harsh look. "Solitary confinement for a decade is a good way to break through delusions."

"Not from what I've heard," Dave retorted.

"Are you asking to try it out?" the Warden hissed.

"No," Dave replied gravely. "I only meant that Buddhist monks live in isolation for three years, not ten. After three years, they return to the world to practice seeing through the myriad delusions."

The Warden studied him. Dave sensed a low-level confusion behind the man's stony expression. He decided to take a leap.

"Buddhist meditation practices have been used in prisons, including this one, to help prisoners remain calm and centered, less prone to fights and violent outbreaks."

"So, I've heard," the Warden commented.

Thus have I heard . . . the opening line of *The Diamond Sutra* echoed in Dave's chest like a heartbeat. *Once, the Bhagavan was dwelling near Shravasti at Anathapidada Garden* . . . Well, Dave sighed silently to himself, here I am. No more, no less than the Buddha, a part of the understanding of reality through which buddhas emerge. He could only do his best, but to attempt anything less was not an option.

He took a breath and surrendered. Chained to the steel chair and bolted to the concrete floor, he surrendered to the reality unfolding before him; surrendered to the full weightless weight of understandings that he carried; surrendered all notions of carrying anything; surrendered the self that carried the notions. He simply sat as the sheer naked reality, nameless, bodiless, and uncontained. Dave Grant was annihilated. Without a conception of a self, there was no conception of an other. The handcuffs held no one. The chair bolted no one into confinement. Self, chair, metal, handcuffs, concrete, Dave, the Warden; all were condensed into a moment of suchness that defied all words or separations.

From this perspective, it was the Warden, not Dave, who was imprisoned. The angular man sat trapped in the confines of his skull, locked in the chains of delusion and separation. Then, for one brief moment, the hardened prison warden caught a glimpse of truth. His eyes widened. His chest clenched. His fingers gripped the edge of his desk as he stared at unbounded freedom. Horror and fascination twisted his face in opposite directions. He saw himself connected to everything in the room. His destiny was linked inextricably to the prisoner who sat chained to the metal chair. He met Dave's eyes -

- and Dave's consciousness crash-landed back in his

breathless body.

The Warden cleared his throat. They stared at each other. A twitch snapped through the Warden's spine. Dave blinked. The Warden stared at Dave, disconcerted and slightly wild-eyed at the sudden shifts of perception. Then he snapped his hanging jaw shut, scowled furiously, and glared at Dave.

"I'll be watching your every move," the Warden warned him as he pressed the buzzer on his desk. A guard opened the office door. "Prisoner one, zero, eight can return to work now."

"I'm Dave Grant. I have a name."

The Warden gave him a sour look, but made no reply. The guard unlocked the handcuffs and pulled Dave up from the chair. The Warden fanned him away like a fly.

"Warden?" Dave asked, pausing by the door. "If you ever wish to talk about - "

"I've more important things to do," the man growled.

"I don't," Dave quietly admitted. "If you ever want - "

"Get out of here," the Warden ordered.

Dave shut up. He glanced back as he passed through the door and saw the Warden staring at him.

"We are not free until all are free," Dave said softly.

The Warden turned his eyes away quickly . . . but not before Dave caught a glimpse of the anguish burning in them.

Released from handcuffs, Dave was led through the corridors to a large workroom. Hundreds of men in gray jumpsuits sat huddled like pigeons. Rows of their heads bobbed and turned slightly as they worked. Low sounds and rustles murmured between hunched shoulders and bent necks. Hands darted out to snatch parts off the worktables and threw the completed pieces down the assembly line. Across the room, the Number caught the guard's attention with a wave and made space for Dave on the workbench. The guard grunted and ordered Dave to sit down. The Number explained their work: assemble the plastic parts to the toy, paint color on the eyes and hair, and pass it down the line for clothes. Dave assembled exactly one plastic toy before he threw it down in disgust.

"This is insane," he declared.

A few curious eyes flicked in his direction, but all heads remained bowed over paintbrushes and plastic pieces.

"Why do they do this?" Dave asked the Number, gesturing at the prisoners bent over their work.

"Because if they work five shifts they can afford a phone call on Saturday to their kids," the Number explained as he delicately touched blue paint to blank eyes. "It's all a racket. Fifteen minute phone calls shouldn't cost a week's worth of wages."

"Why do they buy it?" Dave demanded.

"What choice do they have?" the Number asked with a resigned shrug. "You can't work your way out of prison on fifty cents an hour - not when they're charging you for every day you're locked up."

Dave pondered the plastic toy.

"Do you know how much this costs?" he asked the Number.

"Five dollars and seventy-nine cents, retail," the Number answered. "I asked."

"Wrong," Dave contradicted. "It costs the taxpayers closer to a hundred dollars a piece."

"The prison industry must make billions off this crap," the Number grumbled.

"Only millions, by my calculation," Dave commented.

"One, zero, eight; get your hands moving as fast as your mouth," the guard barked from across the room.

Dave raised his eyes.

"No."

The warehouse stilled. Heads turned. The guard paced over to Dave.

"I said, get working!"

Dave let his hands fall into his lap of his drab, cotton jumpsuit.

"And I said, no. I won't. I won't create profit for your boss while participating in an insane system that unjustly imprisons human beings, forces poverty on their families, feeds the greed of the corporations, and corrupts judges, cops, and lawyers. I won't - I can't - do this work."

"You don't have a choice, smart-aleck," the guard threatened him.

"Wrong," Dave contradicted, "I do have a choice - "

CRACK!

He was backhanded so hard his body smacked against the worktable. Stars exploded in his eyes. Reactions snapped around the room. The Number whipped off the bench to block a second blow from the guard. The startled guard drew his gun. The prisoners tensed.

"Back to work, all of you!" one of the guards ordered from the far end of the room. The other prisoners quickly bent over their work, but their eyes watched Dave, the Number, the gun, and the guard.

The Number stood as still as stone, one hand lowered down toward Dave; the other raised to halt the blow of the guard. The predictions of a Buddhist meditation teacher echoed in his mind: *you killed a man and lost your freedom. You will find your freedom in another man's life.*

"Remember, Dave," the Number said quietly, his eyes never leaving the gun, "in the realm of complete nirvana, the Buddha liberates all beings; but in truth not one being is liberated . . . remember that."

His voice begged Dave to understand. There was no time to explain.

"We are all one, and only one. Remember!" the Number insisted.

Dave didn't dare move his eyes from the guard's pistol.

"Get back to work," the guard repeated.

"What happens next, Dave," the Number spoke softly, "was set in motion lifetimes ago."

The room seemed to hang suspended in time, but the ever-churning wheel of cause and effect turned the Universe forward half a second.

"Get . . . back . . . to . . . work," the guard growled.

Dave's heart thudded woodenly in his chest. He answered the only way he could.

"No."

The pistol swung. A figure leapt toward him. A shot fired.

The torture wheel of suffering halted.

He woke in the darkness. Pain cracked across his body. He groaned. His voice hit the walls with a dull sound. Solitary confinement. He could not remember his arrival - only the Number rising to block the second blow, a threat, a gun, the Number diving - not away, towards him! - and the man who was a statistic crumbling over the body of a man who was all things - the light in the Number's eyes fading, words on the man's lips, *gate, gate, paragate* - the mantra of *The Heart Sutra* - a blow to his head, darkness.

"The Number is dead," he croaked.

The thunderclap of the realization was followed by a rumble of uneasy thoughts. The Number had known. Dave's fist leapt to his mouth. Chills ran up his spine. What had the Number whispered?

What happens next was set in motion lifetimes ago.

And the man had quoted *The Diamond Sutra*, trying in that tense moment to convey a message to Dave . . . in the realm of complete nirvana, the Buddha liberates all beings, but in truth, not one being shall be liberated. And how so?

He heard the echoes of the ancient sutra. When the Buddha enters the realm of complete nirvana, not one being will be liberated . . . for a being is a fiction, a delusion, something that does not exist. Beings are small fantasies constructed in the mind; a being named the Number could not be separated from the being called Dave Grant. Why not call them one being, then, and the guard, and the prisoners as well? When a bullet shoots and strikes, one part crumples, another part lives, and a third part holds a pistol in his hand.

Remember that, the Number said. In the realm of complete enlightenment, all beings are delusions; and delusions are not beings. You cannot liberate what does not exist, so not one being can be liberated. But, delusions can be dropped, and in dropping untrue views, liberation unfolds.

Dave pulled himself upright. Everything hurt. He could not cross his legs, nor would his spine straighten. He leaned against the cold concrete wall and opened his rusty mouth to speak the mantras of the buddhas.

The words would not come.

Tears fell like dharma rain from the fountains of his cheeks. The Number had offered Dave the best of blessings and the greatest of trusts. He had taken a fearless bodhisattva leap off the cliff edge of his life. *Form is emptiness,* the Number's eyes implored. *Emptiness is form.* Utterly non-attached to his body, his self, his being, his soul, he caught a bullet meant for Dave.

Gate, gate, paragate, the Number had chanted as his form unraveled in this realm. *Go, go, go beyond.*

Dave spoke in silent thoughts, chanting a prayer for the sacrifice of the Number.

In whatever realms of existence and nonexistence, he thought, *a being that was once called the Number can be found, by the means of whatever buddha awareness any buddha may have, may the One called the Number be reborn fully enlightened, for his perfection of charity, his perfection of wisdom, his compassion to all suffering beings.*

His head rang like a temple gong. Pain flared in shocks of white lightning. On the breath of his prayer, consciousness folded and he plummeted back into oblivion.

He woke again in the darkness that had no variation, no time, no past or future. His pain throbbed dully. He stank of his own urine. He felt in the dark and found the pipes of a faucet, hauled himself up, and drank in gasping gulps of thirst. He slid back down the wall to his buttocks, smacking a bucket that was mercifully empty. His guts twisted his ribcage with nausea.

How long have I been here? he wondered.

Then swiftly, brutally, he truncated the question. Don't ask, he warned himself. A concept of time gives rise to the madness of loss and fear. Already, anxious sensations jittered in his bloodstream. He clenched his mind around his body like an iron vise.

No past, no future, no being, no body, no life, no soul . . . just be.

He breathed . . . and breathed . . . and breathed.

CHAPTER TWENTY-FIVE

·····

The door swung open. He squinted at the shock of light, unable to see as the guards hauled him to his feet. His weakened body staggered. The guard gripped his arm.

"Thank you," he rasped.

"Can you believe this guy?" the guard exclaimed to his partner. "Three weeks in solitary confinement on water rations and his first words are thank you?"

"What's going on?" Dave choked out.

"You're getting out," the guard informed him.

"Out of solitary?" Dave asked.

"Released. You're being released."

"Maybe he oughta sit down," the second guard mentioned as Dave reeled on his feet.

"Can't," the first man replied, shaking his head. "We got less than an hour to get him fed, showered, shaved, dressed, checked out for release, and up to the Warden's office."

"We ain't gonna make it," the second guard grumbled.

"A glass of water will be fine," Dave croaked out. The food, he remembered, was drugged to keep the prisoners complacent, and he needed his wits about him.

The guards hustled him through the motions of normalcy. He was tossed in the shower and impatiently shaved. A comb was raked through his hair. His old blue jeans, tee-shirt, and sneakers were handed over in a plastic bag. He dressed slower than an old man. His limbs ached. His joints creaked. His bones folded puppet-like. The knobs of his knees, ribs, knuckles, and elbows poked sharply against the empty sack of his skin. When the guards discovered he had difficulty putting one foot in front of the other, they half-carried him up to the Warden's office

"What the hell game do you think you're playing, Grant?" the Warden barked at him as soon as the guards had shut the door and left. "Disguising yourself as a bum to get arrested for vagrancy! Do you realize you could have been killed?!"

"I'm aware," Dave moaned softly. The metal chair, bolted to the floor, seemed more spacious than he remembered . . . his emaciated body barely filled half of it. He swung his eyes up to the Warden and the Number's death flashed before him. He was painfully aware of the dangers of prison.

"If your lawyer hadn't called - "

"Lawyer?" he choked. What lawyer?

"Edward Swenson - "

Susan's lawyer, Dave realized. The attorney had worked for them before the divorce, but then took Susan's side like a winning lottery ticket.

"If he hadn't called, you'd be rotting down to bones in that pit for attempting to start a work strike."

"Does this mean I'll get a trial?" he asked, confused.

"Hell no," the Warden swore. "It means you're getting released with a gag order."

"Ah," Dave tried to compose his face into a look of comprehension. "How did Swenson know where I was?"

The Warden blinked.

"He read about your conviction in the public records."

"But I never had a trial - "

"The clerk is paid to file the forms. It's not her job to verify the data."

"I see," Dave said. "So, Swenson just happened to be reading public records?"

"No, he's been looking for you for months, even set

detectives on your trail."

"Ah," Dave repeated, trying to mask his reeling thoughts.

"Of course," the Warden continued, "if I had a billionaire client gone missing, I'd send out the search parties, too."

"I'm not a billionaire," he protested.

"Your attorney begs to differ," the Warden retorted, frowning. "He paid your fines in full. Says you own a resort up in the Sierras."

The Warden pulled out his desk drawer and offered Dave a Cuban cigar. Dave stared at it, dumbfounded by the gesture. He fought the urge to laugh . . . or weep. He lifted his hand up to scrub his face and discovered he was not handcuffed. There was no need; his limbs hung heavier than iron chains. The situation dizzied him. He took a breath.

"Last time I checked on the resort," he said carefully, "it belonged to my ex-wife."

"Must have had a change of heart and given it all back," the Warden speculated.

A light bulb flickered slowly in Dave's mind. The place must be dead broke, he thought. It was probably floundering in debt and unsellable. The development must be nearly built out, and the massively profitable phase of Gold Mountain would be drawing to a close. The restaurant had always operated at a loss and the resort only pulled in a fraction of what the lot sales and construction company earned. From the start, Gold Mountain resort was just bait to reel in the big fish of real estate. They'd discussed when to sell out even before they broke ground on the golf course.

The Warden shifted in his chair, glancing at Dave uncomfortably.

"I did check on you when you were in solitary, you know."

"Oh?" Dave replied.

"Did you really sit cross-legged the whole time?" the Warden asked.

"I believe I may have," he answered, rubbing his knees ruefully.

The Warden whistled appreciatively. He rose.

"Now, Grant, about that gag order - "

"I didn't sign anything - "

"Your lawyer did," the Warden said sharply.

Dave blinked.

"And what if I don't comply?" he responded.

The Warden tapped his fingers together.

"There might be some changes I could make to this prison," the narrow man said slowly. "Or even to some laws in this area . . . but it could be done quietly - and more quickly - if you and I could come to an understanding."

"Prison reform? Is that what you're going to do?" Dave shot back, skeptical.

The Warden said nothing for a moment, hovering on the edge of stony repentance and hardheaded pride. His eyes flickered. He licked his lips.

"Maybe," the Warden answered quietly.

Dave scrutinized the other man's somber expression. Sincerity lit the hardened features of the man. His eyes flashed with a hint of anguish. Dave nodded.

"You're a good man," he said.

The Warden stared at him, bemused.

"No," he replied. "I'm not. But I may do something decent before my time is up."

He pushed the buzzer on the desk, rose to standing, and stepped around the desk.

"Tell me," he said, gripping Dave's elbow, "are you really a buddha?"

Dave smiled weakly.

"Aren't we all?"

They released him through the south gate. He stared at the road for a long time before slowly, achingly walking northeast toward the county line.

"Get out of the area," the Warden had warned him. "The local kids beat up the homeless. Get a cab, stay in hotels, don't play any of your games around here."

Dave didn't have a dime to his name.

"Money, money, everywhere and not a dime to spend," he chanted as he crossed the county line on foot. He walked bone-weary along the rural road until he came to a busy intersection on the outskirts of a town. He leaned against a metal street lamp and put out his hand to beg.

A car stopped, the window rolled open, and a hand passed out a to-go container of soup and a plastic spoon. Dave fumbled his fingers around the warmth of the container, bowing his head gratefully to the couple in the car, and opened his mouth to speak. Too late! The light changed, they drove forward and never heard his thanks. Dave stepped away from the intersection and sat on the mowed shoulder of the road. The trucks and cars roared past. The air tasted of the black grit that clings to the undercarriage of semi-trucks.

Basho meditated under a bridge, Dave thought, remembering the old Japanese tea seller who chose to practice in the worst of conditions. Unattached to form, he let the traffic and bustle rush over him with absolute equanimity. Dave bowed his head over the container of soup. The heat licked the bones of his hands and slowly spread into his wrists. He opened the lid.

The aroma brought tears to his eyes. The scent of fresh

rosemary and thyme added to boiling broth, the undercurrent of potatoes, a hint of carrots - a whole world pulsed in his nostrils, reminding him of soil and moist leaves, determined plants reaching for the sun, the myriad insects hanging onto dangling fronds, bees resting on green stems as they searched for pollen, the rustling of human hands harvesting, the way they paused around the fibrous stems of a carrot clump, the tensing of sunburned arms yanking carrots free of the earth, orange and audacious.

He couldn't speak. He could barely breathe. A whiff of soup brought him to utter humility and transformed his blood into gratitude.

"Thank you," he whispered to the world.

As the first touch of warmth touched his tongue, he wept. He heaved with messy, ugly sobs as the pain of the past weeks screeched through his limbs and wracked his body with agony. His mind watched these reactions with curiosity as the biological memory of his body protested the pain it had endured. Grimaces twisted over his face; the mortal human being named Dave Grant shuddered at the suffering he had endured.

Then he ate. Slowly, spoonful-by-spoonful, with lengthy pauses when his throat closed and his eyes shadowed with emotion, he swallowed the soup. In between mouthfuls, he sat for long periods of stillness as the beauty of life overwhelmed him. Common things like soup and the kindness of strangers touched his heart. It was not just herbs he tasted in the soup; he chewed on the flavors of the world. He let the sensation of nourishment linger on his tongue along with the bitter twinge of human cruelty. Guilt twanged metallically in his mouth as he thought of his fellow prisoners, waiting for some sign of justice dawning on the horizon.

And, as he licked the last traces of the soup with his finger, he thought of Joan.

"You were right, Joan," he said out loud, "the bodhisattvas don't come back for sex and chocolate."

He started laughing on the slope beside the road.

Soup and kindness were good enough for him.

Without a home, a post office box, an address, an employer, a bank account, or a phone, the simplest of tasks loomed like a mountain of obstacles. Tracking down Joan, he realized, would not be easy.

"Where should she call you back?" the server at the teahouse asked when he called to leave a message for her.

Dave sighed. He had walked four miles across town to find a working payphone. He had begged for a scanty handful of change to use it. He had no cellphone, no landline, no email account, no self, no being, no soul .

"Just tell her to call Gold Mountain," he answered, rattling off the only number he could remember. He hung up and slid another pair of quarters into the payphone. He asked the operator to connect him to Edward Swenson's law office. The secretary answered.

"Connect me to Swenson - " he started to say.

"Mr. Swenson is not available - "

"Tell him Dave Grant wants to talk to him."

"Oh, Mr. Grant!" she exclaimed. "How are you?"

"Reasonably well, all things considered," he replied courteously. He sighed as he stared at his bald toe poking through the worn out side of his shoe.

"Mr. Swenson will be right with you. I'll transfer you now."

A silence. A click.

"Grant!" the lawyer's voice boomed. "You old son-of-gun,

how are you?"

Dave winced as the phone receiver buzzed under the onslaught of volume. He stuck a finger in one ear to block the gas station noise.

"Well, I'm out of jail, thanks to you."

"Oh, that was all Susan," Swenson answered. "I just called the warden."

"Did she really leave the place to me?" he asked.

"Yes, she signed a quit-claim in favor of you."

"Is it broke?"

"Well, I wouldn't say - "

"Hah!" Dave retorted. "It's up to its ears in debt and defaulting on loans, isn't it?"

"Well, yes."

"Did she sign the loans over to me, too?" Dave asked.

"Yes, and the back taxes," the attorney told him.

"Charming," Dave groaned. "That's exactly what I did to her in the old days. Did she tell the Gold Mountain staff what's going on?"

"No, she thought you'd like to do the honors."

"Ah." Dave rolled his eyes. "Is she up at the resort?"

"No, she signed it over and took off for Europe."

"I see."

Dave drew a deep breath. His eyebrows furrowed in thought.

"Swenson, can you loan me some money?"

"Uh, it's not a great time - "

"I'm not looking for a million. I need some pocket change."

The lawyer cleared his throat.

"You could sell Gold Mountain."

"Swenson, I need cash, not a long real estate process."

"It's bordering on foreclosure. You could auction it off in a month."

Dave glanced down at his ribs and worn out sneakers. He didn't have a month.

"I'll think it over," he said to Swenson, signaling the end of the conversation.

"Now, Grant, what number can I reach you at?" the lawyer asked.

"You can't, Swenson," he replied and hung up the receiver.

The attorney could leave messages at the resort - like Joan, like Susan, like the whole rest of the world.

He'd answer them all soon enough.

Rivera Sun

CHAPTER TWENTY-SIX

· · · · ·

A man walked quietly in the foothills of the Sierras. The trees and cows watched him silently. Humanity did not seem to see him. He slipped between realities and walked with one foot hidden in realms the racing drivers could not see. He traveled without asking for rides. The miles were few compared to the thoughts that needed to be considered. He paused often, head tilted as if listening. Quick frowns darted across his face, along with curt nods. An occasional sound escaped his lips.

He traveled long, silent stretches without a word. He sat for a few days in the shadows of a dusty oak. He stood still for an hour, letting the gold seed heads of a meadow read the future in his outstretched palm. The wind told him secrets in the rippling Morse code language of fluttering leaves. A tree tried to kill him with all the violent passion of an assassin, recognizing the billionaire who had spun the wheel of suffering that razed the forests and cracked the hills with drought. He sat with the tree, thinking of causes and effects, ignorance and insight. He saw the world from the eyes of the forests and watched the bodies of their civilization crash to the ground to be loaded onto trucks and carted away to pulp mills and incinerators. He gazed across the continent, remembering the genocide of the native peoples. Six million Jews had died in concentration camps; twenty million natives perished in America; how many billions of trees had fallen to human greed?

He walked slowly, for the Universe is made of a quadrillion moving parts. Each one deserved careful consideration before he moved the butterfly that could affect them all.

He offered a frail, old woman assistance and lost a week of

265

walking and thinking as he drove her up the mountain. The wedge that held back the wheel of change slid out an inch. The mass of the world hung breathlessly on the edge of cataclysm. The old woman could not sense the mounting pressures in all directions. She joked and chattered as humans do before volcanoes explode or earthquakes break or climate change roils the planet in the upheavals of extinction.

Then again, he wondered, perhaps she knew. Like generations of old women throughout human history, perhaps she felt the changes coming. As mothers worry for their children and fathers shore up the house, the old women mutter about simple things like soup, and chocolate, and love.

"Where is Joan?" she had asked as he recounted his story to her late at night.

"On her way, I hope," he answered.

When exhaustion tugged the old woman's wrinkles, he retreated to the quiet of the woods behind Edna's house. She offered him the spare bedroom, but the walls hemmed in his thoughts. The house's electric lights illuminated the hardened edges of tables, bed, refrigerators; too many reasonable definitions of reality, too many points on the human perspective, too many familiar stories that drag people back into the same ruts over and over again. Tonight he wanted to stretch his understanding wider than the sky.

Beyond the frames and boxes of humanity, the planet caressed and curled desperately and deliciously around itself. The creeping vines told stories to the tree trunks. The deer bedded down in the meadows. In the wild raspberry canes, a mother grouse rustled her feathers over the trembling bodies of her chicks. The night air breathed in the scents of a thousand creatures and exhaled a word called nature. Above him lay the night. Around him swirled his questions. Inside him pulsed a silence so strong it would crack the world like thunder when it broke.

CHAPTER TWENTY-SEVEN

. . . . .

Dave eyed the golf course warily as he stepped across the property line between the resort and Edna Lawrence's lot. He wore a clean shirt from Edna's long-buried husband and a pair of too-large slacks cinched around his waist. His beat-up sneakers paused on the asphalt drive, toeing the custom sand blend that colored the roads. His gaze settled on the fairways of the golf course.

Whether they won or lost the round, not one visitor had ever slain the course that curled, green and dragon-like on the crown of the drought-cracked Sierras, guarding the horded treasure of Gold Mountain - the property values of the mansions. Its reputation as one of the toughest and most exclusive courses in North America brought in annual tithes and tributes and assured crucial political alliances. The local officials lived in terror of the beast. They sacrificed virgin lands to new development, sent fealty payments in the form of ordinance exemptions, and bent over backward to keep the owners of Gold Mountain satisfied.

"Your days are numbered," Dave told the golf course sternly.

He turned his gaze to the resort. The shingles on the peaked rooflines had silvered through the years like the edges of his hair. The deeper hardwood siding retained its amber tones. The granite foundation would out-live the world. The windows gleamed from a recent washing. Dave observed details: the greening of the copper weathervane and matching gutter work, the fresh replacement of the pebbles lining the gardens, the one broken sprinkler head that sent a stream of water running down the walkway. He noted the maintenance and upkeep flaws, the poor design of the new gazebo, and the modern style of the new fountain by the front entrance.

The resort had aged like an expensive, older woman who had passed the era of nip-and-tucks and was now descending into health problems and plumbing challenges. Yet, the haughty old matron lifted her peaks proudly and tilted her imperious chin high. The garden sculptures adorned the buildings like fine-wrought jewelry, and she sat, as conceited as an aging dowager, on the throne of the High Sierras.

Dave strode across the circular driveway up to the front entrance of the resort.

"Around the back," the bellhop snapped impatiently.

"Pardon?" Dave asked.

"You're looking for work, right? The manager told me some new applicants might be rolling in. Kitchen staff enters around the back."

Dave chuckled and nodded. He stepped around the side of the building. He had anticipated storming the front gate or laying siege outside, but how convenient to slip in unnoticed, like Odysseus returning home . . . or, he realized, like the emperor-in-disguise. He nodded to himself, a smile curling over his lips. Yes, he decided, after seven years the staff had changed - he had changed! He could walk among his courtiers and employees, unknown to anyone, listening to unvarnished truth.

He circled around to the back of the restaurant, past the garbage cans, and opened the kitchen door.

"Are you the new guy?" a short-tempered manager barked.

Dave nodded.

"Well, get in here then. I haven't got all day."

With a deep breath, Dave Grant entered the belly of the beast.

He scoured endless stacks of plates and cutlery until the caustic stench of disinfectants curled his nose hairs. The hot steam and spray soaked into his sweat. The crashes and bangs and hollering of the kitchen filled his ears. His arms ached. His back screamed obscenities. He mopped his brow on the shoulder of his sopping shirt and plunged back in.

On the first day, he saw only dishes. Heaps of plates flew down the line like rubble from a gold mine. He bent his whole body to the stream that poured from the narrow shaft. He swiped the crystal wine glasses from certain shattering and placed them in the customized dishwasher installed by order of the sommeliers. No trace of soap ever touched these goblets. Boiling water scoured them inside the state-of-the-art machine that cost more than a decent car. No lowly dish boy's hands ever left smudges where a wealthy debutante brought her lips to shining glass.

The plates and bowls received cursory scrapes and rinses before being piled into crates that slid roughly into the industrial dishwasher. Dave dove head first into the enormous cooking cauldrons, wielding the long-necked spraying hose like a fireman as he attacked grease and soot.

He pulled clean dishes from the dishwasher, hot as buns from the baker's oven. The plates and bowls hissed steam as he sorted them into place on the shelves. That evening, after the dinner shift concluded, he looked soberly at the glistening stacks. Tomorrow it would all begin again. Every plate scraped today would return the next, smeared with crème brulé and béchamel sauce. The thought of the endless rounds exhausted him.

Dave slid down the stainless steel counter and laid his head in his hands, knees tucked close to tired ribs. His eyes darted around the empty kitchen as he calculated how many dishes he had sent down the line to unknown dishwashers when he dined in the luxury of Gold Mountain. Six? Ten? Twelve per meal? Several meals a day, most days of the week, fifty-two weeks of the year . . . plus the chef's equipment, knives, chopping boards, pots, frying pans, graters, ladles.

Dave ran his reddened hands through his hair, laying his head back against the cool steel cabinet. There was no grace to this work, no pride or satisfaction. His humanity was chained to the pace of the constant stream of dishes. The pores of his skin felt sullied by the grease and bits of discarded food. His spine wept from the day of bending to servitude.

Dave stilled. It was servitude, there was no other word for it. Like the early laborers of the Industrial Revolution, his heart railed at the injustice of wage-slavery. The lie of capitalism shattered like a crystal wine glass smacked against the hard cast iron of a frying pan. The lords and ladies of the twenty-first century sat out in front, dining in luxury while he sweated and wracked his body laboring for them. Wages were nothing but a cover-up for servitude.

Dave shook his head, trying to clear his thoughts. As a worker, he could find pride in those stacks of glistening dishes, go home, sleep soundly, return the next day, pocket a paycheck, save up, buy a home, become the master of his own little property . . . but he'd still be a servant to the masters - not a tradesman, a householder, a craftsman, or an artist - he would be a servant washing dishes in the estate of the lord.

Does the hypocrisy of America know any bounds? he wondered.

The nation built on the promise of equality and opportunity gave rise to one of the greatest wealth divides on the planet. There was nothing egalitarian about capitalism. The rich got richer; the poor grew poorer. Capital flowed to those who already had it; power followed capital. Upward mobility in the United States was a standing joke. Downward mobility was a statistical reality.

Suddenly, he thought of Joan. An ache of longing wracked his tired body. Her eyes, that cascade of black hair, the wry smile pulling up the corner of her lips; he saw her in the teahouse, bringing hot kettles of water to the tables, sliding into a seat to enjoy a cup with friends. She was neither a master nor a servant, but a companion to all those who traveled on the road of life, an equal among equals.

"To serve and be served," he heard her muse, "to love and be loved."

In his mind, Joan leaned her hips against the teahouse sink, bending slightly as she washed the cups and tea ware. Was it all just attitude, then? Dave didn't buy it. The speed, the insistence of the conveyor belt, the demand of the kitchen managers, the fear of dropping a whole tray of crystal goblets, the scrutiny of his superiors - the notion of superiors! - these elements would challenge the best of the enlightened ones to see the emptiness of the situation.

"Bodhisattvas can awaken in a pigsty," Joan used to claim.

"Yes," he would argue back, "but if you had the option, wouldn't you prefer a quiet, gorgeous temple?"

"Enlightenment doesn't care about the scenery," Joan informed him.

"Yes, but - "

"Dave," she had said, tilted her head to the side and folding her fists onto her hips. "Would you have sex in an abandoned car, rusting in a junkyard?"

"Do you mean, literally? Right now?" he asked.

"Hypothetically," she amended. "We don't have an abandoned car."

"I'd make love to you anywhere," he declared.

"Would you fuck an ugly shrew in a palace?" Joan retorted.

"No," he admitted. "What's your point?"

"Enlightenment will fuck with you anywhere."

The critical manager doesn't matter, nor does the speed of the dishes flying down the conveyer belt, nor the snobbery of the wealthy diners in the restaurant sending dirty salad plates down the line.

"Yes, but," Dave protested as he sat exhausted in the kitchen. If it was all the same to enlightenment, he'd prefer to have every man doing his own damn dishes; every family having enough to live on without spending their lives slaving for the rich; every child receiving equal opportunities of education and employment. He didn't need opulence when he had enough. He didn't need a mansion if a shed could keep him warm. He didn't need chanterelles flown in from France if a small bowl of soup could soothe the ache of hunger. He didn't need a blonde heiress, coiffed and manicured, when there was Joan.

He had once owned it all: mansion, resort, golf course, billions, jewelry, art, servants, sports cars. Everything that money could buy, he'd had and lost and now he couldn't care less. He'd slept in the gutter. He'd soaked in champagne. Poverty did not frighten him. Opulence did not entice him.

If dishes are dishes, Dave thought, why can't everyone just do their own? Why can't we all chop onions, cook soup, eat food, and clean the dishes when we're done? Would that be so bad? Do we really need to work to get wealthy so we don't have to wash the dishes?

Dave stared at the stainless steel industrial sink, imagining a lifetime of scouring those stacks. Day after day, repeating the same monotonous cycle. No one is born to wash other men's dishes. Not the low-wage laborers who showed up in restaurants nationwide; not his mother who endlessly served her husband and sons; not Joan who refused to perpetuate patriarchal cycles; not himself or any others in this world.

At the onset of the Industrial Revolution, agrarian men and women, tradesmen, and craftsmen found the notion of doing menial labor for wages deeply insulting. They objected to wage-slavery, decrying the manipulation of the market, taxes, and politics by the wealthy elite that swept the poor off the land and into factories. They rose up against fifteen-hour days for wages so low that hundreds of thousands perished as destitute as when they began.

They went on strike, boycotted, marched, took over factories, shut down cities, faced brutal repression and violent crackdowns. Every authority in the nation fought them: cops, mafia, private mercenaries, the military, the churches, the social clubs, the newspapers, the elites. Hordes of ordinary laboring mothers and fathers continued their struggle for living wages and jobs that would not kill them with injuries, overwork, pollution, diseases, rapes, disasters, and starvation.

Their top-hatted, silver-caned adversaries in bank offices, mansions, and Congress declared the workers of the United States would go to Europe and fight the good fight in the war to end all wars. The workers of the world shouted an early version of *Hell no, we won't go!* Why should the poor man die in the rich man's war? Why should the worker's blood be shed for the wealthy man's profits?

Congress clucked their tongues and shook their heads. The worker parties were booming, attracting converts by the second.

"We must stop them once and for all," the robber barons growled.

The Espionage and Sedition Act passed faster than any bill in the history of the nation. It swept up all who spoke out against the war. Two hundred labor organizers were arrested in one week. They languished in jails for a decade. The workers floundered. Business boomed. The boys went to the front.

The Second World War echoed the machinations of the first. By the end of it, capitalists had packaged up the vision of equality and opportunity promoted by the workers, and added a white picket fence, a dog, and a brand new car. The American Dream was now for sale, with a price tag on every piece: the lawn, the clothes, the toaster, the kids, Mom's white smile and pearl necklace, Dad's rolled up shirt sleeves-

Ah, those rolled-up sleeves, a touch of brilliance in the painting of the dream. If Dad's cuffs had closed neatly at the wrists, he would have fallen into a different class - the class of servants of the wealthy: the managers, the bureaucrats, the clerks and the lawyers; all those whose shift cuffs buttoned neatly under jackets, paired with clean fingernails and obsequious smiles.

But no, Dad's shirtsleeves rolled up to the elbows; he was a workingman who labored and sweated and by some miracle still had energy to flex his worker's muscles as he tussled with his son on the weekend.

This is the dream, the vision of the worker: that at the end of the day, he has more than when he started; that he'll get home in time to see his kids; that he won't grow old and thin from working overtime to pay the bills; that the kids won't be sent to work instead of school; that the house will be warm and the food will be nourishing; that his wife will be smiling; that the dog will be more than a snarling set of ribs - these are the dreams of the worker. He dreams of them because he does not have them. He joins the struggle to wrest such humble visions from the grip of other men's greed. He is beaten, arrested, fired, persecuted, hunted, hounded, shipped off to war . . . and if by some miracle, he survives decades of that misery, he comes home to a slap in the face.

The Dream has been plastered on billboards and is still out of reach, packaged up by the same capitalists who broke up the worker strikes; the same rich men who enclosed the commons, the same upper class that took the land of Europe and replaced peasants with sheep; the same millionaires who manipulated poverty in America; the same merchants and nobles who impressed starving men into indentured servitude; the same elites who whipped up the poor to massacre the natives; the same ambitious ruling class who rallied the colonists to fight a revolution so the wealthy could seize the Crown's stolen land; the same businessmen who chained desperate immigrants to fifteen-hour work days . . . this self-same lineage has now bottled up the visions of the people and rolled out the advertisements to sell it.

In the stainless steel kitchen of his high-class resort, Dave Grant rubbed his red, aching hands and noted his rolled-up shirtsleeves. History swept over him, swirled, and eddied around him. He thought of the women in skirts singing for bread and roses, children marching with a little old lady to demand school instead of a lifetime in factories. He thought of the daydreams of laborers: living wages, safe work places, healthcare, eight-hour workdays.

Slowly, incredulously, he shook his head. They shortchanged themselves with even the best of those demands. The laborers had struggled and suffered, but in the end, they were still slaves asking for better conditions.

Freedom is what the enslaved cry for, not shorter workdays!

Emancipation is the demand, not better rations!

If we ask for anything less, it is a compromise for the sake of survival. The real vision - if we dare to demand it - is to abolish all forms and causes of wage-slavery.

We sold our labor because we were starving, landless, evicted, foreclosed on, run out of the trades, uneducated, lost. The Earth spreads mightily in every direction . . . but in every direction stretch fences. Property, ownership, control of the common resources by individuals instead of peoples: in a thousand pinpricks of greed seven billion human beings die. Whole populaces are shut off the land, shoved off, locked up in cities, and starved.

If we had dared, Dave thought with ferocity, we should have torn up the fences, the deeds, laws, courts, charters, constitutions, and all notions that carved up the land and gave it to private individuals.

CHAPTER TWENTY-EIGHT

· · · · ·

The next day, he rolled down the sleeves of a borrowed black shirt, buttoned the faux pearls on the cuffs, shook out the wrists, tied a long, white apron around the waist of black pressed pants, and boldly took a place in the line of wait staff standing at attention in front of the manager.

"Who are you?" the manager scowled.

"I'm new," Dave replied. "My paperwork hasn't made it through the office, but they said you're short-handed and I should start today."

The manager frowned, but carried on with instructing the staff.

Dave listened attentively, praying that twenty years of criticizing the service would remind him of the subtle details of how high-class waiters behave. The other waiters eyed him suspiciously as they began gliding in and out of the front of house like sleek-winged crows. Vain and stuffed with simmering conceit, their eyes were ever on the lookout for shiny trinkets dropped from the hands of the rich in exchange for special favors. They glided on the updrafts of their own ironic arrogance, elevated by their proximity to wealth. These were waiters who earned quadruple the average schoolteacher's salary in hundred dollar tips and bribes.

Dave had seen them unceremoniously swipe leftovers off the plates they carried away from silk-lined tables, licking their fingers while their eyes darted to check on the manager, boasting to one another about epicurean tidbits melting on their tongues. The strange and secretive ritual reminded Dave of Catholic Mass, the wafers dissolving the body of Christ into

279

one's own corporal being. The waiters' eyes flicked heavenward as they ingested the discarded food of millionaires, the spittle of billionaires. Their mouths met and mingled with the same bites of desserts that may have brushed the disdainful lips of wealthy heiresses. The last sips of rare bottles of wine never went down the dishwasher's drain. Behind the corner of the staff doors, the drink of the gods slipped down the throats of waiters and busboys.

The resort sat like a temple on the top of Gold Mountain, demanding pilgrimages, offerings, tithes, and worship to the cult of wealth. The ultra-rich attended services and took part in the ritual rounds of golf. The semi-wealthy filled the pews and ate the crusts of the bread and body of fortune. The servants nibbled the crumbs in the back halls. The poor could not approach, though their labor erected the steep cathedral peaks that formed the temple of the resort. All of them, from altar boy to dishwasher to high priest to parishioners sang the praises of money and the glory of wealth and prayed that fortune would bless them.

The waiters, the staff, and the servants of the wealthy held up the pillars that raised the rich to their towering positions. Lawyers, legislators, judges, accountants, and consultants formed the ranks of the wealth defense army. Private security joined the state in guarding the life, liberty, and property of the wealthy.

Our whole nation, Dave realized, is devoted to the cult of wealth.

He stood in the nexus of the temple, watching the priests carry the accessories of ritual through their rounds: crystal glasses, expensive wines, a basket of fresh-baked, crusty bread; the pepper grinder, linen napkins, a lemon wedge, a set of salads, soups, entrées, and desserts. We are worshipping sheer gluttony, he thought, indulging in an obscene mismanagement of resources that deprives the people to provide luxuries to the rich.

A guest interrupted his thoughts with a blunt question.

"What can you do about getting us a golf pass?"

"The membership can be gotten in the shop - "

The man cleared his throat.

Dave's mouth twitched. The skinflint, penny pinchers among the rich defied all logic or comprehension. There were billionaires who demanded free golf club memberships simply because the prestige of their wealth entitled them to it. There were millionaires who were always looking for a deal in over-priced boutiques, where even the discount rack prices cost more than most people could afford.

"Of course, sir," Dave said. "I'll be right back."

Only members could play the course, but there were a stack of "guest" passes in the concierge's desk expressly for this situation. Dave accepted the five hundred dollar tip, slipped a hundred to the concierge, three hundred to the house, pocketed his hundred, and carried on with his work. Par for the course, as the saying goes. In his early Gold Mountain days, he had structured in a whole system of bribes and extras for the resort. Rumors of the extravagances available for the price of a tip reached legendary proportions. Certain staff members were infamous for their ability to arrange *anything*. Just ask for Claire or Jacques, the wealthy told each other.

Dave smirked. Any Tom, Dick, or Harry could work miracles at Gold Mountain. The staff was trained in the system. Long ago, he and Susan had worked out the percentage split for the house and the staff down to the last detail of bribes and tips. He trained the bellhops how to bristle, look worried, or shake their heads regretfully until another hundred-dollar bill slipped into their palms. The Swiss chocolates, roses, exclusive wines, the in-suite champagne baths, and massages from the allegedly "booked up" master masseurs were all part of a secret, itemized list. They pulled the ruse on the wealthy because honesty is boring and subterfuge enticing. Secrecy tantalizes those who own the world.

And, Dave added thoughtfully, some of the rich were notorious cheapskates. Give them a price tag and they'd argue it down. Hesitate due to moral principles, and the money would come pouring out in bribes. Dave had dealt with multi-millionaires who dickered for a lower price on a luxury suite. Many of the wealthy made their fortunes by shortchanging everyone else through outrageously high percentages and interest rates, illegal mortgage scams, tax evasions, overseas labor, sub-minimum wage salaries, part-time jobs without benefits; there were a thousand ways to skim the cream off the milk of economy and industry.

Dave had once scanned a packed opera hall and could not find an honest man or woman in it. A whole society of high-class crooks, raising toasts to each other's swindling, scathingly derisive of the recent crime wave of petty thefts that were wrought by the widespread poverty their business practices induced.

He had yet to stumble upon a stockpile of wealth that had not been amassed through misery and suffering. The trust funds of the past were tainted by unspeakable atrocities. The fortunes of the present were laced with the blood of illegal wars for oil. The speculations of the future rested in the financial enslavement of third world countries.

"I suppose the rich are all very nice people," Joan had once said doubtfully.

"They're not, " he had answered bluntly. "A lot of them are

sociopaths, absolutely insane. A few are very nice people when they want something from you."

"But you're not a sociopath," Joan had protested.

"Maybe I was, then," Dave had replied. "Everyone can change."

"Tables six and nine," the headwaiter snapped impatiently at him.

Dave jolted and nodded. He smoothed the pristine white apron. He ran his palm across his hair. He licked his lips. Beyond the doors of the wait staff entrance lay the compliant faces of monsters. He knew. He had seen them roar in rage and contort their features into grotesque sneers. He had seen the false smile of the Duke's son who had thrown a naked prostitute off a penthouse balcony and still walked free. He had dined with cold-blooded women whose political decisions knowingly starved half a million innocent children. He had seen the face of evil appear as human as any other.

He dispelled the memory, pushed apart the swinging doors and stepped into view of some of the sickest, most powerful people in the world.

Nothing happened.

The soft music continued strumming from the hidden sound system. The fountain splashed gently. The people carried on conversations. Forks lifted. Glasses shone softly. Napkins ran across lips.

Dave snorted silently.

What did you expect, idiot? he hissed at himself. This wasn't the old days - the room wouldn't fall silent when he walked in the door. He glanced at the front entrance almost tempted to try his old stunt. Could he still command the attention of millionaires if he stepped through the arched doorway wearing a waiter's apron? A thin smile stretched over his humorless lips. His eyes glinted in anticipation of the challenge . . . someday!

Dave eyed table six, picked up two menus, and began to cross the room. A hasty mantra pounded through him: good waiters don't carry notepads, good waiters don't forget to ask which salad dressing the lady prefers; good waiters bring the wine over before the glass needs to be refilled; good waiters -

He told himself to stop shaking. He knew from personal experience that the wealthy never glanced twice at the staff unless they were young, beautiful, and possibly for purchase. Eyes slid over him as he crossed the room. No one sees a billionaire where they expect a servant. Dave was the emperor-in-disguise, moving among the courtiers. If he was found out, he'd pull the big reveal, tell them who he was, have a hearty laugh, and toast the prank along with the other wealthy.

He scanned the faces subtly as he walked. Kindness is a thirst that no amount of extravagance can quench. The yearning for simple, human connection makes the rich and powerful wake up crying in the night. Their hearts grow parched and dry as dust, aching with the cracks that split inside them. All-devouring, the wealthy consume to assuage their desperate thirst for kindness. Their material obesity threatens to kill them, but they cannot stop. *It's not enough*, they wail, and irony binds their words to the desperate cries of the poor. They are dying men gasping for a shave of ice to be placed upon their burning tongues. Their bodies scorch with unseen fevers. Hell is nothing more than life without a touch of kindness.

Dave walked among them, a recovering addict shaken by sobriety. He passed by alcoholics drunk on wealth, druggies, whores, pimps and pushers. The ultra-rich perch on the shoulders of the semi-rich who are hoisted up by the upper middle class who sneer at the lower middle class who accuse the poor of being lazy who in turn crush the abjectly miserable in an immense, invisible socioeconomic human pyramid, a circus act of the tallest order, a whole society of clowns and back benders in the greatest freak show on Earth.

What happens if we walk away? Dave wondered. What if anyone at any level - or everyone all together - just refused to perform the circus act of crushing or being crushed? Could we live without the glitz and glamor and the rich men on the top? Couldn't we all just sit down as equals and share a dignified, common meal?

He pondered this as he navigated through his tables, bowing, nodding, taking orders, smiling politely to gruff complaints and humbly answering imperious demands. He served businessmen he had struck deals with and bankers who had loaned him millions. He carried food to women who had flirted with him and politicians he had funded. Not one recognized the thin-carved server as the former owner of Gold Mountain. He was invisible, unnamed, unknown. Without the signs of wealth, he simply did not exist.

CHAPTER TWENTY-NINE

· · · · ·

As he worked incognito, he slept on the slopes of Gold Mountain, stretching out beneath the stars. Night after night, he lay on his back in a grassy alpine meadow, savoring the moment when night moves slower than glaciers and darkness seems absolute. There, as the present hangs in the apex of stillness, the winds ruffle the forest and the stars inch across the sky, and everything changes, as it must.

Late summer days of sleeping outdoors were more rare than precious gems on Gold Mountain. Any night, the frost could sweep down from the peaks, heralding snow. Already, the aspens at higher elevations had been shocked golden by the cold. Even now, he was grateful for the wool blanket that Edna had insisted he take.

Just a few nights, he told the mountains. Let me smell your fragrances and hear the movements of the migrations. Let me know you as a human animal, not the half-dead monster I once was, locked in my tomb of flesh.

At the end of the week, he retraced his steps through the woods and returned to Edna's house. The old woman's station wagon sat parked at the same angle he had left it. He frowned and climbed the loose boards of the porch steps, rapping on the screen door with his knuckles.

"Edna?" he called, laying his cheek to the door to listen for a reply.

A jay chattered from the ponderosa pine.

He tried the knob. The door popped open.

"Edna?" he called again. "It's Dave!"

A muffled voice urged him to come in.

He sighed in relief. She wasn't dead. Her house, however, looked as if it had keeled over in the course of a week and crumbled into disarray. A stack of fallen newspapers lay strewn across the hallway. He pushed them back into a pile and continued down the hall, past the living room, the kitchen, the spare bedroom until he found Edna sitting on the back porch in her gliding chair, staring out at the crested peaks of the Sierras.

"Edna?" he spoke softly, not wanting to startle her. "Are you alright? Did you fall and hurt yourself?"

"No, no, I just got old all of a sudden. Thought I'd just sit here quiet and to hell with the dishes."

"But what about food?"

She shook her head.

"Death is closer than the grocery store."

"Edna," Dave said quietly, "you can't just sit here until you die."

"Why not?" she snorted. "The Buddhist masters died sitting upright, meditating."

"Are you a master?" Dave countered, raising his eyebrow, but leaving himself open to the possibility.

Edna said nothing for a moment, watching the pines sift sunlight through their needles.

"No," she admitted. "But you never know . . . "

"I don't doubt the capacity of your mind to reach enlightenment," Dave began.

"- but it can't reach yesterday's memories," she finished.

"No, no, I wasn't saying that," Dave hastily amended. "It's just that, when the body which hosts the mind slows at the end, I don't want to find you half-starved, pleading for water, protesting the trip to the hospital, and refusing an IV drip. Why don't you have someone help you?"

"Who? The hospice nurses?" she shot back. "They'll pray

like vultures over me, hoping to catch a glimpse of God as I open the door to heaven."

"They're not all like that," Dave sighed.

"They'll call the preacher, too," she insisted. "At the last minute, they won't let an old Buddhist die in peace. How'n the hell am I supposed to navigate reincarnation and come back to help if I can't think straight through all the Christians clogging up the spiritual airwaves praying for my soul to repent and escape eternal damnation?"

"Okay," Dave amended. "Not them. How about a relative?"

"They're all waiting for me in the cemetery, Dave. I'm *old.*"

Dave bit his lip.

"I could - "

"No."

"But - "

"No!" she snapped.

In her fierce glare, Dave saw her outraged pride, visions of bedpans and feebleness, assisted bathing, the last days of needing to be turned by strong arms.

"I'm just advocating some sort of a Middle Path," he tried to explain.

"Hmm-hmm, like a good Billionaire Buddha," she snorted.

"I'm not a billionaire . . . or a buddha," he answered. "I'm just speaking as a friend."

"Are you?" she asked plaintively, her old eyes suddenly large, round, and moist behind her glasses.

He nodded.

"Then let me die in peace," she begged.

"I will," he promised, "but not alone."

She pressed her lips together and her whole body shook. Dave stood up.

"Where are you going?" she cried.

"Just to the kitchen," he assured her.

"Gonna do those dishes, oh Dishwashing Bodhisattva?" she teased to hide her relief.

"Later. First, I thought I'd use your phone."

"Calling the coroner?" she laughed.

"No," he replied with a smile. "I wanted to try the teahouse again and see if I can get ahold of Joan."

"Good," Edna commented. "She ought to be here for the end."

Dave frowned.

"You don't know Joan at all - "

"Not my end, you nitwit," she retorted. "The end of Gold Mountain."

Dave crouched down beside Edna's glider.

"Why do you think I'm going to end it?"

She did not answer straight away. He could see her weighing responses. Finally, she sighed.

"I can see it in your eyes. You're done with it."

"I could sell it," he pointed out.

"You won't," Edna answer matter-of-fact. "That place is bad karma - for you, for Susan, for everyone who visits, for the workers, and for the people who built it."

She turned her watery old eyes toward him so slowly that he felt frozen in place for lifetimes.

"I tried to stop you," she reminded him. "But I didn't understand then, so I petitioned and protested and argued and complained for my own selfish reasons. I didn't want the traffic, the goddamn airport - "

"You stopped that one," he reminded her.

"I didn't stop the rent prices from escalating, nor the dependence of the town on trickle-down baloney, or the hundreds of local nonprofits all jostling to get a piece of the pie, or the artist colony that sprang up to glorify the wealthy patrons."

"Nor the local politicians on the take and the lawsuits between Gold Mountain and the county," he added.

"No," she agreed. "I didn't stop much. I didn't know then what I know now."

"What's that?"

"If you're going to put gold on the top of a mountain, the bodies of the poor will be buried in the mines."

Dave swallowed, seeing visions of pharaohs and pyramids built on slave labor, skyscrapers that rose on immigrants' backs, fortunes amassed on the genocides of natives, and estates stolen through wars of aggression. Under the gilded facade of Gold Mountain lay an Earth full of suffering. Under the jewel on the crown of the richest man in the world lay the sordid truth of squalor and oppression.

"You cannot be free until all are free," he murmured.

He rose.

"You're right," he told Edna. "Joan should be here for the end."

CHAPTER THIRTY

· · · · ·

The stars hung silent overhead. Muffled voices and the sound of shutting car doors trekked across the night. The faint melodies of a swing band pulsed out the windows of Gold Mountain Resort. Dave Grant felt the crisp touch of winter on his skin.

"Almost time," he murmured.

The world turned toward the closing of a season. The resort glistened, hard as diamonds, inscrutable. The glow of lights fell out the windows into the gulp of darkness. The wealthy gathered in their gowns and evening jackets for the annual Gold Mountain charitable soiree.

Dave tied the apron strings around his waist and smoothed the black fabric of his shirt. He breathed the startling clarity of late autumn once more, and then ducked back into the belly of the beast.

He whirred among the guests with a plate of delicacies balanced on his palm. He bowed his head to congressmen he knew quite well, watching their eyes pass over him without recognition. He poured champagne for women who had once tried to seduce him. He served them all, invisible.

Hosting the event cost a fortune, but at the end of the evening, millions would slide through hands as the rich saved hundreds of millions by evading taxes and secured countless deals through the cover of the nonprofit's fundraiser.

The charade weighed unbearably on Dave. A troupe of girls from the women's shelter sang *Ave Maria* to the guests. A senator's daughter screeched *Ode to Joy* on the cello. The CEOs of mega-corporations made pithy toasts about the merits of contributing to worthy causes.

"Lies," Dave muttered. "All of it is lies."

Drunk on their delusions, the wealthy applauded their charity, writing checks and cooing over the wings of museums that would immortalize their names. They applauded generosity while calculating how much tax money they would save. They competed for magnanimity, tittering over the silent auction.

"It's all for a good cause!" they claimed.

And the sycophants hovered, salivating, cajoling, enticing, flattering, convincing the wealthy that giving money in charitable donations justified the immorality of the ways the fortunes had been built.

"Can you be a billionaire and a buddha?" Joan had asked him, once.

Serving caviar to gold-decked hands, he answered silently.

My love, the question is not 'can you?' but 'why would you?'

Anything is possible in the realms of the enlightened, but why would an enlightened being perpetuate the delusions of riches, money, ego, and wealth?

It is all nonsense, Dave thought, and worse than nonsense. Delusions of grandeur were often bought at the price of another person's suffering. Every penny of the wealthy has been taken from the poor.

If the Buddha ran a business, it would not turn a profit. The workers would earn a living wage, the suppliers' children would be well fed, the products would be affordable, and the Earth would not be devastated and destroyed for the sake of profits.

And if even one of these wealthy benefactors understood this concept, lived by it, ran their business by this concept, it would be more beneficial than all the charitable donations of all the rich people in the world.

After all, what is charity but a cruel joke? It's a mockery of the masses - the powerful take all the wealth and hand a penny back to the people. They chastise the poor for fighting tooth-and-nail over scraps from the rich man's banquet table. What is charity but the snobbery of those who have taken more than they need? They give to operas and theatres, art museums, and private schools. They fund a culture of devotion to the wealthy. They support Cinderella stories in which the hero's quest centers on becoming a rich man by hoarding money from the poor. They endow scientific institutions that generate convenient facts. They finance research for technology that serves their profits. That's not charity; it's investment, and tax-deductible at that. They fund education for the specialists their companies will need. They give money to the non-profits of sons-in-laws of influential politicians.

The charity of the wealthy, Dave scowled, is not charity.

It's greed.

Dave Grant stilled in the swirling hall of silks and chiffons. The Number's craggy face rose in his memory. *Remember, Dave,* the Number had said, *what happens next was set in motion lifetimes ago.* Once, the Number had taken a life. Once, he had given his life for Dave. Once, Dave had refused to cooperate with a system that profited from human suffering . . . he could not serve it here.

He put the platter down on a side table, walked back to the kitchen, removed his apron, and paused.

Beyond quitting, there was more that he could do.

Dave Grant drew a shaky breath. He swallowed. He tucked his black shirt into his black trousers and stepped around to the front of the resort. With each step, he picked up the threads of a story he had dropped long ago. He claimed Gold Mountain. He owned his wealth. He took on his privilege, race, and class. He stood taller and gathered up the arrogance, the certainty, the sheer power he commanded. The manager took one look at him and shut his gaping mouth. The hostess moved to ask his name and halted in mid-sentence. The event coordinator saw his face and reached to open the door.

Dave Grant stepped onto Gold Mountain and the room froze in recognition.

"Good evening," he began simply.

A stunned silence hung over the room, pregnant with rumors. Quick, darting eyes took in his leanness, his somber attire, and his quiet, powerful stance. They identified him instantly. For years, they had swapped gossip about the downfall of Dave Grant. Then he fell off the radar of the wealthy class and entered oblivion in the ranks of the poor. Seven years slipped by faster than snowmelt off the mountains. The women nipped and tucked their youth in place. The men panicked and bought sports cars. Affairs sparked, surfaced, scandalized, and subsided. Deals came through and fell apart. Life dragged the wealthy forward by the coattails.

Dave Grant returned to Gold Mountain.

"I thought," he said softly as they leaned in to catch his words, "tonight would be a good time to show up. The stars are beautiful. The night shines clearer than a diamond."

They stirred a little at that. Dave smiled with the look of the ancients.

"I have been gone seven years," he mentioned. "A perfect odyssey, is it not? Tonight is about charity and giving, something I have learned much of in this time."

The guests stood spellbound in place, waiting for the delicious gossip of his past. The man bore nothing reminiscent of the obese patriarch of Gold Mountain . . . except those eyes. Those blue eyes, they all remembered.

In the crowd, a doctor shuddered. Those eyes were

diamonds, sharp and hard, a blue that sparked in the caverns of his face - cutting eyes that slashed through facades of silks and gowns and sliced the soul to shreds.

"I have slept in gutters and mansions," Dave began. His voice fell into a soft intonation, mimicking the rhythm of the sutras. "I have sat in teahouses and redwood forests. I have been locked in solitary confinement and in the embrace of my beloved."

He glanced around the room, almost amused by the frozen figures, immobilized with wine glasses poised halfway to lips and hors d'oevres forgotten in manicured hands. The theatre of the moment swept them up; they were swallowed by his appearance and his story. Their bodies, worries, lives, and conceits dropped from their thoughts for a moment. The element of surprise stuck its foot in the door of possibility. Now it was up to Dave to shove it open all the way.

"I left Gold Mountain with half a fortune - more than most of humanity ever dreams of seeing. I squandered every penny down to nothing. I begged for food and slept in shelters."

His blue eyes implored them to understand.

"I know something of the art of charity. I have given small fortunes to single mothers in rolls of hundred dollar bills. I have received a handful of pocket change and wept with gratitude. I have walked in the ranks of the rich and the poor, and there is one thing I have learned.

"The poor do not need your charity. They need equality and justice. They do not need to be robbed of a decent life so that you can give back mere shreds of their survival. Our wealth devours dignity. Their children's future lies in the mortar of our mansions. Their parents' hard work formed the bricks of our success. We hand out trinkets, baubles, pittances; we throw coins from carriages lined with gold. What we give away is nothing to us; what we take away is everything to them."

The wealthy were balking like sheep that sense the wolf circling their pen. They could smell danger in the night. Dave grasped command of the room with a bark of his voice.

"We have taken hope and turned it into golf courses! We have taken small joys and filled our pools with them. We have taken elements of their survival and served them up as delicacies on our silver platters."

He moved. They were twitching nervously, ready to bolt. He stretched one foot forward and took a step. When the sheep begin to stir, the master must steer them in a direction. He circled the main hall, slowly. Their eyes followed his every move.

"This is what I saw with my own eyes when I descended from Gold Mountain. But there is more and listen closely, for this pertains to you."

He aligned himself with them, with wealth. He clasped his hands behind his back in a gesture they recognized from the Dave Grant of old, the owner of resorts and privileges, the man who had paced their homes that way.

"The masses are stirring."

They flinched at the words all elites fear.

"The people are roiling, rumbling."

Heart rates quickened. Fingernails bit into palms.

"They cry for bread; we stock the shelves with cake." He pointed to the silent auction. "Heads will roll because of this."

Massaged backs stiffened. Mouths pulled into scowls.

"The ingrates," someone muttered.

Dave laughed in a sound as dry as desert sand.

"Why should they be grateful? Their mothers work three jobs. Their schools are crumbling and overcrowded. Their sons are sent to die in wars. Their daughters are forced into prostitution to pay the rent. Their children's fathers are locked in prisons. Their sisters and brothers are looking for work. Drug dealers are the only employers hiring. And they're supposed to thank us for all of this?"

His voice rumbled like thunder, unstoppable, saying words that no one had ever dared to speak in cathedrals of the wealthy. On the street corners, the prophets cried of the coming apocalypse. In the ranks of the poor, the revolutionaries foretold the fall of empires. But in a world of seven billion souls, only one man was poised to deliver this warning to the rich.

"We sit in their halls of power. We own their land. We hold their wealth. We can move mountains or blow them up. We can buy up the stars and name them after ourselves. We can launch wars of utter annihilation. We have the power to make change."

He paced as he spoke, striding rhythmically, circling, mesmerizing, forcing them to turn, turn around the room, turn around themselves, turn in a full revolution, turn and return to the place where everything began.

"They will rise up and take it back. They have to if they are to survive. They may riot. They may organize. But, either way, it is only a matter of time. All our preparations: armies, strategies, surveillance, police, prisons - these are nothing to a father's love for the dying child in his arms. They will not stop determined mothers who see your children growing fat. They will not restrain the righteous youths whose innate sense of equality and justice rebels against oppression. There is only one thing that will save us."

He stilled, suddenly, absolutely, exactly at the starting point framed by the arches of the entrance.

"Give it back to them."

Those diamond eyes swept the room, leaving not one of

them exempt.

"Rebuild equality and justice, pour the profits into the people, restore the public schools and services, pay your taxes, honor debts, take no profit from your work. Pay yourself a living wage and nothing more. Live simply. Be humble. Become one among the many.

"In return, you will receive security in equality; brotherhood in justice; companionship in solidarity; community in mutual prosperity. You will lose your fear of those in poverty. You will lose the unbearable loneliness of our lives."

He stood then as a human being, one who had suffered and struggled, a Dave Grant who had nearly died of loneliness and separation, a man who knew the pain of isolation. He stood as a mere mortal who had lived and lost and learned to love, who had been touched by kindness and restored by soup, who had walked miles in many shoes until he wore all shoes off his footsteps. He stood as one among the many, humbled by them all.

Those diamond-eyes blazed with sharp compassion. The blue ached for the hard words he had delivered. He had stirred uneasy feelings and resentments. He had shattered the evening for them all. The charity would flounder - who could bid on the auction after this? They would stand around awkwardly for a short while then leave as swiftly as they could. He released the power of commanding presence; shock would hold them now. He spoke as gently as he started, beginning with charity again.

"I have learned something about charity in these seven years. We don't need charity, any of us, rich or poor. What we all need is equality, so we can stand side by side again. So we can look each other in the eyes. So we can live and love once more."

But, there was more to say, Dave realized, for the wisdom

of the buddhas began to hum inside his chest. There is the perfection of charity and he must speak to this before they left.

"I want to make a gift tonight," he said. Speeches alone would not suffice. "A perfect gift, an unexcelled gift, one that is unsurpassed."

He walked now to the center of the hall, looking up and around as if pondering which piece of art or statue or gold leafed trim or beams of Mayan temple wood he would sacrifice to show his generosity. They pivoted to watch him, fascinated despite themselves. As in the folktales, some choices might bring disaster; others could shower riches, but only one answer would end all suffering.

What would Dave Grant give?

"I have urged us all to give everything away," he told them. "And now I should practice what I preach."

The breaths caught sharply in throats and chests. Whispered phrases shot out.

"My god!"

"He's insane!"

"He won't do it."

"He's going to give Gold Mountain to charity!"

"Not to charity," he corrected, smiling. "To the perfection of charity."

He paused, for he could feel the buddhas and bhagavans, tathagatas, and fully enlightened ones amassing. The crossroads gathered and surrounded him in all directions like a thousand roads conjoining in a great intersection of the realms.

"Liberation is the greatest gift, but I cannot give what I do not own," he said. "And what I claimed to own was never mine. For the mountains and the forest do not belong to humans. The rivers, birds, and beasts are no more our slaves than our fellow man. How can I claim to own these beings, when in truth, we are part of one another? The deer, the water, the minerals; these are not objects to possess and control. They are part of my interconnected being; I am neither owner nor master of them.

"So, to whom do I give the gift of liberation? Who is being liberated from what?"

He chuckled to himself, for there was only one thing he could give.

"I give up my delusion of ownership, and give everything back to itself: the rivers to the rivers; the trees to the trees; the minerals of Gold Mountain to themselves." His eyes crinkled in an inexpressible burst of laughter. "And though I say, I give everything back to itself, that is not exactly true. There is only one thing I give back to itself . . . and that, of course, is me."

The slave owner emancipates himself from the shame of enslaving other men. He releases the cause of his own confusion, his own suffering, his own agony and living hell. Thus, though he liberates hundreds of beings, he, in truth, emancipates himself.

The same is true for all property, trees, land, objects, wealth. Not one being belongs to another. We belong together, side by side, in an interconnected web of existence, forming the great body of the Earth.

Dave Grant closed his eyes. The room stood silent, shocked. But the realms of the invisible crossroads roared with thunder, for the Billionaire Buddha had finally awakened.

CHAPTER THIRTY-ONE

· · · · ·

She waited. Just beyond the front door, standing calmly, eternally, her feet rooted to the hewn-stone driveway, she placed her hands together and waited. Half concealed in the fold of night, she heard his words tumble out the open windows like beads on a prayer mala.

It is rare, oh Bhagavan, say the sutras, *most rare indeed, to be showered with the best of blessings and trusted with the greatest of trusts.*

The best of blessings is to hear the truth.

The greatest of trusts is to be in the right time at the right place to hear the words of the enlightened ones.

And while the guests inside the hall streamed out and parted like a river around the standing stone of Joan, she stood among the silent assembly of those who honored the words spoken by Dave Grant: the trees, the grasses, the stars strewn across the sky, the creeping beasts and birds rustling in the dark, the unseen hosts assembled at the crossroads, the buddhas, spirits, saints, bodhisattvas, sages, and mystics. Joan stood assembled with them all, listening to the sutra on Gold Mountain.

He left the hall with a consternated horde of mayflies swarming in his wake. Human beings buzzed and whined, appalled by what he said.

Joan waited. As he had once sat against a red door, she now stood framed against a dark night of searching. Cops had run her out of town; the thread of their connection snapped. She heard he had been released. She searched for him by name, by number, by description, but he had simply disappeared. Public records lay in shambles; whole lives slipped between those cracks, so she retreated for a moment, searching the inner realms for clues. In her quiet meditations, she saw him walking - walking upwards, one footstep higher than the next. She recognized the long slope of the continent leading from the coastline to the mountain.

So, she came.

The spill of light from the hall carved gold around his body. The shadow of the night hid his expression from her eyes. Blue, black, and formless, ringed in gold, he took three steps and paused.

The light which hid him, revealed her. It shone on her face, touched the sweep of hair that fell unbound, blazed in the depths of her dark eyes, and illuminated the great patience of her stance.

"Joan," he sighed as relief. Longing pulled his feet into motion and uprooted her from her stance. Like trees torn up in a flashflood, they crashed into one another in a tangle of arms and limbs.

"Joan," he repeated, his voice murmuring in her hair, his cheek damp against her own.

"I looked for you, but couldn't find you," she said.

A chuckle rumbled in his chest.

"It's a side effect of awakening," he teased. "No self, no being, no life, no soul. Nothing to be found."

"You might have left a note," she shot back.

Laughter burst from them both, bouncing off the steeped rooftop of the resort, rustling the pines, startling the people congregated to either side of them.

"Mr. Grant," a man interjected with a tone of indignation. "I don't mean to interrupt - "

"Of course you do," Joan retorted, "otherwise you wouldn't

have."

Dave's grin cracked the horizons of his face as Joan drew her mental sword.

"I'm sorry to intrude, but - " the man grunted impatiently.

Joan spun to face him. A flash of fire glinted in her eyes.

Not as sorry as you're going to be, Dave thought.

"Mr. Grant," the man directed his words to Dave, dismissing Joan. "You can't be serious about what you said back there."

"Why can't I?" Dave replied.

"Well, it's preposterous! You can't set fifteen hundred acres of land free!"

Joan's laughter touched the treetops.

"You're absolutely right," she told the startled man. "It is preposterous to set free that which cannot be enslaved or owned."

"Ah," Dave sighed in delight. "So you heard."

"Every word," she confirmed.

He hugged her to his side, suddenly teary-eyed with gratitude as a contingent of people from the charity dinner gathered around, burning with arguments and questions. Doubters, naysayers, and shocked wealthy patrons of Gold Mountain drew close to demand answers.

Without Joan, Dave thought, they might have torn him to pieces.

But Joan stood like a fighter; fierce, confident, quick on her feet and ready to cross the swords of logic and philosophy. When the man began again, she turned squarely to face him, the defender of the realm Dave set forth in words.

"You can't liberate land," the man argued.

"Did you not hear a word Dave said?" Joan challenged him. "You don't free land. You free yourself from the delusion of ownership."

"Yes, but someone has to own it!" the man insisted. "Mr. Grant must sell it!"

"Why?" Joan demanded.

"Look here, Grant," someone called out. "I'll buy it off you for ten times its worth."

"How can you measure that which has been released from our notions of value?" Joan shot back. It was invaluable, beyond measure, surpassing all comprehension. People balked in utter terror at the idea of liberated land. A senator belligerently threatened to invade and conquer the only patch of free land in the entire world, to take it back into possession of the United States of America.

"We will stop you," Joan declared, the vision of her namesake burning in her, a woman rallying the troops. "We will resist you with every method of nonviolent struggle available. We will bog you down in lawsuits. We will make a public relations nightmare. We will launch boycotts of your businesses until you retreat."

"But it's not legal to give the land to itself," a lawyer protested.

"I'll sign a quit-claim in favor of the natural systems," Dave said, "and leave the land to the land, the trees to the trees, the river to the river, and so on."

"It will never stand in court," the lawyer claimed.

"If it will not stand in court, then it reverts to Dave," Joan pointed out.

"And if it reverts to me," Dave said, "I'll free myself and every other human being from this delusion that we can own it."

They scoffed at him, claimed he had gone mad, accused him of joining a cult.

"You parade around here like you're Buddha, preaching to us about sin - " one woman shrieked furiously at him.

Joan leapt in front of the woman's pointed fingernails, protecting Dave with words.

"The Buddha is not some Asian Jesus," she shot back. "The Buddha is an understanding, not a person. Think of an ecosystem - the shore of the ocean, rocks, starfish, water, salt, sand, seaweed, fisherman, nets - the Buddha isn't the fisherman, no matter how enlightened the fisherman claims to be. The Buddha is the whole ecosystem from the water to the salt to the sea foam spraying in the air. The Buddha is that everything, and also the spaces in between. Occasionally," Joan said wryly, "a human being happens to figure this out. Dave is not the Buddha. The Buddha is Dave and you and me and this resort and city slums and poverty - "

"So, why does the Buddha make poverty?" the woman interjected.

Joan tilted her chin up and quickly fired back a retort.

"You tell me, oh Buddha," she challenged the woman, "and you and you and you," she pointed around the crowd. "Why do you make poverty and starvation, hunger, sickness, wars and prisons?"

Dave put his hand on Joan's arm.

"Forgive them, love," he murmured, quoting Jesus, "for they know not what they do. We've been crucifying ourselves in ignorance."

He hesitated . . . then grinned.

"But now you know. So, stop it."

CHAPTER THIRTY-TWO

. . . . .

The rich left Gold Mountain in utter fury. The event coordinator resigned in tears. The woods and streams rejoiced.

Dave shut Gold Mountain down. The charitable event was supposed to cover the resort's on-going losses. The wealthy homeowners all knew that. Their charity was an investment in the value of their property by ensuring the resort's continuation and earning them a sizable tax deduction. But now that Dave had ended property and values, the worth of the subdivision crashed.

A week dragged by in a tedious stream of supplicants who begged him to reconsider, including the townspeople, the city council, the county commissioners, and the local business association. A couple of the more prosperous artists flew off the handle at him. The wait staff finished up their last days in tight-lipped fury at his lunacy. The sommeliers cursed him. Someone sent a death threat.

But the trees rustled on the mountain slopes and autumn drew golden in a blush of glory. The nights turned taut with frost.

"Maybe you'll open in the spring?" people asked hopefully.

Dave shook his head and shrugged. Spring lay beyond the eternity of winter, shrouded in the shifting mists of now.

One evening, Dave stood up from shutting off sprinkler heads on the golf course and stretched in the sunset. The last fingers of light traced the cheek of free land with a lover's hand. He heard the sounds of footsteps behind him and whirled. A smile broke over his face as he recognized the wiry figure coming up the slope.

"Larry Boggs."

"Dave Grant."

The two men regarded each other in the fading light. The catskinner stood with his thumbs hooked into his belt lops, scuffing the grass with the toe of his worn hiking boots.

"Is it true?" Larry asked. "Did you give the land back to itself?"

Dave nodded.

Larry's eyes shut over his smile. He looked up and reached out a calloused hand.

"Welcome back," Larry said.

"You, too," Dave replied. "I heard you were up in the high country planting trees."

The man's smile deepened in satisfied creases.

"I was. Had both my boys up there with me. The younger one's sixteen - remember how we used to bolt his car seat to the backhoe?"

Dave nodded, stunned by the way time passes. Babies grow into boys; boys challenge the edge of manhood; Larry Boggs had hardly been housebroken when he started working for Dave, now he stood in his prime with his teenage sons working alongside him.

"Did you just get in?" Dave asked.

"This afternoon. My wife told me what you had done . . . and I'd thought I'd come up."

Larry squinted into the sunset.

"You're going to have some time on your hands," Larry mentioned.

"I suppose," Dave agreed.

"You oughta come plant trees with me," Larry offered. "By the time you're a hundred, we'll have replanted everything you cut down."

"I doubt it," Dave replied ruefully. "I suspect there's several lifetimes of planting trees ahead of me to account for all my crimes."

"Mmm," Larry muttered. He snuck a glance at Dave. "Do you . . . do you ever wonder if we were right to build this place?"

Dave stood as still as a statue.

"It just seems to me that what we did up here - " Larry broke off, staring at the peaked roofs of the resort. "It's a thing of the past," he said finally. "Like lords and ladies. Like dinosaurs and dodo birds. I watch my sons - and all the kids - and whether they grow up rich or poor, they've got a world of trouble. Nobody on this earth has time to waste knocking little white balls around golf courses."

Larry spat onto the green. Dave remained silent, letting the other man talk.

"The young folks are different from us," Larry declared. "They're chatting with people all over the world. A fly sneezes in Hong Kong and my son gets a text message about the chain of events that led up to the hurricane in Cancun. Can you imagine? It's a different world. I'm not sure it has a place for Gold Mountains - not when the kids know that half of the Appalachia Mountains have been blown into smithereens. They want to *do* something about that, not ignore it."

Larry smiled shyly and proudly.

"My younger boy, you remember how he couldn't keep his hands out of machines?"

Dave nodded. The troublemaker had pulled apart his golf cart, a lawn mower, and the resort's floor waxing machine before Dave caught onto the cause of his mechanical glitches. He'd hollered at Larry to enroll the kid in vo-tech instead of bringing him to work at the resort.

"He took a green industries course online," Larry told him,

"and that darn kid converted my old pickup to bio-diesel. Can you imagine?"

Larry's smile shown brighter than the golden rays of sunset.

"My older boy, I took him up planting trees in that nasty clear cut someone got through the county permit process. It's my boy's last summer home; goes off to college this year. Says he wants to study poetry. Can you imagine? Me, with a poet for a son!"

Larry shook his head, incredulous.

"We went up planting trees and it was Gary Snyder this and John Muir that. 'Look Dad,' he'd say. 'Look at that cloud! It's a perfection of a poem - that's Ginsberg, Dad.' And I didn't chew him out for thinking I grew up with my head under a bucket - I know who Al Ginsberg is, for chrissake - because the kid was right, that cloud was a perfect poem.

"'You know what's poetry, son?' I said to him. 'This.' I pointed to the burned out slope and the saplings coming back. I gestured to the whole crazy world messed up by people like me and you. I pointed to his strong young back. I rolled his muscles and mine up in that one word, *This,* and I meant that the poetry is both of us working together to set things right.

"'Son,' I told him, 'you study hard, because the world needs great poets to capture these times we're living through. Only poets can do it, not scientists or reporters.'"

Larry laughed at the memory.

"I grabbed hold of his shoulders, all serious-like. 'Son,' I said, 'I'll love you even if you never write a word . . . but if you can write down the changes pulsing through this world, why, the angels in heaven will weep with gratitude until the Earth is washed fresh and clean again.'"

Larry stopped, breathless and smiling.

"You know what that boy said?" he asked Dave.

Dave shook his head.

"'Dad,' he said, 'maybe you oughta start writing poetry, too.'"

Larry's laughter bounded from his chest and startled a flock of birds out from the pine trees.

"Can you imagine?!" he hooted.

Can you imagine? the mountains echoed. *Imagine,* the wind sighed. *Imagine,* the grasses whispered. *Imagine,* the earth hummed. Imagine that a man - a world - could change so much that he begins to speak in poetry. Imagine that one generation could change the course of all the generations of humanity yet to come. Imagine that the human story does not end in the chapter of today.

Can you imagine? the whole world wondered.

Dave smiled and quietly answered.

"I can."

They stood in the growing darkness, talking in somber tones. Larry's voice rumbled down the mountain. Dave's murmurs flowed softly like a stream. He asked Larry for a favor. The younger man's wordless exclamation punctured the quiet of the night. Dave quietly explained. Larry shook his head and spoke. Dave nodded. They shook hands and parted.

Dave locked the doors of the resort and hiked down the hill to Edna's, where the old lady sat quietly with the days, waiting patiently for death. She insisted Joan and Dave stay in the spare bedroom as the nights grew sharp with the breath of winter. Joan helped her around the house, spending hours talking esoteric Buddhist philosophy with Edna, pulling out dusty sutras from the collection in the living room and teasing apart nuances of wisdom.

Dave climbed the porch steps, listening to the creak and groan of the wooden boards. A whiff of wood smoke wafted past his nostrils and his breath turned white on the air.

"It's going to be cold tonight," he announced as he came in the door and kicked off his boots. "From the looks of the clouds, the peaks might get snow."

Edna's thin quaver called back from the kitchen.

"Might even get a few flakes down here. Seems ripe for an early snow."

He poked his head around the doorframe. Soup boiled on the stove and the windows fogged up with steam. Joan wiped her hands on a towel as she came to greet him.

"Oooh," she shivered as he pulled her close, "you brought the night in with you."

"You smell good," he murmured into her hair. Scents of pumpkin and black pepper filled his nostrils.

She smiled and pulled away to remove the soup from the stove.

"Wash up," she suggested.

He ran his chilled fingers under the hot water, shut off the tap, and carefully lathered the dirt-lined creases. His brow furrowed as he scrubbed under his fingernails. The sights and smells of the kitchen seemed sharper than usual. Colors burst with vitality: the blue-gray pottery bowls on the red tablecloth, the sheen of the stainless steel soup pot, the orange of the pumpkin soup. The sound of Joan and Edna's soft exchange touched his eardrums with crisp precision. He rinsed his hands and the sensation of the water flooded him.

Dave joined the women at the table. Joan held out her hands for a quiet blessing. Dave clasped her slender, warm palm in one hand and held the trembling knobs of Edna's arthritic fingers in the other. He closed his eyes and thanked the world

314

for Joan, for Edna's generosity, for the soup, for the warmth. He was filled with the achy feeling that comes with the last streaks of light in a dying sunset. Larry's words about the changing world returned to him. He gave thanks for the ending of centuries of destruction. Emotion pushed against his closed eyelids as he imagined a world beyond everything he had ever known, a world that had no need of Gold Mountains, a world without insatiable cravings for wealth and power, a world that viewed amassing fortunes as an obsolete approach to finding happiness. The women squeezed his hands and a smile burst across his lips.

"Thank you," he said as his eyes opened to the world.

He released their hands and reached to ladle the steaming pumpkin soup into the bowls.

"It took you a long time up on the mountain," Joan remarked. "It was dark when you came in."

"Larry Boggs stopped by," he answered.

"Did he?" Edna asked curiously. "He's down from the high country, then? Must be cold up at that altitude."

Dave nodded. Paused. Dipped a chunk of whole wheat bread into the soup.

"I asked him to plow up the golf course."

Edna dropped her spoon.

"Well!" she exclaimed. "I suppose that'll answer the question of whether or not you'll reopen in the spring."

Her shoulders shook with humor and her eyes turned bright.

"Seems fitting to me. Larry Boggs broke ground on Gold Mountain. Now he'll break greens at the end."

Dave shook his head.

"Larry refused to do it," he commented. "He told me to just shut off the water and let nature take it's course."

Edna's papery lips curled in a smile. After conquering golfers for nearly two decades, the dragon-like course winding sinuously through the forest would be conquered by drought and hardy mountain grasses, hungry deer and shrubs. The old woman sighed. It all comes full circle, doesn't it? Nothing lasts; everything changes. The old gives way to the new. Beginnings and endings and beginnings again. Empires rose and fell. Eras drew to a close. Capitalism breathed raggedly on its deathbed. Consumerism began a cycle of fasting and prayer. Somewhere on Earth, the edge of the night gave way to the dawn. A lonely planet spun silently through the vast darkness of space. Three humans rode on her back, quietly eating their soup.

The moon rose at midnight. Dave tossed restlessly in the bed. The pale light tapped insistently on his eyelids. He opened them. Joan stood by the window, wide-awake, fully clothed, gazing at the round moon as it crested the treetops and rose in the sky. He sat up. Joan turned at the sound of the creaking mattress. The moonlight laid down a river of silver on the black landscape of her hair.

"Are you awake?" she whispered.

He hushed her as he rose, murmuring in her ear.

"Let's go walking."

He fumbled for his jeans and pulled his shirt over his head. They dressed warmly, but the cold snapped their cheeks as they slipped out of the house. They walked briskly up the deer trail, stirring their blood and bringing a flush of warmth into their skin. The trees took on the stature of giants, looming tall and silver, shadowed in midnight blues and blacks. As they moved along the forest trail, Dave shivered at the sense of the crossroads assembling at the intersection of this night. The darkness grew potent with the unknown. The woods seemed alive in the moonlight. Dave squinted at boulders he did not remember, half-convinced that inanimate rocks could walk on such a night as this.

"Where are we going?" Joan asked softly.

He didn't answer, but she knew. The path led to Gold Mountain.

"We built it like a holy place," he murmured, "like a shrine. We used the foundation stones of Aztec ruins and beams of Mayan temples. We were madmen raiding the tombs of collapsed and crumbling civilizations. We built a temple . . . to what? To whom? We never asked. Not consciously. Over time, it became self-evident: we built Gold Mountain to glorify wealth and all that wealth entails."

They broke out of the woods onto the flat expanse of the golf course. In the moonlight, the close-shorn green heaved in silver, ocean-like swells. The larger meadow grasses on the edge of the green rippled in the wind, trembling. It was an ocean of sorrow, a green course that epitomized leisure, wealth, and class. Dave and Joan crossed it quickly.

"Joan?" he began.

"Yes?"

"Would you - can you wait for me by the trees?"

She looked at him curiously.

"I'll be right back," he murmured. "There's something I need to do."

She nodded.

He kissed her and squeezed her fingers before darting down the slope toward the resort. As he drew close, he dug in his pocket for the keys. He unlocked the front door and entered. He stood in the main hall under the high peaked ceiling with the inlaid mosaics of precious woods. Wrested from the empires of the past, designed in the architecture of cathedrals, hallowed by the unchallenged sanctity of wealth and property, Gold Mountain's resort proclaimed itself a temple to the idolatry of greed. Here, the wealthy came to worship wealth. The incense of obsession infused the rooms. The taint of cruelty and callousness seethed beneath the surface.

"So long as you stand," Dave declared softly, "you will spin the wheel of suffering."

In his mind, he bid goodbye to the hall of wealth. He bid goodbye to luxury, to poverty, to inequality. He circled the vaulted dining room, pausing by the main entrance. His fingers clasped the door handles. A smile curled over his lips.

"How should I explain it?" Dave murmured, referencing a line in *The Diamond Sutra*. His gaze passed around the dark shadows of the room as he recited the final words of the sutra.

"As a lamp, a cataract, a star in space,

an illusion, a dewdrop, a bubble,

a dream, a cloud, a flash of lightning

view all created things like this."

He flung open the front doors and spread his arms to the night.

"Come!" he cried.

And the cold rushed into his arms.

"Come darkness!" he invited. "Come creeping beasts. Come daybreak and sunlight and tiny songbirds. Come, make your nests in the rafters of this hall."

He spun and walked slowly through the building, opening the doors of Gold Mountain, one by one. He propped open the sliding doors to the poolroom and stared at the sheet of still, silent water. With the long crank, he opened the skylights in the glass ceiling. A waterfall of cold air poured in, drenching him with chills.

"Come snow," he whispered. "Pile upon the roof until the sun sends you sliding down the glass and through the skylights, along the walls, across the tiles, and seeping into floorboards. Come rain and flood this cavernous building like the mountainsides. Let mold and mildew have their turn."

He opened all the windows, sliding them up with a gasp of sound.

"Come stars," he breathed.

He ran his hand along the polished veneers then bent to the corner of the wall and floor, inviting the tiny insects in. He rose and crossed to the open doors of the main entrance. He flung his arms wide to the sky. Clouds rushed across the black silhouettes of mountains, sweeping in churning masses overhead as the wind flung westward.

"Come!" he called into the blackness. "Come elk; come deer, come lumbering bear. Come take humanity's place."

He stood to the side of the door like a concierge awaiting the arrival of Gold Mountain's newest guests. With a sweep of his arm, he welcomed winged birds, mountain goats, meadow grasses, swaying saplings, buzzing swarms of bees, streams of migrating butterflies, coyote packs and pairs of foxes, solitary cougars, and long-forgotten wolves.

Dave laughed breathlessly into the night. The white frost of his breath hung like prophecies on the air. He whirled and crouched down in the garden. His fingers searched the darkness until a thread of ivy curled around his knuckles.

"Come ivy," he murmured. "Come. The mortar of the building is yours to crumble. The stones and concrete are yours to crush. The roof is yours to climb and collapse. Come, ivy, come."

He rose and backed away from the building. The wind swept in the open windows and rushed through doors, breathing into the hollow structure like a flute. The night vibrated with the low moaning music of the wind through window frames. Exaltation burst in Dave Grant's chest.

"Take it!" he cried, gesturing to the building. "Take it as you take my breath, bones, and body!"

The cold reached down to shake the foundation stones. The night slipped through open skylights. Dry leaves rode the wind through doorways. A mouse cautiously crept across the threshold. The grasses quivered. Roots curled toward the building. The world trembled in anticipation.

"Come!" he called.

Then he ran into the starkness of the night. The taste of snow filled his mouth. His nostrils puckered in the cold. Dark shapes of clouds hung across the sky. Joan waited on the hillside, wool coat pulled tight around her torso, backlit by the determined moonlight pushing through the thinner banks of clouds. As he approached, Dave felt dampness fall onto his cheeks. He reached his hand to touch the unexpected tears, then glanced quickly up.

"Joan, look! *Snow!*"

The flakes tumbled from the sky. Tiny white diamonds clung to the pine trees, to his eyelashes, and to the unbound river of Joan's black hair. She held up her hand in awe. Her fingers gleamed pale against the backdrop of the night. The sky shook with silent thunder. Liberation rose in the voiceless throats of the forest. A lion's roar of emancipation erupted from the earth. Joan's laugh leapt across the slope and resounded on the other side of the mountain.

"Gate!" she whooped.

Gate, gate! the mountains echoed back. *Go, go!*

"Paragate!" she chanted. *Go beyond.*

Parasangate! they refrained. *Go beyond the beyond!*

"Bodhi svaha!" she cried.

Ha . . .hah . . ah, the mountains sighed.

"All together go," Joan whispered quietly. The mountains, trees, Dave, Joan, rich, poor; all together go beyond the beyond of anything you can conceive and something inconceivable will emerge.

Down the slopes of the mountain, an old woman sat in her glider. Her ancient eyes traced the black slope of the ridge. Banks of clouds parted and the moonlight pierced the swirling snowflakes. Impermanence and emptiness shifted the world. The end of an era drew as close as the night. The lineage of gold seekers concluded in her blood. The breath of conquest slowed in her chest. Darkness fell on one cheek. Moonlight illuminated the other. Her eyes flickered once. Then they closed on this world with a smile.

Gate, gate, paragate, parasangate, bodhi svaha!

To all the Billionaire Buddhas awakening:
for the good of the world
and the well-being of all,
give it back,
with love,

Rivera Sun

A Message From
The Man Who Inspired *Billionaire Buddha*

Billionaire Buddha is fiction, but it is inspired by the true story of my life! The beaten little boy, the fabulously rich man, the seeker, the man that gives it all away, and finally the man that sees what it is to have a heart, to care, to love and be loved by others, and to know the importance of telling the world this story – all of those are me.

For much of my life I was extremely wealthy. I had it all. A beautiful wife, a home that had been featured in national magazines, a recreational complex that had been designed by Frank Lloyd Wright, gold, diamonds, golf and ski resorts, tracts of land, stunning art, expensive cars, more money than most people will see in thousands of lifetimes, and the belief that the person that dies with the most toys wins. The problem was: I was so unhappy I wanted to die. Fortunately, I had a wake-up call, a touch on the back (just like in the novel). I was lucky. I turned my back on wealth; I lost much of it and gave the rest away.

Would I give it all away again?

Of course. Being rich in a world where so many are poor is a sickness. It is a disease of the spirit that eventually kills you. Hoarding more than your fair share of wealth means closing your heart to those around you - it means shutting your heart to both the pain and the love of this world. If I had kept my fortune I would be dead by now. My heart certainly felt like it had died back then.

I learned through my own personal experiences that wealth does not buy happiness. Wealth becomes a barrier that keeps you from the true happiness that comes from your heart.

Today I am penniless and have far more than I could ever imagine existed. Each day I am awakened to the joy of being connected and part of all of life around me. I am able to be with other people and with nature in a way that was impossible for me when I was wealthy. I am one with people and the Earth, no longer the dominator, no longer separate and alone, not idolized, idealized or loathed for being rich. I am filled with the true love for the self and others that comes from the recognition that we are all equal in the heart of creation.

Although I would willingly give my wealth away again today, the *way* in which I would give it away has changed. I would not just turn my back and walk off. I would not fritter it away on diamonds and thousand dollar bottles of wine. I wouldn't give it to charities that simply put band-aids on the sicknesses of our society. Instead of *giving it away*, I would *give it back*. I would give it back to the society that created it: the workers, inventors, teachers, artists, families, communities, natural systems - the whole interconnected web of creation that is the basis of all wealth in this world. I wouldn't stop there either. I would, as I am doing today, join with others in building a movement to share the wealth, to fix the systems that create inequality, and help others rejoin the human family.

Our global society is reaching a crisis where the greed of a few is stifling the flow of resources and limiting our ability to confront the challenges our world faces. Currently, a few individuals are hoarding huge reservoirs of wealth for their personal enjoyment, while the planet and the people are suffering to make them even richer. This is an unsustainable situation, and we must resolve it.

We are all part of the Earth system. We are all part of and co-create the system we live in. Creating systemic change takes each person deciding to do differently, educating and organizing others. We can create a culture of care, of love, and of respect for each other and the earth . . . but each of us must decide to do what we can.

The novel was inspired by my life, but the Billionaire Buddha is not one person. The Billionaire Buddha is all of us *together*. It is the awakened understanding that wealth is created by all of us for the purpose of caring for our whole world. I hope you will join me and many others in making this change happen. Whether you can give of your time, your talent, or your treasure, all hands are needed. The world and our people have hurt long enough. Our time for change is here.

Join us at www.riverasun.com or send an email to info@riverasun.com.

We only have one time. Now is the time. The responsibility is ours!

Thank you,

Dariel Garner

Afterword: Open-Hearted Wealth
by Chuck Collins

Billionaire Buddha is a powerful novel. Behind the novel is the inspiring real journey of Dariel Garner. But he is not on this journey alone. There is an emerging movement of open-hearted wealthy people who believe it is in their deeper interest to move our society away from its current trajectory toward greater wealth polarization and ecological catastrophe.

I was born into the fourth generation of a prosperous Midwestern U.S. meatpacking family. In the early 1980s, I considered giving away inherited assets, but I didn't know anyone else who had made such a choice and lived to tell the story. So, I found a few other young people who were also considering giving away wealth and began a series of life-changing conversations.

We asked everyone we knew: *Do you know anyone who has given away substantial assets or all their wealth?* Over several years, we met over twenty-five people, including Millard Fuller, the founder of Habitat for Humanity, and the spiritual teacher, Ram Dass. They were so inspiring that we collected their interviews in a 1992 book, *We Gave Away A Fortune.*

In 1986, I was personally moved to give away my wealth. If I'd held onto the money, I'd have millions of dollars today. But I have no regrets. And I've met dozens of other people who have taken bold steps towards sharing. Like Dariel, they deeply want to live in a world with greater equality, fairness and harmony with nature.

329

Today, we need wealthy people to step forward and boldly support movements to address the twin challenges of extreme wealth inequality and climate change.

Do you think of yourself as privileged or advantaged? What should we do?

Here are some thoughts on steps and actions, based on conversations with many open-hearted people with wealth and advantage.

1. Connect! It is a rare person who figures out how to make personal and social change alone. We encourage people with wealth to talk to others, including Dariel and I. If you can find two or more people, form a support group to share stories and reflect personally on what to do. Such a group could be face-to-face or over the phone or skype. Dariel and I are also available for one-on-one conversations. We can be reached through www.openheartedwealth.org

2. Personal Reflection and Preparation. Ideally with others, reflect on wealth and opportunity. See the tools and organizations that we've compiled at www.openheartedwealth.org. One of our challenges is to understand and counter the deep myths of deservedness and privilege that come along with wealth. Feeling gratitude for the gifts of the commons and our good fortune is a powerful first step. Reflect on the sources of wealth and ways to keep these gifts in circulation.

- **No Shame. No Hubris**. Sometimes there is shame and guilt attached to wealth, especially in the face of

330

inequality. Sometimes there is arrogance and bravado attached to it, as society fawns over you or over-celebrates your gifts. It is important to remember that this is not personal, but a system of rewards that advantages the few and disadvantages the many. Use your story, wealth and networks to create a world without undue privilege and wealth disparities.

- **Opt Into Society Like an Alma Mater.** Reengage your stake in the smooth functioning of societal institutions. Stop privatizing our needs through the creation of private paradises, private education and transportation, gated or enclave communities, and private recreation. Instead develop a personal stake in good education systems, livable communities, and healthy ecosystems for all. Planting our stake in the commonweal will engage our social capital, time, money, insight and our hearts.

3. Change the Story. One powerful myth that rationalizes wealth inequality is the "I created this wealth alone" story. This myth claims that wealth is entirely a function of one's personal character, effort, and intelligence – rather than cornering a piece of the market. You can help change the narratives that justify inequality by telling your own story through the lens of the help you got along the way.

- **Tell True Wealth Stories.** Help demystify the confusion about wealth, success, and privilege by telling true stories about wealth creation. Tell the truth about your own individual gifts, skills and abilities that you or others have contributed to your good fortune. Also celebrate the help you got and the community's contribution to your circumstances. Talk about the cultural discoveries, scientific contributions, inventions, educational advancements, physical infrastructures like roads or electricity, and other collective efforts that contributed to your success. Reveal the ecological roots of your wealth, even if it is several generations back. Finding ways to publicly tell the true story of your wealth is an important part of shifting the culture.

4. Move the Money Those of us with wealth and power vote with our money several times a day for the kind of world we want to live in. Through spending, giving, and investing, we either reinforce the old fossil fuel economy or move society toward a new equitable and sustainable economy. Divest from wealth-extracting industries and ecologically destructive enterprises. Invest in the real economy of goods and services and place-based enterprises. Invest in a generative economy that creates real wealth and livelihoods and respects nature's boundaries.

- **Share the Wealth - Be a Bolder Giver.** Each of us is immersed in cultural assumptions about giving and charity. Whatever the message, it is probably possible to be bolder. Some of us were told "don't give from assets, only income." But many of us will live good lives, even if we share assets. Get help thinking about your giving – and then give deeply.

- **Fund Change, Not Charity.** Support social movements that are working toward addressing the root causes of social problems, not the surface symptoms. Seek out intermediary social change foundations and share decision-making with community activists in identifying emerging movements with a system change analysis.

- **Move Money and Invest in the Real Economy.** Reduce the demand for the highly speculative financial returns delinked from local communities and the meeting of real needs. Walk away from Wall Street. Invest investment capital in real productive and generative capacity, such as community development banks and credit unions, community loan funds, and high impact funds. Connect with "community investment" and "slow money" movements. Help create new capital markets that steer human energy and resources toward a new economy.

- **Divest from the Fossil Fuels Sector.** Some investments in corporations are more destructive than others. There is one particular industry that is hell-bent on destroying the possibility of a shared future – and they must be stopped immediately. Over the last few years, the 200 largest fossil fuel companies spent over $600 billion annually to identify new carbon assets that if burned would lead to catastrophic climate change. Join the movement to publicly move your own money out of the carbon burning industries and revoke their social license to destroy our habitable planet. Enlist friends, family, family-controlled enterprises and charitable institutions to do the same. Use your leverage as an alumni and donor to other endowed institutions to demand the same.

- **Invest in Broadening Wealth Ownership.** Help build a new sector of economic institutions that are different than absolute absentee ownership – but that broaden enterprise ownership and spread wealth around more broadly. Expand worker and community owned enterprises.

- **Advocate for Tax Fairness and Pay Your Fair Share.** Speak out for a fairer tax system and pay your taxes without aggressive tax avoidance schemes. In the last five decades, the percentage of income paid in taxes by the wealthy has dramatically declined. Just because we don't like every activity of government – or have concerns about government inefficiency - does not justify our withdrawing our funds from the system, or using tax-dodging techniques. The tax code is now porous for the wealthy, thanks to systematic lobbying by anti-tax groups. Commit to not complaining about government in an unconstructive and generalized way. Instead be engaged as an advocate for effective government. Explain to others that no matter what size or function of government, we must have a fair and equitable tax system – where those with the greatest capacity to pay should pay more. The moral rational for a progressive tax system is that those with great wealth have disproportionately benefited from society's investments – and have a special obligation to pay back so that others have similar opportunities.

6. **Help Build a Movement of Open-Hearted Wealthy.** We need to reach out to others with wealth and invite them to the

table. Who else will organize them? These include friends, family, classmates, and other social networks. We need to rise above whatever gets in the way of engaging fully with these potential allies, as it is one of the most important and strategic things we can do.

This is fundamentally heart work. This movement is fundamentally about cracking hearts and minds open, starting with our own. Notice when our hearts are beating, when the goose bumps flow down our backs, when the connections happen with other people. Savor them and make more of them happen every day.

Chuck Collins is a senior scholar at the Institute for Policy Studies where he coordinates their Program on Inequality (www.inequality.org). He is author and co-author of numerous books on inequality, social change philanthropy and tax policy. These ideas are expanded upon in his forthcoming book, *Come Home, Wealthy*. Learn more and join the movement at www.OpenHeartedWealth.org

A Note From Rivera Sun

Eighty thousand words danced across the pages of this novel, and still, this author is left with words stirring in her chest.

So, I wrote an essay detailing strategies for the 100%. It spoke of nonviolent strategies to resolve wealth and income inequality, building new economic systems, resisting injustice, standing up for living wages, halting the flood of wealth to the top, returning wealth to the community. It's very practical; you can read it on my website: www.riverasun.com

But yesterday, the full moon rose on a blood-red eclipse and as the eerie darkness blanked out the pale silver light, the Milky Way suddenly blazed in full glory. My breath caught in my chest and truth tripped me up with love and laughed until I heard the voice of awakening.

I wrote an essay on strategies for the 100% and left out most of the equation.

We live in an interconnected web of existence. Every rock, tree, plant, animal, ocean, stream, cloud, mountain, forest, fungi, bacteria, wind, sunlight is a part of the whole. Humans walk around with our big heads chock full of delusion, thinking our being stops at the edges of our skin . . . but if you can trace your breath to the oxygen in the air and keep following the threads of connection, you can find the truth of who you are.

And so, the question of wealth arises. *Give it back*, the Billionaire Buddha urges, and opens the doors of Gold Mountain to the species of this Earth. Humanity has robbed the wealth of civilizations not only from one another, but also from the lifeblood of our fellow species. For thousands of years, we have cultivated philosophies of separation that allow us to own, control, exploit, and dominate this Earth. We have taken our grossly consumptive cultures from the blood and breath of the wolves, passenger pigeons, blue whales, dolphins, coral reefs, ecosystems, watersheds, and marshes.

Can we give it back? Can we not just leave patches of it alone - can we actively give back what we have taken? Can we restore our relationship to all of creation? Can we invest in healthy ecosystems? Can we assist in the repairing of our endangered oceans? Can we plant forests to catch the excess carbon in the atmosphere? Can we give back some of the land humans monopolize, and allow other species to grow, flourish, and rebound?

Can we give back our philosophies of separation and domination? Can we give back these limited notions of a self that stops at the edges of our skin? Can we somehow find the courage to surrender this concept of our small, separate self, and come home to the interconnected web of our true existence?

It might be relaxing. Saints and sages throughout all time have recommended it.

My colleague, Chuck Collins, encourages the wealthy to give their wealth back to the human family. I encourage all of us to give our selves up to enlightenment. Find out the truth about who - and what - you are. Begin to live as if you really are the whole web of your glorious, humble, heartbreaking, spectacular, soul-shattering, breath-taking, unbelievable, inconceivable self.

True wealth cannot be measured. It lies in the understanding of our infinite, interconnected being-ness. Without this awareness, we are all just beggars in the marketplace of existence.

The Beloved said to Rumi, "Why do you steal diamonds, when you are the stardust and the gravity and the earth and the jeweler and the lover and beloved as well?"

Wake up. Ownership and wealth are poor substitutes for the simple opulence of your true being-ness.

Wake up, my friends, wake up.

Love,

Rivera Sun

Acknowledgements

My heartfelt gratitude goes out to so many people who have contributed to this novel and the long conversations that informed it. Thank you, Dariel Garner, for inspiring the story and making my hair stand on end even as my heart leaped with hope for change. Marirose Nightsong, Cindy Reinhardt, and Jenny Bird provided fresh eyes and insights. These wonderful women have done miracles in trying to eliminate my carelessness and excessive creativity. I wish to thank David and Marilee Wright, tea purveyors, for creating the sanctuary of the Empty Boat, and also the many tea drinkers who congregated there. Thank you, Buddy Comfort, for explaining to me the real reason why the bodhisattvas come back. The author and translator, Red Pine, is a stranger to me, but a great teacher through his *Heart Sutra* and *Diamond Sutra* - he is not to blame for my inventive explanations of Buddhist wisdom. I would also like to thank the Occupy protestors for awakening so many people - including me - to the issue of wealth and income inequality. Chuck Collins has been a great support in finding the language to speak about wealth from a heart-centered approach. And lastly, I wish to thank the Buddha, by which I mean the awakened awareness of our interconnected, impermanent reality that encompasses us all.

About the Author

Rivera Sun is the author of *Billionaire Buddha, The Dandelion Insurrection* and *Steam Drills, Treadmills, and Shooting Stars,* as well as nine plays, a study guide to nonviolent action, a book of poetry, and numerous articles. She has red hair, a twin sister, and a fondness for esoteric mystics. She went to Bennington College to study writing as a Harcourt Scholar and graduated with a degree in dance. She lives in an earthship house in New Mexico, where she grows tomatoes, bakes sourdough bread, and writes poetry, plays, and novels on the side. Rivera has been an aerial dancer, a bike messenger, and a gung-fu style tea server. Everything else about her - except her writing - is perfectly ordinary.

Rivera Sun also loves hearing from her readers.
Email: rivera@riverasun.com
Facebook: Rivera Sun
Twitter: @RiveraSunAuthor
Website: www.riverasun.com

343

"*The Dandelion Insurrection* is an updated, more accurate, less fantastical *Brave New World* or *1984*." - David Swanson, author, peace and democracy activist

". . . a beautifully written book just like the dandelion plant itself, punching holes through the concept of corporate terror and inviting all to join in the insurrection." - Keith McHenry, Co-founder of the Food Not Bombs Movement

"Rivera Sun's *The Dandelion Insurrection* takes place in a dystopia just a hop, skip and jump away from today's society. A fundamentally political book with vivid characters and heart stopping action. It's a must and a great read." - Judy Rebick, activist and author of *Occupy This!*

Also Available!
The Dandelion Insurrection Study Guide
to Making Change Through Nonviolent Action

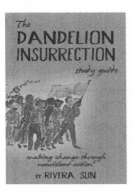

You'll love this lively, engaging journey into the heart of The Dandelion Insurrection's story of nonviolent action! Taking lessons off the page and into our lives, author Rivera Sun guides us through the skills and strategies that created the thrilling adventure of The Dandelion Insurrection. Using your favorite scenes from the book and also drawing on historical examples of nonviolent struggles, this study guide brings the story to life in an exciting way.

Reader Praise for Rivera Sun's
Steam Drills, Treadmills, and Shooting Stars

Steam Drills, Treadmills, and Shooting Stars is a story about people just like you, filled with the audacity of hope and fueled  by the passion of unstoppable love. The ghost of folk hero John Henry haunts Jack Dalton, a corporate lawyer for Standard Coal as Henrietta Owens, activist and mother, wakes up the nation with some tough-loving truth about the environment, the economy, justice, and hope. Pressures mount as John Henry challenges Jack to stand up to the steam drills of contemporary America . . . before it's too late.

"This book is a gem and I'm going to put it in my jewelry box!"

"It 'dips your head in a bucket of truth'."

"This is not a page turner . . . it stops you in your tracks and makes you revel in the beauty of the written word."

"Epic, mythic . . . it's like going to church and praying for the salvation of yourself and your people and your country."

"Controversial, political, and so full of love."

"Partway through reading, I realized I was participating in a historical event. This book has changed me and will change everyone who reads it."

"I am sixty-two years old, and I cried for myself, my neighbors, our country and the earth. I cried and am so much better for it. I would recommend this book to everyone."

Skylandia: Farm Poetry From Maine
by Rivera Sun

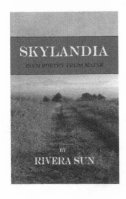

In a collection of writings delightfully and aptly referred to as "farm poetry", author Rivera Sun reveals an intimate portrait of her days growing up on an organic farm in Maine. With wry humor and lavish precision, the words of this volume evoke the essence of pine forests, summer fields, cold snow . . . and the authenticity of a farm girl in Maine.

"You really capture the down to earth (literally) sense of and appreciation of Maine farming."
– Jon Olsen, author of Liberate Hawai'i!

"Skylandia is full of wonder-filled and profound poems just like all of Rivera Sun's other writing is full of wonder-filled and profound prose. And underlying every single word of the writing is grace, courage, and healing . . . stories of how to live boldly and rightly in connection with humor and revolution."
– Marirose Nightsong

"WHEEEE!!! A dazzling volume of poetry . . . Did it make me cry? You bet it did . . . and laugh and sigh and jump up and down excited to share these stories of and love with the world. "Skylandia: Farm Poetry from Maine" is about growing up on an organic farm in Northern Maine . . . not for the faint of heart, but filled with heart."
– Dariel Garner

All of Rivera Sun's books and writings are available at:
www.riverasun.com